PHANTOM ORBIT

Also by David Ignatius

PHANTOM ORBIT

A THRILLER

DAVID IGNATIUS

W. W. NORTON & COMPANY

Independent Publishers Since 1923

For information about permission to reproduce selections from this book, write to Permissions, W. W. Norton & Company, Inc., 500 Fifth Avenue, New York, NY 10110

For information about special discounts for bulk purchases, please contact W. W. Norton Special Sales at specialsales@wwnorton.com or 800-233-4830

Manufacturing by Lake Book Manufacturing

ISBN 978-1-324-05091-9

W. W. Norton & Company, Inc., 500 Fifth Avenue, New York, N.Y. 10110
www.wwnorton.com

W. W. Norton & Company Ltd., 15 Carlisle Street, London W1D 3BS

1 2 3 4 5 6 7 8 9 0

For Sarah, Amy, and Adi

Neither a person nor a nation can endure without some higher idea.

—FYODOR DOSTOYEVSKY, *A Writer's Diary*

PHANTOM ORBIT

Prologue

Ivan Volkov studied the message on his computer screen in the powdery last light of the Moscow afternoon. It was an invitation to commit suicide, wrapped in vanilla icing. "People from nearly every country share information with the Central Intelligence Agency, and new individuals contact us daily. If you have information that might help our foreign intelligence collection mission, there are many ways to reach us."

Volkov had read those words a half dozen times over the past week, on as many different computers. His head was on fire. He was tall, handsome once, an angular, weathered face from the Steppes. He loved his country, but even more he despised what it had become. Now, in the library of the Lebedev Physical Institute, on a virtual private network that Vladimir Vladimirovich himself could not break, he prepared to compose his text. He read the instructions once more.

"If you feel it is safe, think about including these details in your message: Your full name. Biographic details. How to contact you."

These Americans were spoiled, really. They did not know pain. They were Adam, fallen. But they still ruled the ordered world, even more, now. After Russia invaded Ukraine, it was humiliated, hobbled, scorned by the decent world. But it still had its secrets. And it sought to eliminate anyone who might imagine sharing them. The

Chekists had created an organization to kill betrayers that endured, now under a different name. It was the thing that Russia was still truly good at.

Volkov typed: "I am Anonymous. I live on a street with no entrance or exit. Here is my information: You are blind to the danger from above. Satellites are your enemies, especially your own. You have 16 ground monitors and 11 antennas to run your global navigation system. Do you trust it? That is only the beginning. Hidden codes can seem to make time stop and turn north into south. They will freeze your world and everything in it. Warning messages may be tricks. Beware."

Volkov paused. No one should sign his own death warrant. But then he thought: This is not a choice, after what they did to Bucha and Mariupol—and to my own son. These are monsters, who have allied with monsters. Truly, they will turn the world upside down if they are not stopped. He read the instructions one last time.

"The CIA cannot guarantee a response to every message. We reply first to messages of most interest to us and to those with more detail. If we respond to your message, we will do so using a secure method. We go to great lengths to keep these channels secure, but any communication sent using the internet involves some risk. You can reduce some risk by using the Tor browser, a virtual private network, and/or a device not registered to you."

Volkov shook his head. He took off his reading glasses. On his lips was the trace of a rueful smile. These Americans thought they had repealed the laws of gravity. They were the winners. They were so strong that they had become weak. They did not see what was in front of their eyes.

Volkov turned back to the keyboard and typed: "A war has already begun in space. You think you understand, but you do not. The worst has already happened. Only a few people know what I know. If you are smart, you will find me." Then he pushed the button marked послать. Send.

Volkov closed his eyes. He was falling, but he was motionless. His body was heavy as lead and light as air. It was not enough, what he had done, but it was a beginning.

* * *

A young Russia analyst, camped amid a forest of workstations in the New Headquarters Building, was the first person in the agency to read the incoming message. It was from Russia; she knew that at least by the electronic tracings. She scanned the contents, looking for something real that could be examined or traced, but it was mostly a string of worry beads. The message referred to sixteen monitoring stations and eleven ground antennas in the United States' Global Positioning System; but any prankster could find that information on the internet. Otherwise, there was nothing specific, no sources, no contact details, or even hints. Almost certainly it was nothing.

The junior analyst worked in a windowless room in the new annex, sifting through the electronic slush pile that accumulated through the internet portal, looking for bits of real intelligence. She was three years out of college; she was trying to do a good job. Hundreds of messages arrived every day. Half of them offered crazy new conspiracy theories about Russia. That was the drawback of having a public website that invited the world to send information to the CIA; it turned out that every crackpot had something to say. It was like the online comments section at the end of a news story. But they all had to be read, just in case.

The analyst was going to transfer the message to the "Reviewed without Action" file, which was the same as throwing it in the trash. But she read it again, and stopped at the last, dark warning. "A war has already begun in space.... The worst has already happened." Probably that was nonsense; a drunken old crank, a kid stoned on drugs, or a deliberate provocateur in the SVR directorate that spun out dangles and deceptions.

The young woman kept a favorite admonition in a frame on her desk. "The true mystery of the world is the visible, not the invisible." It was a quote from Oscar Wilde. Maybe an older, smarter officer would have discarded the message, sensing that it was a waste of time. But she didn't know enough yet to act by reflex. So she marked the vague, oddly phrased warning for further review and sent it higher up the chain for someone else to take a look.

But riddles don't solve themselves. There were so many other agent reports, intercepts, surveillance photos, and rumors for the Russia experts to sift through in the hideous war for Ukraine. The message from Anonymous sat in a senior analyst's in-box for days. It might have been ignored altogether, if it hadn't still nagged at the younger woman's memory. She sent a query to Russia House asking if they'd found any collateral to support the dire message from the "VW," the virtual walk-in, about killer satellites.

The analyst's query created a paper trail. Now, in the unlikely event that this somber message turned out to contain a real piece of intelligence, someone would get blamed. For self-protection, the officer who oversaw collection and analysis about Russian space operations bumped it to the next bracket of intelligence assessment, at the Directorate of Science and Technology, which studied the vulnerabilities of the U.S. space program among many, many other technology assignments.

The message was reviewed; the box was checked. The responsible desk officer described it as "an unsourced and undocumented warning of vulnerability in the GPS system," and rated its value as "low to moderate," with a twenty to thirty percent chance that it contained actionable intelligence. His supervisor declined to take further action.

* * *

Volkov waited in Moscow for an answer, but none came. The dark of the Russian winter deepened. Soldiers were beginning to return home from Ukraine. Russia's finest units, its paratroopers and special forces, had been shattered in the assault on Kyiv. Thousands more men had died in the meat grinder of Bakhmut. They tried to send the most horribly wounded ones to "recovery camps," so that people wouldn't see them. But everyone knew. You can't keep a secret when people whisper about it every day. The soldiers were ashamed of themselves, even the badly wounded ones. That was the worst of it.

Volkov's son Dimitry had a favorite passage from Tolstoy's War and Peace. Before he died, he had framed it on his desk at the prosecutor's office. "If no one fought except on his own conviction, there would be no wars." Dimitry had fought on his conviction, yes, but he was gone. The powerful man that Dimitry had tried to expose, that man was still alive.

Volkov felt empty. It was as if his soul had left his body. He was just a sack of blood and bones, animated only by cowardice. Fear is a punishment; it robs our dignity. Volkov knew a secret, a real one, that could save lives, but he had been too frightened to give the Americans enough information to respond. What would his son say? Volkov knew the answer.

* * *

After a month of waiting, Volkov sent a second message. He used what CIA officers several generations before had called the "ten-cent pouch." It was an ordinary letter, dropped in a Moscow mailbox. He sent it to an American woman he had met nearly thirty years before at Tsinghua University in Beijing—the woman he had suspected at the time was a CIA spy and someone who now might, possibly, understand what he was trying to say.

Volkov had kept her address all those years, hidden away. Maybe it was insurance, or leverage, or maybe he had really cared for her. Her name was Edith Ryan, and her home, three decades ago, was in a town called Holyoke in Massachusetts.

Volkov wrote her a simple note, nothing incriminating if it was read by the FSB mail monitors. Just a lonely man, in a reverie.

> Dear Miss Ryan:
>
> Perhaps you remember me. I am Ivan Volkov, who studied aerospace engineering at Tsinghua University when we were young and very poor. I am sorry I haven't written for so long. I am 51 years old now, and my son, my only family, is gone. I am quite alone. I work now at the Lebedev Physical Institute. I am always happy to meet old friends. Perhaps you could contact me.
>
> Yours sincerely,
> Ivan Volkov

Volkov sent the letter, and he waited.

BOOK ONE: LAUNCH

I

IVAN VOLKOV AND EDITH RYAN

CHINA, 1995–1996

Dong Fang Hong 1; Launch Date: April 24, 1970

It was the first Chinese experimental satellite launched . . . from a launch facility near Lop Nor. The primary satellite mission was to broadcast the song "Dong Fang Hong" ["The East Is Red"], paying tribute to Chairman Mao, and to announce the time. The satellite was spherically shaped with a one-meter diameter. It ceased transmitting in June 1970. This was the first satellite launched by China on its own booster, making China the fifth nation to put a spacecraft into orbit using its own rocket.

—NASA Space Science Data, Coordinated Archive

1

Beijing, September 1995

Ivan Vladimirovich Volkov arrived in Beijing for the first time on a steamy late summer day. He had traveled from Ulan Bator, the last leg of a journey from his hometown of Magnitogorsk at the eastern edge of the Urals almost to Siberia. He was twenty-four years old and wanted to escape Russia, even then. The Soviet Union had collapsed. His father had died recently, in the rubble, you might say, after a lifetime of drinking too much vodka and eating too many lies. Volkov told his mother the night he left Magnitogorsk that if he stayed there, he would die, too.

Volkov was rail-thin, with high cheekbones and a shock of black hair. Somewhere in his distant past was a Mongol horseman. But in this life, he was a scientist, newly itinerant. He had been studying astronomy and mathematics at Moscow State University until his family ran out of money to pay tuition. He polished his English and looked for stipends abroad in America or Europe. Those were fantasy islands, but it turned out that China was hungry for young scientists. Volkov applied for a scholarship in a master's degree program in astronomy at Tsinghua University in Beijing and was accepted. The university agreed to pay for his travel to Beijing.

He was hungry for the world, but he was also Russian to his bones. When he reached for his seat belt before landing, you could see the name of his local hockey team, METALLURG, tattooed on his forearm. In his backpack, he carried for amusement not a novel or an adventure story, but a book of math puzzles. He closed his eyes as the plane began its approach. He told himself he was free, and he wanted to believe it. But like every child of Russia, he carried a weight.

Beijing was obscured by a haze of smog as Volkov's flight approached the city. When the plane landed, Chinese passengers clapped. As Volkov exited the plane, a blast of humid late summer heat radiated off the concrete runway. He entered a low-rise terminal that buzzed like a convention hall at a party congress. The concrete pillars were trimmed with red bunting; uniformed attendants busily dusted the gray tile floors. At passport control, Volkov waited while officers from the Ministry of Public Security fussed over his visa.

"Russian?" asked the passport control officer. Why would a young Russian want to come to China? "Student," said Volkov in English. The officer shook his head, but he stamped the passport.

A Tsinghua University representative was waiting for Volkov when he cleared customs; he was holding a placard with Volkov's name in English block letters. The man was bald and shook hands very softly; he introduced himself as Lao Wen. "Old Man Wen." Volkov would see him often in coming months, for, as Lao Wen explained, he would be the Russian graduate student's "special friend." Volkov asked if he could eat something; he was famished after his flights. Lao Wen took him to a McDonald's inside the terminal.

The windows of the university transit bus were darkened; through the shaded glass and the haze, the city appeared as a crowded but indistinct blur. The traffic slowed as they reached the congestion of the outer ring road. Beijing in 1995 was a construction zone: the shells of new buildings, topped by spindly construction cranes, lined the boulevards; in the narrow *hutongs* beyond the highways, there was still the whir of old bicycles.

"*Huan ying!*" said Lao Wen brightly, as the bus turned toward a gate with a tall arch framed in white jade. Welcome! Beyond the gate was a broad lawn leading to a great domed auditorium. Farther on were quadrangles of classroom buildings and acres of green grass. Volkov took a deep breath. It was almost as if he had landed in America.

Lao Wen leaned toward the Russian. "You know what people say about

Tsinghua? It is difficult to enter, but easy to exit. Be a good student. Don't make trouble."

The little bus came to a stop in front of the main administration building. The registrar told Volkov that the astronomy program for which he had been admitted was oversubscribed. But they had saved a spot for the Russian student in aerospace engineering. Someone had "placed" him already.

* * *

Volkov was assigned a room in the international dormitories. A single bed, a forlorn bureau, a wobbly desk, a dim lamp. It had a window that looked across the rooftops and tall trees to the university observatory. The tower stood like a lighthouse above the campus, topped by a metal sphere enclosing a telescope. Volkov wandered over to the observatory on his second day at Tsinghua. As he neared the tower, a guard stopped him and shook his head. Looking too closely at the telescope, let alone the stars, was forbidden.

The dormitory cafeteria food was too spicy for Volkov's Russian stomach. He ate plain rice and spongy white bread, along with whatever vegetables weren't too soggy from the steam table. That wasn't enough; he was losing weight, so he began eating hot dogs and hamburgers from an American-style cafeteria across campus.

Midway through his first week, Volkov met another Russian graduate student, from Saint Petersburg. The Russian was too friendly, talking in Russian-English slang words. *Baller! Krypton!* He mentioned his father, in Saint Petersburg, a former party official who knew the people who knew. Volkov kept his distance. He tried to make friends with other foreign students in his first few weeks, but most of them were withdrawn, bookish types who spent their days and nights in the library. *Botanik*, they called them condescendingly back in Russia. Botanists.

Volkov made friends with a Bulgarian from the Mechanical Engineering Faculty, and one night they went to a club in Beijing. They couldn't afford to drink, but they danced with some Chinese girls who thought they were cool, until they got ejected because they weren't buying anything. The DJ played a track from a new Smashing Pumpkins album. Volkov shouted the refrain in English. One of the Chinese girls kissed him on the lips.

The Aerospace Engineering Department had a half dozen other foreign students. Like Volkov, they had come to study in China because it was cheap and academically respectable. Tsinghua had formed a Department of Aeronautics in the late 1930s, before the revolution, and the school had expanded with China's ambitions. Many of its faculty members had studied in America and were publishing academic papers repackaging information they had gathered while at MIT or Caltech.

"Self-discipline and social commitment," advised Lao Wen at one of their weekly meetings. That was the Tsinghua school motto. He commended Volkov for his self-discipline. His marks on the half-term exams had been excellent. He had scored the top grades among master's candidates in his courses on radio astronomy and astrophysical fluid dynamics. Now, Lao Wen said, the university hoped that Volkov would also demonstrate social commitment.

"Of course," said Volkov. He knew what that meant. He had been hearing similar invitations since he was a teenage boy and was instructed to join the Young Technicians Club in Magnitogorsk.

* * *

Volkov was lonely in Beijing in his first months, so he read. One of the few books he had brought with him from Moscow was a history of mathematics, with a foreword by the great American professor Isaac Asimov, which had been published in 1991 and translated into Russian. Volkov had won it as a prize for scoring the top grade from his district in the admissions examination for Moscow State University.

Volkov had no interest in history, usually. The way it had been taught when he was a boy in Magnitogorsk, it was all just lies. But he loved the narrative of mathematical discovery, which Russians revered as a kind of secular religion. And in particular, during his brief stint at Moscow State University, he had become interested in the German astronomer Johannes Kepler.

Volkov liked puzzles. And what had drawn him to Kepler was the German's attempt to solve what was, at the time, the greatest puzzle in the universe—the motion of the planets. Kepler couldn't say no to a challenge, and when the Danish astronomer Tycho Brahe beseeched him in 1600 to calculate the orbit of the planet Mars, Kepler agreed. He discovered that Mars had an "eccentric" orbit, meaning that it was off-center, and elliptical. He had found the "eccentric anomaly" of such planetary motion and developed a formula for relating it to normal circular motion.

"Kepler's Equation," as it became known, was hardwired in Volkov's mathematical brain. $M = E - e \sin E$, where M is the mean anomaly, E is the eccentric anomaly, and e is eccentricity. In his notebooks, he repeated the equations that had led Kepler to an impasse. If we know where a planet is now, can we predict where it will be at some time in the future? Volkov filled pages with his attempts to solve this problem, but he was stumped by the same obstacle that had blocked mathematicians for more than three hundred years. The problem can't be solved directly, because "sin" is a "transcendental" function that can't be represented precisely with algebra. Instead, Kepler and his centuries of students had understood, the expected future location of a body in elliptical orbit can be discovered only through a process of iteration, with ever-closer estimation of its position.

Volkov kept his Kepler doodles in a locked briefcase in his dormitory in Beijing, and he would play with his formulas late into the night, the way some people fiddle with word games. One night, very late, he came up with an idea. It wasn't a formula for direct calculation of an object's course in elliptical orbit; that was still an insoluble problem. But he saw an elegant way to reduce the number of calculations needed for finding the position by iteration.

The next day, with the Beijing sun glowing orange in the hazy October sky, Volkov wrote up his calculations in a brief paper. It was just for himself, he thought at first, to make sure he remembered the formula and the steps he had used to prove it. But he decided to show it to his radio astronomy teacher, Assistant Professor Wu, who had mentioned Kepler and his equations in lectures about telemetry and tracking objects in space. The professor had studied at Caltech and delivered his lectures in good English.

"Who gave this to you?" demanded Assistant Professor Wu when he read the brief paper. "Where did you copy it?" He reviewed it a second time, threw up his hands, and said he would have Volkov expelled from his class for plagiarism.

"It's mine," said Volkov. He repeated the calculation on the blackboard and explained how he had derived the formula after exploring many hundreds of alternatives. He posited the solution as a ratio of "contour integrals" identifying the precise location, rather than approximating it.

Assistant Professor Wu looked at the board, asked some more questions, and tried unsuccessfully to pick apart the answers. "I don't believe it," he said finally, "but I believe it."

The radio astronomy professor told Volkov that he would speak with the dean. He said that Volkov's adviser would contact him with any news. When he shook Volkov's hand to say goodbye, the professor seemed deferential.

*　*　*

A week later, Lao Wen summoned Volkov and told him that he had been invited to meet Professor Cao Lin, a distinguished researcher who could expand his horizons. Lao Wen spoke the name gravely; this was not an ordinary professor. "We want to challenge our foreign students," he said.

Volkov asked Assistant Professor Wu in radio astronomy if he had ever heard of a professor named Cao Lin. The instructor was startled. Cao Lin was a senior cadre. He did work for . . . The instructor stopped, and then he repeated, "He is a senior cadre."

2

Beijing, November 1995

Cao Lin's office was in the Chinese Academy of Sciences headquarters in central Beijing, several miles west of Tiananmen Square. It was a staid old tan-brick building, built in the days of unadorned Chinese communism, with a big Chinese flag, red with five golden stars, flapping above the entrance. Around it now, the city pulsed with the energy of money and ambition. Chinese people understood that they were permitted to be selfish, greedy even, so long as they pretended to be good socialists.

A government limousine drove Volkov downtown. The streets were clogged with cars, bicycles, and pedestrians. Near the Forbidden City, Hermès, Louis Vuitton, and Chanel had just opened branches inside a fancy hotel. The customers thronging the stores were the wives of party officials, using credit cards from banks in Hong Kong and Vancouver. Lao Wen sat in the front seat next to the driver. When they reached the broad stone steps of the academy, a protocol officer opened the door for Volkov. Lao Wen stayed in the car.

The Chinese academician greeted his Russian visitor in his office on the top floor. He was a handsome, well-groomed man in his early fifties; tall for a Chinese, with a full head of hair that was softening to gray, rather than dyed the shoe-polish-black favored by many prominent Chinese. He was dressed in a blue blazer, with a white shirt and striped tie; he might have been an American or Englishman, with his ease and self-assurance. He didn't look like a scientist so much as a businessman.

"Welcome to the new China, Mr. Volkov," said the professor. He spoke in English, with barely an accent. "I am told that you have made an excellent start at Tsinghua. A promising student, they say. Experimental mind. So, of course, I wanted to meet you myself and say that you are most welcome here."

Volkov was several inches taller than Cao Lin. He lowered his shoulders, not quite a bow.

"Thank you, Professor Cao. It's good to be . . ." He stopped and paused. "In a place where I can do my work. That is not easy now back home in Russia. There are distractions."

Cao Lin shook his head regretfully. "So many changes! No more party. No more Soviet Union. We respect our Russian friends, of course, but it is sad, too. Moscow is becoming a gambling casino, from what they tell me. Everything is for sale. Not an easy time for scientists."

Volkov remained silent. The professor offered him a seat on the couch at the far end of his office, overlooking a garden blooming with flowers. Cao Lin took a seat in a big chair opposite.

Volkov surveyed the room; there was an electronic display on the far wall that showed the strait between the island of Taiwan and the Chinese mainland. Next to it was a television screen carrying CNN, which the professor evidently had permission to access. A banner scrolling across the bottom of the screen announced, "China Warns U.S. in Taiwan Crisis." Cao Lin saw his visitor glancing at the display and summoned an assistant. The screens were instantly extinguished. The academician turned to his visitor.

"Have you ever been to Taiwan?" he asked.

"No," said Volkov. "This is the first time I have traveled outside Russia."

"Good," said the Chinese professor. "I would stay away from Taiwan for a while. Trouble is, you know, in the air."

Volkov nodded. "Certainly, sir."

Tea arrived. A butler in white gloves poured for Volkov, then for his host, and placed ceramic lids on both cups, just so.

"They tell me you are interested in aerospace," ventured Cao Lin. "That's my field, too. What specialty will you pursue?"

"I haven't decided," answered Volkov. "I was going to study astronomy, but there were no places, so I switched to aerospace engineering. I have been playing in my notebooks with some old formulas for the orbiting of planets. Number games are better than word games. It's not so easy to cheat." Volkov stopped. He was talking too much.

"Which of your courses do you like best?" the Chinese man continued smoothly.

"Radio astronomy," answered Volkov. "I like finding things in the skies. Planets, meteors, asteroids."

"Satellites, perhaps?" interjected the academician. "They tell me some of your ideas could be useful for tracking satellites."

"Maybe someday. But that is not part of my curriculum. Frankly speaking, that area of study is not for students at Tsinghua."

"For special students, perhaps. It is an important field. The skies are becoming crowded. Russia and America have been in space for a long time. China is still a poor country. We have only a few small satellites. But we are trying to make our way. And we need talent from everywhere, including our foreign guests."

"I am just a graduate student," said Volkov. He was embarrassed.

"I will speak to the Radio Astronomy Department, to see if they can find an opportunity for extra study at one of our institutes. You can use better equipment there. And maybe, I don't know, make a little extra money. How about that?"

Volkov looked at his shoes, then back at his host. He cleared his throat, which had suddenly gone dry. "I am very busy with my work at school, Professor. I am on a full scholarship and my studies must come first."

Cao Lin continued as if he hadn't heard a word.

"I will contact the Chinese Academy of Space Technology. They launched our first satellite. I am sure they could use a good radio astronomy man. Tracking satellites is something we must learn how to do better. So that we can take our place with our Russian and American friends."

Volkov nodded again. He felt very uncomfortable now. People never talked with students about sensitive subjects like satellite tracking in Moscow.

"The sky is the limit, Mr. Volkov. Do you know that expression? Americans use it. I heard it often when I was a graduate student at Harvard, ten years ago. I never understood it. The sky is not a limit. It is the opposite of a limit. It is where things go on forever."

"Yes, sir," said Volkov. He wanted to be respectful of this powerful man who was being so friendly. "In Russia, we say: 'The sea is knee-deep.' It means you can go anywhere. But, of course, the sea is not knee-deep. A person can drown."

"You worry too much, Mr. Volkov," said Cao Lin. "That is a Russian trait. Too much history. Come visit me again, please. Study hard, but leave some free time, too. I will talk with the chair of your department to make sure that your stipend is adequate. We are a poor country, but not so poor as before."

Professor Cao Lin reached out his hand to say goodbye. Volkov mumbled his thanks and followed the professor's assistant out the door. In the hallway, just past Professor Cao Lin's door, was a large photograph of the general secretary of the Chinese Communist Party. In case there was any doubt.

*   *   *

When Volkov returned to the Tsinghua campus, he went to the main library and found the periodicals room. The selection there was limited, but after searching he found back issues of *China Daily* that carried items from the Xinhua news service about recent events in Taiwan. The Chinese reports described a "crisis" after a visit to America in June by the president of Taiwan to address an alumni event at Cornell. Xinhua reported that China had conducted missile tests near the Taiwan Strait in July, prompting the dispatch of an American armada to the strait, followed by more missile tests and more U.S. maritime exercises.

Volkov asked the librarian if there were any newspapers from Taiwan in the stacks. She was startled by the question and said she would have to consult the chief librarian. Volkov shrugged and said it didn't matter. "All I know about Taiwan is that it's part of China," he said. She seemed relieved. Volkov went back to his desk and opened a radio-frequency textbook he had brought in his backpack.

Volkov had been oblivious to political news all of his life. He was a Russian. The only news he knew back home was lies. But now he began paying more attention.

* * *

Volkov was given a bigger dormitory room the next week, with a private bathroom. His instructors now called him "Mr. Volkov." The dean responsible for foreign graduate students offered him a special stipend for his studies in aerospace engineering. Volkov didn't respond at first, but after a week he accepted the grant.

With the extra money, Volkov bought himself a new Samsung cell phone. But he didn't have anyone to call. After carrying the phone in his pocket for a week, he decided to call his mother in Magnitogorsk. It took four tries, but eventually it rang.

"*Ye bogu!*" she exclaimed when she heard his voice. Bless me. She was so shocked to hear her son that she whispered her answers, as if someone might be listening. When he asked her what she wanted, she answered she wanted her son to come home.

Volkov told her to write down the number for his new cell phone, and made her read it back to be sure, and he told her to call him if anything was ever wrong. She was old and getting frail. He worried sometimes that she might be in distress. But the phone didn't ring.

* * *

In the cold of December, when the afternoons were short, Volkov was summoned to the office of Assistant Professor Wu, the man with whom he had shared his doodles about a new solution to Kepler's problem of "eccentric" elliptical orbits. Wu's office was in the astronomy building, near the tall white observatory that graced the northern end of the campus. A bitter wind swept across the bare treetops that lined the approach to the observatory, bringing the chill of the Yangshan mountains that traced a jagged line north of the city.

Assistant Professor Wu had two senior colleagues sitting alongside him in his small office. The moment Volkov entered the room, he felt as if he were on trial. But the three professors greeted him enthusiastically.

"We have reviewed your novel formula," said Assistant Professor Wu. "It is accurate, although it is not more accurate than existing methods. My colleagues who reviewed your work found it very commendable. A credit to you and Tsinghua University. Our committee found that it is similar to work done at Yale University and the Goddard Space Flight Center. Did you know that?"

Volkov edged back his chair. Had he crossed a line?

"I did not know about those others," said Volkov. "I am a graduate student. I don't have access to a proper research library. These were just notions of mine. I am glad they are accurate. I hope they will be useful. I mean no harm."

The senior professor rose from his chair. He hadn't given his name, but Volkov recognized him as the dean of the physics faculty.

"Harm?" said the senior professor. "How would you imagine that this is harmful? You have a gift. That is *helpful*. We hope you will continue to be happy and productive here."

Assistant Professor Wu showed Volkov to the door. A blast of cold from Yangshan braced him as soon as he opened the door. Volkov zipped his jacket tight and made his way toward the student center. He liked China, but he didn't understand the rules.

3

Beijing, January 1996

Ivan Volkov met Edith Ryan in early January, a week before the fall semester ended. The weather had turned even colder. Students hurried to their exams wrapped in coats and scarves and wool hats with earflaps. Volkov had loved to play ice hockey back home in weather like this. But some days it was more frigid in Beijing than it had been in Moscow.

The two met in a new coffee shop on campus that served fancy espresso drinks. Volkov was sitting on a couch nursing a cappuccino before returning to the chill outside when a woman, red-cheeked from the cold, sat down beside him with her latte and introduced herself. She spoke English with an American accent. "You're from Russia, aren't you?" she said. "I've seen you around." Volkov stammered a response. He hadn't talked to a woman in weeks.

Ryan had milk-white skin, a delicate face, and soft auburn curls. Volkov was shy, always, but especially now, so he let her talk. She was studying for a year on a fellowship from Yale, she said. She had graduated last June, and Yale had a partnership with Tsinghua. She was taking classes at the Department of Engineering Physics.

"*Krasota!*" said Volkov.

She leaned toward him and looked up at his hard, narrow face. "What does that mean?" she asked.

"It means, 'Wow!'" The Department of Engineering Physics specialized in nuclear energy. It didn't have many foreign students.

The espresso bar was crowded with students, queuing for drinks and talking noisily in Mandarin accents that, to an outsider, sounded like a gaggle of ducks. The heat had been raised against the cold outdoors, and it was steamy in the couch area where they were sitting.

"Let's move," said Ryan. "This is a zoo." Volkov didn't understand the expression at first, but then he laughed. They walked to a far corner.

"How did you know I was Russian?" Volkov asked when they had found their new seats.

"You're tall and you look like a tough guy," she teased. "And someone told me." She laughed at the last admission. She had a free, easy smile. Despite his wariness about everyone and everything, Volkov was charmed.

Ryan finished her latté and announced that she wanted another. Against Volkov's protest, she brought him another cappuccino, too.

"Here's what you need to know about me," she said when they had settled in with the new drinks. "My family is Irish. On both sides. And we're from Massachusetts. Which means I love the Red Sox. The Celtics. The Patriots. And the Bruins. Do you know who they are?"

"The Bruins are a hockey team, of course. Adam Oates, he is very good. But the Bruins have only one Russian player now, and he is not so good. The Red Sox, everyone knows the Red Sox, even in Russia. We know about 'the curse,' too. It is not Russia's fault."

Ryan laughed again. She talked about her hometown of Holyoke, and how she had been first in her class in high school, and how her parents cried when she got into Yale.

"I'm a science geek," she said "Trekkie, astronaut-wannabe. I wanted to join the Air Force, but I was too short."

"What's a geek?" asked Volkov.

"A smart, maladjusted kid. Sorry, but you're too good-looking to be a geek. What about you, anyway? Tell me about your family."

Volkov cast his eyes down, from shyness more than sadness. "My father is dead. Two years ago. My mother lives alone in a town in the middle of Russia where I was born. She teaches music at a school in our town. She reads books and poetry. She is old, not so well. She has had a hard life, but she is a sweet woman. I miss her."

"What about siblings?"

"I had a brother, but he died when I was young. Our town is not so healthy. You can feel the air on your fingers."

She placed her hand on his and left it there. "I'm sorry," she said. She looked at his face. There were scars on his chin and forehead. She gently touched the one on his chin, grazing his lips with her hand.

"What is this?" she asked. "Were you in a duel?"

"Hockey," he answered. "I was big, so people wanted to take me out of the game."

"Poor boy," she said. "An easy target. But you hung in there."

"Always," he said. He showed her his hockey tattoo, which made her smile.

Volkov would happily have talked with this woman all morning, but he had an exam in thirty minutes, a quarter mile away across the frigid campus. Edith Ryan waited for him to ask the question—when can I see you again?— and when he didn't, she asked her own very forward version.

"What are you doing for winter break?" she asked. The university would be closing for a month when term ended the next week.

"Staying here," he said, shaking his head. "I have a part-time job at one of the institutes. They need me. And I can't afford to go home."

"Want to go to Shanghai for a week? Two other Americans and I are heading there, and then to Hong Kong, and then home. You can come with us for the first week. It will be cheap. We're staying at a friend's apartment. You can sleep on the couch. Why not?"

Volkov frowned. Of course he wanted to go. But he had just met this woman. "Too expensive," he said. "And they would miss me at the institute."

"Are you sure?" she asked, elongating the last word. Her eyes were twinkling. She was a fairy princess, this woman Edith Ryan. Russian girls weren't like her.

"I've got to go to my exam," said Volkov. "I'll see you next term."

"Do you have a cell phone number?" she asked. "I'll call you when I get back. Maybe we can have a coffee date."

Volkov wrote down his number, and she gave him hers. And then he was out the door and leaning into the cold wind of the winter morning.

4

Beijing, February 1996

Edith Ryan returned to Beijing in mid-February at the beginning of spring term. She had sent Volkov a postcard from Hong Kong that arrived a few weeks before. It showed the dazzling harbor arrayed below Victoria Peak. On the back she had scrawled, "wish you were here," with three exclamation points. Volkov tried not to think too much about her. He wasn't used to missing anyone.

Volkov called her phone the day the new term started. She didn't answer, and he worried she wasn't coming back to Tsinghua, but she called him the next afternoon. Her plane had been delayed. They met at the graduate center. It was crowded with returning students, and several stopped to talk with Edith. It was cold outside, but Volkov asked her to take a walk.

Edith looked a bit older, less like a graduate student, but just as beautiful. Her body looked fuller; she was wearing makeup; her sweater was tighter. She said she had been home to see her father in Massachusetts. He was sick. Volkov said his father had been sick for a long time before he died. His throat caught as he said the words. He didn't usually speak about personal things, but he told her about his father's numbing years of work at the immense ruined steel mill back home, and his mother's stubborn persistence there. Volkov touched her arm, and then held her hand for a moment. Edith said she had to go back to her dorm and rest. She had been up all night.

They met two nights later for drinks at a bar near campus. After several rounds, Edith suggested they go to the Harmony Club. They played hard rock there on Saturday nights. There was a cover charge at the door, thirty yuan each. Volkov fumbled for money when they got there, but while he was digging in his pockets, Edith paid with a wad of cash. Volkov was embarrassed, but that went away when they danced. Edith was liquid motion. Volkov didn't really know how to dance, but she grabbed him and swayed her hips, and it was easy. The music got louder, and they drank more. Volkov held her tight during a slow dance, and she wrapped her arms around his neck. When the song ended, he kissed her on the mouth.

After midnight, they caught a taxi back to the university. When they got back to her dorm, Volkov embraced her. Students weren't allowed to have overnight guests in their rooms, but he asked if he could come up anyway. At that moment he didn't think about anything other than her. She let her body relax in his big arms and then stepped back.

"Too soon," she said. "We need to be careful. We're just getting to know each other." Her cheeks were pink from the cold. He moved toward her, but she shook her head. She reached into her pocket and handed him a smooth white stone. She put it in his palm and then closed his fingers around it.

"Hold it tight," she said. "It's a 'Go' stone. One of my 'Edith' things. Russians love chess, but I'm a nut for Go. It's a Chinese game, invented, like, two thousand years ago. Have you ever played?"

"No." He shook his head. "Chess man." He opened his hand to see the perfect white oval in the center.

"Well, there are two things you need to know about Go. Number one, black goes first. That's me. Okay?"

"You go first. I got that. What's the other thing?"

Her lips parted in a smile. "The other thing is that it's a long game."

Volkov laughed. He took her in his arms again, kissed both cheeks and her waiting lips, and said good night. As she walked up the dormitory steps, he took another look at the perfect white stone in his palm.

* * *

Volkov had a visitor early in the spring term. He heard a knock on the door of his dormitory room, an unfamiliar interruption. It was the Russian graduate student from Saint Petersburg, whom Volkov had met in his first weeks in China and to whom he had taken an instant dislike. He began in a genial enough way, calling Volkov by his patronymic, Ivan Vladimirovich, though they weren't friends. He had a message. Volkov must register with the Russian Embassy in Beijing. It was a requirement for all Russian students in the country.

"The embassy asked me for a list of Russian graduate students, so I gave them your name," the St. Petersburg man said. "I assumed you had already contacted them, but they told me no, so now here I am." His eyes were small and set closely together. He was six inches shorter than Volkov, and he was standing on his toes.

"Of course," said "Volkov. "I'll take care of it." He paused and then said, "Thanks." He didn't want to make an enemy of this apprentice informer.

The Russian Embassy was a grand building just inside the second ring road, a half mile from the compound where most foreign embassies were located. There was a fountain outside, surrounded by roses that held a bloom even in the winter. Atop the pillared gray façade was a circular dome topped by a bright new tricolor Russian flag.

Volkov found the consular section on the ground floor and stood patiently in line. When he reached the front and presented his passport, the man behind the window consulted a computer log and told Volkov to go upstairs, to see Mr. Simeon Krastev on the third floor of the chancery. He handed Volkov a pass but kept his passport.

A heavy security door to the chancery buzzed open. Inside, dominating the entry hall, was a big portrait of the florid-faced man who was the first president of post-Communist Russia. The photo had been retouched to remove any blemishes, in the manner of the old-time portraits. The elevator was broken. An escort took Volkov up the stairs.

Mr. Krastev's office was at the dark end of a corridor and guarded by a cyber lock. A plaque outside Krastev's office identified him as a cultural counselor, but when Volkov entered and shook his meaty hand, he knew that couldn't be right. He looked like a secret policeman.

"Perhaps you forgot about us," said Krastev. "Registration with the embassy is, let me be frank, it is a requirement."

Krastev asked how Volkov's studies in aerospace engineering were going. He seemed to have read Volkov's file. He quizzed Volkov about his classes, and his contacts with the Academy of Sciences. Volkov answered all his questions; it would be useless, and also dangerous, to lie. He asked if there were any Americans in Volkov's classes, and the young Russian said no. He didn't seem to know about Edith Ryan.

"Do you trust your new Chinese friends?" asked Krastev.

Volkov shrugged. "I am a Russian. I don't trust anyone."

"Good boy," said Krastev. "Because the Chinese are playing a very tricky game." He reached into the drawer of his desk and removed a folder.

"This document was prepared a few years ago, by the special services of the old regime in Moscow. It's still a good guide to, may I say, the Chinese character, especially for newcomers like you, Mr. Volkov. Here, I will read you a few lines."

He thumbed the pages until he found the passage he wanted. " 'The Chinese have an exaggerated feeling of national pride which can be classed as their most pronounced characteristic.' " He paused, studied Volkov and continued: " 'It is worth remembering that notwithstanding their exaggerated feeling of national pride, many Chinese are still suffering to a certain extent from a complex of "national inferiority" remaining from the last century.' " He paused. "Just so, don't you think?"

Volkov shrugged. "I can imagine what the Chinese say about us."

"Wait, here's another bit. 'The Chinese have for centuries developed the ability to restrain themselves and hide their emotions from others behind a mask of cold tranquility or a polite smile. By common consent, this is a nation of actors; this is why the Chinese are not only able to hide their true feelings but to exhibit them very theatrically.' " He closed the folder. "That's true, don't you think?"

"I only just got here, Mr. Counselor. I cannot say."

Krastev pursed his lips and nodded. "All right. You are a careful man. I can understand that. So I will be frank: We are interested in Chinese technology. They are moving very quickly. They are stealing everything they can from America. Take good notes. We can use China."

"They want to use us, Mr. Counselor."

"Bah! We are a great power. China is a weak power."

Volkov shook his head. "That won't last. I see their scientists."

Krastev rolled his eyes. "Listen, my friend. Russia is an empire. China is a kingdom. Like I said, take careful notes. When you go back home to Russia, people will be interested."

Volkov was silent. He hadn't made plans to return home. He had let himself imagine that if he did well enough, the Chinese might offer him an additional stipend to continue his studies toward a doctorate. Krastev narrowed his eyes. He could see the hesitation in Volkov's face.

"We are sorry about the death of your father. Vladimir Volkov was a man of respect in the party, I am told. A foundation beam of our iron and steel industry, which gave Russia its victory in the Great Patriotic War. You have a legacy. And a duty. And some protection. But the last part is not permanent. It must be earned."

Volkov didn't want anyone's protection. He was between seasons, in that time when the wind came off the Steppes and the last bloom of summer died in Magnitogorsk, and the first days of October began. He shook hands with Krastev and said that he always took good notes, but he didn't promise anything more.

5

Beijing, February 1996

Professor Cao Lin summoned Volkov for another comradely visit at the start of the new term. He requested that they meet at the Chinese Aerospace Corporation, in a new office building a few miles north of the university. The lobby was decorated with a glass-encased replica of China's first satellite, the *Dong Fang Hong I*, barely a yard in diameter, launched in April 1970 and lost less than a month later. THE EAST IS RED read a plaque on the display case. That was the tiny orbiter's name in English.

A guard in the lobby sent Volkov to an office on the fourteenth floor. Cao Lin was waiting in a conference room. Seated at the table with him were a professor from the Academy of Space Technology who had supervised Volkov's work on radio astronomy; an executive from the Aerospace Corporation who said he oversaw "aspects" of the Chinese space program, he didn't say which; and a professor from the Beijing University of Aeronautics and Astronautics, known as BUAA, who said he was connected with some of the "national laboratories" there, unspecified.

Cao Lin was wearing an open-neck blue shirt. He had a lustrous tan, as if he had been visiting a spa resort in midwinter. He looked sleek; a man with money and apparent connections to what mattered in the new China. The other Chinese were dressed severely in white shirts, jackets, and ties. They were cadres, no doubt, but not senior cadres. Volkov wore a dark gray suit he had purchased at a Chinese department store. He might have been dressed for a funeral.

The session was like a job interview, except that Volkov wasn't applying for a job. Cao Lin asked the Russian to describe his background for the group. Volkov answered that his father had been deputy secretary of the Communist Party branch at the Magnitogorsk Iron and Steel Works, known by its Russian initials, MMK. Heads nodded around the table. Good lineage. His father had died two years ago of a stroke, but his mother was still living in Magnitogorsk. He had a brother, but he had died of tuberculosis. Heads bowed appropriately.

"I was good at mathematics, I can say," said Volkov. "I joined the Young Technicians in Magnitogorsk, and then I competed in the All-Soviet Math Olympiad. I won a place at Moscow State University, in the Department of Mathematics, and then I added astronomy, too. It was a very good program, I believe. I won my first degree and planned to continue. But then things changed. My father died. My money had run out and I couldn't afford tuition and board. I had mentors on the faculty, but they left for America and Europe, and they couldn't help me. So I applied for a scholarship to Tsinghua and, you can see, here I am."

"Why didn't you apply for a place at an American university?" asked Cao Lin.

"I did. But they turned me down. I also applied to Oxford and Cambridge. It was the same thing. So I came to Tsinghua." He hadn't meant to, but he had slighted his hosts. Cao Lin smiled.

"We are the lucky ones," said the academician. The others around the table assented. "Your marks in the fall term were very good. What additional courses will you be taking in the new term?"

"Fluid dynamics, astrophysics, and cosmology."

"Cosmology is a waste of time," said Cao Lin, with a wave of his hand. "Too theoretical for a practical man like you. The institute is offering a new course in aerospace propulsion. That would be more ... challenging. Or electrical engineering. But not cosmology. You might as well study religion." Volkov wrote "aerospace propulsion" and "electrical engineering" on the notepad in front of him.

* * *

The conversation became a job fair, with the professors pitching Volkov. The supervisor of the Radio Astronomy Program handed him a diagram for a new radar array that his academy had just completed, in cooperation with an institute in Shanghai, that would investigate the positions and functions of satellites in low-earth orbits. Volkov looked at the writing on the diagram. It was in English. "Perhaps postgraduate study," proposed the radio astronomer.

The Chinese Aerospace Corporation executive described a dozen smaller companies that were under his wing, involved in spacecraft design, propulsion systems, guidance instruments, and electronic controls. He said the company was growing rapidly and was paying salaries that were equivalent to those of Western firms.

The astronautics professor explained his university's network of six national laboratories. He focused on the National Laboratory of Computational Fluid Dynamics. He noted Volkov's decision to study fluid dynamics spring term and mentioned that his Tsinghua professor was a relative. "As you know, computational fluid dynamics is necessary for efficient design of space vehicles," he said. Volkov nodded.

When the three had finished their pitches, all eyes turned to Cao Lin.

"So, my Russian friend, have you thought about what you will do next when you finish your master's program?" asked the academician.

"I plan to return to Moscow. Perhaps I will apply for a job with one of the institutes there."

Cao Lin tilted his head. "There are many good institutes here, as you can see. They pay well, and the work is more, well, you know, stable than in Moscow. And we have some important new projects. We will not be so backward soon. We need to hire the best talent. From everywhere."

"I'm grateful. This has been a happy time for me." Volkov was thinking of Edith Ryan as he said this, but he liked his Chinese studies, too.

"Let me put an idea in your head," said Cao Lin. "To help you think about the future."

"Yes, please."

"What is the most important thing that science might offer to a traveler?

You could give me many answers, but I'll tell you the correct one. The most important gift to the traveler is to tell him where he is, and how to get to where he is going. Don't you think?"

Volkov pondered it for a moment. "Of course, you are right," he answered.

"Finding our way is not so simple. But the Americans have a very good idea. They have been launching satellites to help them find their position on the ground. They called this program Transit. They launched the first of these positioning satellites in 1960, and now the Navy has, I believe, thirty-six satellites in this system. Navstar, they call it these days. It was secret once, but now everyone knows about it. They use it for commercial airlines."

"Russia has such a navigation system," volunteered Volkov. "It's called GLONASS. I had thought I might work on it someday."

Cao Lin shook his head. He wasn't impressed.

"Good luck. But the Americans move very fast when there is money to be made. Next year, they will launch a new version of this technology, much more powerful. Global Positioning System, they are calling it. GPS. We saw the power of these satellites in the war they fought against Iraq in 1991. Such precision. It was not a war, really. Target practice. How can we keep up with these Americans? They are so rich. It is hard for a poor country like us to follow. But perhaps we can contribute to this great endeavor. Perhaps we can help supply the team with the equipment it needs."

The academician let the thought die in the air.

"What do you mean, Professor?"

Cao Lin raised a cautionary hand. "I will explain it another time when it is just you and me. Go back to your classes now. Think about the opportunities that my colleagues have described. The salaries are, as the Americans say, 'competitive.' We need good minds. We have many joint projects, more than you might think. We are building the future, too. We will have the money. And certainly, we have the time."

Volkov said farewell to the institute directors that Cao Lin had assembled. Each of them proffered a business card, holding it carefully with two hands like a delicate object. Volkov was going to follow them out the door, but Cao Lin reached for his elbow so they could talk alone.

"I know what you are thinking. You are a Russian. You want to go back to your country. Your mother lives there. It is in your, what, blood? But you are a young man. Life is long. China is a fragile creature today, but that will not always be so. You will always be glad that you did your graduate studies here, I promise that."

Volkov didn't have an answer, so he remained silent.

Cao Lin walked Volkov to the door of his office. At the corridor, he paused. "There is someone I would like you to meet. His name is Chen Fangyun. We call him 'the father of the Chinese space program.' He has an office here at the Aerospace Corporation. Would you like to see him? It can only be a moment. He is very old."

"I would like that very much," said Volkov. He knew the name. Chen Fangyun was mentioned in all the textbooks. He had founded modern radio electronics in China and helped create the first space telemetry and tracking systems.

Cao Lin took Volkov's elbow and steered the taller man down the hall. "We introduce Academician Chen only to special friends."

*   *   *

They walked to a suite at the end of the hall. Two uniformed guards stood outside, and three assistants sat in the waiting room. Cao Lin approached one and spoke quietly. The assistant nodded, and they were ushered into a grand office, decorated with the Chinese flag and banners and portraits of the party leadership. On one wall were photographs of rocket launches, with names and dates.

Behind a desk at the far end of the room sat a slender man with a high forehead and large wire-framed glasses. Unlike Cao Lin and most of his colleagues, he wore the traditional tunic that people called a "Mao suit."

"Comrade Chen, I would like you to meet my Russian friend, Mr. Volkov," said Cao Lin. "He is studying at Tsinghua, just as you did once."

Chen Fangyun extended his thin hand. The skin was yellow vellum, barely covering the fragile bones.

The old man's lips were thin, and he formed his words slowly and with precision.

He asked Volkov what he was studying, and Volkov answered that he was in the aeronautics faculty, with a concentration in radio astronomy. Academician Chen nodded with evident satisfaction.

"I studied there so many years ago. At the Radio Research Institute. And then, before our glorious revolution, I worked abroad at a radio factory in England. You see, it is good to study outside your country." He gave a thin smile. Several of his teeth were missing.

Volkov moved back from the desk, but Chen put up his bony hand. He wasn't finished.

"They tell me that you read the work of Johannes Kepler about objects in space. Is that right?"

Volkov nodded. How did the old man know about his Kepler studies? The Russian felt momentarily that he was in an echo chamber, where not all the sounds were audible to him.

"Remember what Kepler said," continued Chen. "Before the origin of things, geometry was coeternal with the divine mind. Do you think that is so? I don't believe in a divine mind, personally, but I do believe in geometry."

"That is my belief, too, sir," answered Volkov.

Chen smiled. They shared a fraternity: order, fellowship, purpose. Volkov stood erect, looming over the old gentleman.

"You must be tired," said Cao Lin. "We should leave you."

"I will not forget our meeting, sir," Volkov stammered as he retreated.

But the old man wasn't quite done. He rose, feebly, from his chair. Volkov and Cao Lin halted and returned closer to the desk.

Chen raised his hand, as if toward a blackboard.

"There is one more thing a bright student should understand about the movement of objects in space. Cao Lin knows, and so should you. It is the time problem. Something that Kepler did not consider."

The old man was musing, rambling in his mind with someone he imagined as a pupil and kindred spirit.

"Please, sir," said Volkov. Cao Lin nodded assent.

"Kepler did not consider the reliability of time," said Chen. "Kepler did not ask: What time is it on the satellite? What time is it on the ground? He did not consider that perhaps the two times are not the same. He did not consider what to do if they are different."

The old man's eyes glowed with the sweet mystery of this problem. Volkov knew they should go, but Chen still had his finger pointed toward that invisible board.

"Time and motion tell us the position of things," said the old man. "We need precise measurement of both. Don't forget."

Volkov nodded. Time and motion. He started to bow but stopped. He put his hand over his heart.

"We will leave you, Comrade Chen," said Cao Lin.

*   *   *

When they were back in the hallway, outside the master's suite, Professor Cao took Volkov's hand and sat him down on a couch.

"That was most unusual," he said.

"I won't forget it, ever," said Volkov.

"What did you hear him say?"

Volkov thought a moment. "The essential variable in space systems is time. That means that the most precious thing in space is an accurate clock."

"Clever boy." Cao Lin nodded. "Comrade Chen told you a very big secret. A state secret."

"Why a state secret, Professor Cao? This is science."

"Because this relationship between time and position is the essence of the global navigation systems that the Americans are developing, with us following in their path. If you master this relationship, you control the future in space."

Volkov shook his head. For a young graduate student, this was disorienting. "Why did Chen Fangyun tell me this?"

"Because he liked you. You understand Kepler, who is a god for him. And, I will be frank, because I told him before our meeting that I want you to be a special friend for China."

They rose from the couch and walked toward the elevator. As they neared the door, Cao Lin whispered to his guest.

"Chen Fangyun would never say so himself, he is too modest, but he helped create the '863 Program.' I'm sure you don't know what that is, but the goal is to make China a great technology power. It was announced in 1986, on March third, so '863.' Next month it will be ten years old."

"Happy birthday," said Volkov.

"Come back and see me in a few weeks," answered Cao Lin. "I'll have more to say then, about how we can be helpful to each other." He paused and smiled. "So will you, I hope."

6

Beijing, February–March 1996

Ivan Volkov was at work one afternoon in mid-February in the lab at the Academy of Space Technology when the senior Chinese employees were summoned to a meeting. They returned to their desks silent and glum. Volkov was wary of approaching anyone to ask what had happened. But when he was waiting for a bus after work, he saw Shao Ming, a young woman who had recently graduated from Tsinghua and was his closest friend at the lab.

"Did something happen today?" asked Volkov. "You all looked unhappy."

"*Huai*," said the engineer. "Bad."

"What happened?"

"*Zainan*. Disaster. It will be in the Chinese papers." She looked embarrassed.

"I don't read Chinese. Can you tell me?"

Shao Ming bowed her head. "One of our space rockets crashed. Long March 3B. It hit a village near the launchpad, in Sichuan Province. Many people died. Hundreds, maybe. That's why they cannot keep it secret. Too many dead."

"I'm sorry," said Volkov. He wanted to make his friend feel better. "Rockets crash all the time. Russian rockets, American rockets. Shit happens, as the Americans say, right?"

Shao Ming shook her head. "This was very bad. It wasn't just that the

rocket crashed. It was carrying an American payload. Communications satellite. Big loss of face for China. What can we do? It will be on the news. It is
a . . . setback."

A bus came, and Shao Ming boarded. Volkov had to wait a few more minutes. What struck him, as he thought about it, wasn't that the Chinese rocket
had failed, but that it had been carrying an American payload. The space business evidently had its own rules.

* * *

Edith Ryan called Volkov the next day. The mid-February weather had soft-
ened, and the sun was shining bright over a Beijing that, for once, was free of
smog. It wasn't spring, but certainly a less punishing moment of winter. Edith
asked the Russian if he wanted to take a walk; it was too pretty outside to be
cooped up in the library. Volkov agreed; he wanted company.

They met in the big courtyard that faced the main administration building
at the north end of campus. Edith was wearing a blue skirt, with red tights and a
green sweater. She had a yellow bow tied around a ponytail, but she let her hair
fall loose when she saw Volkov. She kissed him on the cheek, then on the lips.
Chinese passersby stared at them.

They strolled toward the big park just above the campus, side by side and
then holding hands. Edith was in a playful mood, chattering about the comi-
cal personal habits of her dormmates in the international women's graduate
residence. The Romanian woman who needed deodorant. The Cambodian
girl who sang Beatles songs in broken English in the shower. Normally Volkov
didn't laugh much—he came from the land of the unfunny—but Edith's mirth
was infectious.

"Let me tell you something strange that happened yesterday," Volkov said
eventually. "I have this, you know, intern job at an institute. Space, satellites,
and all that. Yesterday the Chinese who work there went crazy. Urgent meeting,
long faces. Nobody talked. Big deal, obviously. Very strange."

Edith was looking up at him attentively. "What was bugging them?"

"A Chinese rocket crashed. A lot of people got killed. My friend said it
would be on the news. That's why she told me, I guess. But that's not the strang-
est part. The rocket that blew up was carrying an American satellite."

"Intelsat," said Edith. "That was the satellite. It was made by an American company called Loral."

"How do you know that?" asked Volkov.

"I told you: I'm a space geek. I wanted to be an astronaut," she said. "Let's walk."

They were entering Yuangmingyan Park at the site of the Old Summer Palace. Ahead of them were the remains of Western-style stone mansions that had been sacked during the Opium Wars. All that was left were pillars and pedestals, decorated with elaborate carvings. It looked like the ruins of a civilization that had been plundered. Beyond the wrecked palaces were ponds and canals that had been part of the formal gardens, their water still frozen in late winter.

"I have a friend," Edith continued. "You should meet him. He knows a lot about space."

"An American friend?"

"Yes. He's older, but we have some friends in common. You'd like him. He's much smarter about this stuff than I am."

"Where does he work?" asked Volkov. He wasn't suspicious. Just curious.

"I'm not sure. One of the American companies that works here. Maybe it's Citibank. He has lots of connections. Who knows? Maybe someday you might need a banker, right?"

"I don't know," said Volkov. "This place is like Russia. People are always watching."

"Come on!" She punched his arm playfully. "Don't be a scaredy-cat."

He shrugged. What could he do? He liked her. And she was right. He was a student. If he was going to make his way in the world, he needed business contacts.

"I can meet anyone I like," said Volkov. "I'm a Russian, and Russia is a free country now."

"Amen to that," she answered.

* * *

They walked back toward campus to the West Gate. New Western-style restaurants were opening along the big boulevard that skirted the university, offering pizza and fried chicken. The police had erected metal barriers to keep the tide of pedestrians from spilling into the street. Volkov pulled Edith toward the gate, a gray stone monolith decorated with Chinese characters, painted in gold.

"Someone is following us," he whispered.

"Why would they do that?" she answered. "We're students." Edith laughed and gave him another playful punch.

"You're right," he said. "They follow everyone. Come on."

The crowd thinned when they were inside the university compound. They walked toward the long green garden that fronted the university's domed administration building. The grass was brown from the February chill. A few months before, a display of flowers had graced the edge of the lawn, arranged to form the year of the university's foundation, 1911, but they had been uprooted when winter came.

They strolled through the quadrangle, two foreign students enjoying a walk on a chilly afternoon. Volkov broke the silence.

"This is a strange question, maybe, but is there some kind of a Taiwan crisis?" he asked. "I see stories in *China Daily*, but I don't believe anything they say."

Edith looked startled for a moment. They didn't talk about politics. She turned away, and then back toward Volkov. "Yes, I think there is. American friends talk about it. China has been launching missiles because it's angry that America gave a visa to the leader of Taiwan, and America has been sending big Navy ships to show that it doesn't like the missiles."

Volkov frowned. Missiles. Ships. "Is there going to be a war?"

Edith shook her head. "No way. America is much too strong. China would be nuts to start a fight. They need America. We're working together. Everyone tells me this Taiwan thing will pass."

"I'm a scientist," said Volkov. It came out louder than he had intended.

"Duh! Of course you are. Don't sound so serious. It's like in Go, things are always changing. A group of stones can be alive, dead, or unsettled. Taiwan is unsettled. It's a long game. Don't worry about it."

"You're not a scientist," said Volkov.

"No, I'm not," she answered. She put her arm through his and they continued their walk.

Volkov after that began visiting the library more regularly to read *China*

Daily and the latest Xinhua dispatches. In early March the paper reported a new set of Chinese missile tests near Taiwan. One Xinhua dispatch noted that commercial shipping and air traffic would be temporarily disrupted in the area. In mid-March, the news agency reported, the Chinese government had protested the dispatch of two U.S. aircraft carrier battle groups to the western Pacific. Then, with this display of American force, the crisis seemed to end.

Volkov wondered whether he should ask Edith more about the news and decided against it. She wouldn't know anything, and if she did, well, then he would not want to ask her any questions.

7

Beijing, March 1996

Edith Ryan wore a business suit and low heels to their next meeting. She had a surprise. She was leaving that afternoon for a few days in Hong Kong to meet a visiting professor from Yale. He was just a teacher, not an old boyfriend, she assured Volkov. And she had good news. She had arranged for Volkov to meet her banker contact, Larry Hoffman, that week at a hotel on the airport road, a few miles from campus. It was a Holiday Inn, and it had the best charcuterie in Beijing. Volkov didn't know what that word meant, so he just nodded.

Edith gave Volkov a card with the address of the Holiday Inn, in Chinese, and the time and day of the meeting. "Take a cab. Hoffman reserved one." She handed him a taxi voucher.

"I wish you were coming, too," said Volkov. "I'm shy." He feigned a tremble in his arms.

"Right," she said.

On the day of the meeting, Volkov went to the taxi queue at the university gate. He gave the driver the card with the hotel address and the voucher. The driver asked Volkov a question in Chinese that he didn't understand, so he just answered, "*Shi, shi.*" Yes. The driver deposited him at the entrance to the hotel.

Volkov asked a uniformed doorman for Mr. Hoffman. He was escorted to a private room. A bottle of Chablis was resting in an ice bucket. On the table was a plate of delicious-looking Italian meats and cheeses. The room was empty when he first arrived, but Hoffman soon entered through a back door. He was in his mid-thirties, solidly built, fancy haircut, trim suit.

Hoffman handed Volkov a business card that said he was a vice president at an investment firm that specialized in technology investments. He said the firm was building a portfolio of joint venture companies in China, especially in the aerospace industry. He poured two glasses of wine. He saw Volkov studying the food and made him a little plate of prosciutto, sopressata, and Genoa salami.

"*Za Zdarovje*," said Hoffman, raising his glass. His Russian pronunciation was near-perfect. Volkov clinked his glass. The food and wine were delicious. The poor exchange student from the edge of Siberia ate and drank heartily.

"Maybe you can help us," said Hoffman. "Edith told me that you're studying astronautics. A lot of smart Chinese are jumping into that sector. We think we can make some money with them. As the Chinese say, it's a 'win-win.' We just need contacts."

Volkov shook his head. "I'm a graduate student. I don't know anybody, really."

"But you meet people," said Hoffman.

Volkov put up the palms of his two big hands. "Mister, please. Like I told you, I am just a graduate student. I am here on a scholarship. The Chinese pay for it. I do some work, part-time. The Chinese pay me. That's the way it is. I'm sorry."

"I heard a Russian proverb once," said Hoffman. "If you don't take risks, you don't drink champagne."

Volkov eased back from the table. "I'm a graduate student on a scholarship," he repeated. "I'm not scared of anything."

Hoffman pressed on. "I gather from Edith that you were interested in the Intelsat crash. Me, too, that was a big fuckup. How do you say that in Russian?

"*Obosrat'sya*," said Volkov. "It means, 'Shit in your pants.'"

"Well, that's what happened. It was an expensive satellite. Made by Loral in New York. We helped put that deal together. Now, blooey. I gather the Chinese are embarrassed. They should be."

They talked for nearly an hour, finishing the bottle of wine and the plate of charcuterie. Hoffman tried several times to draw Volkov out on his work and his Chinese contacts. But the Russian played dumb. He didn't know anyone or anything.

Volkov became animated when they talked about sports. Hoffman was a hockey fan, it seemed. His family was from Detroit. He had watched the great Sergei Fedorov, a star of the old Soviet national team who had defected to play for the Red Wings.

"I watched Fedorov, too," said Volkov wistfully. "Before he went to America, he played for CKSA Moscow. The Red Army Team, everyone called it. When he left, we knew it was over."

"Great hockey player," said Hoffman. "Best skater in the NHL. It's a new world, my friend."

Hoffman wanted to order another bottle of wine, but Volkov said it would be unfair. Americans didn't know how to drink. And he wanted to get back to campus before they closed the gates.

* * *

The day Edith returned from Hong Kong, Volkov met her at the student center and invited her to dinner that night. He had a little money now, thanks to his job at the institute. He suggested a restaurant near the university that served steamed dumplings. "My nickel," he said. He was trying to learn American slang. He wanted to talk. It was time. He didn't want to be "unsettled" anymore.

Edith gave him a coy smile as he made the dinner invitation, and then shook her head. She had a plan of her own. "Come up to my room instead," she said. "My roommate is away." She opened her big purse. Inside was a bottle of vodka, a box of crackers, and a wedge of cheese. "A private party," she said, putting her arm through his.

When they were upstairs, Volkov embraced her passionately. He enfolded her in his big arms, and his hands were under her sweater and then her skirt. She pressed tightly against him, but as he tried to maneuver her toward the bed, she stepped away. "Let's take it slow," she said. He nodded but couldn't resist and came at her again.

"Go slow, baby," she said, backing away again. "I mean it."

Edith sat him down on the bed. She got two glasses from the bathroom and poured a shot of vodka for him and one for herself and opened the crackers and cheese. Volkov didn't want to drink at first. He was wounded.

"I don't get you," he said. "So beautiful. Hot and cold. You're not like a Russian girl. Not like anybody."

"We don't know each other yet, Ivan. You barely know me." She smoothed her skirt and combed her hair with her fingers, so it looked less ruffled.

"Okay. What's your story, anyway?" He took a swig of vodka, and then another. She refilled his glass. She swept her hair back from her face and shook her head slightly to let the hair fall free.

"I told you, I'm an Irish girl from Massachusetts. A town called Holyoke, on the Connecticut River, almost in New York."

"What's it like, this Holyoke?"

"Industrial town. Paper mills. Factories. They've mostly closed down now."

"It sounds like Magnitogorsk. My town. The jobs went away, but the people stayed, the ones who were too old or too poor to escape. I got away."

"Me, too," said Edith. She took a big swig of vodka. She was a drinker, too, in addition to everything else.

"Were your parents rich?"

"Not really. My father edited the Holyoke newspaper, the *News-Transcript*. Peter Ryan, everyone calls him Pete. My mother Kate wrote the editorials. They didn't have much money, but when I was growing up, they seemed smarter than other people. They were Democrats. Most people in our neighborhood were Republicans."

"What is he like, your father?" asked Volkov.

"Well, he likes sports, the way everybody does. And he's patriotic. He sings the 'Star-Spangled Banner' out loud at Red Sox games. He raises an American flag in his front yard every morning. He was wounded in Vietnam, too. He wasn't a big hero, just unlucky. In the wrong place when a shell landed. But, yeah, he's Mr. Red, White, and Blue."

"My father was patriotic, too. 'My country right or wrong.' Isn't that what you say?

"Yes, that's what we all say. What did he do, your dad?"

"He was a steelworker. They wore him out. He was unlucky. Russia was unlucky, maybe."

"I'm sorry." She poured them both another vodka.

In the long pause, Volkov looked at her. "What was it like, your neighborhood?" asked Volkov.

She closed her eyes and bit her lips. It was as if she were fighting something. She opened them and leaned toward the big Russian.

"We lived in the north part of town, near a bend in the Connecticut River. The streets were all named after Ivy League colleges. First there was Yale Street. Go, Eli! Then Dartmouth, Harvard, Amherst, Stanford, Princeton. North of that was Blessed Sacrament, where we went to church. Small world. Too small for me."

He studied her face. He'd had a girlfriend, back in Moscow. But she wasn't remotely as interesting as this woman.

"Did you have secrets? Isn't that what Catholics do? Go to church and confess their secrets."

"Of course. Everybody has secrets." She tightened for a moment and closed her eyes again. "My senior year in high school, my best friend got pregnant. I helped her get an abortion. But I didn't tell anyone. That was a big secret."

"What did you say about it at church?"

"Honestly? I lied. When I went to confession, I said to Father Murphy, 'Forgive me, Father, for I have sinned.' I mentioned that I had shoplifted a purse at the department store, which was true, and that I'd had impure thoughts, which was also true. But I didn't say anything about the abortion. Father Murphy asked me if there was anything else, and I said, 'That is all I can remember. I am sorry for these and all my sins.' And that was it. But I never went back to church."

"So you're a good liar," said Volkov.

"Pretty good."

He put his arms around her once more and kissed her. She relaxed into his embrace at first, and he put his hand under her sweater again. But she shook her head. She looked terribly unhappy, suddenly, as if she had unintentionally broken something precious. He pulled back, wounded again.

"I get it. You don't want to have sex with me."

"Yes, I do," she said. "I've wanted to since we met. But, how can I say this? It wouldn't be right."

"Why not? If it feels right, then it is right. That's what I think. We don't need to have sex. Just let me hold you."

She shook her head. "It's wrong," she said. "I can't explain." She looked away. "It would be using you. Crossing a line."

"What line? I don't know what you're talking about."

"There are things about me that you don't know. Secrets."

"We all have secrets. Like you said."

"But these are different. They could get you in trouble."

He embraced her again and began to kiss her. But there were tears streaming down her face. And then she was sobbing.

"You have to go," she said. "Right now."

"What's wrong? What did I do?"

"Nothing. It's my fault. I don't want to hurt you."

Volkov tried to comfort her, but she pulled back and buried her head in her hands.

"I mean it," she said. Her tears continued, and through her weeping, she moaned, "Please, please, please, just go away."

*   *   *

They saw each other just one more time in Beijing. Edith approached, looking very drawn, outside his dorm. It was in a remote spot, shielded by trees from passersby and from the cameras that were outside every building.

"Hi," she said. He was silent. "I am supposed to tell you something. It's, like, I have to ask, or I'll get in trouble. My friend Hoffman wants to see you again."

"Bitch," muttered Volkov. He was angry. He had missed her, achingly, and this was what she wanted to say to him.

"Tell this Hoffman to fuck off," he said. "And you can fuck off, too."

A vexed look crossed her face. It was as if she had been ordered to do something that she detested. "Please see Hoffman," she repeated. "It could be the best thing, ever. For you, and me, and maybe for both of us."

Volkov looked at her carefully, silently, and played back in his mind the events of the last few weeks.

"It is not possible." He paused, shook his head, and backed away a step. "Do you work for . . ." He halted in midsentence. He didn't want to say the name of the agency. It was death. He started again. "Do you work for . . . the embassy?"

"No," she said. There was the slightest warble in her voice. "I'm a graduate student, like you." That wasn't enough. She knew she had to say more.

"I don't know what I'll do when I go back to the States. Work for the government, maybe. I don't know. But right now, I'm a student. One of my professors arranged it. At Yale."

Volkov nodded. He swallowed hard. He took another step back.

Edith reached out with a piece of paper of paper in her hand. Volkov could see an address and telephone number, written in block letters.

"I probably won't see you again. But if you ever want to talk to me, or talk to people like Larry Hoffman, this is my parents' address and phone number in Holyoke. Call them. They'll know how to get in touch with me. Wherever I am."

Volkov hesitated. His heart was pounding. He knew what this was about now, exactly.

"Please take it," she said. "Life is long. You never know."

Volkov looked around, to make sure no one was watching. He took the handwritten note. She turned and walked away.

At the bottom of the note, below her parents' address and phone number, she had written the words: "I'm sorry."

8

Beijing, April 1996

Professor Cao Lin requested another meeting with Ivan Volkov in early spring when the mid-term exams were over. Volkov had buried himself in his work the month after he said farewell to Edith face-to-face and in his heart. In the numb, solitary precision of his academic studies, he had focused so intensely that he had received the highest grades in all of his classes. His marks in radio astronomy and computational fluid dynamics were "starred" by his professors, which meant that they were exceptionally high.

The meeting with Cao Lin was at the Academy of Sciences. When Volkov was escorted to the big office on the top floor, the academician greeted him warmly, grasping the big Russian's hand in both of his own. Cao Lin was wearing an open-neck shirt and a new pair of expensive shoes. He looked like the host of a variety show.

On a table, Cao Lin had arrayed some gifts for his visitor. A bottle of Japanese whiskey and another of Russian vodka, a new laptop computer, and a fine cashmere shawl. There was a thick envelope, too, stuffed with cash.

"For your mother," said Cao Lin, pointing to the shawl. "You must miss her. We can bring her to China to visit you."

Volkov stroked the soft fabric with his hand. His mother wouldn't know what to do with something so elegant. She had only known roughness in her life. And it was impossible to imagine her visiting Beijing. She had only traveled to Moscow once.

"You are very kind to think of my mother, Professor Cao. But her health is not good. I do not think she could leave her home."

"Pity," said the academician. He motioned for Volkov to sit. They talked about his recent academic performance and his work at the institute. He noted particular areas where Volkov was proficient. He seemed to have received a briefing from every professor.

"A Russian man named Krastev from your embassy came to see me last week," said Cao Lin after a pause. "He told me the Russians have an interest in you. A future engineer in the new Russia, I think he said. Is that true?"

"I went to see Mr. Krastev when I first arrived in Beijing. I was told it was necessary. I haven't been back to see him since then. If he has an interest in me, it's not reciprocated."

There was a long silence, as if Cao Lin were waiting for his guest to say more, and when he didn't, the Chinese man broke the silence.

"How is your personal life, if I may ask, Mr. Volkov?" Cao Lin ventured.

"Nothing to say, sir. All I do, really, is work. No time for anything else. That's the way I like it."

"No girlfriend?" asked the academician gently.

"I did, sort of. But I stopped seeing her. She is a big *nyet* for me now."

"An American girl?"

So he knew. How could it be otherwise? The Chinese watched everything.

"Yes. An American. Edith Ryan. I did not feel comfortable with her. So now I stay away."

"Yes," said Cao Lin, as if he already knew that they had separated, as well. "Probably for the best. Having a girlfriend can be a burden for a young man. Too many, what, choices? Probably better to be alone, until you find, we can say, the right girl."

Volkov nodded. The Chinese had been observing her, too, inevitably. He worried, for a moment, about Edith. But she was a student, like him. She had told him so. He put it out of his mind.

"I am going be very un-Chinese, and say something direct," said Cao Lin.

"I want to trust you. I need someone like you, who is smart, very smart. But who is not Chinese or American. Someone who can go places where these people could not go. Who could act on my behalf."

"To do what?" asked Volkov.

"It is too soon for me to explain that. Much too soon. But would you be interested in working with me, as a special friend?"

"I don't know," said Volkov honestly. "I need to understand better what you are doing."

"Ha! Of course you do. You are too smart to be stupid."

Cao Lin went to his desk, picked up his phone, and said a few words in Chinese. Then he returned, a more serious look on his face.

"Do you remember, at our last meeting, we talked about the new American Global Positioning System, this 'GPS'"?

"Yes, certainly. I told you about our Russian GLONASS. But you didn't seem to think it was very good."

"It isn't. Take my word. But this GPS will change the world. It will be so powerful everyone, everywhere will depend on it. Right now it can tell an airplane or a ship where it is, in an instant. But maybe someday soon it can tell each of us the same thing. So that we know exactly where we are, always."

"How would it do that?" asked Volkov.

"I think you must have a mobile phone."

Volkov pulled his Samsung phone from his pocket.

"Before too long, the whole world will have one of those. And do you know what? The phones will all connect with this GPS. Everything will. It will be the arrow that points everyone in exactly the right direction. And the clock that orders every encounter, every business transaction. It will be an essential part of, what do the Americans call it, the 'connected' world? But do you know what? This GPS is not always, you know, reliable."

"Why not? I thought you said it was the best."

"It is. But sometimes there are gaps. They make us wonder."

Volkov leaned forward. The Chinese professor was trying to tell him something, but he didn't understand. "What gaps?" Volkov asked.

Cao Lin tilted his angular face, as if measuring his guest. "Do you follow the news?" he asked.

"Not really," answered Volkov. "I read *China Daily* at the library sometimes. But I'm not very interested in the news."

"Smart fellow. Stick to your studies. But perhaps you have heard about the recent difficulty in Taiwan. Chinese missiles and American ships and all of that. CNN can't stop talking about it."

"Yes," said Volkov warily. He remembered the silent CNN broadcast that had been playing on the professor's video monitor the first time he visited. "I read some Xinhua stories. They call it the 'Taiwan Strait Crisis.' But what does that have to do with GPS, Professor?"

"Maybe nothing. But researchers in our academy tell me that there have been some interruptions in the GPS signals over China recently. Who can say why? I fear they stopped the signals deliberately. But perhaps they have other problems. Maybe the Americans need some Chinese help. So that the system is more reliable."

Volkov raised his eyebrows. "How can you do that?"

"Mr. Volkov, this GPS cannot run without parts. Circuits, routers, connections, a whole chain of little things. And we can make all these things more cheaply than anyone. Have you been to the new economic zone at Shenzhen? We are making all the *little* things. Phones for this company and laptops for that one. We are very good at it, really.

"And this GPS," he continued. "It will have ground stations that will need the cheap computers and routers that we make so well. Its satellites in space will need solar panels for electricity. Who makes the cheapest and best solar panels? It is China. So we will have our place in this new world if we make the right contacts."

"Good business," said Volkov. He didn't understand the point of the conversation, but he didn't want to be impolite.

Cao Lin rested his chin on his hand as he pondered something. "I want you to meet someone," he said after a few moments. "An American fellow who works on these products. Let's make a date for next week. Someplace where we can relax. You must be getting tired of dormitory food. I'll think of something."

The Russian said he would be happy to meet Cao Lin's friend, wherever he suggested. His head was spinning. It was as if he were watching a play in a language he didn't understand. Back at Tsinghua, he visited his usual kiosk in the periodicals section of the library. But he couldn't find any mention of an interruption of GPS signals over the territory of China.

9

Beijing, April 1996

Professor Cao Lin invited Volkov to lunch at the Palace Hotel downtown. It was the fanciest place in town, a few blocks from Tiananmen Square. The management was based in Hong Kong, and they dressed the Chinese doormen like footmen from colonial times, with braided buttons on their jackets and round hats atop their heads. The Chinese academician was sitting at a table in the far end of the restaurant, shielded by an etched-glass partition. Sitting next to him was a younger man, with Chinese features but wearing a baseball cap with the logo of the New York Yankees.

"I would like you to meet Arthur Wang," said the professor "He is a Chinese American. He grew up in one of those places they call 'Chinatown.' But that was very long ago. He is forming a new company. Building products in China to sell to America. The best business. He wants to hire smart engineers and scientists. Arthur, meet Ivan. Two clever young people. Brains are in short supply, always."

After handshakes and polite small talk, the food began to arrive. It was a French restaurant, the fanciest of the fine dining establishments that had become popular with the Chinese elite. The academician had pre-ordered the meal, and the dishes began arriving. Duck liver pâté; caviar; steamed lobster; Wagyu beef, along with wines for each course. Volkov wasn't sure which of the

half-dozen knives and forks arrayed before him he should use. As they ate, Cao
Lin invited the Chinese American to explain his business plans.

Arthur Wang was one of those young entrepreneurs who was born to make
a pitch. It was part Power Point, part soap opera. He recalled his childhood in
New York's Chinatown, the Regents Scholarship that took him to Cornell, the
doctoral program at Berkeley.

"I was a satellite nut, always," said Wang. "Give me *Star Wars*, or *Star
Trek*, or star anything. But I was never just a Chinese lab-nerd. I wanted to
make money."

"Tell him the subject of your thesis," interjecteded Cao Lin.

"High-frequency radio waveforms for communications and navigation satellites. It seemed like a hot topic. I was ABD. Do they have that in Russia? It
means 'all but dissertation.'"

"Why did you quit?" asked Volkov.

"Because I needed money. My family was poor. Silicon Valley was getting
rich, and it was almost in my backyard at Berkeley. Graduate school was a bore.
So I got a job designing routers, and then I left and got a better job, designing
more advanced routers for a smaller company. But then I got, like, angry."

"Tell us why," said Cao Lin, who already knew.

"Because people using my ideas were getting rich, and I wasn't, and I was
smarter than they were. So, I thought: Arthur, why are you acting dumb? I quit
and formed my own company to make components for satellite systems. I had
a friend who had studied finance at business school. His name is Roger Birken.
Nice guy. All-American."

"What's the company?" asked Volkov.

"We named it Satellite Supply Systems. Like plumbing supplies, or hardware, except that it's for the satellite market. We sell ground stations, cables,
dishes, all the uncool stuff that nobody remembers. What do you think?"

Volkov tried to conjure the right answer. There wasn't an obvious correct
one, so he said what he thought.

"You have *yaytsa*. That means 'balls.' In Russia, people don't take so
many chances. It's not healthy. There are too many people who want a slice
of your pie. You need a roof, that's what we call it. Something over your head,
for protection."

"In America, we have roofs, too. The Department of Justice. The Securities Exchange Commission. Boards of directors and general counsels and compliance officers. We don't get wet. Not so dangerous as in Russia. So, Ivan, if I can be informal, American-style, Mr. Cao said you might be willing to talk about the space business."

"I am listening, for sure." Volkov was wary, too. Hearing the speech about American roofs, he wondered if Arthur Wang had friends in Washington.

"My company needs engineers and scientists. Mr. Cao has been helping me make contacts, and he said that you have a lot of talent, so I asked him if I could talk to you."

Volkov looked at Wang, then Cao. "Do you work for Professor Cao?"

Cao laughed, but it was the American who answered.

"Hell, no," said Wang. "He's helping me, introductions, permissions, party contacts. Roofs, right? And I'm helping Mr. Cao's family, who want to get settled in America. His daughter in Seattle is going to have a baby. His sister is moving to Vancouver. Maybe she'll work for Satellite Supply Systems. We're a start-up. We can do whatever we like."

"Well, okay, tell me about the company, then," said the Russian.

"Our headquarters will be in California, but our production operations will mostly be here in China. It makes business sense. People get goo-goo when they talk about space. It's all those years of looking at astronauts and their families. But space is about money, Ivan. Satellites will be like telephone poles. They will carry all the wires. We want to be part of that business. A low-cost supplier, but high-quality, too. Are you interested?

Volkov was flustered. He had never pursued a real job. He knew hockey rinks and libraries. But not money.

"How much will you pay?" he asked.

"Senior technical staff in China will make fifteen thousand yuan a month, about three thousand dollars. So maybe fifty thousand dollars a year, with a bonus. But that's just the starting salary. And it's negotiable."

Volkov did a quick calculation. That salary would be worth nearly three thousand rubles. Not a fortune. But enough to buy his mother a new television. And a dishwasher. And an airplane ticket to China.

While he was thinking, Arthur Wang broke in.

"We'll pay for an apartment, too. In Guangzhou. That's worth another five thousand dollars, easy."

Volkov's eyes widened.

"I need to think about it," he said.

"Ask for stock," said Cao Lin.

Volkov raised his eyebrows. "What?"

"Shares in the company. That's how you'll make real money. Isn't that right, Arthur? So, if you want Mr. Volkov, offer him stock options."

Volkov nodded. The point of this exercise was to get as much money as possible. That much he understood. "Yes, stock," he said.

"Absolutely. Give me a couple of days. I need to talk to my partner, Roger, about dilution. But that's probably doable. Let's confirm it on Monday. Can you give me an answer then?"

It was Thursday. That was four days. "Sure," said Volkov.

Wang gave him a business card, with a U.S. number and a Chinese one. "Call the '86' number. But you're going to say yes, right?"

"Maybe so. I will tell you Monday, after you talk to Roger about the stock option thing."

Cao Lin was all smiles. The dessert had arrived. A vacherin, with coconut ice cream, mango sorbet, and passion fruit caramel custard. Volkov went home in Cao Lin's limousine with his head spinning.

*   *   *

That Sunday, the day before Volkov was going to talk again with Arthur Wang, he got a call on his cell phone. It was his mother, telephoning from Magnitogorsk. Her voice was weak, but insistent.

"I'm very sick," she said. "You have to come home now."

II

IVAN AND VERONIKA

RUSSIA, 1996–1997

Failure [in space] came badly to a [Russian] people fed on a diet of success.... The Mars 96...spacecraft was shipped to Baikonur during the summer. Even then, finishing the probe off in the hangar in Baikonur presented its own problems. Baikonur was suffering from power shortages as utilities tried to keep going in the face of unpaid bills. At one stage, in a telling parable of the state of Russia at the time, there was no electricity, so technicians found themselves trying to complete the ultramodern Mars probe in the cold and the dark by candlelight and kerosene heaters. Many engineers were never paid for their work.

—BRIAN HARVEY, *Russian Planetary Exploration: History, Development, Legacy and Prospects*

10

Magnitogorsk, May 1996

Ivan Volkov emerged from the salmon-pink façade of the Magnitogorsk train station in the first rays of the morning. He had traveled almost four days, with a bus passage through Kazakhstan in the middle of the trip. Magnitogorsk looked almost beautiful in the early light. Steel production had collapsed, so the air was nearly clean. The lake to the east of the station was heavy with filth, yet it glistened as a breeze off the Steppes striated the water into tiny waves. Across the boulevard from the train station was a giant statue of a metalworker with his upraised hammer.

Volkov took a taxi to his family's apartment near the western bank of the Ural River. He lugged his case up the stairs and found the key that his mother always left under the mat. He opened the door and shouted her name. But the apartment was empty. The rooms were tidy; she had scrubbed the simple flat before leaving. A note on the kitchen table explained that she had gone to Regional Cancer Hospital No. 2, in the northern part of the city. She had left two moldering sandwiches of meat and cheese in the refrigerator, and a bottle of vodka.

Over the mantel was a portrait of his father Vladimir in a suit with a red tie, knotted too big, taken at a meeting of the Magnitogorsk city party committee.

He was wearing his two medals, the Order of Labor Valor, and the Order of the Red Banner of Labor. The frame around his father's portrait had dulled, but the glass was still shiny. His mother polished it every week.

Volkov ate the two sandwiches. He didn't drink the vodka at first; it was still early morning. But there was something about being home, in the emptiness of the apartment where he had grown up, that made him want to do as his father had in too many times of despair. He opened the bottle and drank a glass, and then another. Sharp, astringent, deadening. He dragged his suitcase into the room that he had shared with his brother. He debated whether to unpack and then decided, yes.

From the window of his bedroom, Volkov could see in the east the "Magnetic Mountain" for which the city was named. It was so rich with iron ore that compass needles and migratory birds lost direction within its pull. Stalin constructed his steelmaking colossus on this remote spot in 1929. A famous German architect was imported to design a workers' paradise, but his project stalled, partly because the party couldn't make up its mind on which side of the Ural River paradise should be constructed.

"When can we leave this place?" Volkov sometimes asked his father as a teenager, when it was hard even for the old man to pretend that the socialist dream was going according to plan. But it's a truth about places like Magnitogorsk, or Pittsburgh in America, that people don't leave, even when everything around them is yellowing with rust.

Volkov's mother was stoically loyal to her husband and his comrades. She had a secret bourgeois life, reading mimeographed pages of poetry and fiction passed among friends; she played the flute in a chamber group with neighbors who were violinists and cellists, who met in the basement of her apartment building. Suffering was the norm, and every happy day was a precious accident, unlikely to be repeated.

*   *   *

Volkov took the bus to Regional Cancer Hospital No. 2. It was a five-story concrete block, as charmless as a prison. There was a little garden out back where the patients could walk. Next door stood a small Orthodox church whose onion dome had been given a new coat of gold paint since the fall of the Soviet

Union. Volkov asked for his mother Marina at the front desk. "Lung cancer," he said. The nurse nodded. That affliction was a local specialty in Magnitogorsk.

Marina Volkova was in a room with three other women. She was asleep when her son arrived. Volkov approached the bed quietly. He felt unsteady for a moment as he watched her breathing through an oxygen tube affixed to her nostrils. She was so thin. Her skin was the dull color of gray ash. The woman he had left a year before was gone. He touched the frail, veined skin of her hand, afraid she might leave him in the next moment. To his astonishment, she opened her eyes and smiled.

"*Golubchik*," she whispered. My little dove. "You have come home."

Volkov held his mother's hand. His eyes filled with tears. It had been a very long time since he had cried, but he did now. His mother was right. He had come home.

11

Magnitogorsk, June 1996

The dean for foreign graduate students at Tsinghua contacted Volkov soon after he returned to Russia. The first email was a gentle inquiry about his mother's condition, but that was followed by a sharper note reminding him that he was expected to sit for his final examinations in early June, at the end of spring term. Volkov responded to both messages in similar language: that his mother was seriously ill, he was the only family member present and could not leave. Meanwhile, an email arrived from the Tsinghua bursar's office, copied several days later in a registered letter, warning that if Volkov did not complete his final exams, he would be expected to repay his fellowship.

Beijing seemed very far away, and unimportant. When Volkov wasn't seeing his mother, he worked out at a local gym or visited several friends from his old youth hockey league team. The Steel Foxes, they were called.

Seeing his hockey teammates was a mindless pleasure. The others hadn't gone on to college, let alone graduate school. Too many pucks to the head, perhaps. One had moved to Moscow and then returned broke. Another played briefly for Metallurg, the city's premier team, and then was cut. He had the team's name on his forearm, too. When Volkov pulled up his sleeve and showed his tattoo, the friend sang out the team's name.

His friends spent their days and nights now snorting methamphetamine and drinking. They seemed glad that Volkov was back, assuming that he, too, had failed to escape the gravitational field of this imploding Russian steel town. They made him laugh, with their cynical obscene jokes, just as they had a decade before, and they took his mind off his mother's troubles.

Volkov was wondering what to tell the dean at Tsinghua when an email arrived from the assistant to Professor Cao Lin at the Academy of Sciences. She wanted to arrange a telephone call between the academician and Volkov. He was dreading an arm-twisting session, or another demand for reimbursement. But when Cao Lin called, he was gentle and supportive.

"Of course, we understand," said the academician. "We will call this 'compassionate leave.' I have instructed the institute to keep paying your stipend. If you give me a bank routing number in Russia, I will wire the money immediately."

Volkov mumbled thanks. He apologized that he had not kept up with his work in radio astronomy, fluid dynamics, and the other courses. But the academician told him not to worry. He would call the dean. Exams could be handled later.

"Family comes first," said Cao Lin. "We would just like to be sure that you will be coming back to us. We think you have a wonderful future. As the Americans say, we would like to buy stock in you." He chuckled.

Volkov promised that he would contact Tsinghua as soon as things were clear. Cao Lin clucked his tongue in sympathy. Of course, of course. Just let us know. When the Chinese professor ended the call, Volkov had an odd sense that someone else might have been listening.

The next day, an elaborate bouquet of flowers was delivered to Marina Volkova's room at Regional Cancer Hospital No. 2. The card said it was from the Chinese Academy of Sciences. Later that day, Madame Volkova was moved into the hospice ward.

* * *

In the final week of his mother's life, Volkov had an unlikely visitor. His name was Sergei Shulman, and he said that he was a dean at the Faculty of Physics at Novosibirsk State University, farther east in Siberia. Volkov was impressed.

During Soviet times, Novosibirsk had been a closed city, where some of the country's most advanced scientific work had been done.

Volkov took his visitor to a café nearby that overlooked the Ural River, to escape the now-dirty apartment..

"I gather you have been doing some interesting work in China," said Shulman when they were settled. "People say you are talented." He was a small, intense man with wiry hair.

Volkov stared back at him. His mother was dying, his only desire was privacy, and here was a man he had never met, intruding himself and making flattering comments about his research.

"How do you know anything about me? You are a professor. I am a graduate student who couldn't pay his tuition at Moscow State University. Why would you care?"

Shulman shrugged. "Scientists like to gossip." That wasn't an answer, but Volkov got the message. People watched everything in Russia, even when it was coming apart at the seams. His phone calls, his emails, probably his entire academic transcript, were available for anyone who was curious.

"The Chinese have been good to me, you know," Volkov said. "I was planning to go back."

"China, China. The Chinese are like a clever little brother, but not a big boy, not really. They are good at copying things, but they are not inventors. Do they play chess? No. I hear you are interested in space. Is that right?"

Volkov nodded. Someone had gone to considerable trouble to research his file.

"China in space is nothing. They have no astronauts. Their rockets crash. They steal other countries' secrets, and maybe they steal their researchers, too, like you. But they are nothing. They have big eyes but no mouth. But Russia, in space, we are the king. The first satellite, the first astronaut, the biggest rockets. Even now, with our troubles, we are still the best. The *vory* who run Roscosmos, they may be big crooks, but they have money to pay for talent. They can provide scholarships at university. *Research* grants. You hear me?"

"I am already working in a lab in Beijing. It's clean there. No games."

"Come on, Ivan Vladimirovich. You make me laugh. What is Beijing? It is a colony of America. Come home. You will work in a better lab in Moscow.

I promise you. Apply for readmission at Moscow State University. They will admit you. With a scholarship. I know. I am on the committee."

"But you're at Novosibirsk."

"It's another committee. Never mind. Just trust me. Why do you think I am here? People want you back. You know the saying: Visiting is good, but home is better. So come home."

Volkov said he hadn't decided what to do. He was thinking about his mother. He would make up his mind soon. Shulman gave him an envelope stuffed with rubles. "For the funeral," he said. When he counted later, it was the equivalent of nearly a thousand dollars.

After Shulman left, Volkov went to a funeral home near his apartment and bought a lacquered wood coffin with gold-painted handles and a silk crèche for the body. He thought: This will be the nicest home my mother has ever had.

12

Magnitogorsk, July 1996

Marina Volkova was buried next to her husband in a plot that Vladimir Volkov had been assigned by the party while he was still an active member. It was on the eastern side of the river, in the shadow of the steel plant. The ground was flat and there were few trees. The distinguishing feature on the landscape was the hulk of the rusting blast furnace and the metal frame of the conveyor belt that had carried iron ore to the top.

Volkov bought a stone monument for his mother, engraved with her name and the dates of her birth and death, and a photograph of her from just after her marriage when she looked almost young and carefree. There was a picture of his father on the adjacent monument, too, weathered, the image barely visible. On his mother's tombstone, he thought of placing an Orthodox cross below the name, the way people were doing now; but he had never once seen her pray, and he decided that if he could have asked her about the cross, she would have said no.

He told the funeral home instead to craft a metal plaque with the words of a poem she had read aloud to him when he was a teenager in the 1980s, when the Soviet world was opening, even in Magnitogorsk. It was a few lines from a poem by Anna Akhmatova called "A land not mine," published when the government first allowed her works to be circulated openly. Volkov traced the words with his finger. "Sunset in the ethereal waves: I cannot tell if the day is ending, or the world, or if the secret of secrets is inside me again."

Several dozen people were at the graveside. Neighbors from the apartment building, a few of his father's friends from the metalworkers' union, several teachers from the school where his mother had taught music, one of Volkov's mentors at the Young Technicians Club, and several of his hockey friends.

There was no priest to say any words over the grave. Volkov asked one of the neighbors upstairs, who was a violinist in the conservatory orchestra, to play a violin solo written by Nikolai Rimsky-Korsakov, which the neighbor had played in private for his mother and other friends in the basement of the apartment building, back when it was not permitted in public.

Volkov shook hands with each of the mourners as they departed. Many of them appeared to have been weeping, but perhaps people always did that at funerals. When all the guests had departed, Volkov sat at the foot of his parents' graves and thought about whether he should leave Russia, perhaps forever. A month before, that had been an obvious choice. But now it seemed impossible.

* * *

Several days after the burial, when Volkov was closing his mother's bank account and settling other details of her modest estate, he received a hand-delivered request from the Magnitogorsk office of the Federal Security Service, known as the FSB, which had been created the year before as the domestic successor to the old KGB. The letter asked him to visit the head of the local office at ten the next morning.

Volkov wasn't frightened so much as curious. He had done nothing wrong. His papers were in order. His only worry was that someone might want him to pay a bribe or do a favor, in exchange for something he might need. The rules of the new Russia weren't clear yet. People were making them up as they went along.

Volkov arrived for his appointment fifteen minutes early. The security headquarters was a solid block on a divided highway bisected by a trolly line. It had a high fence and a guard booth out front. The façade had been freshly painted, in an incongruous sunny yellow. Volkov showed his papers at the gate and was taken upstairs to a waiting room outside the chief's office. He had been seated for five minutes when a uniformed man strode into the room, carrying some papers in his hands.

"Dr. Volkov," he said, extending his hand to the visitor. Volkov didn't correct him. "I have been asked to deliver something to you. It is an airplane ticket to Moscow. Here." He handed over the ticket.

"You have been invited by the dean of the Department of Astrophysics and Stellar Astronomy at Moscow State University to enroll for the fall semester. The dean has sent you a letter. Here." He delivered a second packet of correspondence. "I have for you, also, an invitation from the director of the Space Research Institute of the Russian Academy of Sciences, offering you a stipend. Here."

Volkov gathered the papers. Moscow State University had put together what in business terms would be called a "matching offer" equivalent to what he had been receiving in Beijing.

"Thank you," said Volkov. "I want to think about it, before accepting the airplane ticket and the rest."

The FSB officer looked startled. Why would anyone turn down a gift from powerful people? "They are expecting an immediate answer."

"What if I say no?"

"Dr. Volkov," said the officer gently. He was trying not to get angry. "I don't think you understand. This is an offer from, I can say, people of some importance. They have reviewed your file. They do not want you to return to China. They want you to be a good Russian and stay in your country, where your talents are valued. Frankly speaking, this is a matter of special interest. That is why I, as a representative of the special services, am delivering the message."

"It's very sudden, that's all. My mother has just passed. I want to do the right thing."

"I feel sorry for your loss. My condolences. I think, Doctor, that your mother would want you to stay in your country. I have read your file. Your parents were patriots. If you say no, you can never come back to Russia."

"I want to be a free man. Can I be free here? In the new Russia."

"Yes," said the officer. "Why not?"

Volkov closed his eyes. Suddenly he knew that it wasn't really a choice. He was not born for permanent exile. He swallowed hard.

"I accept. Please have your colleagues in Moscow tell the dean's office that I will contact them to arrange my housing. It will take me a week. I will write the dean a personal letter of thanks."

The FSB officer was relieved. He didn't have to use persuasive methods. He shook Volkov's hand and then patted him on the back.

Volkov looked at his handler with an odd sense of comradeship. Russians were frightened. Their world had been turned upside down. The idea that their brightest minds were abandoning the country made people in a town like Magnitogorsk worry that the very foundations of life were crumbling.

Volkov contacted Professor Cao Lin. The academician was disappointed, and also incredulous. Didn't Volkov know that he was betting on a loser? The young Russian had big talents and big dreams. "It is the stress of your mother's death, of course," he said eventually. "When you think things over, maybe you will change your mind. You will always be welcome."

Cao Lin said he would speak with the administrators at Tsinghua. They messaged Volkov a day later that they would be leaving his file open pending future word from him.

Volkov flew to Moscow two weeks later. He stopped by his mother's grave on his last afternoon in Magnitogorsk. One of the furnaces was wheezing smoke that day, and the hot July air was filled with soot. To the west, a summer storm was gathering, with distant illuminations at the horizon. Volkov thought of his mother, reading poetry in the flickering light of their apartment. "You will hear thunder and remember me, and think: she wanted storms," Akhmatova had written. His mother had wanted calm, in truth, and now she had it.

Volkov flew west toward Moscow with the certainty that he could not escape the suffering that was Russia.

13

Moscow, September–November 1996

Ivan Volkov's reentry gate in Moscow was a formal debriefing about his year in China. Volkov had no secrets. He was exactly what he claimed to be: a Russian student who had returned to his old university. He had put on five pounds since returning home. He had regained a ruddy color, too, in the wind and the dry cold of his homeland. As with so many Russian faces, the hard set of his eyes and lips gave him a look of skepticism bordering on surliness.

The examination was conducted by the deputy administrator of security at Moscow State University, in the spike-domed tower that dominated the campus. His examiners gathered in a conference room with a window overlooking the Moscow River to the north and, beyond it, Red Square.

Accompanying the university representative were two FSB security officers, who asked most of the questions. The administrator apologized for the inquiry. It was a relic of the past, he said. This was a new era! But it was a requirement for Volkov's part-time work for the Faculty of Space Research, which the university had arranged as part of his admission package.

The government security men silently attached wires and galvanic sensors to his body and inserted graphing paper in the polygraph machine they had brought along. The polygraph had become legal in the new Russia. In the old days, the KGB favored torture as a means to obtain the truth, but now the security services, the police, and even private companies were strapping people up to these "modern" machines to chart their truthfulness.

Volkov took his seat in the conference room. He wanted to make a clean start. He liked being back in Moscow. He had arrived in late summer, before the chill descended. The university had assigned him a dormitory room in a building near the campus, close to the Moscow State Circus. At night Volkov could see the neon lights surrounding the circus building and the long lines waiting to enter.

The polygraphers' questions began with simple biographical data to establish a baseline. What is your name? Where were you born? Have you ever visited China? The polygraphers watched the needle and calibrated the settings. Volkov answered every question truthfully. He listed the names and positions of the Chinese researchers he had met. He detailed the level of scientific progress he had observed in their space program. When asked if he had met any Americans at Tsinghua, he mentioned Edith Ryan and described her background. He said they had both decided to end the relationship because it had no future.

The examiners pressed a little, but not very much. Volkov would have told them about his meeting at the hotel with the American banker, Larry Hoffman, but they didn't ask.

When the examiners asked Volkov if he had received any job offers while he was in Beijing, he mentioned the Chinese American from Silicon Valley, Arthur Wang, and his space infrastructure company, Satellite Supply Systems. That prompted a string of additional questions about Wang's job offer, his company's future plans, and the Chinese government's interest.

But none of Volkov's answers seemed to raise suspicions, and the examination ended after ninety minutes. Nobody told Volkov that he had passed, but he quickly received permission to review "confidential" information, and soon after that he was given a clearance for what was known as "completely secret" material. It would be a long four years later, after he had taken a research position at the Lebedev Physical Institute, that he would be cleared for the highest level, categorized as "particularly important."

*   *   *

Volkov's classes that fall were mostly in the Faculty of Physics. The institution had the solemnity of a museum. An ornate wooden cabinet displayed the photographs of the eight faculty members who had won Nobel prizes. The faculty's journal remained classified, so it was hard to do even the simplest research without special permission.

Moscow had gotten hipper and crazier in the year Volkov had been away. New clubs played techno music, and drugs were plentiful and cheap. Russia had rediscovered sex since the fall of communism; it was in the air now, hot and steamy, on campus, in bars and clubs, even in the stacks of the library. Women relished their new freedom; birth control pills, once hard to obtain, were as cheap as aspirin. Volkov had a string of one-night stands that fall with women who liked him, and not for his brains.

Volkov's faculty adviser was a hard-boiled middle-aged professor. She had ridden the roller coaster of late-Soviet life and planted her feet in physics, the only academic area where Russia remained an undisputed world champion. She told Volkov bluntly that the university had agreed to take him back and pay his way because, as she put it, "certain people, I do not need to say who," wanted him to develop the satellite specialty he had developed in Beijing.

"Can I do what I want?" Volkov asked at their first meeting.

She looked at him curiously. From what planet had he arrived? "Of course," she said. "So long as what you want is what they want."

She studied the course catalogue and constructed for him a first-semester program that included more radio astronomy, as well as astrophysics, laser physics, and a special tutorial in the physics and engineering requirements of satellite telemetry.

"That's what I want," said Volkov. He was trying to make a joke. She shook her head.

"Ponyatiya," she muttered. It was a word that criminal gangs used to describe the unwritten rules that were more important than any statutes. "Be careful," she said. "The people you will be working for are running out of money. Everything is for sale."

* * *

The Russian Space Research Institute was styled like a technology park in America, with a big green lawn sloping up to a modern glass office block. The lobby was decorated with space vehicles from Russia's vaunted early days, and photographs of the first cosmonauts and their capsules. A visitor could see that a common feature of the pioneer space travelers, from Yuri Gagarin on, was that they tended to be very short, and thus able to fit in the tiny capsules the Russians were able to launch in the late 1950s.

The institute's obsession that season was a space project known as Mars 96. The launch date was scheduled for November, two months hence. The plan was to do something that even NASA had never done, which was to land a rover on Mars and explore the surface. For a country whose empire had disintegrated on earth, this space dream was precious.

On the day in November when the Mars rocket was set to launch, Volkov managed to squeeze into the back of the institute's command center. He hugged his colleagues when the television monitor showed the liftoff of the huge Proton rocket. The lander was due to arrive on Mars a year later, and the Russian television commentator talked of putting cosmonauts on Mars by 2015.

The spacecraft was parked in earth orbit waiting to rocket toward its target when something went terribly wrong. The upper stage misfired, and the capsule began an erratic, uncontrollable descent back toward earth. It eventually crashed in Chile.

Volkov watched the agony from the institute command center. When mission control reported (secretly, at first, but then everyone knew) that the capsule and its two landers were gone, Volkov was upset. Russia had failed in many things, but not space. As he looked around the command center, some of his colleagues were crying.

"What is wrong with our country?" Volkov muttered to himself but loud enough to be heard by his colleagues nearby.

"Things will get better," said the payload specialist who sat in the next cubicle, when they had returned to their desks. Volkov nodded. Of course they would get better.

14

The Space Research Institute closed for several weeks, for "renovation."
Volkov's classmates at the Faculty of Physics didn't talk about the Mars mission. It was like a death in the family. When the institute reopened in December, Ivan Volkov was summoned to meet a "visitor."

Volkov didn't recognize him at first. It was only when he introduced himself that Volkov recalled an encounter, a year earlier, in the Russian Embassy in Beijing, with an embassy officer who had quizzed him about his research program at Tsinghua University. The man had put on weight since then. The veins in his nose were bright red. He reminded Volkov vaguely of someone from his childhood.

"Welcome home," said Simeon Krastev. "I told them that you would not return to China. They were worried. They cannot afford to lose talent. They are interested in you." It was obvious that by "they," Krastev meant what Russians liked to call the "special services."

"We are all sad about Mars 96," Krastev continued. "But let me be frank. The future of Russia's space program has nothing to do with these scientific missions to collect Martian dust and measure the size of its craters. You know that, of course."

Volkov was a head taller than the pudgy intelligence officer. He leaned toward him. "I am a science student. We gather knowledge, and if we are successful, we also create knowledge. What people do with that knowledge is not my responsibility."

"Yes, I know. Nice speech." He clapped his hands silently, in pantomime. "But, Ivan Vladimirovich, you need to see facts as facts. The future of space is a military domain. We have always known that, among reasonable people. But now it is obvious. Russian space efforts will continue, but not to put pictures of cosmonauts on the front page of the newspaper. No more of that. We can't afford it."

"What does that mean for me? I am a researcher."

"There is no pure research. That is a fantasy. We want you to continue your work. But for the greater good. Always."

Volkov shifted his weight in his chair, thinking. He had a momentary desire to punch the corpulent spy in his bulbous nose. He cleared his throat.

"I am interested in satellite telemetry," Volkov said. "I was thinking that I might apply to work on the GLONASS system. That is useful to the nation."

"Perhaps." Krastev shrugged. "Who can say where talent will be most useful? For the time being, we hope you will continue with your studies. We have spoken with your adviser at the physics faculty and also at the institute. I told them that I will be your special friend now."

Volkov felt a turn in his stomach. He realized now who Krastev looked like. The overfed party branch secretary in Magnitogorsk, whom his father had called, "the commissar." When his father was sick, the commissar had denied him care at the party's special hospital in Chelyabinsk.

"I would like you to meet with one of us regularly, but not here," continued Krastev. "Write down the address of your dormitory room, and the number of your cellular phone." He handed Volkov a blank piece of paper and a pen. "One of my colleagues will contact you, to suggest an appropriate meeting place."

Volkov left the meeting with Krastev and went to the park outside the office. He sat on a bench in front of the institute until it got too cold. He had a momentary desire to flee, to go back to China or to head to Europe. He knew that was impossible. His passport had expired, and he had no money. But it was more than that. He was a Russian, attached to his country with sullen, stubborn pride. The worst days were past, he told himself.

He returned to the office block and settled back at his desk. He had been working on a telemetry problem, calculating the angle of insertion of a spacecraft into medium-earth orbit at an altitude and speed that would match those of the existing Russian constellation of navigation satellites.

The researcher in the next cubicle wandered by in the late afternoon and asked Volkov what he was working on. Volkov explained that he was trying to learn the basics of GLONASS architecture.

"You're wasting your time," said his colleague. "There's no money left for that. Those satellites will all die."

* * *

Volkov was in his dorm room late one night, completing a physics assignment due the next day, when there was a knock on his door. He wasn't expecting anyone. His mates down the hall had left hours before to go to a club. He gave his face a slap to wake himself up and opened the door, but there was nobody outside. A piece of paper had been left on the floor. On it was written the address of a flat block near Gorky Park and a date and time, two days hence.

Volkov arrived at the specified time and place. It was a cheery apartment, much nicer than his own. Sandwiches and cakes had been laid on a side table; atop a big coffee table stood a pyramid of ice chilling a bowl of caviar and bottle of vodka. Sitting on a couch, behind the caviar and vodka, was a man in a black suit.

"Alexei," he said, extending his hand. He gave Volkov a card; it didn't have a name or address; just a phone number. "I work with Lieutenant Colonel Krastev. He is very busy these days, so he asked me to take care of things."

"What things?" asked Volkov.

"We have found a part-time job for you at Roscosmos. They are responsible for GLONASS. Good luck, I may say. They do not hire too many people."

"I thought GLONASS was a civilian project," said Volkov.

"Don't be silly. Nothing in Russia is civilian. Everything needs protection. Now you will have protection."

"I'm a scientist," said Volkov.

Alexei nodded politely. "I am an intelligence officer. But these are new days. There is no more KGB. Poof!" He made a sound like he was blowing away the petals of a flower.

Alexei looked at his watch. He was not a man for small talk. He handed Volkov an envelope. "Count it," he said. Inside were five thousand rubles.

"Why are you giving me this?" asked Volkov.

"It is a stipend. The people at Roscosmos have no money. They won't pay enough for your meals. So we help them out. Their projects are still important, even if some of them are rascals. We will give you names of people there you can trust. Do a good job there, and someday, for you, there will be a nice job in a real research institute. Mr. Scientist.'

Volkov took the money and, on the way out, ladled himself a big spoonful of caviar. With the cash, he rented a new apartment, farther from the university. He worked weekends for a bank, writing computer code for their back office. For the first time in his life, he had some money.

*   *   *

Roscosmos was headquartered in a tower block northeast of the city center. The space agency had moved there after leaving its old home at the Ministry of General Machine Parts. The new offices had the unfinished look of a start-up business that had run out of capital. The company's urgent mission now, as with every other enterprise in the bankrupt former Soviet Union, was to sell things to the West.

The first floor was gaily decorated with mementos from the old trophy days, when its bosses were featured in lavish spreads in *Izvestia* and broadcasts on All-Union television specials. Now it was a premature relic; on many of the upper floors, proper ceilings hadn't been hung, and naked light bulbs dangled from the plaster.

Volkov received an introductory briefing from a woman manager who looked bored as she mechanically recited the architecture of the GLONASS system. Volkov asked how precise the system was in its geolocation. He had been studying the American version, which was accurate to about one foot, but the Russian data wasn't published yet.

"Ten meters," said the manager. She shrugged. "Maybe twenty. It is not perfect, frankly speaking. We have a better system that can be accessed by, we can say, 'special users.'"

On his second day at Roscosmos, Volkov was summoned by a man whose demeanor suggested that he was from the "special user" section. He had a round Turkic face; he said he was from Baikonur, near Kazakhstan, where the Russians launched their satellites. Everyone called him by the Turkish honorific "Pasha."

Pasha's office was in a bunker several stories underground, reached by a special elevator. The room was dominated by an illuminated satellite tracking screen that displayed the GLONASS array, and also American GPS satellites.

Pasha pointed to the two constellations. He shook his head in a way that conveyed disgust, with his budget, his thieving circle of employees, and the slow-motion collapse of what had once been the world's pioneering program in space.

"You're the new astrophysicist?" asked Pasha.

Volkov recited his credentials.

"Can you fix our satellites?"

"Yes. Maybe. What's wrong with them?"

"Russian satellites are shit. Too sloppy. Imprecise. What use are they? If I want to shoot a deer, and I'm a dozen meters off, what do I hit? I hit my friend's ass, probably."

He grabbed Volkov and pulled the big man closer. "You're supposed to be smart. How do I make better GLONASS satellites?"

Volkov thought a moment. This was a door opening. The Kazakh space boss was right about precision. He recalled something that an aging scientist in China had said to him a year before, which had never left him.

"You need better clocks," Volkov said. "Satellites can't measure distances unless you know precisely where they are in space. But you can't calibrate that accurately unless the clock in the satellite and the one on the ground are synchronized. That's why GLONASS is sloppy. Time is precision."

"Time is *money*," muttered Pasha. "I can't fix anything if I can't pay for it."

The Kazakh was pondering what to do with Volkov when an aide summoned him. A Russian businessman was pitching a deal to sell space on Russian rockets to a new consortium of European and Indian companies. The "rent" for Roscosmos would be in the tens of millions of dollars, and the *dan* on that, the skim, would be in the millions.

Pasha retreated to his office to make the deal. Volkov's proposal for more precise clocks was forgotten.

*   *   *

Because Volkov could speak English, they sent him that winter to the head-quarters of the European Space Agency in Paris. The Europeans were planning their own geolocation system, to be known as Galileo, and the Roscosmos team hoped to sell them components of the Russian commercial system.

The Europeans politely conveyed their lack of interest. A Dutch scientist eventually said it out loud: GLONASS was so imprecise it was useless; the average working life of the Russian satellites was just three years, when they worked at all; and the electronics were knockoffs of technical hardware from the West. GLONASS was so short of cash it had reduced the number of satellites in its constellation.

The sales trip was a bust. But for many members of the Russian team, that had been a secondary objective. Their deeper mission had been to purchase goodies they could sell back in Russia. Before departing, many visited the big Fnac electronics store off the Champs-Élysées and stocked up on television sets, disk drives, Sony PlayStations, and other marvels that they could resell for a hefty profit back in Moscow.

Volkov's colleagues got drunk at the airport and bought pornographic magazines at the news kiosk. They weren't embarrassed. They were playing by the new rules. Several colleagues asked Volkov why he wasn't joining the free-lance smuggling scheme. What made him special? He assured them that he wouldn't tell anyone, and that seemed to be enough.

Volkov didn't talk to anyone on the flight back. He played chess against himself on a plastic board he'd brought on the trip. Solitude was his new friend. He found that talking to himself in his head was more interesting than talking to most "real" people.

15

Moscow, February–June 1997

In the frigid midwinter of February 1997, Volkov was invited to a party at a new club called Titanic, in an underground cellar in the suburbs, near the stadium where the Dynamo soccer team played. Volkov went with an old friend named Lev, who had gotten rich buying up commercial rights to hockey stadiums around the country that were now up for grabs. Lev, the new king of the rinks, was buying shots of vodka for everyone near his table, and party girls were gathering around him, dancing with each other and traipsing off to the bathroom to get high.

The underground bar was hot and noisy. The DJ was playing an amped-up techno-disco mix. On the dark walls were posters of Russian grunge bands. One of the girls, very drunk, got up on the bar and danced topless until she slipped and fell. There were plenty of hands to grab her.

Volkov was drinking shots and watching the show when a woman with sleek jet-black hair and a short, tight skirt began dancing next to him. She was tall and slender like a model. Volkov watched her; she was a good dancer, confident about her body, just drunk enough to let it go. Volkov watched her for a long while, until she gave him a smoky look back, lips parted, head moving with the beat but her eyes right on him.

She pulled him toward the dance floor. Volkov didn't like to dance. Dancing was for girls. But this wasn't a night to hang back. She kept hold of his hand, pulling him into the maw of the crowd. The music was still playing loud and fast, but she began to dance slow, holding his waist.

Her name was Veronika. They kept drinking and dancing, even after Volkov's hockey friend Lev had left with two of his party girls. It was biting cold when they finally left the club, so he had to hold her tight to keep her warm.

It took a while for a cab to arrive, and as they huddled together on the street, she embraced him. Volkov kissed her tenderly. He was a big man, but gentle in his movements. She kissed him back hard, her big lips moist with a fresh gloss of lipstick. When a cab came, she pulled him into the backseat and put her hand on his crotch.

Volkov asked if she wanted to come back to his apartment. She laughed and stroked him. Volkov told the driver his address.

Veronika was a secretary in the office of one of the new business tycoons who were buying up Moscow property and any other assets they could find. She was street-smart; she had studied at one of the polytechnics, and then danced with a small ballet company in Tula before coming to Moscow. Her chief asset was her beautiful long-legged body, and she knew it.

They were drunk with sex. Volkov had never had a steady girlfriend, and he was always hungry for her. They would make love before breakfast, after dinner, and times in between. Volkov didn't exactly stop working, but he stopped thinking so hard about physics and telemetry problems. Where he had once fallen asleep with numbers in his head, now all he could see in his mind's eye was Veronika's body.

"You need to make money!" she scolded him one night as he was pulling her jeans off. "I want to live in New York. Or Cannes." Her boss, the real-estate vampire, had just bought himself a place on the Riviera.

"I want to make love," he answered. But she pouted and got dressed again and went shopping.

"Make money," she admonished him as she walked out the door that night, wagging her finger.

* * *

Veronika was pregnant by that summer. Volkov saw the change in her body before she told him. Her cheeks were flushed, and her breasts were fuller. She bought a home pregnancy test from the pharmacy. When she showed Volkov the test stick, he teared up.

"We need to move," Veronika said a few weeks later, after they'd been to the doctor for a prenatal check. "My boss can get us a flat near Tverskaya Street. He just bought a building there. I want a nursery, and two bathrooms."

"Will it be expensive?"

"Of course," she purred. "This is the new Russia. We can have the good life, but it costs money. You are a smart man. Special talents. Everyone says that. And you love me. So we will move."

Of course he loved her. He was in thrall to her. He would find the money, or borrow it, whatever it took to keep her happy.

The apartment building was in a rapidly gentrifying neighborhood near the Mayakovsky underground station. A remodeling crew was stocking the flats with all the things Russians had lived without in the Soviet days and now craved. They installed new bathrooms with showers, modern stoves, refrigerators, and dishwashers; they knocked down walls to combine small apartments into big apartments. They double-glazed the windows so people wouldn't have to wear overcoats indoors during the winter.

Volkov had been planning to rent his new flat. But Veronika's boss decided to sell the units as condos only. Volkov wanted to back out of the deal, but Veronika insisted they take the apartment. She convinced her boss to front them the down payment for a mortgage loan, and an extra sum to pay for furnishings. She hired a decorator; she installed a bidet.

They were married in October, when the baby was beginning to show. Volkov wanted a wedding in the old, no-frills Soviet style: go to the registry, sign some documents, and then have a big party. But Orthodox Church weddings were part of the neo-czarist Moscow style, and Veronika wanted that piece of post-Soviet life, too. She arranged a wedding at St. Michael's Church, where one of her model friends had been wed the year before.

The bridal couple was crowned, in the Orthodox fashion, in a traditional ceremony that showed how quickly the moribund church, too, could adapt to changing times when there was money to be made.

Veronika's parents paid the tab for the church and the party afterward. They were aspiring members of the new class: Her father had left a job with the interior ministry in Moscow and moved to Sochi on the Black Sea, where he and his wife started a business renting beach umbrellas, paddleboards, and other holiday gear to tourists. Now they were buying up hostels near the beach that had previously belonged to the Young Pioneers youth group.

* * *

Alexei from the special services continued to meet every other month with Volkov. He seemed to know all about Volkov's new bride, and about his money problems, too. He offered Volkov an additional stipend if he would provide information about his colleagues at Roscosmos.

"But that would make me a spy," protested Volkov.

"No, no," corrected Alexei. "I am a spy. You will be my informant. It is harmless. Everyone does this in Russia. Simple information. We want to know who is stealing money. Who is vulnerable to pressure. Nothing more."

"Everyone is stealing money," said Volkov. "That is the system."

Alexei wasn't interested in hearing about the sociology of the new Russia. "Just give me some names. I will give them to Lieutenant Colonel Krastev. He will give you more money. It is easy."

Volkov made a halfhearted effort to collect information at the office. He asked the GLONASS director why some of Roscosmos' European customers were doing business with a subsidiary in Cyprus. He queried Pasha about the export-import agency in Saint Petersburg that was purchasing electronic components at a substantial markup from the costs listed in original tenders.

Volkov hated being an informant. But the bills were stacking up in his new apartment near Tverskaya Street. He prepared a report with as many details as he could remember and presented it to Alexei. His reward was that he was summoned to meet Lieutenant Colonel Krastev at the safe house near Gorky Park.

* * *

The coffee table was empty this time, except for a bottle of Armenian brandy. The fancy spread of iced caviar and vodka was only for first dates, apparently.

Krastev was even fatter than Volkov had remembered. His stomach bulged underneath his belt. The skin under his neck had begun to sag.

Krastev brandished Volkov's thin report in his hand. "Acceptable," he said. "But frankly, not valuable. We know all this. In some cases, we are the recipients of these contracts and special payments. This sort of petty corruption is part of capitalism, and of course we are a capitalist country now. But I am encouraged by your attempt. It suggests you may provide better results."

"What do you mean?" asked Volkov. He had hated his first foray as an intelligence collector, and he didn't want any more assignments.

"We would like you to go to China and see some of your old contacts. We think we can, well, do some business with them. Russia and China are friends. And friends help each other, you know."

Volkov sat straight in his chair, across from the bloated intelligence officer. Usually he was a careful man. Life in the old Soviet Union had taught him the value of keeping his mouth shut. But not this time.

"No," said Volkov.

"I cannot have heard you correctly." Krastev rotated forward. "From what I know, you are not a man who should refuse an offer from, let us say, those who have been generous to you in the past. Please reconsider."

"No," Volkov repeated. "I am a scientist. I came home to do scientific work for my country. I have financial needs, like everyone. But you cannot buy me so cheap. In fact, you cannot buy me at all."

Krastev's face reddened. His assistant Alexei, standing in the shadows, moved toward Volkov as if he might strike him. But before he could get close, Krastev rose from the chair.

"You will regret this," said Krastev. He turned and walked out the door.

*   *   *

Volkov began reading fiction. He had never had time for his country's great writers when he was a boy. He was playing hockey or studying for math competitions. When his mother talked about the Russian soul, or his neighbors discussed Pasternak secretly in the basement, Volkov had thought it was a waste of time. But now he wanted something to reassure himself that his spendthrift wife and her money-chasing friends weren't what the Russian story was about.

He read Tolstoy first. *Anna Karenina*. He devoured the book, stayed up until two or three a.m. reading. Veronika complained, so he stopped reading in bed and went to the kitchen. Toward the end of the book, as Anna staggered toward her fatal walk along the railroad tracks, Volkov thought he was inside the woman's head, experiencing her interwoven love and madness.

Veronika's mindless chatter about clothes and music was annoying. But Volkov was as enraptured by her body as ever, so he tuned out the words and felt her on his skin.

He read *War and Peace* next, engulfed in the grand tragedy of Russian history, and then Dostoyevsky and Chekov. When he read Gogol's play *The Inspector General*, it occurred to him that its main character, Khlestakov, the bogus inspector, was an avatar of Russia's rising new leader, a former KGB officer from Saint Petersburg who had the same banal wickedness.

The more he read, the more he understood the degradation of post-Soviet life. Every personality of the new Russia was a caricature of someone in the old Russia. History was a loop.

Volkov's son, Dimitry Ivanovich, was born in April. Veronika didn't want to nurse. She said it would spoil her figure. So Volkov spent long nights holding a bottle to his son's lips and rocking him gently while his wife slept. He was a sweet boy, who bonded with his father from infancy and seemed to know Volkov's smell and touch as soon as he took the baby in his arms.

Veronika was happy enough as a mother, as long as it didn't interfere with the pleasure of being a beautiful young woman; she bought an expensive baby stroller and took Dimitry for walks in the park, where people gave her the compliments due a new mother.

She joined a health club to get her body back into a ballet dancer's shape. She had quit her job when the baby came, but she still hung around with her former boss and her old office mates. She began disappearing for long periods in the afternoon and evening. Volkov didn't think about it at first, and when he did, he willed himself to ignore it.

16

Moscow, August 1997

Volkov's debts mounted, as he wandered in a fog of loneliness and what felt like single parenting. When the bank cut off his credit card, Veronika was enraged, calling him a failure and a loser, and threatening to take their son away to live with her parents in Sochi. He missed a mortgage payment, and then another. Veronika's boss sent an associate to warn Volkov that people who didn't pay their debts faced serious consequences.

Veronika refused to make love with him. His world was collapsing. He had his son, Dimitry, but the child cried all the time now, as if amplifying the tension in his home. Volkov momentarily considered visiting Krastev, the spy, and repenting somehow. But the thought disgusted him.

He worked hard on his classwork. He had a new professor of astrophysics, who was teaching him the dynamics of orbital maneuver. Space was a string of paradoxes. It was very large but precisely bounded. Objects moved very quickly, but any attempt to move or reposition their orbits was very slow. It was the sort of mathematical game in which Volkov had always excelled, and his professor was happy. But it didn't bring him any extra money.

Volkov asked for a private appointment with Pasha at Roscosmos. Volkov said the meeting was personal and urgent. He took the elevator down to the secret workspace underground. It was less tidy than the last time he had visited. Computer monitors were blank. Cubicles were empty. The place seemed to be in liquidation.

"Comrade Pasha, sir, I need to make more money," said Volkov.

Pasha shrugged. "Everyone needs more money. Starting with Roscosmos. Our budget has been cut, again. We can't keep our satellites in orbit. We are space whores. Unless you know a way to earn dollars, I don't want to hear about your problems."

Volkov bit his lip. He couldn't afford his pride or dignity anymore. His story was always going to come to a moment like this.

"I can help you," Volkov said. "Maybe you need to bring something over the border, from Finland or Estonia, perhaps. Someone who can carry it through customs. Do a business service."

Pasha looked curiously at the tall Russian. "I am confused. You are the scientist who wanted to help me build a better clock. Now you want to be a smuggler. What happened to you?"

"I need money," answered Volkov.

"What a fucked-up country this is," said the Kazakh, shaking his head. "I'll think about it."

Pasha summoned Volkov two days later. He gave him a plane ticket for Helsinki and an address downtown. "A package will be waiting for you. Don't open it, don't drop it, don't shake it, don't let it get wet, don't get caught."

Volkov nodded. He was a smuggler now. He should act like one. "How much money will I get?" he asked.

"Ten thousand rubles."

"I need more. Twenty thousand."

Volkov's eyes twitched at the corners as he made his demand. He wasn't good at talking like a gangster.

"Fifteen," countered Pasha.

Volkov steadied himself. "Twenty. Or you can get someone else."

Pasha reflected, smiled, and then nodded. "A new passport will be waiting at the Foreign Ministry tomorrow. Line D."

* * *

Volkov was arrested by Russian customs agents when he arrived at Sheremetyevo Airport after his return flight from Finland. As the officers examined the boxes in his suitcase, Volkov saw the contraband material he had carried: Scores of tiny computer circuit boards; transistors wrapped tightly in plastic; A dozen bubble-wrapped computer screens. He wasn't just a mule. He was a dumb one.

"You knew I was coming. Who told you?" Volkov said to the head of the customs details. The official stared at Volkov for a moment, and then slapped him. One of his men punched Volkov to the floor and kicked him until the chief said it was enough.

* * *

Volkov was arraigned at a Moscow district court branch near the airport and sentenced to thirty days in a prison in central Moscow. It was a light sentence. Even the judge seemed to realize he had been set up.

Veronika didn't attend most of the trial, but she asked to speak to Volkov after the sentencing. She looked like a movie star. Pump heels, tight slit skirt, no bra under her silk blouse. She was dressing for someone else now.

"I'm leaving you," she said. He made her repeat the words and then asked why. "We will lose the apartment in a month, when you are released," she said. "You are not the man I wanted. You are a student and a part-time engineer with a state company that is going bankrupt. You are a failure in every way."

Volkov absorbed what she had said. It was all true. "What will you do?" he asked.

"I am getting a job with my old company. The boss is opening a new office in London. He needs me there."

Volkov looked at her blankly, stupidly. Everyone needed a roof in the new Russia. His had collapsed. What did he have left?

"Don't take Dimitry," he said. "Please. Take everything else. I don't care. But I need my son."

"I don't want Dimitry. He reminds me of you. I am starting a new life. I will have someone write the legal papers."

A big man in a bulky suit, her bodyguard, maybe, or her boss's, walked her out of the courtroom.

* * *

Lieutenant Colonel Krastev came to see him in prison. He was Volkov's first visitor. He brought cigarettes, which Volkov didn't smoke, and a bar of dark chocolate, which he devoured.

"You need to eat more," Krastev said. "Don't they feed you?"

"Of course, Lieutenant Colonel. I am content." He had been running his head at the wall long enough. No more fights.

"We know what happened, of course. Your colleague from Almaty, who calls himself the Pasha, thought that he could use you to make business. He didn't share. He is gone now. But frankly, when you are released, I don't think you should go back to Roscosmos. That place will be about stealing money, now and forever. You don't have the stomach for it."

"What should I do, then? I am still a doctoral student. But I have a son. I have debts."

Krastev sat back in his chair. He put his hands on his round stomach. "I have been talking to my colleagues about you," he said. "You are an interesting case. People say that you are quite intelligent. They assume that because you are a big man physically, you know how to take care of yourself. So they try to use you, like a hammer.

"But that seems to be a mistake," Krastev continued. "It leads nowhere. One of our Communist forebears, I should not say the name, but I believe it was Leon Trotsky, said once that you should not use a gold watch to pound a nail. You ruin the watch, and the nail doesn't go in the hole anyway. So my colleagues think that you should try a different approach."

"I won't work for the KGB, or whatever you call yourself now."

"Certainly not. We tried that. I think we can all agree that it didn't go very well."

"So, what, then? I want to finish my studies, but I need money."

"Let me explain something. The Soviet Union is dead. And, frankly, good riddance. But Russia is eternal. Its best days are ahead. And what it needs most is brains. That is our only natural resource, other than oil and pretty women.

So we need to put these good brains in a bank, where we can draw on them. Receive interest. You understand."

"Not really, Lieutenant Colonel. It sounds like a different way of saying that you want me to be a spy."

"Bah! You are a terrible spy. Why would we want that? No, we want you to be a scientist. In particular, we want you to master the details of space operations. This is the future of everything, basically. That's what my colleagues think, and they are much smarter than I am. They want you to finish your studies in physics at Moscow State University, with a particular focus on the physics of astronautics."

Krastev paused. If he had extended his hand, Volkov would have kissed it. "Thank you," he said.

"A committee of scientists will review your work," Krastev continued. "When you finish your doctorate, they will expect you to go to work for one of the closed institutes. They mentioned several. The Lebedev Physical Institute is one. Very prestigious. The Central Scientific Research Institute of Chemistry and Mechanics. Not so famous, and more secret. But special. They mentioned others. The GPRZ instrument factory in Ryazan. The State Institute of Optics. At all of them, the work is interesting, and the pay is good. These are the jewels in the crown."

"I'm a criminal. I've been in prison. How could I ever work in one of these places?"

"Your record will be cleaned if you agree. None of this customs business will have happened, officially. Your security clearances will be restored and, if you are trustworthy, they will be enhanced. Work hard, obey orders. A state committee is offering you a fellowship. If you accept it, there will be certain rules. But that is always the case with any fellowship."

Volkov nodded. The afternoon light was disappearing from the visiting room where they had been talking. "Let me think about it," said Volkov.

Krastev laughed. It was almost a snort. "For a smart man, you are an idiot. You don't have a choice. This is 'it.' "

He removed a document from his briefcase and laid it on the table before Volkov. "This is a contract. It is legally binding, but in Russia that is not the important part, because what is law? It is an agreement of trust. If you violate it, the consequences will be severe. If you don't sign it? Well, I cannot say, except that you will have made yourself useless to everyone, and I cannot predict, frankly, what will happen to you."

Volkov took the contract in his big hands. It was, as Krastev had said, like one of the research contracts that a graduate student would sign with a research institute. In exchange for money and the assurance of academic support, the recipient would cede control. A shadowy state council making the grant would, in essence, own the products of Volkov's mind. He could think for himself, but if he ran a lab, or attended a conference, or published a paper, it would be an endeavor controlled by the state.

Volkov leafed through the pages. Krastev rose from his seat, spoke to the guard, and came back with a thick piece of honey cake. Volkov kept reading while the lieutenant colonel ate his food. He looked up, finally, as Krastev was taking the last bite.

"I don't have a choice, really."

"No. That's what I told you before. A sane man does not have a choice. An insane man could refuse, but that is not you."

"Do you have a pen?" asked Volkov. Krastev handed him a thick fountain pen. Volkov initialed each page at the bottom and signed and dated the final page.

Krastev shook his hand. It was sticky, from the honey cake.

"You are doing the right thing, of course, Ivan Vladimirovich. Just because it is compelled upon you does not mean that it isn't a good choice."

Volkov stood up straight. He towered over the intelligence officer. He bowed his head slightly, in thanks and in recognition, too, of altered status. Krastev was nodding in satisfaction.

"A happy life for you and your son!" said Krastev, raising an imaginary glass. "You will be released from prison tomorrow. Your furniture and other belongings will be moved to a new apartment, smaller and less fancy, but more than adequate. Your son is in the care of state protective services now, but he will be brought to you in several days."

"And that's it?" asked Volkov.

"Yes," said Krastev. "Nothing is ever over, really. But yes, we can say: That's it."

III

CAO LIN
CHINA, 2000

Chen Fangyun took charge technically of China's first satellite tracking and measurement system and participated in the design and build-up of the system in a comprehensive way. He proposed and designed new schemes for the microwave integrated telemetry, tracking, and command system used for the launch of China's communications satellites, and was responsible for the research and development of the system as well as for the coordination of the satellite–Earth technology, thus to have made great contributions to the build-up of China's satellite network. In addition, he was one of the founders of China's 863 Program and the founder of the theory for BeiDou Navigation Satellite System....

"I work to seek innovations and render my services without the intention of fishing reputations for myself. I usually feel ashamed when I see others work harder than me!" Those are lines written by Chen Fangyun, which well reflect his virtuous personality and selfless spirit.

—BEIDOUCHINA.ORG.CN

17

Huangyan, April 2000

The senior members of the Chinese Academy of Sciences, flanked by representatives of the state technology ministries, stood in two tidy rows on a makeshift reviewing stand overlooking a waterfall in the hills above a provincial river town. They had gathered to bid farewell to their departed comrade, Chen Fangyun, who had been born in the valley below. They were getting wet, as mist from the falls splashed against the iron-gray rocks above them, but they stood as still as sentries.

The dignitaries listened as each speaker extolled the virtues of Comrade Chen. They were mopping their damp faces with handkerchiefs now. They surely wanted to be back at their institutes or ministries or fine homes in the elite districts in North Beijing, and not in this humdrum town along the central coast of China. Behind them, the sound of the water was a continuous splash like a faucet jet hitting a washbowl. A protocol officer offered umbrellas, but the chairman of the academy shook his head and the others then demurred, too.

The party leaders would have preferred to place Chen's urn in Beijing, where they could build a proper monument to him with flowers freshened year-round, and an iron fence, and restricted access. But Chen said in his will that he wanted his ashes to rest in his hometown, near the meandering river that emptied into the sea at Taizhou. This low river valley was filling up now with tall apartment buildings and ribbons of concrete, like everywhere else along the coast, but not so long ago it had been just another rural town.

The Chinese characters written on Chen's memorial stone told his story. He had been born here in 1916, attended the local middle school, and then, a brilliant boy even at that early age, had been planted in the hothouse of Shanghai's Pudong High School, where so many Chinese prodigies had done their studies. Then to Tsinghua University, the best of the best, where he took a bachelor's degree in physics, followed by his stint working for a British radio company. He returned to China in 1948, just in time for the revolution.

Speakers took turns recounting all the fields of science that Chen had shaped. He founded the Institute of Electronics at the academy. He developed the measuring devices used to monitor China's first nuclear weapons. He devised the tracking systems that controlled China's missiles. He helped imagine China's satellite program when most Chinese were still riding bicycles.

A People's Liberation Army general rose and placed on Chen's funeral monument the medal awarded to him and twenty-two other founding fathers in science, with the unlikely name Two Bombs and One Satellite, commemorating China's first tests of nuclear and hydrogen weapons in the 1960s and its first satellite launch in 1970. Chen Fangyun had helped create all three.

Watching the proceedings from the second row of dignitaries, standing at the far end so that he was barely visible, was Cao Lin, a former member of the Academy of Sciences who had "disappeared upward," as people liked to say, to head a committee on "special projects" that reported to the Central Military Commission. People still called him "Professor," but his dress was less casual, no more fancy shoes, now that he was a gray man from the ministry of "no one knows."

Cao Lin stood as if in a trance. He reached into his pocket and removed a message that had arrived at his office in Beijing three days ago from Russia. It was a commercial telegram, sent without a cipher. Cao Lin was surprised that the censors had allowed it to be delivered. He unfolded the wrinkled paper and read the script.

Dear Professor Cao: I share my condolences with you on the death of Chen Fangyun. He was a great man. I grieve for you. I. V. Volkov, Principal Engineer, Lebedev Physical Institute. Moscow.

The Russian had remembered Chen, with words that were simple and true. "He was a great man." That brief message said more than the florid testimonials from the dignitaries on the stand.

Cao Lin recalled the brief encounter when Chen had bonded with the young Russian. They were both devotees of the German astronomer Johannes Kepler. Chen had shared a momentary, almost mystical insight into the physics of time and space, which young Volkov had said he would not forget. And indeed, he had remembered. The visit, little more than a minute, had stayed embedded in the Russian's mind.

Why had Volkov sent his message now, on Chen's death, when he had ignored Cao Lin's entreaties before? It was a question to explore later, when the bland encomiums and the party business were done.

Cao Lin was roused from his reverie by a nudge from Teng Guomeng, the deputy minister of State Security, who was standing next to him in the shadows.

"Greetings, Comrade Professor," Teng said. They exchanged half kisses on each cheek. "What a sad day," he said, patting Cao on the back.

Cao Lin acknowledged the show of condolence from the intelligence man. He was the sort of party careerist that Chen would have detested.

Teng edged closer. "Can we talk a moment, Comrade Professor? Just a word while they make their speeches."

Cao nodded. There was no refusing State Security, even on a day of mourning. They stepped back to the edge of the riser, and down a wooden stairway. Teng put his hand on his colleague's shoulder and pulled him close.

"Comrade Cao, I must ask you a question. It is for you only. Are our space secrets safe? Are they protected from the eyes of others?"

"Yes, of course," answered Cao brusquely. "Why do you ask me that?"

"Because the Americans are everywhere. My colleagues at the ministry are concerned. I thought I should warn you."

"Warn me of what?" asked Cao Lin, pulling back from the intelligence chief's embrace.

"Choose your associates carefully. Soon China will be very powerful, but today it is weak. All the leading cadres saw how vulnerable we were during the Taiwan crisis, when the Americans cut the GPS navigation signal. Why were we such an easy target? they asked."

Cao bristled. This was as close as it came, in his circle, to receiving a reprimand.

"Of course, Comrade Deputy Minister. I will be careful. Thank you for your warning. Perhaps we should get back to the group on the stand, before we are missed."

The rebuke stayed with Cao Lin. It reminded him that men like Teng would turn China into a nation of spies and informers, if they had their way. The clever young Chinese men and women who were building the future would run away. If they had their way, the deputy minister and his friends would create a nation of robots.

*　*　*

The band had begun to play "March of the Volunteers," the Chinese national anthem. A chorus of professional singers brought from Beijing sang the words, against the martial sound of trumpets and drums. "Arise, all ye who refuse to be slaves! Let our flesh and blood become the new Great Wall." Most of the dignitaries joined in, even the deputy chief from State Security. But Cao Lin remained silent, and he stepped back a few feet deeper into the depth of the podium crowd. So many liars.

As the anthem ended, the notables moved quickly toward the stairs to exit the platform. Their limousines were idling in a parking lot below; they wanted to get back to the fine meals and young women who surrounded the lives of most senior cadres in Beijing these days.

Cao Lin took a long gaze at the monument to Academician Chen; he was no one's comrade, really. He was a singular talent. He had lit a spark that had ignited a hundred fires, dazzling China and soon the world. And no one could say where the spark would land.

18

Beijing, June 2000

The headquarters of the Central Military Commission was a tall concrete building capped by an immense tile roof in the style of a traditional Chinese building. It was called the August 1 Building, or "8-1," because the People's Liberation Army had been formed on August 1, 1927, back in the days when Chinese communism was a dream of desperate, hunted men and women. Now the PLA structure dominated a district of western Beijing that was given over to the military and its growing empire of power.

Cao Lin arrived at the building's underground garage and was escorted to an elevator that carried him to an upper floor; he couldn't see where he stopped because the floor numbers were obscured by a uniformed elevator operator. When Cao exited, he was met at the door by a senior officer. His shoulder bars identified him as a colonel, and he wore the badge of the PLA Rocket Force, a red-tipped rocket trailed by a plume of red-rimmed exhaust.

"Where am I?" Cao asked the colonel. "Your new headquarters is so big, I get lost."

Cao spoke in a friendly tone, not challenging but not deferential, either. That was the useful thing about secret power. It allowed people to say what they liked, softly. The colonel in his starched uniform didn't answer.

The colonel led Cao down a carpeted hallway, past heroic paintings of men in battle, to a conference room where two men were sitting at the table. One was dressed in a military uniform, the other in civilian clothes. The civilian was a familiar face: Deputy Minister Teng from the Ministry of State Security; his eyebrows slanted in permanent skepticism. Cao nodded to him, no more than polite.

The colonel whispered into the ear of his military colleague, whose name badge said ZHANG, and whose insignia identified him as a three-star general in the Rocket Force. On the wall was a large screen that displayed the few Chinese satellites that were orbiting the earth at that moment, their paths illuminated in red.

"Welcome, Professor Cao," the general said grandly. "They tell me you are lost, so I will explain: You are in the offices of the General Armament Department, which oversees all satellite and strategic technology under the authority of the Commission on Science, Technology, and Industry for National Defense."

Precise, bureaucratic, dismissive.

"Yes, yes, but which office?" pressed Cao Lin. "I am here for an oversight meeting, and I want to know who is overseeing me."

"This particular office belongs to the Science and Technology Committee. I run that committee. I report directly to the chairman of the General Armament Department."

"Ah!" said Cao. "My respects to the Comrade Chairman." He looked across the table to the civilian and nodded again. "Fraternal greetings, Comrade Teng. The last time we met was beside a waterfall. Now all we hear is the whir of the air-conditioning on whatever floor this is."

The MSS man frowned. Cao was here as a supplicant; it was not his place to make jokes.

The general cleared his throat. He was not a big man, probably spurned by his more robust classmates at the PLA military academy, but he had obviously found a comfortable niche in the Rocket Force and kept his hands clean—no, that was too much to ask of any senior PLA officer handling expensive procurement—but not too dirty, at least.

"We are grateful that you have come to see us, Professor Cao," the general began. "We know the sensitivity of your work in the 'special projects' commit-tee. We do not mean to intrude. But we have been asked to provide an update for other senior cadres on your progress. Some guideposts."

"Where to begin, my friends?" said Cao. "Perhaps I will explain some basics about space, and then about counter-space. Yes? I will tell you the things you 'need to know.'"

The general bowed his head slightly in assent. Teng was still glowering.

Cao pointed to the computer screen and its display of Chinese satellites in orbit. "Can we see American satellites, too?" asked Cao.

"Not normally," said the general. "But yes, it is possible."

"Show them," said Cao. The general signaled to an aide, and the screen was suddenly a jumble of lines, a thick band closest to the earth, and then ellip-tical bands looping in medium-earth orbit, and finally, at a distance of more than twenty-two thousand miles from earth, the satellites in geosynchro-nous orbit that remained at a fixed point over the equator as the earth hurtled through space.

Cao Lin sighed in what seemed genuine admiration.

"The Americans are so clever," he said. "And they had such a head start. Look at all their little eyes and ears in the skies over us right now. It should have been obvious long ago what this would mean. These Americans could command their military forces around the world, communicate with them instantly, wherever they were. Poor Iraq. Nine years ago, we watched their destruction, their humiliation, by an enemy that was coming at them from space. But they didn't understand it. Nobody did, or almost nobody."

"The Central Military Commission understood it," said Teng. "That's why they gave you special authority."

"The commission, of course. But I was thinking of our dear comrade Aca-demician Chen Fangyun, whom we honored so recently."

"Two Bombs and One Satellite," recited Teng.

"Academician Chen began thinking about a Chinese global positioning system back in the 1980s, before the Americans gave the world a demonstration of what they could do in Iraq."

"An easy target!" scoffed the general.

"Perhaps. But a brilliant technology. My dear friend Chen took me aside, when I came home during my studies at Harvard, and told me what to look for, how to understand, how to see where the treasure was."

"Hurrah for the great Academician Chen," said Teng. He was getting impatient.

"So, as you know, China will launch its first navigation satellite soon, before the end of this year, I hope," Cao resumed. "And we will begin to have our own central nervous system that extends from our earthly body to our body in space."

"Noted," said Teng. "Hurrah for BeiDou."

Cao raised a finger, to say: Pay attention. He was getting to his point.

"We needed more than our own system. We needed to weaken the Americans and make them vulnerable. So we began to think: How can we confound our adversary? Where are the trapdoors that allow us to enter his precious network of global control? That is when the most senior cadres encouraged me to create my 'special projects' office. To take quiet measures that, if they were exposed to others, would evaporate like a raindrop on a summer's day."

"We don't want to evaporate anything," muttered Teng. "We just want a briefing."

Cao stared at Teng with an unspoken disdain. In fact, the Ministry of State Security had always wanted to control anti-satellite operations, but they were blocked by the PLA. The military hated the spy service, and the generals had the ultimate power, because it was the PLA that controlled the hardware.

"As we thought about penetrating the American systems," Cao continued, "we considered the individual components. There are the satellites, of course. We would never get inside the places where the Americans actually make them, but each satellite needs solar panels for electricity. And little motors to run the solar panels. And computers to run those motors and every other operation of the satellite. And inside each computer there are, what, chips, wires, capacitators, relays, batteries, transformers. So the satellite, really, is not one thing but many things.

"And that is only the beginning," Cao Lin said expansively, widening his hands. "Each satellite must communicate with ground stations. How many of them exist? Where are they? And in each of these ground stations there is so much equipment. Big dishes to receive and send signals, of course, the wheelbarrows of space, and so many other things. Cables and routers and relays. For everything there is a power source, which connects to a grid, which people may imagine is secure, but not against clever operators. So, you see, that's how we started to think, in our 'special projects' unit."

"I do not need the little details," said Teng. "I want to hear the big plan."

Cao gave him a trace of a wink. He disliked the man. He didn't have to tell him anything, really, but he would say a bit more.

"Well, of course, we thought about the satellite signals that are downloaded by the ground stations. How to capture them? But first we needed to think about where the signals were sent once they reached earth. Well, some of them bounced back up into space to be relayed to other receivers. But some were transmitted by broadband cables. It happens that many important ground stations are located on remote islands. So, inevitably, many of the signals were transmitted by undersea broadband cables."

"A vulnerability," said Teng.

"Certainly. I do not need to tell my friends from the General Armament Department and State Security that undersea cables can be accessed by certain technical operations."

Gen. Zhang thumped the table in approval.

"So, you see," continued Cao, "as we proceeded with our 'special projects' work, we had many targets of opportunity. We tried to ask ourselves: What would the Americans do to protect themselves? How would they harden their systems, so they were not vulnerable to creative methods of attack? How would they anticipate our attacks and construct clever defenses?"

"And the answer?" asked Teng. He was leaning forward now, wanting to suck the juice out of Cao Lin.

Cao's first response was a chuckle. "The funny thing, my friends, is that the Americans really are quite careless. That is what we are discovering. They got to space so early, and their dominance has been unchallenged for so long, that they really didn't think much about their weaknesses. Perhaps it was laziness, or overconfidence. Or that unthinking openness and generosity of spirit that we find in our American friends.

Cao Lin trailed off for a moment, thinking about the Americans. What did it say, that they were so trusting?

"I don't know why they were so open," he continued, "but we discovered that there is quite a lot you can get just by walking in the front door and asking for it. That was the joy of being a physics student in America. They believe in sharing knowledge to make the world better. That is the wonder of their power—it makes them so generous that they give things away."

"And their supply chains?" asked Teng.

"Another surprise! The Americans are good at protecting the big secrets. Too good. They put them in a gold box, inside a steel box, inside an iron box. They have so many layers of classification that they can't get inside, themselves. But the little secrets—or, more, the things that connect the little secrets together—those they barely protect at all. That is what we are learning, in our 'special projects' office."

"All right, all right," said Teng impatiently. "What is the method of attack?"

Cao lowered his head. He had been waiting for this moment, savoring it, really.

"Ah! I am sorry, Comrade Deputy Minister and Comrade Lieutenant General. That is the one thing I am forbidden to tell you. I have told you everything that I am authorized to say. You can turn me over to the special services and let them do their worst, or take me up in a helicopter and threaten to throw me out the door. But it won't do any good. I cannot tell you more unless I am given an order by the proper authority."

"And who is that? asked Teng, arching those heavy eyebrows.

"It is the general secretary of the Communist Party, Comrade Deputy Minister. Advised by the premier and the State Council. I am bound by their instructions. I cannot deviate, even at the request of most esteemed and senior colleagues such as yourselves. I invite you to check. And, let me be frank, comrades, there is a reason for this extreme secrecy."

Teng narrowed his eyes. "Don't tell me about secrecy, Professor. I run the house of secrets. What are you talking about?"

Cao Lin leaned toward him. He didn't like this man. He shouldn't embarrass him in front of his colleague, but he couldn't resist.

"There is always a danger of what I believe the British and Americans call a 'mole.' That's why there must be compartments, to prevent the advance of this burrowing creature. And I inhabit one of those compartments. If you don't like it, complain to the general secretary."

"Who are you to tell me of moles?" responded Teng with a mixture of anger and defensiveness. "I am responsible for rooting them out!"

"Just so," said Cao Lin. "Please, do your job."

There was a long pause, perhaps twenty seconds, while the intelligence and military men separately pondered their options and then for a minute more, as they whispered back and forth. Cao Lin could have overheard, if he wanted, but instead he pulled his chair farther back from the table.

Eventually General Zhang turned to Cao Lin.

"Thank you for your briefing, Professor. We are grateful for your work to protect the motherland. We have no further questions at this time. We will report to the commission and the State Council that the 'special project' is proceeding. The deputy premier, Hu Zimo, has asked for a personal report. I will share with him our most interesting conversation."

Cao Lin nodded. There was something wrong here. These men were too smug, too certain of their bureaucratic power. They were not creators but controllers, and they resented his freedom from bureaucracy, he could tell. He rose and walked to the door, and then turned back.

"I'll need help getting out of here," he said to Zhang, with just a trace of a smile. "This place is a maze!"

19

Xichang, October 2000

The first BeiDou satellite was scheduled to be launched on an autumn day from the Xichang base in the distant reaches of Sichuan Province. The PLA had invited leading cadres to travel there to witness the historic event. Cao Lin thought of declining, but a friend with very good connections advised him that he was expected. This was his project; it would be a sign of disrespect to others not to attend the launch ceremony. So he agreed to the long flight on a military plane.

It was a nearly four-hour trip to Xichang. The former academician closed his eyes, but he couldn't sleep. He asked the general sitting next to him about his children, to pass the time. The man, a farmer's son from Hainan, said he had one child, a daughter, who was attending Stanford. She had applied for graduate school there but had been refused. Did Cao Lin know anyone who could help? His assistance would be very . . . valuable.

The former academician smiled and said he would see what he could do. It was so common to offer bribes now in China that people didn't even pretend to be embarrassed.

The plane landed at Xichang in the dry, grainy light of the Sichuan highlands. The dignitaries climbed aboard a bus to the launch facility, aided by a protocol officer who told them where to sit. They passed through three rings of security. Finally, as the sun illuminated the foothills of the Himalayas to the west, they reached the launch site.

The Long March rocket stood slender as a bamboo shoot atop the platform. Its metal skin caught the rising light of the morning. The cranes and ladders were still attached, but they fell away as the members of the launch party took their seats in a reviewing stand a half mile from the pad. The VIP boxes were clad in red bunting; in the middle distance, streamers bearing party slogans trailed in the breeze: THE EAST IS RED. RESOLUTELY DEFY ALL OBSTACLES. THE HEAVENS ARE THE COMMANDING HEIGHTS.

An announcer's voice blared from a bank of speakers near the reviewing stand. "Today, a red-letter day, the People's Republic of China will launch the first satellite in its new global positioning system. Success is certain!" The announcer reverently spoke the name of the new project. "BeiDou." The guiding star. On that cue, a chorus from the Young Communist League sang a song especially composed for the occasion.

The announcer read a long list of names that included most of the dignitaries who were attending the ceremony. Cao Lin's name was not spoken. But more than a few members of the audience knew that he was the bridegroom at this wedding. He had helped to imagine the system, and then he had helped to steal the technology that made it possible.

The group listened to the Chinese national anthem, and a chorus of "The Sky Above the Liberated Zone," a famous revolutionary song. Then they awaited the countdown to the launch. Some were nervous that this might be another mishap, with the rocket veering off course and exploding in a fireball that incinerated its precious cargo, as had happened too often in the past. But Cao Lin was calm. He had stolen the best rocket technology from America, and his engineers had monitored a dozen tests.

The rocket carrying the first pieces of China's new heavenly compass lifted slowly from the pad, and then quickly traced a flawless arc toward its orbit. The dignitaries cheered. Cao Lin popped into his mouth a piece of hard candy that he had purchased on his last trip abroad and sucked on its sweet center as the assembly dispersed for its return to Beijing.

Hu Zimo, the deputy premier of the State Council, the most senior official attending the event, pulled Cao Lin aside as the crowd was departing and offered him a ride in his limousine. Cao Lin watched the envious eyes of the other officials who were boarding the bus. A PLA adjutant opened the limousine door.

"This is only the beginning," Cao Lin told the deputy premier. "Someday we will own space."

The deputy premier nodded faintly and gestured for Cao Lin to take a seat in the back of the big Mercedes limousine. It would not be quite so easy as that.

*   *   *

On the car ride back to Xichang, the deputy premier was silent for a few minutes, as if composing his thoughts before delivering his message.

Hu Zimo was a party man, of course. They all were, but the deputy premier was a particular model of the bland but ruthless collective leadership that was emerging as China grew more prosperous. As at every public occasion, he wore a neat blue suit and crisp white shirt, immaculately cut by the tailor who dressed senior officials. They were like Mafia lieutenants, these senior cadres. They did their business, took their cut of the spoils, left no fingerprints, and always protected the boss.

"We are very pleased with how far you have come, Cao," said the deputy premier. He spoke as if they were members of a family, not just party comrades, but something more intimate.

"I have done my duty," said Cao Lin. "And I have been rewarded, too. They don't always go together."

"Now it is time to share," said the deputy premier. "That is what we think."

"Please be more specific, Comrade Hu. I don't understand."

"We think that it is time for the military to take control of the satellite operations that you have developed so effectively." Hu solicitously patted Cao Lin on the knee. "It is too much for one man to oversee so many sensitive programs."

"You mean I'm being fired?"

"Not at all. Promoted. There will be more money for you. More face. You will still have your 'special project.' But you will not control the systems. Forgive the Western term, but your finger will not be on the trigger. I am sorry. The PLA insists. The Central Military Commission agrees. I have been asked to give you this message."

"The PLA insists," Cao repeated. "I see."

Cao Lin made small talk. He asked about the deputy prime minister's family. He didn't protest that the mission he cared most about in the world had just been stripped from him. The thing about collective leadership was that once it had made a decision, it was set in concrete. If you didn't like it, you could run your head at that concrete, but you would only bloody yourself.

*   *   *

When he returned to Beijing, Professor Cao took a long walk in a park near his home. It was late, but groups of Chinese men and women were still out on the lawns, some doing ritual Chinese exercises to stay fit, others puffing away at cigarettes while they played furiously at board games. Chinese people were disciplined, like an army of ants, but they also liked to win.

Cao Lin wasn't used to losing, but he had unquestionably lost his battle with the PLA. He had been naïve to think he could challenge the military. In the end, they ran everyone and everything in China. The leaders might call themselves generals or admirals, but they were political commissars. They tolerated other enclaves of power only as long as it suited them.

Cao strolled toward the old imperial garden that bordered the park. Its filagree of ponds and temples predated the revolution. Time moved very fast in the new China; most of these relics had been bulldozed and forgotten. Cao wondered if he was anchored to anything at all. His ancestors before 1949 were a blur. He stopped at a pond where golden-pink carp were feeding in a dense cluster, two-deep as they wriggled toward extra morsels of food. The prize was to eat, but what then?

Cao was a steady man. But he felt precarious. His demotion reminded him that he stood upon a small platform that was unstable. He needed his own place to stand. He let himself think forbidden thoughts about how he might accomplish that.

20

Beijing, October 2000

Cao Lin was a man for all seasons. His public face was so well composed that people rarely looked for another side. He did much of his work in secret, in a private office hidden away in a building managed by the Commission on Science, Technology, and Industry for National Defense, in the northeast district of the city. The building was set far back from the road, in an unfashionable area, where people traveled only if they had a very particular reason. He never received visitors there.

But Professor Cao had a grand second office, too, where he met guests, in the compound of the China Aerospace Science and Technology Corporation in the Haidian District of Beijing. That was a glamorous modern complex, built to show off China's new ambitions in space. The sign outside Cao's office door read VICE PRESIDENT, in Chinese and English, but it didn't say what he presided over.

It was here, at this public office, that Cao Lin received a visitor in late October, just after the launch of the first BeiDou satellite. The guest was his old friend Arthur Wang, a Chinese American entrepreneur whose company, Satellite Supply Systems, was active in the growing market for satellite peripheral equipment in the United States and around the world. His partner, Roger Birken, the chief executive, stayed behind in San Jose; he signed the documents and, when necessary, received the clearances from the U.S. government. Which left Arthur Wang free to travel in search of new customers and manufacturing locations.

Cao Lin welcomed his guest with a BeiDou commemorative plaque, showing the stars of the Big Dipper over a stylized rendering of earth.

"Kudos," said Arthur Wang, whose speech and manner were so thoroughly American he might have been born in a fast-food restaurant. "This is a big deal!"

"We are pleased," said Cao modestly. "We launched our first satellite two weeks ago. It will not surprise you that we have big plans, because you know China. We have plans for everything."

"I'm all ears."

"It's no secret: The State Council has approved the plan. In three years, we will complete the experimental navigation system with three satellites. In ten years, we will have BeidDou 2 with seven satellites, enough to cover China and the neighboring regions. And then, before long, BeiDou 3, with thirty-five satellites, a global system. It is written in the stars, you might say."

"Good business," responded Wang. "China is my best customer and supplier." He spoke with trace of a New York accent, dropping the r's.

"We'd like to do even more business," said Cao. "We hope you will produce more components in China that you can sell to customers. That is a double win."

"For sure," agreed Wang.

"Tell me, Arthur. Where does Satellite Supply Systems sell the products that it makes in China?"

"Everywhere," answered Wang. "I mean, everywhere that uses satellite dishes, for a start. Our factory in Shenzhen makes low-noise block downconverters, LNBs we call them. They're attached to every dish, big, small, simple, fancy, whatever. They all do the same thing, which is to take the signals from space down to a frequency that can connect with the receiver. The low-tech that makes the high-tech work."

"I remember visiting your Shenzhen factory when it opened, what, four years ago. This LNB gadget is simple electronics, as I remember."

"Very simple. A low-noise amplifier; a frequency mixer; an intermediate-frequency amplifier; a local oscillator. That's it. But it has to be reliable, and it has to be cheap. Because people want to save their money for the fancy stuff."

"You have some high-end customers, as I remember," continued Cao. "Customers who want a more precisely calibrated version of this LNB. How is that market doing?"

"We're killing it. Television networks. NASA ground stations. Government customers. Even the Pentagon. They all want price and quality, which we can deliver."

Cao gave a thumbs-up sign. "What about our government inspectors in Shenzhen? I hope they're not too intrusive."

"They're invisible. They do their checks. Health and safety. Fire security. And they help arrange maintenance, too, when we need it. In and out, no problem. They have their own access badges to make it easy."

The muscles on Cao's face relaxed. But he had a few more questions.

"Satellite Supply Systems opened a new factory recently, as I remember. Farther north, in Guangzhou. How's that going?"

"It's doing great. The satellite market is booming, so we're making more specialized products. Engineered for what customers need."

"What's selling? If I may ask."

Cao's amiable manner gave no hint that he already received monthly reports from his agents in Shenzhen and Guangzhou on precisely what the factories there were producing, and with what subtle modifications. That was the advantage of running a "special project." You could touch anything and anyone.

"Thermal controls. People don't think about it, but space is a nasty environment. It's very hot and very cold. Satellites need to monitor temperature constantly and accurately. The thermal control isn't a very fancy product, compared to what's in the satellite. But it has to be good, and ours are the best. We also make controls to move and monitor antennas. That's another junk business, you'd think, but every satellite needs antennas. We have process control software, simple stuff, to run the gear."

"Making money?"

"Millions. Hundreds of millions. Maybe billions, soon."

Cao Lin shrugged, as if the business details were all too complicated for him to understand. "Do you make sales trips?" he asked. "To go see the high-end customers, the people who buy your fancy dishes and thermal controls and all of that?"

"Of course," said Wang. "I'm leaving on one next week, after I visit our factories in Guangzhou and Shenzhen. I'm trying to sell gear to government customers that operate ground stations, to receive signals from space. They buy a lot of our high-end dishes."

Cao already knew about the sales trip, of course. And he understood that it would be to places that a Chinese visitor could travel in relative safety, without too many curious American eyes. Cao smiled. He pressed Wang about his itinerary.

"I'll be flying out of Hong Kong. To Australia first, then New Zealand and Tahiti. Ground stations in each place. Want to come along?"

Cao feigned indifference. "I'm very busy here. I don't know. How long would it take?"

"Less than a week. One day in each place."

He paused, as if deliberating. "Well, a trip like that would be useful. And timely. We will be building ground stations soon for BeiDou."

They shook hands. Professor Cao Lin, a former member of the Chinese Academy of Sciences now working for the China Aerospace Science and Technology Corporation, would accompany Arthur Wang, his sometime business partner, on a commercial tour of the southern rim of ground monitors for the United States' GPS monitoring system.

"A business development trip," said Cao.

21

Adelaide, Australia, November 2000

Professor Cao made just one stop abroad, as it turned out. He was careful, as always, in preparing his trip. He used a passport in the name of a supposed Hong Kong resident named Fang Bao. He cleared the trip with his new supervisors at PLA headquarters, telling them he had a rare chance to visit elements of the "special project" network he had created, which was now under the military's command.

Before he left, he contacted several old friends abroad, from years ago, who were surprised but happy to hear from him.

Cao traveled on a Gulfstream jet that had been leased by Satellite Supply Systems. Wang tried to make conversation, but Cao ignored him. He was lost in thought; a man between two worlds. It was like the dizzy feeling he remembered from his first semester at Harvard, when his mind was pulled into another realm but his body felt like it was still tethered to China.

The group stopped first in Adelaide, on Australia's southwestern coast. They stayed in a grand old hotel called Gentle Winds that looked out over a broad bay, offering handsome views through the stucco arcades. The hotel had been built in the 1880s as a way station for sea captains and wealthy tourists. It had once been an outpost of a new world, but it now looked very old.

Cao Lin excused himself from his travel mates. He sat on his balcony and watched the waves churning in Largs Bay and the foaming sea beyond. He didn't smoke, normally, but he lit a cigar he had bought at the gift shop downstairs. He wore a silk scarf against the chill. He put his feet up on the balcony railing as he smoked and watched the shifting shapes of the clouds.

Through the pine trees that skirted the bay, Cao could see the old pier where several centuries of arrivals had come ashore. Some of them must have been Chinese. This city, like nearly every urban area around the world, had its own Chinatown, selling medicinal herbs and strange spices and cheap trinkets from home. Cao had taken a walk there when they first arrived, to stretch his legs, he said, but really to remember the inescapable fact of Chinese-ness in a foreign place.

Chinese had come to this land a century and a half before, kidnapped in Fujian Province and transported as slaves in what the locals called "the sale of pigs." And then more waves of Chinese arrived, many thousands, to seek their fortunes in the gold rushes in Victoria and New South Wales. They indentured themselves to pay for their passages and most were impoverished from the moment they arrived. If they had the uncommon luck to find any gold, the locals tried to run them off their mines. This island, populated by the sons and daughters of British convicts, became so frightened of Chinese immigrants that its parliament greeted the twentieth century with what it called a White Australia Policy.

Cao took another puff of his cigar. The long ash fell to the lacquered floor of his balcony. The light was fading, but he could still see a few ships, making their way up from Port Adelaide into the bay.

The British white men who governed here imagined they were the kings of this ocean. Just as their kinsmen in America believed now that they were the kings of space. But Cao Lin knew better. In the 1750s, decades before the British had settled Australia with their paroled ruffians and debtors, this island had been a regular stop for Chinese traders. Yes, brave Chinese captains had plied the northern coast, as they did most of the world's oceans. They sailed into natural harbors, did their business, and slipped away. They were happy when their power was limitless but invisible.

The waves were crashing louder, as the tide rose to the rocks above the

sandy beach. Cao Lin's mind wandered forward, to the bad time that had followed the good time. The Chinese of that trading empire had become greedy
and corrupt. Their culture did not keep pace with the West. Their military came
under the control of warlords who thought more about their own power than
the good of the nation. They had invented science in ancient times, but they
forgot it. Knowledge survived in the minds of Chinese who studied in the West,
like Chen Fangyun and, yes, Cao Lin.

Which world did Cao Lin inhabit? The answer had once seemed obvious
to him. But he was beginning to wonder.

It was late. Cao Lin threw what remained of his cigar from his balcony
onto the neatly mowed grass below. He was tired from the airplane flight. He
had brought along a new Tom Clancy novel about Jack Ryan stopping a war
between Russia and China. He tried reading a few pages but fell asleep. The
book thudded to the floor, awakening him long enough to brush his teeth and
turn out the lights.

*   *   *

Cao tagged along the next morning on a round of appointments at the dish
farms that had grown up around Adelaide. They were all customers. Wang's
company provisioned satellite ground stations scattered around the globe: Australia, obviously. But also, Alaska, Uruguay, South Africa, Bahrain, Ascension
Island, Diego Garcia, Kwajalein. They were specks of nothing, many of them,
except that they were positioned in just the right spots to exchange signals with
the satellite fleet that sailed the skies.

Wang announced that, after a lunch break back at the hotel, he had arranged
afternoon visits to the wholesalers and retailers who sold satellite dishes for the
Australian home market. Cao Lin politely declined. He should catch up on
paperwork back at the hotel, he told the group. He would meet them for dinner.
His voice was calm, as always, but there was a tautness in his face that suggested
anticipation and perhaps anxiety.

22

Adelaide, Australia, November 2000

Professor Cao Lin, in truth, had scheduled an appointment that afternoon. He left the hotel in the early afternoon and wandered, aimlessly, one might have thought. He browsed shops along King William Street, one of Adelaide's busiest thoroughfares. He took buses in one direction, then another. He strolled into a department store and browsed on several floors, before exiting by the stairwell. He settled down for afternoon tea and a sweet biscuit at a small café near the university. He took a seat in the back, facing the door, thumbing a day-old copy of the *Financial Times*.

Cao Lin drank his tea and ate half of his cookie. He lingered for a while, and then took a stroll back toward the park near the university. He took a seat on a park bench, near the river that bent past the university. When Cao Lin had been seated for nearly fifteen minutes, a man approached and took a place next to him on the bench. He was wearing a gray cap with a crimson red H on the crown.

Cao Lin spoke to the visitor with animation. They were friends, it appeared. Old classmates, having an accidental reunion. Eventually the gentleman in the hat rose and departed. He left behind, on the slats next to Cao Lin, a manila envelope. Cao Lin took the envelope with him and, in the safety of his hotel room, he read its contents.

* * *

That night at dinner, after the other members of the sales team had finished their meals and gone up to bed, Cao Lin told his host that he wasn't feeling well. Something he ate, perhaps.

"I think I may return to China tomorrow," he said. "I'm very sorry."

"But sir, I want you to see our offices in Wellington and Papeete. They're expanding, too."

"I'm sure. But I've learned so much here in Adelaide. Worth the trip."

"We'll send you back in our plane, then, and the team will fly commercial to New Zealand."

"Don't be silly. I've already booked a flight for tomorrow, via Singapore. Very comfortable."

Wang looked dejected. He stared at the dining table for a moment and then looked up. "Did I fuck something up?"

"Not at all, my friend," answered Cao Lin. "You have opened the door. We have a saying in China, when we want good luck for a new venture: May you live as long as the Southern Mountain and your fortune be as boundless as the Eastern Sea."

23

Hong Kong, November 2000

Cao Lin stopped in Hong Kong on the way back from Australia. He wanted to buy some new clothes from his tailor in the Mandarin Hotel and several cases of red Burgundy. On the long flight home, he relaxed in his first-class suite and let his mind wander about the tasks ahead of him. He broke his task down into components, the way his physics professors at Harvard had taught him.

Space was the right problem. Cao Lin was certain of that. This was the future of warfare, certainly. The Americans had taught the world that truth in their 1991 war against Iraq. They could put a missile down a stovepipe if they wanted to, guiding its trajectory from a satellite hovering over the earth. And they could command forces halfway around the globe, bouncing their messages off satellites as if they were telegraph wires. This command-and-control system was untouchable by normal means of interception. Certainly the Chinese had tried.

Space was the future of commerce, too. The Americans had perfected their global-positioning system, and rather than keep it a military secret, as the Chinese would have done, they were making it a commercial platform for the whole world—just as they had done with the internet. They were giving away the most precious secrets, and in the process building new realms of industry.

It had always worked that way, really: Build the highways, and soon they will be filled with cars and trucks rushing to make business. Space would be the same. America was creating a satellite infrastructure that would support a new era of commerce.

So, then, what about America? What made this nation so open and generous, perhaps to a fault? Cao Lin had often wondered about this puzzle. When he was a student at Harvard, he lived for a year in Winthrop House by the Charles River. He had read the famous words of Governor John Winthrop, the pilgrim father for whom the dormitory was named: "We shall be as a city upon a hill, the eyes of all people are upon us."

Was it vanity, this American idealism? Probably so. They liked to be in the city on the hill, certainly, but they also liked to be watched and admired there. When Americans talked about their country's "exceptionalism," they seemed to take it for granted that they were better than other people. Chinese people thought they were special, too, but they didn't boast about it. It would be bad luck. When the Chinese appeared generous, it was chiefly to mask their intentions. They were selfish to the core.

Cao Lin was a man in between. He liked nice things, fine wines and good clothes. But he could live without them. In his heart he thought of himself as an intellectual—a man who pursued universal things, rather than ones belonging to a particular tribe or nation. Like his mentor, Chen Fangyun, his knowledge was in service of larger goals. But he didn't want his epitaph to be: TWO BOMBS AND ONE SATELLITE. There was a higher ambition, surely.

Cao Lin knew that the mission of his "special project" was to help China become selfish in space—to act today, when it was weak, in a way that would someday secure its power. It was like shooting a bird in flight. If you aimed right at it, you would miss. You needed to fire at the place where it would be in the future.

Cao Lin had understood that telemetry several years ago when he began thinking about the American space enterprise. He considered the ways that China might enter the supply chain invisibly, with parts that would seem as reliable as a light bulb—until they switched off at a moment of opportunity.

He had been building this capability through his "investments," as he called them, like Arthur Wang and his Satellite Supply Services company. They had already given Cao Lin and his engineers access to satellite dishes in sensitive locations; they were selling routers into which Cao's team could insert bits of code, and communications software with malware baked into the code, invisible until the instant it was cued.

That was the advantage of being a "weak" country, where wages were low and global investors were eager to build factories to make the tools of the new century. It simply wouldn't occur to these investors that China was attaching every wire invisibly to another unseen control panel, to be activated later. What would China do with this hidden power? Cao Lin had never thought about that too much.

*　*　*

But just as Cao Lin was succeeding in this subtle ploy, the PLA generals had taken it away from him. It gnawed at him, this loss of control. The commissars were selfish. They didn't care about the shining city on the hill; they just wanted the keys. They didn't understand Cao Lin's aspirations as a scientist; they wanted to own the product.

When he was a student at Harvard, Cao Lin had wondered for a time if he should stay in America and make a life there. But he had decided, back then, that the Americans were unreliable. They had stars in their eyes. They wanted to make the world better, but they weren't tough enough to accomplish the task. That was what Cao Lin had concluded as a young man. He was Chinese, strong enough to make a new world; he had returned home to serve with men like Academician Chen.

Cao Lin had assumed, as decent people do, that his good work would be rewarded. But when it was taken from him, something broke. He didn't know how to fix it.

24

Beijing and Moscow, December 2000

Cao Lin was alone at home in early December, before the "holidays." His wife was at their new second home in Vancouver, with his children. He had hoped to join them, but his security officer advised that it was "not convenient" to go to North America that year. The FBI was making headlines chasing Chinese spies. A Chinese American scientist who had worked at Los Alamos had just been released from prison after pleading guilty to mishandling classified documents. They didn't have any real evidence. The Americans would calm down, Cao Lin told his handlers. But he agreed to stay home.

Cao Lin, in his solitude, pondered a problem that he had been considering for months, and, more truly, for several years. How could he send a fraternal message to the young Russian physicist Ivan Volkov? Brainpower was a strategic asset, to be cultivated and harvested, especially when it was foreign-born. And that was especially true now for Cao Lin when the PLA had taken away his operational control. He needed a helper.

Cao pondered how he could solicit this Russian's interest, without scaring him off. He wanted to send him an object that would have emotional value, recalling his time as a student and researcher in China, without exposing him to danger from the Russian special services as a possible security risk. He needed something that would feel true, emotionally, and not false.

Professor Cao thought first of sending a gift that would evoke the special personality of the great Chinese scientist Chen Fangyun, whom Volkov had met in Beijing, and whose death had moved the Russian to send a brief but powerful note of condolence. But what sort of gift would convey the special qualities of the late academician?

Cao searched the records of the Academy of Sciences, where Chen had been among the most esteemed members. The archivist there said that Chen, like many men of his generation, including Mao Zedong himself, had been an amateur calligrapher. He wrote out the lines of favorite poems, and composed a few himself, in brushstrokes that were themselves works of art. But only a few of these brush paintings survived, and they were zealously guarded by the academy. The only one in private hands belonged to Chen's son, and Cao Lin couldn't ask for such a treasure.

He considered sending one of Chen's books. But the physicist had done his most creative work in his head, on a blackboard or computer, not in the pages of scholarly monographs. Cao found a few journal articles, but they were on absurdly technical subjects. "Characteristic Analyses for Millimeter-Wave Diffraction Antenna with Continuous Phase Construction." Volkov might be able to understand the arcane science of such a paper, but it would have no emotional meaning for him. Cao might as well send a picture of the bland tan-brick façade of the Academy of Sciences.

And then it was obvious. Ivan Volkov had attracted attention at Tsinghua because of his attempt to solve a puzzle set nearly three hundred years before by the German mathematician and astronomer Johannes Kepler. That was his link with Chen, too.

Professor Cao set about trying to find something that would evoke the majesty of Kepler's vision of mathematics. That would be his calling card. It would say between the written words: Join me, Cao Lin, in the pursuit of ideas for themselves, not as instruments to create wealth or impose domination.

Cao consulted historians and museum curators; he reviewed the bibliographic record of Kepler's own works. And at last he found what he was looking for in a notice of a planned auction of rare first editions.

An auction house was soliciting bids on a "first edition" of Kepler's 1619 treatise *Harmonices Mundi*, "The Harmony of the World." The catalogue included an appreciation by the writer Arthur Koestler: "The Harmony of the World is a mathematician's Song of Songs . . . What Kepler attempted here was, simply, to bare the ultimate secret of the universe in an all-embracing synthesis." What better gift could Cao Lin make to the young man he wanted to apprentice than this: the ultimate secret?

Cao Lin submitted a bid on the rare book and raised it twice, until he had acquired the item. He had it shipped to the Chinese Embassy in Moscow, which had obtained Ivan Volkov's current address.

Professor Cao sent a note to Moscow, to be included in the box along with the precious manuscript. It was a brief personal letter.

> Dear Mr. Volkov:
>
> I think of you when I read the disturbing news from Russia. It is a difficult time for your country.
>
> Johannes Kepler, the author of the work enclosed, composed an epitaph for himself several months before he died. He wrote: "Sky-bound was the mind, Earth-bound the body rests." You are earth-bound in Russia. It is too early for you to rest. Your friend in China sends you this gift as a recollection of your sky-bound mind, and with an offer to support your work in any way that is appropriate.

Cao Lin left the note unsigned.

25

Moscow, December 2000

Ivan Volkov's son Dimitry was tall for a three-year-old, and musical. At the day-care center where he spent the day while his father worked at the institute, he sang to the other children after story time. At home, he listened to classical music and hummed to himself while his father played solitaire chess. He was the joy of Volkov's life, and truly the only person he genuinely cared about. He hadn't dated anyone seriously since his wife had left him, only an occasional *perepikhnut'sya*, a quick lay. His colleagues bored him. People were a waste of time, except for his son.

Volkov lived in a new apartment block a few miles south of the Moscow River, a hundred yards from a park where his son could play. The apartment was near his office, and on a nice day he could walk to work. Since the intervention of the special services and his release from prison, he had worked diligently at the Lebedev Physical Institute. This was the pinnacle of the Russian science establishment. Its predecessor institute had been established by Peter the Great.

Volkov was transferred after a year to a branch of the institute called the Astro Space Center, on Profsoyuznaya Street. It was to that address that the package from the Chinese Embassy was delivered in mid-December. It had been opened, of course. You could tell from the misaligned creases in the wrapping paper.

Volkov read the note first, smiled, and put it aside. He opened the layers of bubble wrap that protected the book, and then opened the wooden case. He was afraid to touch the book. The title page seemed almost to glow in the light. "*Ioanni Keppleri. HARMONICES MVNDI.*" Below the title was a wood-cut image of a celestial angel blowing life into the space that surrounded her. And below that the publication date, in Roman numerals. "*M.DC.XIX.*" 1619.

Volkov gently removed the book from its case and touched the cover page as if it were a living thing. It had been re-bound in vellum, but the pages were fragile. He held the volume close to his chest. Then he put it back in the wooden case.

He took up the accompanying letter and read it again. It was true. He was earth-bound. His mind still looked skyward, toward the questions of telemetry and motion through space that had obsessed Kepler. But his assignments at the institute were practical, even mundane. Lebedev, prestigious as it was, had to pay its way. Nothing in the new Russia was free.

Volkov thought of Cao Lin, who had sent him this lavish gift—as an inspiration and also a bribe. He remembered his first visit to the Academy of Sciences. How smooth and Western Cao had seemed. The sheen of his cotton shirt; the softness of his cashmere blazer. The years studying in America had given him a confidence that was unusual among academics in China, or anywhere.

Volkov had wondered then whether he was something else. He didn't know about spies, other than Russian novels about heroic KGB agents and James Bond movies that were memorable for women with big bosoms. But it was obvious that Cao Lin came from a world that was larger, and smaller, than science.

He put the book gently on a shelf behind his desk and waited for a visitor. It wasn't long before the secretary of the Astro Space Center buzzed him and said that someone from outside the institute had come to see him.

* * *

Krastev knocked on Volkov's office door. He was wearing a fur hat, against the winter chill, marked with the FSB insignia of an imperial eagle, backed by a sword. He removed his hat and coat and laid them on a chair in a corner of the room. His uniform displayed the rank of a full colonel now. He was a man on the way up.

"Your Chinese friends are very generous," said Krastev. "They bought that book at auction for nearly one hundred thousand dollars. We checked."

"I didn't ask for it," said Volkov quietly. "It just arrived."

Krastev nodded. "You can't keep it, of course."

Volkov looked away, to hide the sadness in his eyes. "I don't want it."

"But I would like you to write a thank-you letter, just the same. I have prepared a draft. I want you to rewrite it in your own hand, in English. In your own words, we could say."

He handed Volkov a typed letter. Volkov read it, with surprise at first, and then a somber recognition of what he was being asked to do.

"Read it aloud," said Krastev.

" 'Dear Professor Cao.' " Volkov had to clear his throat, which caught with the first words. " 'Your gift moves me profoundly. You know my fidelity to 'the harmony of the world.' To hold that pure light in my hands is a miracle. You expressed a wish in your note. I share that wish. I would like to be sky-bound again. Perhaps we can explore how that might be possible. With my deep thanks and sincere best wishes. IV.' "

"That's rather good, don't you think?" said Krastev. "Your voice. Sweet. A bit lonely. Eyes in the sky. That is our Volkov."

Volkov shook his head in disgust.

"You want me to be a spy. You asked once before, and I said no. I told you that I was a scientist. I'm still a scientist."

"Yes, yes. But that was before you went to prison. We own you now. You signed a contract. If you violate it now, you will lose everything. Your job, your son, your country. Everything."

Volkov closed his eyes to think. What options did he have? He could refuse, but eventually they would make him comply. Or he could cooperate and keep a space in his mind that was separate, a free part that could observe what was not free.

"What do you want me to do?" Volkov asked. "Other than send this letter."

"Do what your Chinese friend asks. Help him. Find out what he's doing. You won't be able to travel to China, I must tell you that frankly. Not unless we trust you, and, well, that will take a very long time. But perhaps he will come here to see you."

*   *   *

Volkov sent the letter, and soon he received a new message. It didn't arrive in the same way, in a box delivered to his office, but in a manner that was meant to be clandestine.

One afternoon when Volkov was pushing his son's stroller in the park near his apartment, a man with Chinese features approached from the other direction. As they passed, he leaned toward Volkov and slipped something into his coat pocket. He said, "Excuse me," as if he had bumped him by accident, and continued on.

Volkov walked another quarter mile, toward what was left of the winter sun, and then removed from his pocket the object that had been placed there. It was a small communications device, like a cellular phone, accompanied by a brief note telling Volkov that his friend in Beijing wished to talk with him and specifying a time, just over a week hence.

When Volkov returned to his apartment with his son, one of Krastev's men was waiting. The colonel arrived an hour later with a technician who examined the communications device. Volkov had put his son down for a nap and was singing to him, even after he had fallen asleep. Krastev summoned him from the boy's bedroom.

"We want you to do just as he says. Contact the number and ask your friend what he wants."

"And then?" asked Volkov.

"Then tell him that you'll do it. Whatever it is. Our Chinese friends want to use you, which is fine, so long as we are using them. You are in the game now. You work for me. Don't forget it."

*   *   *

The Chinese request was simple enough. Professor Cao Lin, speaking through an intermediary, said that he wanted Volkov's help in protecting China's new BeiDou global navigation system. He was gathering expert advice on the vulnerabilities of such a system to disruption. This research would be helpful to

Russia, too, and to the world. The intermediary solicited Volkov's suggestions and said that the China Aerospace Science and Technology Corporation would use them to improve security.

Volkov prepared a response, carefully vetted by Krastev's team. The mathematics of this problem were complicated, Volkov explained. The issues involved the number and location of ground stations in this system, and the synchronization of the timing clocks. He had examined this same problem for Russia's GLONASS array, he wrote, but the project had been abandoned for budget reasons.

Volkov asked for coordinates of the ground stations, and the transmission frequencies, and the timing mechanism used for synchronization.

An answer arrived on the communications device. The message described the coordinates as "test data." When Volkov researched the data provided, he found that it matched the footprint of the publicly disclosed ground stations of the American GPS system. It wasn't much more than could be found on the internet.

Volkov asked Krastev for guidance.

"Push him for more," Krastev said. "You need the specific radio frequencies on which this system operates, and the geographical coverage of each satellite." The colonel patted Volkov on the back. "Take your time. If you make it too easy, they will know you are a fake."

Volkov prepared the data request just as instructed. He waited for an answer. When the message finally appeared on his communications device, it was not what Volkov had expected. The message was from Cao Lin, and it was brief.

I regret that we cannot share data about satellite operations in this channel. Russia and China are friendly nations, but these are sensitive issues that require a political decision. It is not in my control. Please share this message with your Russian government friends.

Volkov told Krastev that he had been rebuffed. Cao Lin had realized that he was being played. Volkov shared Cao's message and gave him the communications device, to disassemble as he liked.

Krastev was disappointed, but patient. "They will contact you again. When they are strong and think we need them. Who knows, with these crazy Chinese? We will be watching them. And you."

Volkov decided that he was lucky. He would have made a very bad spy if Cao Lin had accepted him. He had developed an intense dislike for his "handler," Krastev. After every talk with him, he felt he should rinse his mouth and wash his hands. These covert fabrications were the opposite of knowledge. Someday, perhaps, he might encounter something so important that he would have to transmit it by hidden means. But for now, he despised secrets.

He returned to his work at the institute. Russia these days felt less like a wooden roller coaster about to splinter, and more like a regular, modern corrupt country. He raised his son. He taught him to play chess and soccer.

Volkov looked for a woman he could love, but he never found one. He thought occasionally of other paths he might have taken, people who might have helped him escape this desolation. But it was a vain exercise. And whatever the emptiness of his inner life, he had his son Dmitry.

IV

EDITH RYAN

Asia and America, 1998–2023

The Petticoat Panel: CIA's First Study—in 1953—
on the Role of Women in Intelligence

Director Allen W. Dulles fielded a slew of questions [in 1953] from a group of "wise gals"—a name given later by a senior CIA manager—who wanted the Director's thoughts on the role of women at CIA.... Lyman Kirkpatrick, CIA's IG at the time, decided—following discussions with Dulles—to convene a panel of women employees who could analyze the issues of representation, discrimination, recognition, and general barriers to advancement for women at CIA.... "The Petticoat Panel," as the group would be known, was charged ... "to determine for themselves whether they believe there is any discrimination as such against women for advancing professionally."

—CENTRAL INTELLIGENCE AGENCY WEBSITE,
posted March 8, 2021

26

Singapore, March 2000

Edith Ryan celebrated her twenty-fifth birthday alone on a sunset cruise in the Singapore harbor. It was a sticky-sweet evening just after the end of the rainy season. The maître d' didn't want to give her a table near the water because she was alone, so she bribed him with a crazy-big tip and told him to start bringing the drinks. She had a gin martini, then a rum punch, then a "Singapore Sling" because . . . it was her fucking birthday, that's why.

The cruise was advertised as a romantic getaway, and Singapore couples were dancing and smooching in the nighttime heat. The playlist was predictable brand-name nostalgia: Elvis, Frank Sinatra, the Beatles. As Edith sipped her cocktails and played with her food, she stared at the bland, compact cityscape across the water, like a Lego version of a modern metropolis. She waited for the velvet hammer. By the time the boat docked at midnight, she had fallen asleep.

The Singapore station chief had sent her a "happy birthday" message on the agency computer system, but she ignored it, for all sorts of reasons. Friends at the embassy had wanted to give her a party, but she had said no to that, too. She would have said yes to the young case officer from Texas who had wanted to date her, but he had been transferred away two months before. She thought of working out in the embassy gym, taking care of her body, looking beautiful on the outside so it wasn't so obvious what was on the inside. But she was afraid someone would come by the gym and ask her what she was doing.

It was better to be alone. Safer, easier, better protected. She called her parents in Holyoke before she got on the boat, so they would have a chance to wish her a happy birthday. They asked what she was going to do to celebrate, and she lied and told them she was going to a party. She did her best to sound cheerful, and she succeeded. She was good at that. But she didn't fool herself.

Sometimes mistakes go away quickly. We make errors in judgment, large or small, but time covers them over. People forget, even if we remember. The present grows over the past like an ever-replenishing forest. But other times, mistakes compound themselves. The holes don't get filled in. We do something wrong, and people find out, and we begin trying to explain ourselves or make amends. And then the real trouble begins.

*   *   *

When Edith Ryan left Tsinghua University at the end of spring term several years before, the agency brought her back home. She wasn't really a case officer yet. Her year in Beijing had been an unusual experiment in pre-employment. She had been spotted during her junior year by one of her Yale professors as a likely CIA prospect, and her intake interviews with the agency recruiters had gone splendidly.

With the professor's encouragement, the clandestine service decided to try something unusual, which was to encourage Edith to apply for a one-year Yale exchange fellowship at Tsinghua on the promise of a job with the agency after she returned. It would be like a gap year. During that time, she would have the advantage of being genuinely undercover, and could report any useful contacts or information like an asset, rather than as a case officer. She would be a butterfly encased inside a chrysalis, her professor said. "Caterpillar," Edith had corrected him.

After Edith returned from Beijing, her first debriefings were at a covert location far from Washington, where the agency processed deep-cover officers. It was an ordinary office building until you got to the third floor and the cyber-locks. After the first week of interviews back home, the agency dropped the idea that she could become an officer under nonofficial cover, as they had once planned. She was too young and inexperienced to operate on her own overseas. The counterintelligence staff wondered, too, whether her cover had been compromised in Beijing. Chinese surveillance had been intense in the final few months.

Then there was the problem of the botched development of the Russian graduate student. The debriefer raised that subject on the first day of his interviews with Ryan. The Russian had been a promising developmental: Edith had spotted him as a prospect, advised her handler in Hong Kong about him during a Christmas trip out, arranged a promising introduction to an experienced deep-cover case officer, Larry Hoffman. It had been a textbook operation. And then suddenly the case stopped. The Russian broke off contact. Why? It was a puzzling question; worth a scrub for "lessons learned."

*   *   *

Edith's difficulties began when she lied about her interaction with Ivan Volkov. When the debriefer asked if there had been any romantic involvement between them, Edith had said no. That was the "correct" answer. Sexual relationships between officers and potential recruits were strictly off-limits. Too many crossed wires. And for a young woman like Edith, there was the embarrassment of using her sexuality in a way that was unprofessional.

When a second debriefer asked if Volkov had ever proposed sex with her, Edith said no again. He had never asked, she insisted, and she would never have let it get to that point. She would have broken it off long before. Those denials might have held up, but as the senior officer pressed her about her meetings with Volkov, asking her to explain where they were in her dorm room, what he said, whether he had touched her physically, Edith started crying and wouldn't answer any more questions.

The agency brought in a woman psychiatrist then, a sympathetic ear. They went through Edith's recollections of her encounters with Volkov, one by one. Sometimes Edith had to make up answers to cover what had really happened.

Eventually the fabric of all those little lies frayed, and Edith confessed to the big lie. She had made a mistake, yes, but she tried to fix it. She knew that it was wrong to have sex with a recruit, so she had pushed him away, refused him. That was the right thing to do, wasn't it? She conceded that maybe Volkov had suspected something after she rejected him; perhaps he had guessed who she worked for. He didn't quite say it, but he probably knew. The psychiatrist asked Edith if she had been in love with Volkov, and she said no—and then, in tears again, said yes.

Now there was an investigation. If Edith had misrepresented the interaction with Volkov, what else might she have lied about? A Support officer requested her consent to take a polygraph exam, and she agreed. She still wanted to be a case officer, all the more now to redeem herself. Two long polygraph examinations followed, covering each intimate detail of her interactions with Volkov, and a half dozen men she had actually slept with, before him. It was a degrading feeling of nakedness and vulnerability, like being abused but coming back for more. Yet she did it, because she wanted to feel good about herself again, even if that meant living inside her shame.

The case took much of that summer to resolve. Women managers intervened. There were "equities." The agency had made its own mistakes. Edith was young and inexperienced. She hadn't been adequately briefed before she went to Beijing. Her handler in Hong Kong hadn't elicited the necessary information from her about Volkov; they didn't have a proper operations plan for development of him.

And what about the experimental arrangement to send her to Beijing as a witting asset before she was actually hired as a case officer? Was that legal? Should it be reported to oversight committees in Congress?

A first review board concluded that Edith Ryan was unsuitable for the clandestine service and should be offered compensation if she withdrew her employment application and signed a nondisclosure agreement. But a member of that first panel protested to the general counsel's office that she was being treated too harshly, the rules would be different for a man, and a second panel was convened. This time the group agreed that Edith Ryan should be offered a job in the clandestine service, as she had originally been promised at Yale, but under official embassy cover.

The final question was where Edith should be assigned after she finished the career trainee program at Camp Peary. She spent a first year on probation on the East Asia desk monitoring Chinese efforts to steal technology, and she got good marks.

The East Asia Division chief liked her. She had "pluck," he said. He decided to send her back in the field as a China targets officer. Her Beijing stint, whatever its mistakes, gave her useful background. But which station made sense? The East Asia Division chief said she would need a strong boss, no-nonsense, someone who would teach her how to do things the right way. Otherwise, the clandestine service would bust her out after two years. That was the deal.

The right man was Frank Conway in Singapore, the division chief decided. He was a new-model station chief. Not a Yale professor, god forbid, but a hard man who could close a billion-dollar deal for Boeing or General Electric if he wasn't a spy. Edith's start date was set for June 1999. Singapore would be her test. Up or out.

27

Singapore, June 1999

Frank Conway reminded Edith of her first boyfriend when he welcomed her to the station in the embassy on Tanglin Road. He had the cut body of an athlete and a studied self-assurance, like Teddy, the boyfriend, who had been captain of the Yale lacrosse team. Teddy had been a senior when she entered Yale as a freshman, and he had plucked her from the vine in her first month on campus. She had wanted so much to please him, but he made her feel awkward and stupid, which only made her try even harder.

Edith recited her verbal résumé that first day in Singapore, but Conway waved her off. Don't rush it! He rattled off some administrative details, this desk, that apartment, and then criticized her clothing. Didn't she realize how hot and humid it was in Singapore? She should put her button-up suit in the closet; this was the tropics, for god's sake! Edith tried to establish a professional distance in that first meeting, but he was in control, and she couldn't escape— and didn't want to. She wanted to please him.

Edith left that first meeting feeling flushed and vulnerable. She had no power in this relationship; only need. But this was her chance to make it as a case officer and the only imperative was: don't blow it.

Conway told her that she should report to the operations chief for assignments, but he was away on vacation in Hawaii. Wanting to show Conway that she was a self-starter, she decided to task herself. The East Asia Division had said back at headquarters that part of her assignment would be tracking Chinese tech companies that were setting up offices in Singapore, so she would get started.

She ran traces on the Chinese nationals who had come to work in those companies: engineers, technicians, executives, secretaries. She was looking for people who might be vulnerable to recruitment. It took her two days to gather the information. She sent a message to Conway telling him what she was doing, but he didn't respond.

Edith went ahead without permission. When she had assembled a list of Chinese names, she ran it against a database of recent graduates of Tsinghua University. She came up with a match. A man named Hu Xinhuang had graduated from Tsinghua in 1995, the year she had arrived there, and he now worked for the new Singapore office of a Chinese engineering company.

A query to the East Asia Division turned up an intelligence report that the company was bidding on an airport signaling system. The hardware had been designed by a French company and built in China. The French-Chinese joint venture was based in Singapore. Perfect.

Edith typed up an operational proposal for Conway. She explained that Tsinghua had an alumni association in Singapore. It held a monthly social gathering. Edith would have a station asset send a pretext message to Mr. Hu Xinhuang inviting him to the next gathering. Edith would attend and have a "chance" conversation. She would send him a follow-up email and see if he was willing to meet for coffee.

Conway waited a day before answering and then summoned Edith into his office.

"This is a stupid idea," he said sharply. He seemed angry. "We have to assume the Chinese made you in Beijing. Or at least, I do. This would blow you up before you even started. Wait for the CHOPS to get back from Hawaii."

* * *

Edith walked out of Conway's office feeling like a kicked dog. After hiding behind her closed door for twenty minutes she steadied herself and asked

Lynette, a reports officer in the station, to come have a coffee with her. Lynette was an older Black woman, married to a diplomat. A big sister, maybe. They went to an empty café in the nearby mall.

Edith asked about Conway; she felt she was getting off to a bad start with him.

"Be careful with him, honey," the older woman advised, her voice just above a whisper. "His wife just left him. She couldn't deal with him anymore. He's on the prowl."

"What's his problem?"

"Aggression, ambition, too much testosterone. How should I know? This is your first station, right? Well, welcome to Fight Club. And you know the first rule, okay? Your colleagues are spies, sweetie. They get paid to steal shit and lie about it. That's just the way it is. If it gets bad with Conway or anybody else, then you tell me. But it is what it is. You hear me?"

Edith nodded. She got it. Fight Club. Deal with it.

She was reworking her ops proposal later that afternoon when she received a secure message from Conway. He apologized for rejecting the plan so quickly before. Worth a second draft. He asked her to have a drink after work. She responded with a note summarizing her revised ops plan, in which she wouldn't make initial visual contact with Hu Xinhuang but leave that to a station asset.

Conway said fine, good change. He repeated his suggestion that they have a drink after work. A get-acquainted session. Standard practice with every new arrival.

Edith agreed to meet him. Alcohol was mother's milk in the agency, everyone knew that. Over a drink, agents were recruited, bonds of trust formed, mentorships developed. She asked Conway where he wanted to meet. He suggested his apartment, for security reasons.

She knew that was a bad idea, but she agreed. Maybe it was better security. She left the office soon after to go home and change into an outfit she thought he would like.

*　*　*

Conway's apartment was a penthouse in a new high-rise that overlooked the central district of the city and the glow of the harbor beyond. Edith arrived in a cotton party dress, the kind she might wear to a club, and heels that were an inch higher than sensible. Conway was dressed in black slacks and a black T-shirt. He had the glow of a man who'd just come from the gym and a sauna. He asked Edith what she was drinking, and she answered, "A gin martini," thinking that sounded sophisticated.

He made two martinis, poured to the brim, and carried them to the enclosed, air-conditioned porch that overlooked the water. Beyond the giant cranes of the port, you could see the ships at anchor in the Singapore Strait, waiting to unload their cargoes.

"Where's your wife?" asked Edith.

"Back home," answered Conway. "We've been having some issues." Edith already knew that much. She had been curious what he would say.

"I'm sorry," she said. He shrugged.

*   *   *

Halfway through the first martini, Conway got talkative, leaning in close and telling her war stories. He had started off in Ground Branch. An ex–Army Ranger. She figured that, looking at him. He gone into Iraq before the '91 war started, eating dirt with his Kurdish agents, blowing up Republican Guard communications sites. What else? He had been in Berlin when the Wall came down. He had exfiltrated agents in rubber boats from Russia, China, Iran. Even if just half of it was true, it made a hell of a story.

Edith didn't usually swear, but she did so as she was talking with Conway. "No shit!" she said about one yarn. "No fucking way!" about another. She thought it sounded cool, and her enthusiasm jazzed him to tell her more stories.

When they finished the first round of drinks, Conway proposed that they have another. She shook her head; she knew she was getting blasted. But when he said, "Just a little one," she nodded assent.

He was bringing the second round when it happened. He set down both drinks, and then, from behind her chair, put his hands on her shoulders.

"What are you doing?" she asked. She could have said, Stop! or just walked out, but she didn't.

"How tall are you?" he asked. That sounded like a crazy question, but she was in his power now, and she stood up.

That was when he embraced her and pulled her toward him. It didn't begin as an assault. It was more like a hug.

"No," she said. "This is a bad idea." Still, she didn't say stop.

"Sometimes you should roll with it," he said, backing away but only a little. "You should have learned that in Beijing with your Russian friend."

"What do you mean?" She was embarrassed and a little ashamed. He must have read all the debriefings.

He wagged his finger at her. "You know."

Then he was on her, hands on her breasts and then her bottom. She tried to resist, but he was a big man, and her struggle only seemed to arouse him more.

"Come with me," he said, pulling her toward the bedroom. When she wouldn't move, he picked her up in his arms and carried her into the bedroom. She wanted to fight, but she didn't. He lowered her on the bed and began taking off her clothes. Not ripping them but unbuttoning them. She let herself go limp, and when he was on top of her, his lips against hers, she kissed him.

"Be gentle," she said. That was something she used to say to Teddy, her first boyfriend. He didn't listen, either.

28

Singapore, January 2000

They didn't talk about what had happened. But they continued to see each other. Once a week, sometimes twice. It was a secret inside a secret. He was a hungry lover, exploding with energy and desire, and the need to exert control. He brought her stylish gifts. A coat from Max Mara. A purse from Piero Guidi. He gave her expensive lingerie that made her look like a princess, he said, but she thought he really meant a fancy whore, which was what she often felt like. She wanted to stop feeling ashamed. She gave him books, military history at first, and then a poetry book that he pretended to like. Lots of people had affairs with their bosses, she told herself.

She read Sylvia Plath out loud to him after they made love one night. "The Couriers." A tear rolled down her cheek when she read the last line. Love, love, my season. But she knew it wasn't love, really. It was a rite of passage. It was instrumental. He was getting what he wanted, and she was getting what she wanted. That was the way the world worked, and the agency was an intensely compressed version of the world.

Edith reported to the chief of operations, the CHOPS. The Hu Xinhuang plan didn't go anywhere. The Chinese target was on a short leash. As soon as he saw foreigners at the Tsinghua alumni event, he bolted. But Edith had more luck with a new social media company from Hangzhou that had just opened a branch in Singapore. Many of its executives and engineers had been to university in America; they had friends who needed green cards. They had sick relatives. They needed favors.

Edith's world seemed tightly compartmented, all the lies going in the same direction, until the Christmas holidays. Conway left on home leave to see his children and finalize his divorce, he said. Edith, as a junior officer, was low in the queue for leave, and she didn't want to go home anyway. In Singapore, the Christmas season was on steroids. The city was alight; twinkling bulbs in the trees and atop the construction cranes that overhung every boulevard.

Christmas Eve, Edith went to mass at the cathedral downtown near the water. She had been to church once after leaving Beijing, when she worried that she was cracking up and hoped that confession and absolution might help. It only left her feeling emptier, and she wasn't sure why she wanted to be back in church again. But it was Christmas. She didn't have anything else to do.

She spent a long time in the confession booth. She hadn't reckoned on how hard it would be. She was honest, up to a point. She told the priest that she would sin no more, but it was like an alcoholic proclaiming that he would never drink again. She was an addict; she knew it. She craved the sense of shame as much as pleasure; that was the part that lit her up. But still, she had promised the priest she would stop. She wasn't sure what she would do when Conway came back.

That evening some people from the embassy were planning to go to a fancy party at Raffles Hotel. It was overdone in the way of Singapore events. Icing on top of icing. The colonial façade of the hotel was decked in garlands of green holly and enormous Christmas wreaths. Inside the main lobby a lavishly decorated Christmas tree filled the atrium.

In the hotel bar, most people appeared to be drunk by the time Edith arrived. The inebriated included American and British expats, Singaporean Chinese and Malays, most of Edith's embassy colleagues. The embassy group included Averill Hart, the new officer who had recently joined the station.

Hart was tall, skinny, his face framed by big black Buddy Holly glasses, awkward but wicked-smart. He had attended the University of Texas at Austin and then Harvard Kennedy School. He was Edith's age, and when he'd had several drinks and taken off his glasses on the dance floor, he was kind of cute. They didn't really flirt. It was known in the station, even by the newbie, that Edith was dating someone, nobody quite knew who.

They shared a cab on the way home, and when they reached Edith's flat block he got out and tried to kiss her. She countered him with a jujitsu move, the way they were taught at the Farm, whipping his arm behind his back, but not so it hurt. She laughed as soon as she did it, and he did, too.

"You're good," he said. There was a slight Texas twang in his voice. They hugged and wished each other Merry Christmas and said good night. She felt better falling asleep that night than she had in a long while. He invited her out to the movies two nights later, and she said yes. When he asked if this was a date, she said no, not yet.

*   *   *

Conway returned just after New Year's. He invited Edith to come for a drink, but she begged off. She had a developmental agent meeting. That was true the first time, but the second time she refused Conway it was a made-up excuse. Conway checked the logs before he called Edith into the office.

"What's up with you?" he snapped. "The sheriff's back in town. I want to see you. You don't seem very happy about that."

Edith lowered her eyes, held her arms tight against her chest, steeled herself. This was like going cold turkey. She wasn't sure she could do it. But then he made it easier.

"Come on, damn it," he shouted. "What the hell is going on?" He reached for her arm to grab it. She took a quick step back.

"I'm seeing someone else," she said.

"Who? Tell me!" he demanded, his jealousy now surging up his throat like reflux acid.

"It's none of your business," she said. Each word she spoke came out a little stronger.

"Oh yeah? Fuck you. It's not that little dipshit who just joined the station, is it? Averill. What a fucking loser. Someone warned me about that when I got back, but I didn't fucking believe it. I didn't think you would date a high school guy. What a cunt you are."

"It's none of your business," she repeated coolly, ignoring his profanity. "I'll see whoever I want. Averill and I aren't dating, anyway."

She hated herself for saying that last part as soon as the words were out of her mouth. It was true, they weren't dating. Just talking. But it was a concession to Conway. And it only empowered him.

"Hey, Edith, you know what? I can guarantee that you're not dating him. And you know why? Because I am transferring him out of this station. He came here on probation, one month, to be extended at the discretion of the station chief. He's not cutting it. He's going back to Mommy in Texas."

"You wouldn't dare."

"I've already done it, bitch. His last day is Friday."

Her lips were trembling. There were tears in her eyes.

"You can't," she said. "I'll file a complaint."

"No, you won't," said Conway. "Nobody would believe you. It's 'he said, she said,' and you've already lied about your Russian boyfriend, so why would anyone believe you when you challenge your boss, who is a member of the Senior Intelligence Service? Answer: They wouldn't. So, if you try that, I guarantee you'll commit career suicide. Assisted suicide, actually."

This last assertion of his power over her broke whatever reserves she had left. She knelt to the floor and began weeping, a low sob, like an abandoned child or a grieving mother. He ignored her and went back to his desk while she continued to moan. The office was soundproof. Nobody could hear. There it was: she could keep crying while he typed on his keyboard, but nobody would come.

After several minutes, she got up, straightened her hair, adjusted her skirt, and went back into the office. She took a coffee break ten minutes later. Hart asked her if he could come along, but she said no.

Friday was indeed Averill Hart's last day in the office. He left on the Monday morning flight to Washington, via Los Angeles. He tried to see Edith before he left, but she refused. She felt doubly ashamed now that she had ruined his life as well as her own life because of her weakness.

29

Singapore, March–April 2000

Edith Ryan was a shell person for the first two months after Averill Hart's reassignment. Even Conway seemed uninterested in her. She was so inert she didn't even have the energy to be submissive. Or perhaps he was frightened of her. She didn't care. He stayed away and let her continue with a roster of uninteresting operations. She stopped eating. Starving herself was the only means of exerting control over her life. She began to feel light-headed as she grew thinner. She liked that.

Edith would have done better if she was less self-aware. She understood how powerless she was. Even if she had found the strength to report the incident with Conway, she feared it would backfire. She would have to disclose the months of submissive "consensual" sexual relations with him. She couldn't bear the humiliation of another interrogation about her personal life.

And she wondered if she even had a case. It turned out that Conway hadn't given Averill Hart a negative performance evaluation; that would have been stupid and dangerous. No, Conway just said that his skill set didn't fit with the station's current priorities and, talented as he was, Hart would be more useful elsewhere in the East Asia Division. He got the CHOPS to sign off on it, and the personnel people back at headquarters didn't say boo.

It was that easy: You could coerce a needy subordinate into sex. You could transfer the man your subordinate wanted to date to another station. Edith had no doubt that if Conway himself was transferred to another station, he could arrange to have Edith transferred there, too. The CIA wasn't the Boy Scouts, certainly not the Girl Scouts. Bad behavior was a positive attribute for a case officer. This was like the college fraternity that all the badass kids joined. Being a prick was the whole point.

*   *   *

An agency psychiatrist paid a visit to the Singapore station in early March. It was a routine visit. She was the regional shrink, based in Tokyo, available to help with assessments of neurotic agents, alcoholic or drug-dependent case officers, marital breakups, stress meltdowns. One of her most useful services was to write prescriptions for controlled substances—uppers or downers, sleep aids or anxiety relievers—which were available for the CIA "family" like M&M's in a candy store.

Edith wasn't planning to see her, but it turned out that the psychiatrist had scheduled short visits with everyone in the station, so she had no choice. The visitor held her "consults" in the medical office, down the hall by the communications suite.

"You don't look so good," the shrink told Edith after a few minutes of conversation. "How have you been sleeping?"

"My sleep is bad. Everything's bad," said Edith.

"You want to talk about it?"

"Honestly, no, I don't," answered Edith. "I've had some personal issues. But everybody does, right? If I decide I need help, I'll ask for it."

"Is it something here in the office?" asked the shrink. She had that sixth sense, maybe, knowing which rock to look under.

"I don't want to talk about it," Edith repeated, more sharply. "I'm responsible for myself and my actions. I don't want to let the agency or my colleagues down, and I won't. Period. Let's change the subject. Don't you want to ask me about my parents, or traumatic childhood experiences?"

The shrink shook her head. Tough cookie here. No point in trying to make her talk until she was willing. She had read Edith's file. She knew about the Beijing case, and the two panels that had reviewed it.

"May I call you Edith?"

She shrugged. "Sure."

"You know, Edith, things are not always your fault. I know that people asked questions about your decisions when you first joined the agency, but they decided to hire you. Because they trusted you. They still do."

"That's nice. If true."

"Stop it!" the shrink said. "Stop being a victim. If something bad happened to you, then you can file a complaint. If you don't want to talk to me, then send a message to the inspector general. It's on an anonymous channel. Nobody in the station or at division headquarters can see it. It's there if you need it."

Edith studied the shrink's face. For the first time in weeks, there was a spark in her eyes.

"Really? Is that true?"

"Yes. Really. It's your call. But if you could see yourself through my eyes, you would know that something is very wrong. You need to do something, or it will eat you up."

"I'll think about it," said Edith. "Until I decide, nothing in my file, right?"

"Of course," said the shrink. "Our conversation is protected by doctor-patient privilege."

"Right," said Edith. This was the CIA. Who was the shrink kidding? "It doesn't matter, because I didn't tell you anything anyway."

"Think about it," the shrink said one final time. She said farewell to Edith and waited for the next member of the station to visit for a chat.

*   *   *

Edith did think about it, intently, for the next ten days. Her birthday was approaching. She told herself that this was the time for a decision. Up or down, in or out, crazy or sane. She bought a ticket for the sunset harbor cruise that left from Clarke Quay the night of her birthday. She kept thinking that she would decide by then and celebrate. But she was still torn, all that night, and the only relief came when she guzzled so much booze that she passed out while the Singapore couples were dancing to Frank Sinatra.

When Edith woke up the next morning, she knew the answer. She walked through the early morning mist up to the embassy's verdant campus, buzzed into the station, and entered the passwords for her computer account. She logged on to the red channel that was used for the most sensitive communications and found the address of the inspector general for the clandestine service.

"I am writing to file a formal complaint about sexual harassment by the chief of station in Singapore, Frank Conway," she began. It took her nearly an hour to catalogue every detail of abuse that she could remember, with dates of each specific event. Alone, in her office, she spared nothing.

By that night, she had received a confidential reply from the inspector general's office. Two days later, a lawyer from the IG's office at Langley arrived in Singapore, along with two people from the Office of Security who had been instructed to safeguard relevant files.

And then Edith waited. It was 2000. A new millennium. Things had changed. She kept telling herself that.

30

Langley, May 2001

It took more than a year for the investigation of Frank Conway that Edith had launched to be completed. It was a big secret, a charge of sexual harassment against a chief of station, but people heard rumors. Edith was pulled from Singapore, but Conway remained as chief of station. That suggested the imbalance of power. There was no contemporaneous record to support Edith's charges; obviously not. She had refused to talk with Lynette, the reports clerk, other colleagues, or even with the visiting shrink. The lack of a record was itself evidence of trauma, but the lawyers didn't see it that way.

Edith was given a temporary assignment as Support liaison for the East Asia Division. It wasn't a demotion, she was assured. But access to some compartmented information was closed. When she tried to follow the operational traffic on the cases she had initiated in Singapore, she was denied access. She busied herself with her tasks: arranging airplane flights, renting safe houses, scheduling appointments for polygraph sessions. She didn't even do the real work; those services were provided by the Support officers. She was a go-between. It was as low on the totem pole as you could go without falling off.

The inspector general's office summoned her for two "informal" interviews, which were formally recorded and transcribed. The lawyers asked about each sexual encounter with Conway. There were several dozen; she couldn't remember them all. Did he slap you during intercourse? Did you tell him to stop? Did you tell him that anal intercourse was painful? Did he continue? What did you say?

The interrogation was humiliation upon humiliation, but Edith knew that it was necessary. Once you've jumped out of a plane, you can't jump back in. You just have to hope that the parachute opens.

*   *   *

The general counsel for the clandestine service asked to see her personally after her second interview with the IG's office. He was a nattily dressed man, wearing a pin-striped suit, cuff links, and a pocket square that matched his tie. He had a big face and a receding hairline that was not quite bald. He looked like what you imagine from the movies a mob lawyer would look like.

"Hiya," he said, when she was seated across from his broad mahogany desk. "My name is Mike Lugano. How's life?"

She looked at him quizzically. This wasn't what she had expected. "It's pretty bad, actually," she answered. "I want to get back to my real job. What's happening with my complaint?"

"It's making progress, from what I hear. Takes a while. Complicated set of facts. Mind you, that's separate. The IG's office and the general counsel's office are not the same, regardless of what you may have heard." He flicked an invisible piece of lint off his suit jacket.

"So why did you want to see me, if you're not handling my complaint?"

He leaned forward, bridging his chin on his folded hands. "Do you plan to file a lawsuit?" he asked.

She paused a moment before responding. "I haven't decided."

Actually, she hadn't really thought about it. She had talked to an agency lawyer, who had advised against seeking outside counsel for now, and she had followed that advice. But she had wondered about talking to her own lawyer. For all she knew, they might be coming after her, and she would need serious legal advice.

"Okay, so let's talk," continued the general counsel. "To be clear: I represent the agency. Not you, not Frank Conway. I am not here to make any findings of fact. Understood? I want what's best for the Culinary Institute of America. Period."

She nodded.

"So I am going to lay this out for you as clearly as I can. So that you can think about your options and make a good decision."

"Right." She sensed that he wanted something. "Go on. I'm listening."

"If you file a lawsuit, the agency will immediately move to have it sealed. And I can pretty much guarantee that we will win. You are an officer of the CIA operations directorate, which means, by law, that you can't talk publicly about your work. Neither can we. We'll file in the Eastern District of Virginia, which is our backyard, and the case will be sealed as soon as it's filed."

"So what?" she said sharply. "I expected that."

"Wait a minute, Miss Ryan! I'm just getting started. Before you ever get to filing the lawsuit that will be sealed, you will have to retain a lawyer who has the necessary clearances to prepare your case. Frankly, that takes a while. I'm not bullshitting you here, just telling you the facts. There are some attorneys who are cleared for agency matters, who handle HR complaints and things like that. But this is different because it involves so many operational details."

"Like what?" pressed Edith. The more he talked, the more she realized that she had some kind of leverage here, though she wasn't sure what it was.

"Like what happened in Beijing, for starters. In any lawsuit, Conway's lawyer would raise that. To 'impeach' your testimony. And by the way: We didn't talk about how long it would take for Conway's lawyer to get cleared. So add that in."

"I might not sue Conway. I might sue the agency. For breach of supervisory duty. And for tolerating a workplace environment where sexual harassment is condoned."

"Yeah. Whatever. Be my guest. The point is, whoever you sue, it's going to take a hell of a long time. And it may have the opposite outcome from what you want."

"Meaning what? Is that a threat?"

"Of course not. Meaning that you might lose in the litigation and have substantial legal bills to pay, that's all. Please! I am not trying to intimidate you. I hate what happened to you, off the record. I want to make it better, not worse, that's all."

Edith took a deep breath. He was gradually getting to the point after the preliminaries. "What would be an alternative path?" she asked. "If I decided not to file a lawsuit in federal court."

"Ah, well, now, that's an interesting question," he said, looking skyward, as if such an alternative had never occurred to him. "Let me think. The alternative, presumably, would amount to an out-of-court settlement. A kind of private arbitration. Except there wouldn't be an arbitrator. On behalf of the agency, someone—me, I guess—would try to find a solution that would be acceptable to both parties."

"Say more. You have my attention."

"Well, the starting point for any settlement is to think about terms. What would you as the complainant think would be a fair basis for resolving this matter, rather than pursuing it through litigation?"

"Frank Conway should be fired from his job as chief of station for sexually harassing an employee, for starters. He's an abuser."

"But that would require a finding of fact that he sexually abused you. He denies it. He says it was consensual. I've reviewed your interviews with the IG's office, and there's nothing there about rape or forcible assault. And you didn't tell anyone about it at the time."

"But he was my boss." Her voice grew louder. "He had power over me. I couldn't refuse. Don't you get it? That's the point. He abused a subordinate by pressuring her for sex. That's not right. That shouldn't be allowed. If that doesn't violate the rules, then the rules should be changed."

"Look, Miss Ryan, I get it. Really. I'm trying to think of a way to get to yes. Seeking Frank Conway's dismissal for sexual harassment is going down the same road as filing a lawsuit. It's going to take a long time and it may not be successful. And in the meantime, it will damage the agency."

"What about his transfer of Averill Hart? That wasn't consensual. It was arbitrary. The vengeful act of a jealous man who didn't want someone else to date one of his subordinates. There is no universe in which that's acceptable."

"Interesting that you mention Mr. Hart. We've been thinking about that. Talking with him, actually."

Edith's eyes brightened. "And what does Mr. Hart say?"

"Off the record? He thinks his removal in Singapore was arbitrary and unfair. He doesn't know anything about your relationship with Mr. Conway, obviously, because that's confidential. But he has, in fact, filed a complaint with the personnel selection review board."

"I didn't know that."

"Of course you didn't. And unlike your complaint, the one he filed has some collateral evidence. Testimony from members of the station that his performance had been excellent, evidence that his Chinese language skills more than qualified him for the position, evidence that his dismissal conflicted with an evaluation made two weeks before that his initial performance exceeded expectations."

"You have all that in writing?"

"More or less. Mr. Hart has a strong and well-documented case."

Edith shook her head. She could see what was coming.

"Let me guess. The lawyers will support Averill's claim, but not mine. And you'll use that as a basis for firing Conway."

"Reprimanding him. Not dismissing him from the agency. Though he won't stay for long with the reprimand in his file. That, I can predict."

"What about me? I'm the victim, for god's sake. What happens to me?"

"You keep your job. Not in East Asia Division. Somewhere else. We'll find you a lily pad. A fresh start. There will be compensation, of course."

"For what? I thought my complaint was a dead letter."

"If you agree to withdraw the complaint, the deputy director for operations has authorized me to offer you a payment from his 'contingency fund,' in the amount of two hundred fifty thousand dollars, for operational expenses that you incurred. Last time I looked, that would be enough to buy an apartment in D.C., which is where you would be stationed."

"So, let me make sure I understand this arrangement, hypothetically speaking: You want to uphold the man's claim that his rights were violated but reject the woman's claim that she was sexually harassed. And you want to buy the woman's silence with a cash payment. Why on earth would I agree to that?"

"Well, let me think." He adjusted his tie, patted the pocket square, adjusted himself in his chair. "Because it's a good settlement, hypothetically speaking. You get what you want. The man you say wronged you is reprimanded, you are allowed to remain in the agency, and you get a substantial cash payment to compensate you for the damage you say you experienced. It's done a little sideways, but that's where we live."

"Sideways. More like backwards, or upside down. Let me ask again: Why would I agree to the humiliation of this sideways arrangement, in addition to the humiliation I've already experienced?"

Silence. He didn't fidget with his tie or shuffle the papers on his desk. He just waited, while he thought it through.

"Because it's the best deal you're going to get," he said finally. "The inspector general is almost certain to reject your complaint. The East Asia Division will be poisonous for you. A lawsuit will take forever, probably fail, and expose you to the risk of publicity. Not from us, but from 'do-gooders' who think they are helping you. It is, as we lawyers like to say, a 'no-brainer.'"

Edith waited a good while, too, before responding. The only power she had was to say no. She rose from the chair.

"Let me consider it," she said. "Give me an hour. I'll be back."

Lugano, the nattily dressed lawyer, widened his eyes as she walked to the door. He was good at this. When he crafted a deal, people usually said yes. What was wrong with this woman?

31

Langley, May 2001

When Edith Ryan returned to the general counsel's office, she was composed and confident. She had taken a walk outside, in the light and fragrant May air, along the grassy periphery of the agency compound. She thought of herself, but also the dozens of other women who had faced similar situations before, and the hundreds who would come after. She knew it, everyone knew it.

Lugano had removed his jacket, but he put it back on when she entered the room. He was about to offer a flowery greeting, but she spoke first.

"Here's what I am prepared to offer. I will support the deal you described to me, with amendments. Conway is reprimanded in the Averill Hart matter. Okay. His status as a member of the senior intelligence service is withdrawn. I want that, too. I agree to withdraw my complaint from the inspector general's office, without agreeing that I'm wrong. The agency commits in writing that I will remain in the clandestine service as an operations officer, not in the East Asia Division but in another division or directorate that both sides agree is a good fit."

She studied Lugano. "Good so far?"

"Yes," said the lawyer. "That all works."

"Next, I refuse to accept two hundred fifty thousand from the director of operations 'contingency fund.'"

"Why on earth would you do that?"

"Because it's dirty money. It doesn't feel right. So I'm not doing it. But I reserve my right to seek compensation in the future."

"That doesn't make sense. Why hold on to a right that you don't want to exercise?"

"To keep you honest. If anyone tries this kind of shit again, I am going to sue their ass. And win."

Lugano shrugged. "I could tell you about taking a bird in the hand, and all that. But it's a small point. Obviously, we can agree to not paying you money."

"There's one more thing, and it isn't a small point," said Edith. She sat back in her chair and swept the auburn-brown hair back from her face. That was a tell. She only did that when she was about to say something from her heart, not just her head.

"The agency must agree to establish a new committee within the directorate of operations to review sexual harassment policies and update them. When the new policies are written, the DO will hold training sessions for every employee, to make sure they understand the rules. The director of operations will state that violation of these rules will result in disciplinary action, which may include dismissal. This committee will be secret, like everything else in the clandestine service. What the rest of the agency decides to do is up to them, but I assume they will adopt similar policies."

She stopped there and rested her hands on the table. "That's my demand for settlement. Otherwise, deal's off."

Lugano pondered it for a moment, as if he were weighing an invisible object.

"I have to talk to the seventh floor. Obviously. The director of operations and the DCI, too. I don't know what they'll say."

"Come on! They'll do it if you recommend it as a necessary part of settling this matter. Which it is. So I want your assurance—a handshake promise—that you will recommend it. Got that?"

"Otherwise, no deal?"

"Correct. Negotiation ends now."

"Hmmm." There was a long pause, but it was theatrical. He eventually extended his hand.

"One last thing," she said, raising her hand like a guard at a crosswalk. "I want to be a member of that committee."

"A committee member? That's it? You're not going to hold us up for more?" Lugano still had his hand out.

Edith laughed. Really, that was all. A committee to hear sexual harassment complaints with her as a member. She grasped his meaty hand, jarring his jeweled cuff link as they shook on it.

32

Langley, January 2003

Edith Ryan found her lily pad. It was called the Directorate of Science and Technology. The move was suggested by one of her mentors in East Asia Division, a Chinese American woman who knew that she was a space geek. Edith was leaving the East Asia Division, for reasons nobody quite knew but everyone accepted, and she needed a good place to land. Support talked to her, but they wanted someone with experience using firearms. The front office wanted her, thanks to Lugano. They dangled congressional affairs and human resources. But Edith declined. She still wanted to be a spy, and S&T was as close as she would get.

Edith loved her new home. S&T was part of the clandestine side of the agency but separate from the operational network of stations around the world. It was a quirky niche, where people worked on puzzles that the operators needed to solve. How to extend the battery life of a surveillance bug so that it wouldn't require external power? How to trick a passport control sensor so it flashed green, no matter what the passport data said? How to support agency officers in the field, with overhead imagery, real-time signals interception, and even communications devices in their earpieces when they went on surveillance detection runs?

Edith embraced her new workplace. She was a mischievous person. An elf, more than a leprechaun. Her colleagues in S&T were nerds and screwballs, not ball-busters who had transferred in from the Special Forces. She untied knots at S&T, performed the intelligence equivalent of magic tricks to get officers in and out of hard places and steal the information that the agency needed.

Edith's work increasingly involved spy satellites, which S&T had pretty much invented back in 1960, with the crazy but effective plan to drop spools of exposed overhead-reconnaissance photos from orbiting satellites and retrieve them with airplanes far below. Like much of what S&T did, the bottom line for the project was: It worked.

Edith had been a satellite groupie as a girl. By the time she was born, Neil Armstrong had already landed on the moon. As a little girl, she dressed up in a white outfit one Halloween and pretended to be an astronaut. The *Challenger* shuttle crashed when she was thirteen, and America's civilian space program began an accelerating downward arc. But the intelligence side remained robust.

Edith had been thinking about satellite intelligence as far back as Beijing; it was hard, occasionally painful, to remember that time. But now she began working on technical issues in space that mattered to S&T. She led a small "tasking" group that matched reconnaissance satellite orbit schedules with collection needs; she led a project on improving maneuver systems to move available satellites more quickly to where they were needed to support operations officers. She explored systems for space counterespionage—spying on other spies in the sky. She was a member of a "red team" that thought about possible vulnerabilities in upload and download links for America's satellite architecture.

*   *   *

Edith was in a meeting with counterintelligence officers from the East Asia Division, two years into her job with S&T, when she saw a Chinese man's face on the screen. He was handsome, mid-fifties, dressed expensively in well-cut trousers and a tweed jacket. The camera had caught him on a tour of the family compound in Vancouver, Canada. Chinese often look wary and opaque in surveillance photographs; this one looked confident and sleek.

"Who's that guy?" asked Edith.

"His name is Cao Lin," answered the chief of East Asia counterintelligence.

"He's a physicist. Studied at Harvard, a space guy, protégé of Chen Fangyun. He used to be a member of the Chinese Academy of Sciences, maybe still is. He went off the grid in the mid-1990s. He surfaces occasionally with China Aerospace Science and Technology Corp. He hangs out some with Westerners, a few Americans. We pinged the Bureau. We think maybe he's a recruiter. Why do you ask?"

"I've seen that man before," said Edith, trying to clear the fog from her brain. "In Beijing, when I was studying for a year at Tsinghua University. I think maybe my handler in Hong Kong showed me a picture of him. I had a friend who was spending time at the Chinese Academy, a Russian guy. The Chinese were just getting started with satellites, and they thought my Russian friend could help them. So he saw lots of Chinese scientists, including this guy, maybe. That's all I remember."

"I gather that Beijing tour didn't go too well," said the CI officer. "I read the file."

Edith stared at him. She was tired of being intimidated and second-guessed about the Volkov case. "Beijing had its ups and downs. Listen, why don't you see if you can get traces for me on Cao Lin? We know the Chinese are obsessed with satellites, but we don't know what they're doing. Maybe I could help untangle the Cao Lin thread."

The CI chief shrugged. He didn't say no, but you could tell from the look in his eyes that he was dubious, suspicious even. "I'll put in a request with the deputy division chief. He would have to sign off on it."

"Thanks," said Edith. Two weeks later a response to her request came back from the East Asia Division: "Access denied."

33

Chantilly, Virginia, March 2008

As Edith Ryan gained expertise in overhead collection, she was detailed to the National Reconnaissance Office, where nearly a third of the workforce was actually on loan from the CIA. The NRO was an austere, ultramodern operation, set apart from the rest of the intelligence community like a piece of Scandinavian furniture. It was out in Chantilly, Virginia, beyond the CIA physically and operationally, too. Secrets went into NRO, but they never came out.

Edith loved it. She traveled to Vandenberg Air Base for launches of satellites whose mission details were unknown except to her and a handful of other people. She was trusted. *Supra et ultra.* That was the NRO slogan. Above and beyond.

Edith began working on counterintelligence assignments while she was at the NRO. The United States had established such total mastery of space that people didn't think much, even at S&T and the NRO, about how our technology secrets might be stolen. That became a specialty for Edith, thinking about the unthinkable in space. Sometimes people listened to her, but mostly they didn't.

During her stint at the NRO, Edith encountered a reminder that male power dynamics were a part of life not just in the operations directorate of the CIA, but everywhere, including America's supposedly spotless spy satellite agency. Or, at least, that's what she thought explained her exclusion from the inner circle.

Edith had been in Chantilly for several months when she was invited to join the "Threat Assessment" Task Force. It was an elite group, presided over by a fastidious scientist named Robert Gallant, who liked to wear tweed suits and bow ties. He regarded the word "unbending" as a compliment. He had been an assistant professor of applied physics at Caltech earlier in his career, and lecturing was still what he did best.

Edith was the only woman in the group, and for the first several meetings she just watched and listened. But after a month of meandering and inconclusive threat assessments, she spoke up.

"Can the Chinese sabotage us in space? Get inside our heads. Mess us up." It was 2008. China had conducted its first anti-satellite test the year before, by demolishing a weather satellite named Fengyun 17 with a kinetic kill vehicle.

"The Chinese are trying, but they are sloppy," said "Dr. Gallant," as he liked to be addressed. "The strike on the weather satellite left two thousand pieces of debris. It was irresponsible and immature."

"But aren't we vulnerable, even to a sloppy attack?" asked Edith. This was a touchy subject. A few naysayers had begun criticizing the NRO for relying on a small array of satellites, configured with what were always described as "exquisite" surveillance capabilities.

"We are vulnerable, just as they are vulnerable. That is the essence of deterrence," answered Dr. Gallant. He meant that to end the conversation. But Edith persisted.

"Obviously there's deterrence, in terms of a direct attack. But suppose the Chinese had somehow gotten inside our systems. How would we turn them off?"

Gallant was peeved. These were very sensitive matters. This woman was not part of the family.

"What do you mean, 'inside'? We have trusted foundries. We assemble every piece of secure hardware ourselves. We are the most secure intelligence organization in the world."

He paused a beat. "The CIA and FBI should be as lucky as NRO." That was a shot. The other intelligence services had been rocked over the previous decade by two catastrophic Russian penetrations agents.

Gallant had already clicked on the next PowerPoint slide, but Edith wasn't finished.

"Right, but, excuse me, let's just imagine that the Chinese are very smart, as opposed to just medium-smart. I lived there a year, and think they are, yeah, very smart. And let's assume that they have been thinking about this a long time, and that they have capabilities that we don't know about. And it's a crisis and, like, they try to turn out the lights. What would we do?"

Gallant slammed his fist down on the table. He was furious. "I'd like to adjourn this meeting for ten minutes," he said. "Miss Ryan, would you stay behind here in the conference room, please?"

Everyone else filed out. Edith stood meekly before him.

"Don't ever do that again," said Gallant. "This is one of the most sensitive topics in our agency. Most people in that conference room are not cleared for the special access program in which this issue of counter-threat capability is discussed. I am *quite* certain that you are not cleared for this SAP."

"So long as you've thought about the problem, that's all," she said. He was still bristling, and she couldn't resist taking another shot. "I mean, I know I don't have a doctorate, and I'm just a stupid woman on temporary duty from the CIA. So, I guess I should leave it to you."

"Jesus lord!" His face was red. His neck was bulging, just above the bow tie, straining the collar button. He was ready to start shouting at her. But instead a self-preservation impulse intervened, and he turned and walked toward the door.

Edith was back in her chair when the session resumed. She didn't say anything more at that meeting. But at the next gathering, Dr. Gallant was nice to her and encouraged her to speak up. She assumed that Gallant must have learned something of her past history and was afraid of getting caught up in a "women's lib" protest.

It never occurred to Edith that she might have stumbled into a very big secret, and that Gallant was trying to protect her from causing unintentional damage.

* * *

After the stint at the NRO, Edith returned to the lily pad at S&T. She was a manager now, with a small staff of officers assigned to help her solve technical problems with surveillance requirements. "Mr. Fixit" was what she called her group, even though it was run by a "Miss." Her office became a reliable go-to for problems that nobody else could handle. She liked that. After so many years, she had found a specialty that suited her, because it wasn't too specialized.

She dated men, even lived for a year with an assistant professor from Georgetown University. They went on long bicycle trips and cross-country skiing vacations, and she sensed that he would have proposed to her, if he had thought she would say yes.

But she had scars. The men who were good for her didn't excite her. And the men who aroused her were trouble. She tried therapy several times, but the raw places remained. She stayed happy by getting exercise, carousing with her friends, dating for fun, and not beating herself up for her mistakes.

* * *

And she had her Workplace Behavior Committee, founded in the Operations Directorate but now agency-wide. She served on the committee for five years and consulted informally for ten more.

Men at the CIA still did bad things to women. An agency officer in the Mexico City Station drugged and assaulted twenty-four Mexican women before he was caught. A station chief in Algiers assaulted two local women: same thing, he drugged and raped them. A senior officer was videoed in the agency parking lot molesting a woman employee. A senior officer got caught in an affair with a subordinate after her suspicious husband hired a private detective who took photos that captured them in the act.

The CIA was like America, in other words. But now at the agency, at least, women had somewhere to go with their complaints, and reasonable confidence that people would listen to them. It's hard to say, "me, too," in a house of secrets, where any hint of vulnerability can be an exit ticket. But Edith's committee helped drive the dinosaurs into retreat.

34

Life moves in a hurry when we're young, but then it slows down. Things that seemed excruciating when they were happening become cauterized, and they don't bleed on through time. The secret, perhaps, is just to turn the channel. You reach an impasse where there's no possibility of winning the argument with yourself or someone else, no possibility of release or forgiveness in the stall where you're seated. So you move. Begin a different conversation in your head. Stop one thread; start a different one.

That was the gist of what Edith Ryan told her colleagues when she decided to retire. The rules said she could retire on full pension after twenty years in the clandestine service, and she did. The agency invited her parents and friends to a retirement ceremony in the lobby, with the anonymous stars carved on the wall for fallen heroes and the CIA seal embedded in the marble floor. It was the place everyone had seen in the movies, and the agency liked to allow family and friends of retiring officers to get a taste of the secret world, or at least the entrance lobby of it. Edith invited her parents; that was it.

Edith received the Career Intelligence Medal, for "substantial" contributions to the agency's mission, but they gave that to most people who made it through without blowing the place up. It was like an honorable discharge, with a ribbon. Edith hadn't planned a farewell speech; she hadn't let herself think in the past tense about the agency, really, so she just used as a valedictory the biblical quotation that was carved on the wall: "And ye shall know the truth and the truth shall make you free."

* * *

After the retirement ceremony in the marbled CIA lobby with her parents, Edith cleared out her desk in the Science and Technology directorate. Some friends had asked her to come meet for a farewell party, for real, at a restaurant on Route 123 not far from the agency. The party invitation had a cartoon of a woman in a green hat and striped stockings marked "Ryan," and a note at the bottom that said, "Warning: Alcohol will be consumed."

Edith Ryan arrived at the farewell party wearing an elf hat. She gave her guests paper horns and glasses with flashing lights, as if it were a New Year's party. People from all over the agency had shown up. Not just from S&T, but from the East Asia Division, including Lynette, the reports officer who had tried to wise her up. They had a private room at the back of the restaurant, but even then the manager asked them to keep the noise down, because other guests were complaining. But Edith's guests kept honking and singing, and eventually the agency crowd in the restaurant gave up complaining and joined the party.

When everyone was good and drunk, people started making toasts. Mike Lugano from the general counsel's office showed up, nattily dressed, as ever. He clinked his glass to give a speech but it was only three words. "You done good!" It was mostly a blur for Edith, who loved her colleagues but was also glad to be leaving and starting a second career in her early forties. "Clowns in Action," a colleague said as people began to get smashed, using one of the most derogatory nicknames for the agency. Edith just smiled.

She was thinking it was time to call it a night when a woman arrived late from the office. Heads turned when she entered the room; she was a celebrity in their world. She had put on a name tag, as if people didn't know who she was. Laura Oden had just been named director of operations.

Oden was slender and self-assured, with long silken hair, and a body somewhere between a kickboxer's and a ballroom dancer's. She had served as an operations officer in a half dozen stations overseas. Tough places, where you had to make the right decisions under pressure every day.

Edith greeted her. "Thanks for coming."

Oden took a glass of wine from the bar and walked toward Edith. She put her arm around her colleague. "For a long time, nobody in our shop would listen to people like you and me," she said, raising her glass. "Now they do."

"Yeah," said Edith, allowing herself a smile. "They do."

35

Manhattan Beach, May 2017

Edith Ryan took a slow walk out the CIA door. She went through the standard exit process: debriefings; being read out of code-word programs; signing forms pledging never to divulge secrets, on pain of criminal prosecution. She was in employment purdah for a few months, not allowed to talk to any of the intelligence or military contractors that were eager to throw money at her. But she had pretty much decided where she wanted to go before submitting her resignation letter. "I'm not sure what the question is, but the answer is California," she told a friend in S&T. And there was a particular place she had in mind.

When she got a formal job offer from Apollo Space Laboratories in Manhattan Beach, she said yes twenty-four hours later. That probably wasn't cool; you were supposed to imply that you were weighing other options to leverage a higher starting salary. But Edith had worked with engineers and analysts from Apollo when she was seconded to the National Reconnaissance Office, and she liked everything about them, starting with the fact they seemed smarter than the government officials for whom they worked.

Apollo was "the place for space," as its recruiter liked to say. It had been created in the early 1960s, to supplement the work of its more famous cousin, Aerospace Corporation, just up the road in El Segundo. Apollo was now so tightly interwound with America's secret space programs that, like Aerospace, it had its own office in Chantilly, down the street from NRO's cool cube of a headquarters.

Edith moved to Los Angeles. She wanted to live near the Apollo headquarters in Manhattan Beach. She hunted for a home in Santa Monica, ten miles up the coast, and found a little house just north of Venice, near the beach. The people on her block included a failed actor, a wannabe surfer, and a part-time bodybuilder, who all had unglamorous jobs in the entertainment industry. It was a five-minute walk to the beach, past the palm-lined boulevard and the sidewalk crowded with roller skaters and boarders, and across the sand to the blue Pacific.

She spent much of her first week lying on the beach, hanging out later in scuzzy bars drinking beer and looking for the right hookup. If anyone asked what she did for a living, she told them she had just quit the circus. "Trapeze," she would answer if they pressed any further. She was still lithe at forty-two. After that first week on the beach, her tan glowed. Like most Angelinos, she lived in her sunglasses.

One night after her afternoon swim, she let a good-looking man, fit but not too ripped, pick her up in a bar. They went home to Edith's new house, tight and tidy as a hotel suite. He was about her age, not inappropriate, but the sex wasn't very good, and she didn't ask for his phone number. Her new rule was "no bads"—don't drink bad wine, don't eat bad food, don't have bad sex.

Edith drove to work. Of course she did. It was Los Angeles. It took her thirty minutes on a good day. Most people took the 405, the monstrous north-south freeway, but Edith liked Route 1, which hugged the coast. It took her right to the Manhattan Beach Pier, where the surfers hung out and the water stretched from the sandy beach to the edge of the world.

When she turned east from the coast road toward the Apollo Space Labs campus, the neighborhood got weird. Edith would drive past warehouses and railroad tracks and cheap taco stands before arriving at the sleek offices of Apollo, tucked away in this industrial zone like an emerald hidden in a stack of plywood. One thing she noticed on her very first visit was the forest of satellite dishes of different sizes and configurations at the west end of the campus, all pointing skyward. Silent, essential, always running, like the plumbing of this establishment.

Apollo had as much security as any three-letter agency. Edith had to get cleared, badged, drug-tested, pre-interviewed, and then interviewed. It was a familiar routine, and comforting in its way. Edith liked having secrets and she had always been passionate about protecting them. When the Edward Snowden affair broke a few years before, she had loathed the man. She felt not simply dislike but an almost physical repulsion at someone who would so cavalierly steal the secrets she had worked for two decades to gather and protect. That wasn't a popular position among liberal Californians, so Edith didn't express it openly. But she burned inside every time a new leak was reported.

*   *   *

Edith had been at Apollo Space Laboratories for several weeks when the company held its quarterly get-acquainted meeting for new employees. They gathered in a large auditorium that was much nicer than any conference facility at the CIA. The hall was past the gleaming entrance lobby, which was decorated with trophies of Apollo's work with the government: satellites suspended by wires from ceilings; models of several generations of rockets; photo displays of the unclassified parts of projects the company was managing now.

Edith took a seat near the front of the auditorium. She wore a new employee badge that read EDITH! She introduced herself to everyone she encountered, and they were as welcoming as awkward, geeky people can be. The members of the senior management team gave presentations; they looked like characters in *Mad Men*, dressed in slim black suits, men and women alike, tight haircuts, fixed smiles. The employees in the audience were looser. Nearly half the people in the room were women. Some people had piercings, black T-shirts, and pastel streaks in their hair; they would have looked at home at a *Star Wars* con.

The main event was a lecture from a woman named Anna Friedman, whose title was space operations chief. She was slender, with sleek black hair, high cheekbones and large, sensuous lips. She had the exotic look of a Russian émigré a decade or two earlier, with the brainpower of Odessa filtered through the fine grains of America's schools, secret agencies, and now corporate science.

The title of her talk was "The Physics of Space." Edith was afraid it would be like the extra-credit problem on an exam. But it was a lucid, easy-to-understand explanation of some of the very complicated problems the engineers struggled with at Apollo Space Labs.

"Hey, everybody," she began. That was a better start, right away, than "Ladies and gentlemen."

"Hey, Anna," people shouted back.

"Most of us have worked for a while in space science," she began. "But because this is the 'new employees' town hall, I want to go back to some basic issues of physics that we don't talk about very often, but are crucial for moving satellites around in space, which is a big part of what we do. Is that cool with everyone?"

"Cool!" several dozen people called back.

"Okay, so the first thing is that space is *big*. I mean, that's obvious, right? It's infinite. But let's think about what that bigness means operationally. For starters, think about the space that's between geosynchronous orbit, GEO, and the earth. That's where we operate most of the time. That band of space, let's forget all the rest, is a hundred and ninety times bigger than the volume of earth. It's huge! And that's the distance within which we have to maneuver our satellites.

"The second big point is that movement in space is *hard*. Directing a satellite isn't like flying a plane or driving a car. It's more like operating a train. Because a satellite is basically on *tracks*. The momentum of its orbit is like a pair of rails, and the rails only go in one direction. You can't turn the wheel left or right. If you want to move to another course, you have to use some energy, a little rocket burn, and move to another set of tracks that fixes the new orbit. Someday we'll have better propulsion systems and it will be easier to move, but not now.

"Third point, even though you're going at super-speed in space, targeting anything is *slow*. You can't just move from A to B. There are no straight lines in orbit. Let's say you want to move your LEO satellite to a slightly higher orbit. Well, you need at least two burns. The first one pushes you up, farther out in space; the second one levels you onto a new orbital plane. That takes a while. And if you wanted to move all the way to GEO, it would take at least five hours. So, dogfights in space, forget it.

"Fourth point about space is that for satellites, it's *flat*. It's two-dimensional. We think of space as, what, three, four, five dimensions? The Fifth Dimension, that was a sixties band, right? But each satellite, as it spins around the earth, is on an orbital plane like a plate that's carrying its own slice of the sky. You can change the tilt of that plate, or widen or narrow it, but it's complicated, and it takes time.

"And that's the fifth point about space. It requires *patience*, as a military domain. You can do simple things quickly. Like if you just want a flyby, all you need is to intersect the target without actually matching its orbit. To take a local metaphor, forgive me, let's say you're on the 405, going north-south, and your target is on the 10, going east-west. You don't have to get off the 405 and onto the 10 to have proximity. You just need to time your trip so that you're at the point where the two highways—let's say the two orbits—cross at the same time. Which would be, I think, the overpass that's in, like, Culver City.

"But let's assume that you actually want to intercept your target, and be together on the same orbital plane, so you can inspect the other satellite closely. Fix some stuff, if it's one of your satellites. Or play games if it's someone else's. Or, maybe, just snatch the damn thing out of the sky. Well, that's going to take a long time—changing altitude, changing orbital plane, changing speed, lining up so you're in just the right lane on the 10, at just the same speed. It could take a week to get into just the right position. And that's assuming that your target doesn't take evasive action and move to Orbit B just as you're closing in on Orbit A.

"Sixth point about space is that it's scary-*fast* when it's crunch time. Yes, all the other things are true. It's big, hard, slow, flat, and requires patience. But when things happen, it's incredibly, catastrophically fast. An object in low-earth orbit is moving at fifteen thousand to eighteen thousand miles per hour. It goes from New York to London in ten minutes. In GEO, a satellite moves slower, at sixty-seven hundred miles an hour, so it takes thirty minutes to get to London. The margin for error at these speeds is tiny. If one object hits another, it can scatter, what, two thousand pieces of debris that will stay in space for twenty or thirty years.

"So, colleagues, when you think about space, think physics. This is a domain, like land or sea, that has its own rules. Movement is constrained. Things that you think are easy turn out to be very hard. Clausewitz said that combat was like moving through water. Movements are slower, more complicated. Well, operating in space is as slow as moving through maple syrup, even though it's just plain air.

"And another, final thing about this domain. For all the previously mentioned reasons, it's *stealthy*. It's incredibly easy to hide what you're doing, mislead observers, make your adversaries think you're going to New York when you're really headed for Miami Beach. And if you think I'm overstating things, I suggest that you visit the China team at the Operations Group. I will say no more."

The audience was starting to clap, with a few hoots and whistles, but Anna put up her hands for them to stop.

"Hey, thanks, guys," she concluded. "Welcome to space operations. Big, hard, slow, flat, fast, sneaky. Yeah! Have fun."

*   *   *

Edith moved to the front of the room to meet Anna when she finished speaking. She had heard similar talks about the physical aspects of space operations, but never one like this.

"I'm Edith Ryan," she said, pushing her way past other fanboys and fangirls. "I just joined the company. Your talk was awesome. Just, wow!"

"Hey, thanks," said Anna. "Where are you coming from? A university? Think tank?"

"I've worked twenty years for a government agency. Its name begins with a *C*."

"Cool," said Anna. "Where have they assigned you at Apollo?"

"I'm doing government liaison right now. Talking to the people I used to work with, basically. Pretty boring, to be honest. Can I be totally shameless?"

"Sure," said Anna. "This is California."

"I'd like to work in your part of the company. In space operations. My clearances are still solid. I had to read out of some programs, but I could read back into most of them pretty quickly. Listening to you just now I thought, Yeah! This is what I want to do. I think I'd be really good at it. If I'm not, you can fire me. Right?"

"Do you have a card?" asked Anna. That was always the default answer when someone was pumping you for a job. Give me your card.

"No," said Edith. "My cards aren't ready yet. Blame the company. So I wrote my contacts on a piece of paper." She handed Anna a small sheet with her name, cell number, Apollo phone extension, and email. "Can I have one of your cards?"

Anna handed one over. "I'll see what I can do," she said.

"I know China, too," said Edith. "I lived there for a year. I was a China targets officer. It's all in my résumé."

"Now you've got my attention," said Anna Friedman. She flashed a Vulcan salute, middle fingers parted, from *Star Trek*.

Edith tried to match the sign, but her fingers wouldn't stay in place.

Anna laughed and waved her off. "I hate that show, actually. I'll be in touch."

36

Manhattan Beach, August 2017–September 2020

Edith Ryan didn't have to wait long. She soon received a message from Anna Friedman, the space operations chief, suggesting that she apply for a position in the Operations Lab. The lab was in a separate building apart from the main campus, air-gapped from the company's other computing and communications systems.

Edith still had many of her agency clearances, but joining the lab required her to describe her foreign contacts. She listed several dozen Tsinghua classmates from twenty years before, including the distant but still vivid encounter with a Russian who had studied there. The process took weeks, but Edith was eventually offered a position as senior analyst with the China operations team.

The China team was run by a Vietnamese American named Linh Phan. Her parents had fled Saigon in the late 1970s as boat people. Linh had been born just after the family arrived in America. She hated Communist China the way a Holocaust survivor's daughter would hate Nazi Germany. She was several years younger than Edith but had worked earlier in her career for both the NRO and the National Security Agency.

Edith's first day on the new job, she put her hair in a ponytail, something she had rarely done at the agency. She wore black jeans, black sneakers, and a black hoodie to surprise any new colleagues who might think of her as an ex-government goon. Linh took Edith into her office for an initial briefing. Edith signed more forms, and then Linh explained the peculiar analytical work that would now consume Edith's workdays.

"I want you to think of yourself as a detective," Linh said. "Our group tails Chinese satellites. Unfortunately, the target is twenty-two thousand miles away. We'd like to cruise in for a close look, but we don't have that authority yet. So we use other monitors. Telescopes on the ground and in space; signals collection to monitor what they're uploading and downloading. Radar and lasers to track position and movement. When we see things that don't make sense, we flag them."

"China: Menace or threat?"

Linh laughed. "I assume the worst. I think the Chinese are developing advanced anti-satellite capabilities in space. But a lot of people don't agree, so we need proof."

"I'm a worst-case person, too," said Edith. "I smell the flowers and look for the funeral."

* * *

When Edith joined the lab, the pandemic hadn't begun, so she could see people's faces and get to know them a bit before the curtain came down. It wasn't a chatty office, in any event. Most of her colleagues were engineers. Normal vocabulary range was, "Yup," "Nope," and "Awesome."

A large screen dominated the far wall of the lab, charting orbits of known Chinese satellites around a green-and-blue image of earth. Next to the main screen were separate panels for closer examination of LEO and GEO orbits. A smaller screen conveyed current location data about Chinese satellites, drawn from radio frequency, radar, and optical monitors. Another panel presented real-time information from Chinese launch facilities at Jiuquan, Taiyuan, Wenchang, and Xichang.

Pointing to the display of launch facilities, Edith told her new colleagues that back when she lived in China, they had just one launch site, at Xichang. Heads shook. No way. The other locations must have been hidden.

Linh escorted Edith to a small office along the side wall of the operations room. Two monitors sat atop her desk, displaying smaller versions of the images that were on the main displays.

"Your new home," said Linh. "As a senior analyst, you'll be monitoring all Chinese launch and tracking data. The Chinese have about five hundred satellites in space. You'll help prepare our weekly report, and topical analyses for our clients in the USG. But while you're doing the daily grind, I want you to focus on one special project."

Edith leaned toward her new boss. "What makes it special?"

"Meet Shijian 17." Linh handed Edith a photograph of a satellite. " 'SH-17,' we call it. This is your new best friend. You're going to be stuck like glue."

Edith was perplexed. "Why do we care so much about SH-17?"

"SH-17 was launched in November 2016 from Wenchang. The Chinese officially called it an 'experimental' satellite. They haven't said any more about it. It doesn't do communications. It doesn't do earth observation. We don't know what it does, honestly. It has a robotic arm, that's one odd thing. It makes people nervous."

"What's my assignment?" asked Edith.

"Track it and surveil it with every sensor we have. Review its history since launch, interrogate it, the way a detective would. Who, what, where, when, and why. Figure it out."

"How long will this take?" asked Edith.

"Months. This assignment is LTI. Meaning: Long. Tedious. Important. Weeks could pass without any movement from your new friend SH-17. You have to be patient. Someone else had this project before you. He went wiggy on me. Don't do that."

Linh retreated, leaving Edith with her new best friend blinking on the monitor screen.

* * *

Edith spied on space from her workstation in the Apollo operations lab. There was a daily routine of gathering and assessing data about the range of Chinese satellite operations, looking for signatures and vulnerabilities. But one eye was always glancing at SH-17 and meticulously plotting its course through space.

Taped to her monitor was the picture of the satellite that Linh had given her, which had been published by Xinhua, the Chinese news agency, when the orbiter was launched: A square core, flanked by two blue wings of solar cells to collect power from the sun. Above the capsule rested the robotic arm stored in a white sleeve.

SH-17 had started its life normally enough. But as Edith tracked its history, she found that it had a peculiar signature: It was a wanderer, and it liked to visit other Chinese satellites. Why was it doing that? Answering that question became an obsession.

* * *

After many long months, Edith presented her research in a secure videoconference for her colleagues at Apollo, and CIA and NRO officials in Washington. The pandemic was in full swing now. Apollo employees still came to work at the campus near the Pacific, but they always wore their masks. A cough in the office brought dirty looks. For her video presentation, Edith settled into a conference room alone, removed her mask, and queued up her PowerPoint deck.

"Meet Red Rover," Edith began, displaying on a shared screen for her colleagues a copy of the Xinhua photo of the boxy satellite and its solar panel wings. "As I will explain, this little satellite gets around." She launched into her narrative, with each section accompanied by a slide mapping the satellite's position and movement.

"Let's go back to the beginning." Edith continued. "After its launch, SH-17 powered up to the GEO belt. It looked pretty normal. The first odd thing was that it rendezvoused right away with a communications satellite, catalogued as Chinasat 5A. Here, take a look." An image of the communications satellite clicked on the screen.

"Nothing special about 5A. Like every GEO, its longitude was fixed above the equator. Its latitude gave it a signals footprint over China, India, Korea, and Southeast Asia. But why did SH-17 meet up with 5A right away? I've thought about that a long time, and my answer is: Because it could." Click, next slide.

"Red Rover continued its wandering. After finishing its proximity operations near 5A, it moved farther east. A few months later, it settled near the orbit of another Chinese communications satellite, Chinasat 6A." Click. Another image.

"Our little traveler stayed with 6A a few months, and then it moved again to rendezvous with Chinasat 20, yet another communications satellite in the GEO belt." Click, a new slide.

"My Chinese friend stayed put for months. Taking a rest. Saving fuel, maybe. Then, almost a year after its last repositioning, it began moving again. Maybe the Chinese thought we weren't looking. Who knows? This time it rendezvoused with yet another communications satellite, Chinasat 6B." Click.

"And then a few months later, it visited another 'experimental,' satellite, a younger brother, which the Chinese had designated SH-20." Click. The screen displayed another box with wings. "And finally, Red Rover shifted course sharply eastward and positioned itself near GF-13, a Chinese earth-observation satellite."

One more click, and the screen share ended. It was just Edith Ryan looking at the camera.

"So what on earth has SH-17 been doing up there in space? Forgive the pun. That's what I have been trying to understand, and I'll give you my two hypotheses." On the group screen, the faces were in rapt attention, waiting for Edith's explanation.

"Hypothesis One. The benign version. China was practicing its ability to rendezvous precisely with other satellites in geocentric orbit so that it could develop satellite-maintenance capability. SH-17 showed that they could find another satellite and approach it closely, in theory allowing the robot arm to replace defective parts or provide more fuel or deactivate a satellite that was failing.

"Yes, that's certainly possible. But I would bet the ranch, if I had one, on Hypothesis Two. Which is that SH-17 is an experimental attack satellite. Let me repeat those last two words for emphasis: *attack satellite*.

"Here's the bottom line for me as an analyst: I think SH-17's maneuvers in space were tactical training exercises designed to perfect space-combat skills. The Chinese have shown us, with SH-17, the ability to move an attack satellite into position near a target, close on that target, remain as long as needed, and then move toward another target, sometimes at a higher apogee in GEO, sometimes lower.

"Consider, please, what the Chinese could do in a close encounter with one of our satellites. Using high-powered microwaves or lasers, they could insert malicious code. That code could disable the satellite, or disorient it, or alter its instructions. Cyberwar in space is much creepier than on earth because it's so hard to verify and impossible to attribute. But the people in this audience know the danger. That's why you're here."

Edith paused. She was briefing people who were in more senior positions than any she had ever held in government herself. She took a breath and raised her voice.

"My judgment is that the Chinese are very good, eerily good, at the basics of space warfare. I don't know much about U.S. capabilities. I'm not cleared for that. But from what I've seen, I worry that in this domain, China has the high ground."

People actually clapped when Edith finished her presentation. She quickly scrolled through the cameos of the attendees to get a sense of her audience's reaction. The only person who wasn't visibly conveying approval was the senior NRO representative. Robert Gallant. He didn't look angry so much as startled—as if this conversation shouldn't be happening.

Once again, Edith thought she knew what was motivating Gallant: A discomfort with a woman who was making a provocative comment on a subject that he wanted to control. As she scrolled back through the approving faces, she forgot about Gallant's scowling look of reproach.

*　*　*

Edith loved her California life. It was easier to be single there; many of the married people she knew seemed miserable. She worked out most days at a gym near her house in Santa Monica. She joined a book club and a tennis league. She interviewed West Coast applicants for Yale. She babysat her friends' children when they went away on weekends, took vacations with pals from work, visited her parents in Holyoke.

Her favorite hobby became Go, the game she had started playing as an undergraduate. She carried her board and boxes of black and white stones to conventions up and down the West Coast. Many of the players were Asian American. They were surprised, occasionally offended, but generally appreciative that she was so good at the game.

People who didn't know her tried to advise her about tactics for enclosing the opponents' pieces and gaining advantage. "The ladder," one man would admonish. "The net," counseled another." "The pin."

At the beginning of every match, Edith would bow. She would keep playing until she dominated the board or lost. She would thank her opponent, always, when the game ended. If asked, she would explain moves that her adversaries hadn't seen coming. "The tiger's mouth." "The bamboo joint." Ah—her opponents would nod.

Then she would collect her stones, excuse herself, and go to a bar. She would flirt with men who interested her and ignore those who didn't. Almost always, she would go home alone.

A Go player seeks what is known as "liberty," when she can move her stone freely. A player loses when she has "no liberty." Edith had liberty.

*   *   *

Edith visited her parents in Holyoke the first Christmas after she moved to California. Her father had just turned seventy, and he was slowing down. He had enough shrapnel inside his body from his year in Vietnam that he set off the metal detector at the airport.

She worried about him. He still raised the flag in front of their house on Harvard Street every day. He and his wife wrote joint op-eds occasionally for the News-Transcript, but the paper had a new owner now, and it was little more than a shopper. He watched cable news more than Edith had remembered, and he groaned aloud at the stories about the Republican braggart who had just been elected president.

"I hate that man," he said. "I can't bear the thought of dying while he's president."

"Then don't die, Dad," Edith said. But when they played tennis at an indoor court the week after Christmas, she noticed that he was very short of breath. She asked him if he wanted to take a break, but he won every game after that, and she decided not to worry about him.

37

Manhattan Beach, January 2022

Edith Ryan's research into the Red Rover made her a minor celebrity at Apollo Space Laboratories. The Pentagon and the intelligence community, after years of lowballing the dangers in space, were now eager for information and analysis. The White House had pushed the creation of a "Space Force" on a reluctant military, and White House and congressional staffers were eager for briefings. Covid was still raging, so Edith didn't travel much, but she had become a star on the secure video-teleconference circuit.

Anna Friedman, the head of the Operations Lab, pulled Edith away from her usual China work to conduct a special analysis of the strange behavior of a Russian satellite named Cosmos 2542. Edith took several months to prepare her analysis for a video briefing. This one had an audience of more than a hundred people, all watching in secure facilities. Edith had dropped the black T-shirt look, and as her hair began to go gray she had cut it shorter and dyed it the auburn color she saw in her high school pictures.

Edith presented her Russia satellite report in an election year, at a moment when the country seemed to be coming apart at the seams. At the time, Russia was discussed mainly as a partisan issue—a country name followed by the word "scandal" or "hoax," depending on which party affiliation the speaker professed. Edith's research was a reminder that the Russians, however feeble or corrupted, still had a few tricks to play in space.

Edith stared into the camera as she introduced herself to the unseen audience and began her briefing. Apollo had built a little studio for her and other regular briefers as videoconferences became the primary form of communication.

As Edith began her briefing, she took a gaily painted figure of a Russian peasant woman from the table in front of her and held it toward the camera. It was nine inches tall, bulbous on the bottom and narrowing only slightly at the waist and top.

"I'm sure most of you have seen one of these. It's called a 'matryoshka' doll. Russians have been making them for their children since the nineteenth century. It's a cute doll, a little chubby maybe, but nothing unusual except, see, when you twist it in the middle, it opens up and, look, out comes another doll. And then another, and another, and one more."

Edith lined the five dolls up in front of her so the camera could see.

"Very cute. And you've probably seen the crazy versions they make in Russia these days. Politicians, football players, characters from *The Simpsons*. So maybe it was inevitable that the Russians would eventually put a matryoshka doll in space.

"Look at the screen, and I'll show you the babushka, the mommy doll, Cosmos 2542." The screen showed an image of a Russian satellite, with the usual rectangular body and the giant solar-panel wings.

"This space story began several years ago when Cosmos 2542, which I'll call the Inspector, was launched. Its initial orbit worried us, because every week or so, it passed within several hundred miles of one of our KH-11 spy satellites, one that we designate as USA 245. But space is big, so people thought maybe it was nothing.

"We began to get worried two months later, when the Inspector moved much closer to the KH-11, so that it could take good photos. We only had four KH-11s in space at the time, so that upset people. And the Inspector could have done more than inspect, as you'll see." A click, and the screen displayed tracking data, with little flags next to the two countries' satellites.

"And then, zap! The Inspector went matryoshka—and ejected another satellite, Cosmos 2543, which I'll call the Attacker." Click, and another satellite image appeared on the screen.

"Now, the Attacker turned out to be a very nosy satellite. It kept changing its orbit to line up with other satellites. First it flew alongside a Russian bird called Cosmos 2535, and then it wandered over to check out another one called Cosmos 2536. The Twins, I call those two. And then, after a month of these maneuvers, the Attacker fired a projectile near 2535. It was an anti-satellite test, unmistakably. It showed that the Attacker, nested inside the Inspector, could have killed our KH-11 if it had tried." Click, and an image of a space-fired projectile.

"The Attacker eventually moved away. But the Russians kept playing games. The Twins, 2535 and 2536, flew so near each other they may have docked. We thought we saw a joined image from an earth telescope, but we're not sure. Then the Twins split, and a few days later they were fifteen miles apart. But then they moved back to less than a mile away." Click, and the screen displayed the orbital paths of the neighboring Russian satellites.

"Many members of this audience have military experience," Edith continued. "So, when you look at these images of satellites moving in and out, adjusting location, I want you to think of an artillery battery bracketing mortar fire.

"To conclude: What does the matryoshka case tell us? The Russians can hide an attack satellite inside an inspection satellite. They can move easily among potential targets, gathering intelligence. They can get close enough to inject malicious code into a target satellite or fire a disabling projectile.

"I've been using the matryoshka metaphor, which makes us think of cute Russian dolls. But really, ladies and gentlemen, this is 'Spetznaz in Space.' These are killers."

Edith asked if there were any questions. The screen was silent for a moment, and then there was a flurry of raised hands, and Edith called on them in turn, starting with the most senior officials. The discussion lasted nearly a half hour, which in secure government briefings was a very long discussion.

The day after the Russia briefing, Anna Friedman summoned Edith and gave her a $20,000 merit pay increase and a two-spot promotion to senior manager.

* * *

Edith's winter darkened when her father Pete got Covid. His blood oxygen level dropped below ninety, and his internist was about to put him in the hospital, maybe on the way to a ventilator, when he recovered. Edith flew back to be with him as soon as he tested negative. He was happy to see her but visibly depressed. Like everyone in America, he was sick of the virus.

It was a snowy, slushy winter in western Massachusetts. A neighborhood boy had been shoveling their walks, but then he got Covid, too, and the snow piled up. Edith cleared it when she arrived, and she built a fire each night for her parents and took them for walks along the Connecticut River.

"Is this it?" her father asked Edith when they settled down one night over a cocktail. "Am I just going to sit at home and watch television, and wear a mask when I go to the grocery store, and as for going to a movie theater, forget about it? Is this what I have to look forward to? Because, frankly, I'd rather go out swinging."

Edith tried to encourage him. He had always liked to write. He was a newspaperman. He should try writing about what interested him from when he was a young man. Bob Dylan. The Beatles. Getting stoned. Vietnam, even. He tried it for a while. He sent Edith several of his essays, and she told him she would put them together in a book.

But he lost interest and settled back into a funk. He was getting all his shots and boosters. But every few months it seemed there was a new variant. Edith had a dreadful thought that, yeah, maybe this was it. She called him on FaceTime from California and tried to make him laugh. And usually, he did.

* * *

Apollo assigned Edith another Chinese space puzzle that spring. Beijing had launched a new GEO satellite in its "experimental" series, Shijian 21. A Xinhua news release said the satellite's mission was "On-Orbit Service, Assembly and Maintenance," and that it would be used "to test and verify space debris mitigation technologies." In other words, clean up debris in space.

That sounded like a good idea, but Edith didn't believe it for a minute.

After its launch from Xichang, SH-21 moved into GEO orbit, and then the anomalies began. First, trackers noted that it released a mini-satellite, known as an "apogee kick motor," or AKM. That was like a power pack that could attach itself to other satellites and move them to new orbits. For weeks, SH-21 kept moving around its subsatellite, as if it were performing tests.

The cat-and-mouse game with its subsatellite was just a warm-up. A few weeks later, SH-21 began moving toward a Compass G2 satellite that was part of China's BeiDou array. It had been launched back in 2009 but had appeared to be stillborn electronically.

SH-21 flew some reconnaissance passes around Compass G2 and then delicately docked with the old satellite and began moving it deeper into space, two thousand miles beyond the GEO belt, into what was known as the Graveyard Zone, where it parked the seemingly dead positioning satellite.

* * *

"What's Really in the Graveyard Zone?" That was the title of the analytical report that Edith prepared on the Shijian 21 case. China had demonstrated the ability to transport satellites into a distant region of space where all the orbiters were assumed to be depleted and useless. SH-21 was a space tug taking them to a final anchorage.

Edith concluded that report with a haunting question: What if Compass G2 and the Chinese occupants of the graveyard were only sleeping—and could be powered back to life to mount sudden surprise attacks from deep space? What if they were the space version of zombies—the living dead?

Space hawks back in Washington loved Edith's latest report. The White House proposed a "deep dive" on America's vulnerability in space. It would be an all-day meeting in the Situation Room, attended by members of the National Security Council and their deputies. The morning session was billed as "Chinese Threats in Space," and the afternoon one was "Responses to Chinese Threats in Space."

Apollo sent Edith as one of its representatives. She flew back to D.C. for the briefings with a sense of accomplishment and anxiety. She was returning not as a mid-level career CIA officer, but as a leading analyst from one of the most respected think tanks studying classified activities in space.

38

Washington and Holyoke, Massachusetts, Spring 2022

Edith Ryan approached the White House complex from the southwestern gate, facing the Washington Monument. Even with her clearances, she had to pass through five checkpoints before she entered the residence under the awning that shaded West Executive Avenue. Senior officials were gathering in the Situation Room. Inevitably, one of them was Robert Gallant. For the senior officials, there were folded name cards around the table. Affixed to a chair against the back wall was Edith's name.

Washington was budding in early spring. The city felt quieter than it had when Edith left it six years before, as if air had escaped from a balloon that had been about to pop. The pulse was slower; the histrionic narcissist who had haunted the White House with his misspelled Twitter postings and threats in CAPITAL LETTERS was gone. The new administration was about "normal order." But intrigue continued under this placid surface, especially on contentious topics where information was precious, and bureaucracies were battling for control.

The Situation Room was the place where little problems became big ones, and that was happening now with space policy. China was demonstrating new space warfare capabilities every month. The military had wildly expensive new ways to spend money, but they were so secret that they couldn't easily be discussed in detail.

The hawks made their case: America depended on its network of assets in space for every aspect of its national well-being—its military power, its intelligence activities, its financial system, its transportation infrastructure; in sum, its very economic existence. America's future survival depended on electronic wires suspended from the sky, and China had demonstrated that it could cut those wires.

Edith remained silent for most of the morning session. She had helped prepare some of the threat analyses that were being discussed, and the facts spoke for themselves. Space Force briefers made elliptical references to "counterforce" programs—meaning America's own arsenal of inspection and attack satellites. But they were in compartments so restricted that many of the attendees, though senior officials and analysts, hadn't been read into the programs.

Edith had a thought as the morning session was ending. If the past was any guide, the U.S. military would respond aggressively, if belatedly, to the threats that they could see. That was the whole history of America's role in modern warfare, from Pearl Harbor to the "*Sputnik* moment" with the Soviet Union, to the explosion of ISIS in the Syrian desert. America might slumber, but when it woke up to the danger, it mobilized resources for an obliterating counterstrike.

But what about the dangers that America didn't see? If they never surfaced, there was no "wake-up call." Edith began making notes to herself about possible hidden surprises, as she sat silently in her chair against the back wall. She started her list with commercial space. Private satellites were ringing the globe these days. They were doing all the things that governments used to do—collecting optical images, gathering signals, forecasting not just the weather but crop yields and migrations of fish at sea. That was the visible part.

But what if these satellites also carried government capabilities, perhaps unwittingly? Satellite components were modular now. There was a whole division at Apollo that did nothing but create such modular hardware for satellites. Edith had never been allowed into that lab, but she could guess what they were making. Little boxes that would drop plug-and-play intelligence capabilities into commercial orbiters that would be unknown and unseen except to a handful of people who had signed off on the covert operation.

At the end of the morning session, Jason Wolf, the national security adviser, opened the meeting for questions. He was young for the job, so people often made the mistake of assuming he wasn't tough.

Edith wanted to join the discussion. She felt she knew more about space operations than many of the others in the room. She wasn't cleared for the afternoon session of this "deep dive," which would focus on the hyper-classified subject of "Responses" to Chinese space threats. So she decided to ask her question while she still had a place at the table.

She raised her hand, but after several men ignored her and spoke without being recognized, she just blurted out: "Excuse me." All the heads turned toward her.

"I've been studying these threats for years now," she began, "and I'm glad that you're reviewing them at the highest level. But I want to ask this group a contrarian question. If the Chinese are doing all the things that we've been discussing—things that we can see—what else are they doing that we *don't* see?"

"What do you mean, Miss, uh . . ." Wolf consulted his seating chart. "Miss Ryan."

"I mean, what are they concealing, perhaps under commercial cover? Maybe the threats are planted in Russian satellites, or French ones, or Indian, Israeli, Japanese, Saudi, Brazilian, or Iranian spacecraft. More than one hundred countries have satellites in space."

"Point noted. Let me just say: we have considered this problem," said the NRO representative at the far end of the table, Robert Gallant. He was the senior scientist at the meeting. He spoke in a clipped voice.

"I'm sure you have," said Edith modestly. "But I want to make sure that we assess deep-cover capabilities in space, the way we would if we were counterintelligence analysts. There are so many places to hide."

"Where is this going?" asked Gallant.

Edith continued as if she hadn't heard him. "Let's think about the numbers. The United States has, what, thirty-five hundred active satellites in orbit, but fewer than two hundred fifty of them are military. Obviously, our commercial satellite array gives the United States enormous opportunities for nonofficial cover. NOCs in space, you might say."

"What do you know about NOCs?" asked Gallant sharply, his face reddening.

"I used to be one!" she answered. "I know what such undeclared assets— 'illegals,' as the Russians call them—could do in space."

Gallant had risen and moved toward the national security adviser at the head of the table and was whispering in his ear.

Wolf, when he had heard Gallant's urgent advice, raised his hand, palm open, in a gesture that said: Stop.

"Sorry, I'm going to have to close the conversation here. I have been advised that we have a classification problem. We will return to this subject this afternoon with a smaller group."

This was Edith's last chance. She wouldn't be at the afternoon session. People were already rising from their chairs.

"One more thing, before we end the session. What about our vulnerabilities on the ground? We spent a whole morning talking about threats in space. But what about the ground stations? Aren't they open to cyberattack? Or missile attack? Or plain old supply chain attack? That would be the easiest."

Gallant, who was among those standing, responded in a way that was meant to close the discussion once and for all.

"Madam, you are one sentence from being arrested for a security violation. We spend enormous time and energy protecting our ground stations. As for supply chains, we have had a 'trusted foundry' system in place since 2007, the year the Chinese launched their first anti-satellite attack."

"What about before that?" shouted out Edith. But she had lost them. Most of the group was already out the door.

As she was leaving the meeting, climbing up the stairs past the White House Mess, she passed Robert Gallant. He was shaking his head. He leaned toward her.

"You really don't know what you are talking about, Miss Ryan," he said.

Before Edith could think of an answer, he was gone.

* * *

Edith had planned to fly back to California the next morning, after an afternoon run in Rock Creek Park. She wanted to escape all the people in the government, and at Apollo, too, who would be angry at her for being so outspoken. But her plans changed—her life changed—when her mobile phone rang as she was walking up Pennsylvania Avenue toward lunch.

It was her mother. Her father had contracted Covid again. His blood oxygen had fallen below eighty, the lowest it had ever been. He was weak and feverish and having trouble breathing. She had called an ambulance, and he was on the way to Holyoke Medical Center on Beech Street. Edith had to come right away.

She flew that afternoon to Hartford and rented a car. They wouldn't let her see her father. He was on a ventilator and locked away in the intensive care unit. She talked to the attending pulmonologist who had ordered the ventilator.

"Your father is very sick," he said. "We're trying to stabilize him."

The next day, he seemed to be recovering. An orderly wheeled his gurney to the window of the ICU, and Edith was able to see him. She waved, as tears streamed down her cheeks. He wasn't able to smile or wave back because of the ventilator. But she saw a light in his eyes of contentment, maybe from the drugs they were feeding him, but Edith thought it was something else. A kind of peace. He was ready to go.

*   *   *

Edith asked if she could say something at her father's funeral at Blessed Sacrament. The Catholic Church frowned on eulogies. Too hard on the family, the priest said. Edith asked if she could read a psalm that her father had loved, and the priest agreed.

Her father hadn't been all that religious, but he had gone to mass sometimes with Edith's mother, and he liked the idea of God presiding over an ordered world, even if he had lost faith in the miraculous parts about virgin birth and resurrection. He was one of those people who had seen so much pain and suffering as a young man in Vietnam that it was hard for him to believe that a benign spirit animated the world.

Edith tried to talk with him about Vietnam when she was a teenager. Usually he made jokes about it. How terrible the food was. How many cans of soda pop he drank in a day. How the shrapnel from his wounds set off all the alarm bells at Bradley Airport in Windsor Locks. He made it sound funny.

But he showed Edith one day the psalm he had kept with him through his year in hell. It had been given to him by his mother, who seemed convinced it had magical powers.

Edith read it at the funeral. The passage began like so many psalms: "The Lord is my rock, my fortress and my deliverer." But it was toward the end that she could hear her father's voice. "To the pure you show yourself pure, but to the devious you show yourself shrewd. You save the humble but bring low those whose eyes are haughty. You, Lord, keep my lamp burning; my God turns my darkness into light. With your help I can advance against a troop; with my God I can scale a wall."

As the priest delivered his homily, about a man he hadn't really known or understood, Edith bowed her head in prayer and asked herself what wall she might climb.

V

DMITRY VOLKOV
MOSCOW, 2020–2022

Life is bearable in Moscow but travel 100 kilometers in any direction and everything's a mess. Our whole country is living in this mess, without the slightest prospects, earning 20,000 rubles [$265] a month. And they're all silent; they try to shut people up with these show trials. Lock up this one to scare millions more. One person takes to the streets, and they lock up another five people to scare 15 million more. . . .

The only thing growing in [Russia] is the number of billionaires. Everything else is declining. I'm locked up in a prison cell and all I hear about is reports that butter is getting more expensive, pasta is getting more expensive, the price of eggs is rising. . . . You've deprived these people of a future, you're trying to cow them. . . .

This is what happens when lawlessness and tyranny become the essence of a political system, and it's horrifying.

—ALEKSEI NAVALNY, excerpt from a speech in a Moscow courtroom
printed in *The New York Times*, February 4, 2021

39

Moscow, June 2020

A few days before Dimitry Volkov graduated from the law faculty at Moscow State University, Russia celebrated the seventy-fifth anniversary of its victory over Nazi Germany. There weren't many Russians still alive who could remember the Great Patriotic War, but young people tried to be respectful, as one would be in the presence of an aging grandparent. There was a military parade with thousands of Russian troops goose-stepping through Red Square, in unlikely cadence with the nation they had crushed in 1945. Frankly speaking, as Russians liked to say, it was a moment of nostalgia for a lost time when Russia was a great nation, and a good one, too.

The sheer scale of that conflict was hard to imagine in a softer century. More Russians perished during the siege of Leningrad than all the American and British casualties during the whole of the war. More than twenty million Russian soldiers and civilians died, all told, during World War II, one in every ten people. These were incomprehensible numbers, and young Russians didn't comprehend them. They knew that the motherland had been something worth fighting for, but they weren't sure what it was.

Dmitry had a hangover that morning, and the noisy flyover by Russian jets made his head hurt. He had been up with his friends celebrating his impending graduation with ritual pranks—burning class notebooks in a bonfire, tearing his exam papers into confetti, dragging drunken classmates down the stairs in a laundry basin.

Dmitry didn't normally drink very much. Drunkenness was like smoking cigarettes, an addiction wedded to an unhealthy past that had been killing Russians for centuries. But as graduation approached, he gave way. His classmates would have poured vodka down his throat if he had refused, and he might have hit one of them, and because he was strong, he might well have hurt them, which was no way to start a law career.

The law faculty was in a new building, just south of the U-shaped bend in the Moscow River. It was a modern block of glass and stone, a showpiece that the university boasted about, maybe because it looked like a new campus building in Palo Alto or Berlin. Dmitry hated everything about it, but most of all its sham Westernness. He preferred the baroque wedding-cake tower of the university's main building, all thirty-seven floors of it a Stalinist palace. At least it was honest about its roots.

The New Academic Building was light and airy, decorated in blues and pastels; it had computer labs and cafeterias, fitness centers and dance studios. Dmitry tried to imagine how much money had been skimmed by the *vory*, the thieves, during its construction. The pile of looted rubles would have risen up the building's fancy lobby all the way to its skylight dome.

Dmitry's ambitious friends were applying to fancy law firms in the United States or Britain and taking special courses in the nuances of the U.S. Foreign Corrupt Practices Act and the latest rulings of the World Trade Organization. "This is a puppet show," Dmitry told one of his classmates who was on his way to an investment arbitration moot court competition in Frankfurt. His friends were apprenticing to become compradors, representatives of a lawless state that wanted the benefit of global rules without having to observe them.

Dmitry had liked these would-be internationalists well enough during law school; he played basketball and volleyball with the global men; he dated some of the global women. But he was a separate breed. His father had taught him to loath hypocrisy above all things, and his father's authority was unquestioned. Once when Ivan caught his son reading a copy of a Western magazine that had a photo spread of the house in the south of France where the boy's mother and her gangster husband lived, he burned it.

Ashes. That was his mother's residue. Veronika never wrote to him, visited him, or showed any sign that she had ever carried him in her womb. They were embarrassed by each other, mother and son, and pretended that the other didn't exist.

Dmitry was tall, like his father, but more supple, like his mother. He had her sandy blond hair and ash-blue eyes. He had skipped a grade in grammar school and excelled in his classes all the way to university. His teachers at the prestigious State School 57, near the Kremlin, were proud of him, but he was shaped more by the homeschooling he had received every day from his father than by any elite classroom.

As Dmitry approached graduation, he sought the job he believed his father would have wanted if he had been a lawyer rather than a scientist. He applied for a position as a criminal prosecutor with the Investigative Committee of Russia, the only organization that had a shred of credibility in pursuing corruption. Its main job was investigating the police force, but its mandate had spread to cover bribe-takers in every government department and region in Russia. Its emblem showed a knight riding on a white horse.

Dmitry's friends thought that he was nuts. Russia was a gangster state, everyone knew that. If these prosecutors on their white horses got too close to anyone powerful, they would be skewered. Dmitry had good grades; the professors liked him; he could have protection if he wanted it. He could easily find a *krysha*, a cozy roof to hide under. But Dmitry loved his Investigative Committee all the better for its lost-cause mandate to reform Russia. He was an idealist of the sort that Russians sometimes called a "holy fool."

* * *

Dmitry went to see his father the night before graduation. "*Papochka*," he shouted through the apartment door as he turned the key. Daddy. Sweet Daddy. He was the only parent Dmitry had known his whole life.

Ivan Volkov came to the door. He was dressed in sweatpants and a T-shirt with the logo of Metallurg, the hockey team in his hometown of Magnitogorsk, toweling himself off after a run in the park near his flat block. He was still a handsome man just shy of fifty, chiseled features, short hair turning to gray.

Ivan kept to himself, as his colleagues said of him at the Lebedev Physical Institute. He didn't take bribes; he didn't accept "consulting" contracts with wealthy men who wanted a piece of the space business. He was one of Russia's leading experts on the tracking and telemetry systems in the country's still-functioning GLONASS navigational system. He was an active member of a chess club and a book club; he wrote poetry for magazines that nobody read. He still played hockey in the winter for a pickup team of *chudaks*, aging misfits like him.

"*Papochka*, I am a prosecutor!" Dmitry announced. "I got the job. I start in July." The hiring letter from the Investigative Committee had arrived a few hours before.

"Wait until September," answered Ivan. "There will be plenty of crooks left."

"They want me now. They're starting a new strike team. That's the gossip. Maybe they'll want me on it. I know it sounds crazy, but it's what I want to do."

Ivan smiled. This was a moment for which he had been waiting for two decades. "Be careful," he said. "Don't tell anyone else."

"Of course," said Dmitry. "Keep this to yourself, Papochka, but I bet they're looking at one of the ministries. They had to give me a background check before they accepted me."

"*Vot chort!*" said Ivan, shaking his head but inwardly proud. Damn! My son is walking into fire.

* * *

The law school graduation ceremony was held under a perfect blue sky near the statute of Mikhail Lomonosov, who had founded the university in 1755 during what people hopefully described as the Russian renaissance. It was Ivan Volkov's favorite spot on the campus, the place he had come to be alone when his father died in Magnitogorsk, his wife left him, his son was born. He would sit on the stone steps nearby and read Russian novels while Dmitry slept in his stroller.

The graduates marched out in their robes and red shawls. Ivan sat down with the other parents, but he was a head taller than most of them, so he moved to the back row so that shorter mothers and fathers could see. A speaker from the Association of Jurists talked about "the law of the future," with a naïveté that Ivan found chilling.

Prizes were awarded. Dmitry won a medal from the Faculty of Criminal Procedure, Justice, and Public Prosecution for an essay examining a recent case in which the son of a former prosecutor general had embezzled millions and invested it in a luxury hotel in Greece. Dmitry had used social media posts on the internet to confirm that the prosecutor's son and his sleek second wife were the owners. "A bold inquiry," said the professor in describing the winning essay. He might have called it dangerous.

When the ceremony ended, the graduates threw their mortarboards up into that robin's-egg sky. As the other graduates hugged each other, popping corks of the champagne bottles they had hidden under their robes, Dmitry found his father in the back row. He invited Ivan to join him at the law faculty's post-graduation party. It was an event where, they both knew, everyone would get very, very drunk.

Ivan declined. He shook his son's hand. Then, with more emotion than he usually showed in public, he embraced Dmitry for nearly thirty seconds, whispering in his ear his pride and satisfaction. What he had experienced that afternoon, watching his son take wing, was better than anything he had ever dreamed or imagined.

40

Moscow, September 2020

The headquarters of the Investigative Committee of Russia was a modern office tower, faced with ice-blue glass, in a district northeast of Moscow center. If this area was known for anything, it was crime and punishment. Lefortovo Prison, one of the harshest in Russia, stood just west at a bend in the Yauza River, with its notorious courthouse nearby. Dmitry showed up for work the first day in a black suit and tie, but the administrator's office issued him a blue uniform with a gold trim on the lapels and told him that he was an officer of the law now.

The first week, Dmitry wondered if he had made a mistake joining the committee. He was assigned to a desk in a windowless room in the basement with five other newly minted prosecutors, all dressed in their blue-and-gold uniforms. They were given paper files from oblasts around the country to sort by hand. The files described low-level kickbacks: a corrupt contractor in Krasnodar; a state property manager outside Saint Petersburg who had received a bribe on the sale of a tract of land; a judge in Khakassia who was paid to deliver a lighter sentence for a drug dealer.

All illegal, certainly. Worth prosecuting, probably. But this was the sort of petty corruption that had been habitual in Russia since the first czars. Dmitry had imagined that his work would take him to the heart of what was hobbling the new Russia. These cases were at the distant periphery.

Arkady Byk, one of his supervisors, invited him for a drink after work near the end of that first week. He was not much older than Dmitry, with intense blue eyes and closely trimmed hair that framed a steely face. He might have been a musician or a writer, with his mix of *kultura* and disdain. When the two exited the headquarters building, Arkady removed his prosecutor's jacket; Dmitry wanted to do the same, but he was afraid that might be against somebody's rules.

Arkady led them to a pub near Lefortovo Park. He took a seat at a lone table in the far corner. A punk rock band was rehearsing in a back room; otherwise, the place was nearly empty. It was hot inside. Dmitry removed his blue wool jacket and draped it neatly over the chair. Arkady leaned toward him and opened his hands, as if to say: This is it.

"We've been watching you, of course," said Arkady. "People want to know if they can trust you."

Dmitry thought a long moment. "You should try me," he said eventually. "That's the only way you'll know."

"Good answer. We've been checking on you, for sure. We saw what you wrote about the prosecutor general's son and his Greek hotel. We even helped you with that, although you couldn't see it. When you went to *Novaya Gazeta* to do some research on the Swiss bank that passed the money to Greece, that was us. We had the information. We want to trust you. What can I say? It's high stakes, my brother."

"Can you tell me about the case you're working on now? The one that has a strike force." Dmitry didn't want to rush it, but he wanted to find out whether he had a chance to get on the team.

Arkady put his finger to his lips. "A little. If any of it leaks, we'll kill you."

Dmitry's face went white. Arkady gave him a soft punch on the shoulder. "Don't be a mouse. We don't kill people, first thing, and I would never have invited you here if I didn't trust you."

Arkady gave Dmitry a fist bump.

"So, yeah, I will explain a few things," Arkady continued. "We're looking at someone in the Defense Ministry. Very high up. Everything goes through him. He signs all the checks. He's a Maytag, you know, a washing machine. We are gathering records. We need someone who knows how to use a computer and can read English."

"Check, and check."

"Make sure you're ready. These are big boys. They aren't like the old *vory*. No tattoos, no gold chains. These are whales, you understand?"

Dmitry nodded. This was what he had wanted. To prosecute the big men who ran the country and stole the people's money.

"I'm not a white hand," he told Arkady. "Most lawyers are *beloruchka*, people who don't want to get dirty. Not me. I want to do the work."

*   *   *

They drank for a while longer, and the place began to fill up with young people who most definitely didn't look like cops. Arkady downed a last vodka and led his new colleague to the back room, where the punk band was still rehearsing. A pretty girl in a tiny miniskirt and stripped leggings was jumping up and down as she sang the chorus of a Russian song that sounded like "Fuck the Police."

She handed Dmitry a joint when she was done with her set. Dmitry was going to refuse—this wasn't really the time or place to get wasted—but then he took a puff, and so did Arkady.

The band unplugged, and people sat on the floor with more dope and some vodka. Some of them were undercover cops, it turned out. Arkady whispered that one of them, a bearded man dressed in a black leather motorcycle jacket, was the leader of the task force.

"You can call me Yuri," said the man in the leather jacket when Arkady introduced them. He sat next to Dmitry on the floor, asked him questions for a while, and eventually filled another joint with tobacco and hashish and torched it with his lighter.

"We're like them. You see? A *bratva*, a brotherhood," Yuri said as handed over the joint. As Dmitry looked back a few months later, he knew this was the moment, sitting on the floor, when he joined the task force that was investigating a senior official in the Ministry of Defense.

* * *

When Dmitry arrived at the office the next Monday, he didn't return to the windowless crypt in the basement. Arkady gave him a room number on an upper floor. The task force's technical chief issued Dmitry a laptop with the latest VPN and encryption software, a burner phone with a Proton Mail account, and an MP-443 Grach pistol.

Next, Arkady gave him the address of an office building a few miles north, on Rusakovskaya Street on the way to Sokolniki Park.

"The cave," he said. "You start tomorrow morning. Don't wear your uniform."

The address was an anonymous office block astride a divided highway in a new suburban area that already looked shabby. Dmitry wore jeans and a hoodie. An old babushka was sitting at a desk on the ground floor smoking a cigarette when he arrived. She didn't ask Dmitry where he was going, and he didn't volunteer.

The task force occupied the eighth floor. Dmitry arrived at eight-thirty, before most people started work in Moscow, but the office was already filled. Most people were young and fit. Many of them were dressed in T-shirts, men and women both. The place looked more like the offices of *Novaya Gazeta* than a law enforcement organization. People wandered between desks, stopping to talk, arguing with each other.

A secretary showed Dmitry to a desk where he could plug in his laptop. He was just settling in when Yuri came by and yanked him by the arm. "Staff meeting," he said. He led the new arrival toward his office in the back of the room. On the wall were photos of some of the notorious senior leaders of Russia, arrayed without comment. The room was soon crowded with more than a dozen people, Dmitry's new colleagues.

* * *

"Well, I think it would be a good time to introduce our new target," began Yuri, in the usual roundabout Russian way. "The gentleman we are examining is, I can say, a scion of the new Russia. He is close to the president. His best friend is the Kremlin chief of staff. He has a second wife, of course. She was a model and then a television host. But marrying such a woman is expensive. Our servant of the people needs money to afford his lifestyle. What does he do? That is our mission, to find out."

He looked around the room. "Guys, does this sound like fun?" Heads nodded. He smiled at once whimsical and red-hot, and continued.

"So, Yuri, you ask me, who is this servant of the nation? Okay. Our man is named Danil Kuzmin. He runs the Federal Service for Defense Contracts. He is responsible for all military construction. Yes. All construction. Every military airport, training camp, submarine base, military hospital, special railway line. All of it requires his signature.

"There is nothing that this man does not touch. This would not be possible in a normal state. But this is Russia.

"Behold the devil," said Yuri. "As you will see, he has had some surgery."

A screen behind him displayed a photograph of Kuzmin. He had a broad face, graying hair streaked by black highlights, the skin smoothed and buffed by cosmetic injections in the way that had become popular among wealthy Russian men. He was wearing a powder-blue uniform with the insignia of his contracting service next to the Ministry of Defense pin.

"And the devil's wife, Madam Nadia Kuzmina." The screen showed a beautiful woman, with a figure too perfect for God's hand alone, dressed in a glittering ball gown. "Kuzmina just turned fifty. She pays a lot of money to look, well, we can say, younger. Where does she get it? I wonder." He smiled again, the gleaming teeth of a panther.

"Poor Kuzmin," said Yuri. "Think of how hard he must work at stealing the people's money to keep this princess happy."

* * *

Yuri pulled Dmitry aside when the meeting ended. He gave him a manila folder and a USB drive. "Flash drive. Don't ever put one of these in your computer. Except this one, which you put in your computer."

"What's on the drive?" asked Dmitry.

"Our dossier on Madame Kuzmina. It's small now. I want you to make it big. Get inside this woman's world so we see all the connections. Can you do that?"

"Yes," said Dmitry. Like many of the decisions that affect us most in life, he barely thought about it.

41

Moscow, October 2020

Dmitry immersed himself in the Kuzmin dossier. He was good at puzzles, like his father, but this one was maddeningly unformed, like a crossword with only fragments of questions. He had a few hard facts that his colleagues had obtained from public records: the Kuzmins' airplane flights every summer to Nice on the French Côte d'Azur; the address of their town house in Moscow; the bank accounts they admitted to having; the names of the people who worked for them legally, whose salaries they paid.

Dmitry's first step deeper was to harvest the Kuzmins' social media data. Neither of them had accounts in their own names on VKontakte, or VK, the Russian-language equivalent of Facebook. But by using facial recognition software, Dmitry was able to find a VK account that Kuzmina maintained under a false name. That same false name had an Instagram account, too.

Vanity leads people to do foolish things. Nadia Kuzmina could not resist the urge to post glamorous photographs of herself, often with her husband in tow. She shared images on social media, "anonymously," of herself at wedding parties at lavish hotels, fashion shows, government ceremonies, celebrity events. There wasn't a red carpet in Moscow, it seemed, that Nadia hadn't graced. With each new photo, her face looked tighter and her figure more voluptuous.

Dmitry began examining the records of the family's employees. He focused in particular on a young woman who had been Nadia Kuzmina's personal assistant and social secretary for a year, until payments to her suddenly ceased a few months before. She had been fired, evidently. Her name was Vera; she was twenty-six.

Dmitry did some digging and found her address in Tsaritsyno, a new suburb south of the city. He took the information to Arkady, who called a quick meeting in Yuri's office.

"I want to knock on this lady's door tonight to see what she knows," said Dmitry. He was learning to talk like a cop. He explained the work the secretary had been doing and the possibility that she might have access to records. That would make her an uncommonly valuable source.

Yuri put his arm around the young prosecutor.

"*Bratan*," he said. Brother. "Go get her." As Dmitry was leaving, he added: "Take your gun."

*   *   *

Vera opened the door a few inches after twenty seconds of pounding by Dmitry. He was wearing his pistol in a shoulder holster. It felt like a tumor bulging from his armpit. He showed her his badge from the Investigative Committee and asked if he could come in. She was still holding the door warily. But when he told Vera that he only wanted to ask some questions about her former boss, Nadia Kuzmina, her face brightened.

"Kuzmina? You mean, I'm not in trouble?"

Dmitry nodded, and she opened the door and beckoned for him to sit on the couch.

She was young but aging fast. Her blond hair was darkening; her face was puffy, from drinking or crying.

"That bitch," she said, barely audibly. "She fired me. You know that, of course."

"We know a lot," said Dmitry, staring her in the eye as he played his bluff. "We think you can tell us more."

She shook her head scornfully. "You have no idea. I could destroy that woman."

"How do you mean?" Dmitry said. Slowly, slowly, he told himself.

He saw a bottle of cheap Georgian wine open on the counter. He asked for a glass, hoping that she would take another for herself. She reached for the bottle and filled two goblets up to the rim.

"I am not a fool, as Madam thinks. I knew that she might come after me, and that I needed to protect myself." She took a sip of wine, and then another.

"Quite sensible," said Dmitry.

"I am a loyal Russian, you know. My grandfather fought in the Great Patriotic War. My uncle was in Afghanistan. These people offend me. Who do they think they are? They are supposed to protect our men in the army. Where does the money really go? Furs. Icons. Rolls-Royce cars. Trips to the Riviera. They even shit differently. They buy Japanese toilet seats, so their bottoms don't get cold. Horseradish! They think they are the new nobility. All with stolen money."

"Stolen?" asked Dmitry gently.

"Yes. And I can prove it!" She pounded the table.

Dmitry steadied the wineglass and poured another measure from the bottle. "How can you prove it?"

"Because I have her emails!" Vera roared. "That's why. What do you think of that, Mr. Prosecutor?"

"Please?" queried Dmitry, wanting to make sure he had heard her correctly. "What do you have?"

"Her emails! Her communications. Are you deaf?" She pounded the table again. "They show everything. Her hotel in Cannes. The meals she eats with that pig of a husband. The clothes she buys. The paintings. The furniture. The rugs. My god! The payments to the doctor who makes her boobs big and her tummy small. The wines in the cellar. The jewelry. All the invoices, she kept them electronically, you know. And Kuzmin! She managed his secrets, too."

"What do you mean? Do you have Kuzmin's emails, too?"

She had nearly finished her glass. He took the bottle and poured the rest into her cup.

"Oh yes!" Vera couldn't stop herself now. "Madam was her husband's accountant. She sent the messages to their private bank in Geneva. Numbered accounts. No names. Secret messages on Proton Mail. But do you know what?

She kept copies on her computer. She said I was a stupid secretary. Ha! See who is stupid!"

"These emails, I wonder, do they show where the money comes from?"

"Yes, certainly. They had a lawyer in Switzerland who created fake companies for Kuzmin, where the contractors would pay the bribes. Want to build an airport? Okay. Ten percent goes to Kuzmin's Swiss bank. Want the winning bid on a new camp for recruits? No problem, charge what you like, but ten percent, please. The money goes into the numbered account. Then some of it goes out. Of course! He has to pay other *vory*, his fellow thieves at the ministry—and probably pays you-know-who, too. But my, my, he keeps a lot for himself."

Dmitry reached out and touched her hand. His manner was comforting, reassuring.

"You are brave, Vera. And a true patriot. You protect the Russian people. The decent people. The nation is in your debt." He patted her hand.

A tear rolled down her cheek. "Thank you," she said. "I do my duty."

"One more thing. Do you have those emails that you protected so courageously?"

She sat up straight on the couch. "Of course I do. I kept them. It was my responsibility."

"Where are they, I wonder? Maybe you could show me."

Her eyes widened. "Will you take care of me? These people are not pussycats, you know."

"I give you my word," Dmitry said solemnly. He knew that wasn't worth much. He had only been a prosecutor for a few months, but she seemed comforted and nodded her assent.

Vera retreated unsteadily to her bedroom and returned with a cardboard box. Inside were hundreds of sheets of paper, on which she had printed the most incriminating email messages. She reached into the box and extracted a flash drive. She held it between her thumb and forefinger, just in front of her face, as if it were a tiny scepter.

"All here," she said.

Dmitriy nodded. "Brava," he said, clapping as if it were a performance at the opera or ballet. She was holding the key to the kingdom. He took his burner phone from his pocket.

"May I call one of my colleagues? I want to make sure that we can protect you and this great gift to the motherland."

"Yes," she said dreamily. "Why not?"

She was still holding the flash drive before her face as he dialed. She began singing softly to herself.

"Russia is our sacred state," she sang in a whisper. "Russia is our beloved country. A mighty will, great glory—Your dignity for all time!"

Dmitry listened as he waited for Arkady to answer. He knew that song. It was the Russian national anthem.

A team from the strike force arrived forty minutes later and began making copies of the documents, the flash drive, and everything on Vera's computer. She had fallen asleep on her bed before they finished.

42

Moscow, April 2021

Dmitry Volkov was a hero in the squad room on Rusakovskaya Street after the Vera breakthrough. Yuri boasted about the newly minted prosecutor's success in getting the documents the task force needed to begin building a case it could take to court. "*Cherchez la femme!*" he would say in badly accented French when he wandered by Dmitry's desk.

The members of the team were building out the case now as fast as they could. They examined contracts issued by Kuzmin's agency, construction sites, bank accounts of executives of the contracting firms that performed the work, Kuzmin's own accounts. They issued warrants, sealed, but subject to review by higher-ups. Dmitry wondered if his boss was making too much noise about their investigation. As the months passed, the case gathered momentum; but it also garnered attention.

Just before the holidays, Yuri asked Dmitry to join a five-person team that would brief the Investigative Committee. He wore his blue-and-gold uniform, as did the other task force representatives. The committee chairman presided over the meeting. He had been in the job for ten years, and even Yuri seemed wary of him. He was accompanied by three vice chairmen who were responsible for forensics, analysis, and document processing. They appeared to be solid, self-effacing technocrats.

Another, more ominous figure joined the group: the deputy prosecutor general, representing the big law enforcement bureaucracy from which the Investigative Committee had been launched. He was a bull of a man, with a cannonball head shaved clean and a look on his face somewhere between a sneer and a smirk. He had three stars on his epaulets, a reward for service in some of the trickiest places in Russia. The freewheeling casino of Saint Peterburg; the charnel house of Grozny; and Moscow, where he had held a string of ever-ascending assignments.

Yuri asked Dmitry to summarize the investigation into personal corruption involving Kuzmin and his wife. Some of Dmitry's colleagues might have said that this was the good stuff, the sexy part, but he knew better. This was the aspect of the investigation that would make other members of the elite squirm. It was one thing to punish a sloppy and excessively greedy bribe-taker at the Defense Ministry. It was another to expose his wife's personal spending for interior decoration, at-home catering, and cosmetic surgery. Dmitry spoke carefully, but he could see the uneasiness on the faces of the committee chairman and, even more, the deputy prosecutor general.

As Dmitry was closing, he could see the deputy prosecutor general whisper something into the ear of the chairman. A moment later, the chairman interrupted Dmitry with a question. The investigative records of personal spending that the task force had gathered, how exactly had those been obtained?

Dmitry answered that the material had been provided by a confidential source who was now under the protection of the task force. He hoped that would be enough, and Yuri tried to move on, but the chairman pressed harder. Were these records obtained through legal process? Dmitry looked to Yuri, who answered that the records had all been confirmed through legal warrants. But still, that wasn't enough, and Yuri finally conceded that the records had initially been obtained by the confidential source who was acting as a whistleblower.

"Whistleblower?" snorted the deputy prosecutor general. "What kind of American shit is that? We don't have whistleblowers in Russia. We have citizens."

The committee chair tried to calm the proceedings and get back to a presentation of the evidence. But the point had been made. Later that day, Yuri ordered that the protected location of their prize witness, young Vera, be changed. And he asked all the members of the task force to get new SIM cards for their phones.

*   *   *

A week later, Yuri was replaced as leader of the task force by a career member of the prosecutor general's office who had joined the committee six months before. At a farewell party, with lots to drink, Yuri gave Dmitry, the youngest member of his staff, as a joke gift, a comic book called *Demonslayer*, from the Bubble series that was popular with Russian kids.

"Color within the lines," said Yuri, handing over a box of crayons. But it was too late for that.

*   *   *

Dmitry celebrated Orthodox Christmas with his father in January. Ivan Volkov saw the stress in his son's face when he arrived at the apartment at midday. He proposed that they go ice-skating at the huge outdoor rink in Gorky Park, something they had done often when Dmitry was a boy.

The "rink" was a lattice of glistening paths stitched through the park. The temperature was near zero degrees, but Ivan gave his son layers of his own clothing. They skated until past dark, when the lights in the trees were glowing and every young woman preened like an ice queen.

Ivan was a powerful skater, even in his fifties. He still played occasionally in a senior hockey league. He remained a gentle man in most ways, ascetic and disciplined like his son. But on the ice, he displayed the ferocity he usually kept inside as he worked in the astrophysics lab or in the GLONASS control room.

Father and son came home happily fatigued, faces red from the cold and the exercise. Ivan opened a bottle of vodka, something he did rarely and only on special occasions. They exchanged presents. Ivan had bought a fine new suitcase for his son, an elegant model made in America that must have cost him a thousand dollars.

"For foreign travel," he said.

When his son answered that he didn't travel abroad for work, his father suggested, "For vacations, then." He had other gifts for Dmitry: sweaters, ties, a new sports jacket. Ivan had money now, and very little to spend it on.

Ivan hadn't asked his son much about his new job, but that night he did. Dmitry bristled at first; he wasn't sure what he could safely say; and now that he was making his own decisions after a lifetime of coaching and concern from his father, he wanted independence. But his reserve melted with each toast of chilled vodka in the warmth of Ivan's living room.

"How are things at the Investigative Committee?" Ivan began. "From what I hear, the people there aren't as bad as the ones that are very bad."

"We're the good guys, Papa. We have the right enemies."

"Maybe. But you know the saying. A thousand friends are too few. One enemy is too many."

"Some talk from you! You aren't happy unless you're making enemies, Papochka. You like telling people no."

"Saying no is my secret power, *zaika*." He kissed his son on his forehead. "I never want anything, need anything, ask for anything. If anyone says he wants to do me a favor, I tell him to fuck off, that's all."

"Isn't that lonely?" It was an unfair question. Dmitry knew that his father was lonely. He lived inside his head, which was the only reliable and unpolluted space he could find.

"Sometimes. But I have you. And I have my self-respect. That's enough. They say that you can either have a broken heart or a shriveled heart. Maybe I have a broken heart. But that was a long time ago."

Dmitry gave his father a long hug. "Sweet Papa," he said.

Ivan was embarrassed. He wanted to change the subject. "I hear that you have a big case."

Dmitry bristled. "Where did you hear that?"

"Someone at work. He's on loan from the Defense Ministry. He said the Investigative Committee was working on something big."

Dmitry shook his head and smiled. One of his father's most lovable but also maddening qualities was that he always knew more than he said.

"I can't talk about it, Papochka. I'm sorry."

"I know. Don't tell me anything. But I worry about you. There are snakes under these rocks."

"We'll kill the snakes, then," answered Dmitry.

"This is Russia. Trouble never comes alone."

Ivan's hand trembled slightly as he raised his glass for another toast. He was worried for his son. Dmitry was all the things that Ivan cherished in life. Principled, fearless, incorruptible. He had dreamed of having a son like that. But now it frightened him.

"Be careful," he told Dmitry as he poured him the last drops of the vodka.

The young man raised his glass. "I will. Always. But you know, Papochka, if you're afraid of wolves, you shouldn't go into the woods. I made that decision. I'm in the woods now."

43

Moscow, June 2021

Russia moved troops to the Ukraine border in April. The president of the Russian Federation described it as an exercise, and most analysts assumed that it was a theatrical show of strength, like his hunting a Siberian tiger or swimming bare-chested in a frigid lake. But the White House was concerned and hastily organized a summit meeting in Geneva. American officials said they were hopeful about a new dialogue on strategic stability. But for cynics in Russia, the events in Ukraine looked like a rehearsal for something, though few dared to predict what form it might take.

The Investigative Committee continued to prepare its case against Danil Kuzmin, the director general of the Federal Service for Defense Contracts. The task force had sought permission to bring an indictment in February, and then again in April. Each time the chairman of the commission said he needed more evidence before making public charges against such a senior official. The case was very sensitive. Kuzmin had friends in the Kremlin. As the case was delayed, records of past contracting transactions began to disappear. Requests for documents went unanswered.

And then the catastrophes began. Vera, the star witness for the prosecution, disappeared after the task force made its second request for an indictment.

She had been living under police protection in Nizhny Novgorod, about three hundred miles east of Moscow. She vanished one night while the guards were sleeping. A letter purportedly from her arrived at the committee a week later, saying not to worry, she was safe. She had decided of her own free will against testifying against her former employers, the Kuzmins.

Dmitry thought the letter was a fake. The Defense Ministry had made her write it, or simply forged it. Maybe she was safe, maybe she was dead; he didn't know. The point was that someone in the Kremlin didn't want this story of corruption in the Defense Ministry to be prosecuted. Powerful people were attempting to obstruct an inquiry and intimidate the investigators and witnesses.

The task force held a meeting, away from the office on Rusakovskaya Street, and without informing the stooge who had been installed as leader after Yuri was sacked. They met in a basement room that had once been a gym for a Komsomol basketball team and was now abandoned. Arkady Byk, who was now the informal leader of the group, spoke first. You could see from the narrow set of his eyes, and the way they darted from side to side, that he was frightened.

"Our investigation of the Service for Defense Contracts has encountered difficulty," he began. "Our most useful witness is unavailable. The Defense Ministry has protested directly to the prosecutor general's office about our investigation. We have worked together as a team, so I ask all of you to decide jointly: What do we do?"

"Look for another target, at another ministry," muttered one veteran prosecutor. "We should be realistic," recommended another gloomy voice. Nobody else spoke for a moment, and in the silence, a consensus for abandoning the case seemed to be building in the room. But then a voice spoke up in the back. It was Dmitry.

"I think we should find more evidence," he said. "I made a promise to Vera that I would take care of her. I failed. I don't know what has happened. Maybe she is okay, maybe not, but either way, I feel that I broke my word after she agreed to give us information. If we stop this case now, I will feel like a liar. Worse than that. Like a coward."

Another long silence, broken by Arkady. "Let me ask: What would shame Kuzmin's bosses so much that they wouldn't dare to interfere?"

"The army," answered Dmitry. "We need to show how Kuzmin's actions damaged the troops. That's who he's stealing from."

"Too dangerous," said Arkady. "You could never get close enough." Several others agreed. If the Defense Ministry had rallied to protect its logistics chief, what would the generals do to protect their own reputations and legitimacy?

Dmitry cut them off. "I'll do it. I have a friend from law school who's from Voronezh, near the Ukraine border. Kuzmin was supposed to build a base there. It's in the documents we got. They planned a new garrison for the army. Big project. I'll go see what actually got built. What about that?"

"You're crazy," said Arkady. Then, after a pause: "I'll come, too."

"It's better to go alone," said Dmitry. "I'll go quick. Stay with friends. Find evidence. Come home. Nobody will notice."

The task force agreed that Dmitry would go to Voronezh. If he could find any evidence of misdeeds, the team would present a new draft indictment to the Investigative Committee. Or to anyone else who would listen.

*　*　*

Voronezh was a pretty provincial town on a broad stretch of the Voronezh River. The city center had a few graceful old structures, but the banks of the river were lined with cheap, showy apartment towers. The Ukraine border was 150 miles west.

Dmitry had lied to his colleagues about having friends in the city. When his train arrived in the afternoon, he found a room in a cheap hotel on a rise above the river. He bought a sandwich and a beer in the lobby and retired to his room with his briefcase to prepare for the next day.

He had brought along some documents that had been gathered early in the investigation. They included contracts that Kuzmin had signed two years before to build a new headquarters for the Twentieth Army, which had been transferred in 2015 from Mulino, east of Moscow. The complex was supposed to be built within the compound of a big air base south of the city. Dmitry had architectural drawings, plat markings for where streets and barracks would go. It was a little city on paper.

Voronezh Oblast had a small office of the federal prosecutor general's service, with one lawyer and a few cops. Dmitry had called the afternoon he

arrived and said he would be conducting a confidential official investigation at
the direction of the Investigative Committee. He requested support. The aging
local prosecutor didn't have time to protest. He said he would be waiting for
Dmitry at nine a.m.

The oblast's legal headquarters was along a broad boulevard next to the
city museum. The chief prosecutor unlocked the door and admitted Dmitry at
nine sharp. He looked like a Chekov character: a wizened face, a thick handle-
bar mustache, his old blue uniform flecked at the shoulders with dandruff. It
appeared to please and worry him to have a visitor from the capital. He might
have done something wrong. He had no instructions from his supervisor in
Moscow, whom he had messaged the night before. He was on his own, which
was an uncomfortable position for a provincial bureaucrat.

Dmitry greeted the old man and presented his badge. He was wearing his
own uniform for the first time in weeks. It felt too big. He showed the local prosecutor the orders that Arkady had drafted for him on the committee's statio-
nery, date-stamped with an official seal warranting the investigation. He asked
for a car and a police escort with authority to enter the military compound on
the southwestern bank of the river. The local director promptly agreed. Orders
were orders. He was relieved that Dmitry hadn't been sent to chastise him.

A police car arrived, white with a thick blue stripe across the middle. A
major joined Dmitry in the backseat, while a sergeant drove the car. Dmitry
had his maps and plats open on this lap. He directed the driver to the north
entrance of the base. The guard at the gate telephoned his commander. There
was a brief delay until the police major got on the phone and said this was an
official request from the Voronezh prosecutor general; the visitor from Moscow
had the proper documentation and should be admitted.

The guard waved the car forward. The police car, accompanied by a military escort, drove along the main road toward the airfield. Two concrete run-
ways lay just ahead. Farther east, the planes of the air wing were parked: big
bombers, smaller swept-wing fighters, a dozen helicopters.

Dmitry's map showed that the planned complex for the Twentieth Army
headquarters was farther south. He directed the driver to turn right down a
long road that led to the top of a hill, beyond which the project had been sited.
On the other side, he expected to see rows of barracks, the officers' houses, and

the army's command center. In the architectural drawing, there had been a war memorial in a park, just in front of the Twentieth Army commander's residence.

The police car crested the hill and Dmitry leaned forward to get a better view. He saw only an open field.

Scrub grass stretched from one perimeter of the base to the other, broken by a few trenches where construction had begun but was later abandoned. The grand new headquarters designed for the Twentieth Army was, in fact, an empty lot. The contracts had been issued. The money had been paid out. But nothing had been built.

"We've got him," Dmitry said under his breath.

Dmitry had brought along a camera. The military escort scrambled toward him and warned, no pictures of the aircraft, even for the prosecutor general. Dmitry explained that he only wanted to photograph the empty part of the base. The military officer agreed, and Dmitry began snapping pictures of the scene.

When Dmitry was done with the photos, he asked the police major to sign an affidavit, using a standard form he had brought along, attesting that he had been present and observed that the southern sector of the Voronezh base was not occupied.

The visitor got back in the police car and they returned to the entry gate. The policemen dropped Dmitry back at the oblast headquarters of the prosecutor general, where he thanked the mustachioed chief and asked him to sign more paperwork for the Investigative Committee. Still without instructions from Moscow, the old man complied with what he assumed were official orders.

Dmitry returned to the hotel and retrieved his bag. He was on the train back home by the time the prosecutor general's office in Moscow sent a frantic message telling the local chief in Voronezh to ignore any request from committee investigators. Poor man: his world was about to collapse.

*　*　*

Ivan Volkov received an unscheduled visit from an officer in the security services two days later. The man was in his early forties, a decade younger than Volkov, charmless and impassive. Colonel Krastev, the man who had handled

Ivan Volkov's file ever since he was in Beijing two decades ago, had died of a heart attack a few years before. The services had left Ivan alone after that. But his story was still in the files, and the points of leverage remained.

The officer's badge said he was from the FSB, but who really knew anymore? He had removed the name strip from his uniform. He asked Ivan to close the door. The man's square stance and folded arms conveyed gravity. So did the weapon bulging from a holster.

"Your son Dmitry is doing something very foolish. He is interfering in a matter of national security. He must stop the investigation he is conducting. We want you to convey this message to him immediately. It is a matter of great urgency."

Ivan's demeanor remained calm, but inside he felt a vertiginous sense of falling through space. He had spent a lifetime measuring orbits, and now his own was wobbling dangerously.

"Dmitry is a government official," Ivan answered slowly. "I believe he works for the Investigative Committee, which acts under the authority of the prosecutor general. He's a representative of the Russian Federation. If you have a concern about some investigation of his, then you tell him."

The security officer took several steps toward Ivan, so that they were closer to each other than Russian men usually stand. It was a gesture of menace.

"This is serious, Ivan Vladimirovich." He pointed a finger at Ivan's face. "We can say that it is a matter of the highest interest. The Presidential Administration is aware. They do not want this investigation to go forward. You are Dmitry's father. I have read the file. He listens to you only. You can get him to stop. I am asking you. Telling you. Do this or there will be severe consequences."

Ivan stood back from his visitor, to regain some distance and time to think. He knew the reality: If he told his son to back off, he would do so. It would have to be a personal request from father to son. That was the only obligation that Dmitry would accept, beyond his professional duties.

"I'll think about it," said Ivan.

"That's not enough. I need your commitment. As I said, this is a matter of high concern. People will demand to know your answer."

"I'll think about it," repeated Ivan. "More than that, I cannot say."

The security officer shook his head. He stepped back toward the door.

"I must caution you, Ivan Vladimirovich. You do not have very much time to make your decision. This is an urgent matter."

"I know," said Ivan. "I understand."

*   *   *

Ivan Volkov never made the call to his son. He came close several times, taking up his mobile phone and composing the number his son had given him. But he could never press the button to connect. He didn't want to follow the FSB man's instructions.

It wasn't just that. He knew it would be wrong. His son was young, but he had a clear vision of his moral and professional duty. A father's interference now would reverse a lifetime of encouragement to find the truth and act upon it. His son Dmitry would do the right thing, for his own reasons. The gift a father could give was silence.

44

Moscow, July 2021

Dmitry Ivanovich Volkov was found dead on the pavement below his apartment building near the university. It was a hot July afternoon. The police report said that he had slipped off the roof while sunbathing.

Ivan Volkov heard the news late that afternoon when a police captain came to his office at the institute, handed him a hastily written death certificate, and quickly left. Ivan fell to the floor as if he had been shot. He couldn't breathe at first, as if there were an enormous weight on his lungs. He only began to draw regular breaths as he started sobbing, gasping for air with each choke of tears. He felt a pain that was like a knife cleaving his innards, but the evisceration was in his mind and soul. He locked his door and stayed in his office until early morning, when he stumbled home. He didn't sleep for two nights. He felt the emptiness of utter loss.

Novaya Gazeta wrote a story about Dmitry's death. The newspaper reported that he had worked for the Investigative Committee pursuing official corruption but said no more. The article noted how many investigators had recently died from falls: in Yekaterinburg, a thirty-two-year-old probing political corruption had fallen from a fifth-floor balcony; in Moscow, a woman broadcaster had tumbled from a fourteenth-floor window; and a Moscow lawyer investigating tax fraud had slipped out of a fourth-story window, supposedly while trying to move a bathtub.

People knew the truth, even if nobody dared to say it. The director of the Investigative Committee asked Ivan if he could personally organize the funeral. Ivan at first resisted. It was too much. He wanted a simple cremation, and then he planned to scatter the ashes in the Ural River at Magnitogorsk. But the director said that too many people loved his son, they needed to grieve, too, and Ivan relented. His son was a public person. That was another choice he had made. He would have wanted to be mourned by his friends and colleagues.

The director of the Investigative Committee made a special arrangement with Donskoye Cemetery to hold the memorial there, even though the cemetery had been closed to new burials for decades. The red-brick gates of Donskoye were just east of Moscow State University, in the academic district where Ivan and Dmitry had spent so much of their youth. It was the place where decent people were buried. Russian soldiers who died during the Battle of Moscow; political prisoners who had perished during Stalin's time and were dumped in a mass grave; writers and poets and others who had dared to think for themselves.

Many dozens of Dmitry's colleagues gathered for the memorial, not just Yuri and Arkady and the other task force members, but the staff of the Investigative Committee headquarters on Bauman Street, and even a few guilty souls from the prosecutor general's office. They knew that this man was, in ways they dared not admit, a martyr for the work they had pledged to do. They shook Ivan's hand, reaching up to the big man with tears in their eyes. Ivan, so hardened to the world, could see the power of decency that his son had represented. Evil might triumph, but people knew what it was.

Dmitry's mother Veronika asked if she could attend the funeral with her husband, the wealthy businessman who luxuriated in the south of France with people like Danil and Nadia Kuzmin.

Ivan refused her request. She hadn't visited her son in two decades, and now she wanted to be seen at his memorial as if she were a loving mother. She sobbed and pleaded, but Ivan demanded that she stay away and said he would have her arrested by representatives of the Investigative Committee if she dared to show her face.

The wooden casket was open in the Russian way, friends covering the body with garlands of summer flowers, as bright as the corpse was colorless and cold. People brought sweets and cakes to dispel the sadness. Mourners walked by the casket and murmured ancient Russian phrases: May the earth be soft to him. May the kingdom of heaven be open to him. Some bent down to kiss his cold forehead.

Dmitry hadn't been a religious man, any more than his father. An Orthodox priest was in attendance and said a few ancient words over the body. "It is better to make one's exit as a free man than to seek liberty after one is in chains," he chanted. "We should, therefore, despise this world with all our hearts as though its glory were already spent."

Ivan had told the director of the Investigative Committee that he wanted no eulogies at the funeral. In truth, he wasn't sure he could bear it. But he asked if Arkady, who was Dmitry's best friend at work, would read a favorite passage from Dostoyevsky's *The Brothers Karamazov*, the immensely long book that Ivan had read to his precocious son, a chapter a night, when he was young. The reading was one of the homilies given by the mystical elder Zosima, whose spirit animates the book and, in truth, haunts Russia.

Arkady read: " 'Yet the Lord will save Russia, as he has saved her many times before. Salvation will come from the people, from their faith and their humility. Fathers and teachers, watch over the faith of the people—and this is no dream: All my life I have been struck by the true and gracious dignity in our great people, I have seen it, I can testify to it myself . . . I dream of seeing our future, and seem to see it clearly already: for it will come to pass that even the most corrupt of our rich men will finally be ashamed of his riches before the poor man, and the poor man, seeing his humility, will understand and yield to him in joy, and will respond with kindness to his gracious shame.' "

When Arkady finished his reading, the priest returned and made the sign of the cross over the body and blessed the congregation. People filed forward to heap more flowers on Dmitry or touch his body. Ivan waited until they were all gone and then placed a kiss on his son's cheek.

45

Moscow, September 2021

Ivan Volkov entered the iron gates of the Lebedev Physical Institute for the first time in more than a month, after taking a bereavement leave following his son's death. Returning to the compound was like passing through a time warp into the preserved remnants of another Russia. Two tall fir trees framed the Corinthian columns of the old administration building. Through the door was a grand salon enclosed by marble pillars, which had the eerie quiet of a library. Along a wall were sacramental portraits of the institute's Nobel Prize winners. It was a shrine to the one thing that Russia's venal leaders couldn't kill.

Volkov would have stayed away from work longer. But he had been jolted back to the reality of modern-day Russia by a visit to his apartment a week before. There had been a loud rap on his door. Volkov hadn't wanted to answer. It was just four weeks after his son's death. He hadn't shaved in days, and he had closed the curtains of his flat tight against the summer sun, whose brightness seemed unbearable. He thought that if he ignored the pounding on his door, the visitor would eventually go away. But the knocking only got louder, and Volkov eventually shuffled to the door.

The figure at the door was the same FSB man who had visited Volkov in the days before his son's murder, telling the father to intervene with his son to halt the Kuzmin investigation. His name tag and rank were missing, as before. The security man didn't wait for an invitation; he simply entered the apartment and closed the door behind him.

Volkov had stared at him through eyes dulled by tears and sleeplessness. He hadn't talked to another soul in days. But he raised his body to its full, commanding height and spoke.

"How dare you come here?" he said. "Leave my home."

The security man stood in the entryway. He spoke some ritual words of apology. Forgive the intrusion on a grieving father. He could imagine the pain. To bury one's own son. How terrible.

But then he had looked Volkov cruelly in the eye.

"I will be honest, Ivan Vladimirovich. This was your fault. You could have saved your son. You could have protected him. But you were too vain. Too righteous. How sad, that you let this boy die."

Volkov's hands trembled, but his voice was firm.

"Get out! I cannot call the police, because you are the police. But I will kill you myself if you don't leave, with these two hands."

Ivan moved toward the security man, who backed away but at the same time raised his hand to say: Stop.

"I have come here to give you some advice, Ivan Vladimirovich. Not to scold you. I don't care about your pain, frankly. I am warning you not to seek revenge for your son. Let him be. You can continue with your work at the Lebedev Physical Institute. They are willing to have you back, as before. But don't seek publicity, don't speak out, don't imagine that you know things that you don't know."

"I despise you," Ivan said.

"I'm sure that you do," the visitor responded, his voice cold and flat as stone. "Just don't act on that emotion, and you will recover in time. This is Russia. Pain is as certain as the winter snow. Get some sleep. Drink some beer. Play some hockey. After a while, the world will get fuzzy for you, like everyone else."

The security man left. Ivan sat in a chair in his living room for several hours. His odious visitor had been right in one respect. He needed to go back to work. Otherwise, the barely flickering light of his consciousness would expire, and the people who had killed Dmitry would claim another victim.

* * *

Volkov's office was in a new building beyond the formal courtyard. His coworkers welcomed him back with hugs and expressions of condolence. On his desk was a bouquet of flowers and a plate of cookies left by his administrative assistant. In midmorning, a colleague brought him some new volumes of the Lebedev Physical Institute Series, which had been published while he was away. *Theoretical Problems in the Spectroscopy and Gas Dynamics of Lasers. Materials and Apparatus in Quantum Radiophysics.* Volkov thanked him and began reading the first volume.

There was a comforting numbness in the technical details of science, and Volkov embraced it in those weeks of mourning. There was always something new in space research. Volkov tried to stay current with the technology. He read American publications on the internet, and he knew that the paradigm for space was changing. The scientific and military missions that had been the dominant theme through Volkov's career were giving way to something different.

Now it was the "space business." American money was financing networks of small satellites that could provide internet service, optical imagery, thermal measurements. The satellites were in a constant, dizzying flow of commerce. Volkov tracked and mapped the commercial satellites, thousands of them now. He worked with his colleagues to update and improve GLONASS, so that it would have something to offer in this new age of commercial space.

But Russia brought little to the table. Volkov knew that his country, slow and corrupt, was losing its way in this new space race. And though he would never whisper the thought to his colleagues, he was glad of it. China was now the great power that would contest the Americans in space. Russia might ask for help, but it had little to contribute.

* * *

Volkov was an adviser to the Pushchino Radio Astronomy Observatory, sixty miles south of Moscow. He visited there once a month to meet with the engineers on site, and he welcomed the chance to escape Moscow. On his third day back from work after bereavement leave, he drove down the M2 highway toward Pushchino in the Korean car he had bought himself several years before. He looked for surveillance along the way but didn't see any.

He visited the Pushchino campus for most of the day. He talked with the technicians who tended the dishes of the four giant radio telescopes and walked the length of the phased-array antenna complex, nearly a mile long, through the woods. People stopped him along the way. They had heard about his son out in Pushchino, too. Colleagues patted Volkov on the back and told him they were sorry for his loss.

When the sun was low in the sky, Volkov headed back to Moscow. He pulled off the highway once, took a side road for several miles, and then doubled back. Nobody appeared to be following him. He didn't know what he would do with this freedom of movement, but he was happy to have it.

* * *

September was mild, with steel-blue skies. It was the brief season that Russians call "*baba*'s days," the window of sunlight when the grandmas could take a pleasant walk or finish their chores outside before the long blast of winter began. Volkov rose early most mornings and took a walk in the park near his apartment just after sunrise, when there was a bright sheen on the trees and grass. He liked to read his morning newspaper sitting on a park bench that was hidden away off the path but caught the full glaze of the morning sun.

Volkov was reading the sports pages, studying the soccer scores, when a man sat down beside him on the bench. He was wearing a Dynamo cap, so Volkov didn't see at first that his features were Chinese. He edged away from the interloper, but the man touched his arm and spoke softly.

"Mr. Volkov." He bowed his head. "May I offer you sympathy on the death of your son."

Volkov was startled by the intrusion. As he mumbled thanks, the man handed him a letter. When Volkov had received it, the Chinese man rose and walked away. Volkov opened the letter. He scanned the missive, neatly typed on plain paper. He knew before reading the first words who it must be from.

Dear Mr. Volkov:

I send you deep condolences on the untimely death of your son Dmitry, which was mentioned in news reports. I recall many years ago that the illness of your mother brought you back to Russia, and it was duty to your son that kept you there. You are a good son and father, a quality prized everywhere but especially in your country and in mine.

We have always had the greatest respect for your scientific ability, and in the years since we communicated, your knowledge of technologies involved in space operations has only become more valuable. Perhaps you will recall that once long ago in Beijing I encouraged you to join a company that was just beginning its work in the business of satellite supply. And I repeated that suggestion a second time, after you returned to Moscow. Perhaps you will recall a book meant to convey my affection. "The Harmony of the World." But events intervened. It was not the time for us to work together.

This is a new season. Perhaps it would be a good time to renew contact with the firm that sought to hire you. I understand that their foreign sales representative, Mr. Arthur Wang, will be visiting Moscow in late September. He will be staying at the Kempinski Hotel in Moscow. He will be arriving on Saturday, Sept. 24. I am sure that he would be pleased to see you in the hotel lobby on the afternoon of September 25 at 4:00.

We have a saying in China that the usefulness of a cup is its emptiness. I send you deepest sympathy for the emptiness that you must feel now. But I hope that it will not always be so.

With regret and warmest wishes,

Cao Lin, Academician

Chinese Academy of Sciences

46

Moscow, September 2021

The Kempinski Hotel was one of the elegant façades that Moscow used to cover its ugly wounds so that visitors wouldn't see. It was a creamy palace on the banks of the Moscow River across from the onion domes and red-brick walls of the Kremlin. Its guests came from many countries, but they shared a brotherhood of wealth and ostentation. It was a place that Ivan Volkov had never once entered before the Sunday afternoon that he met Arthur Wang in the lobby.

Wang's belly had grown and his hair had thinned since the two first met in Beijing twenty-five years before. But he retained the relentless good cheer of a born salesman. He expressed well-rehearsed sympathy for Volkov's loss. They ordered tea. The waiters were wearing Covid masks, but the clients were unshielded and conversing in many languages. Volkov sipped his tea and ate a bite of a madeleine. A piano player at the far end of the lobby began playing Broadway show tunes.

Volkov suggested that they take a walk. The evening was pleasant, and the late afternoon sun cast golden ripples on the river. Volkov wanted to be out of the hotel lobby. It wasn't so much that he feared surveillance as that the vulgar splendor of the place disgusted him. He looked for followers or watchers as they moved toward the embankment but saw no one. His son had been dangerous; he was simply an afterthought.

They strolled along the banks of the river for several hours, up and back, until the sun set and the lights illuminated the Kremlin and Red Square like a fairy kingdom. Wang enthused about how wonderful Russia was, doubtless thinking that would please his companion. Volkov gave polite answers, but eventually, at a bend in the river where there was no one within thirty yards in either direction, he put the matter to the visitor:

"What did Cao Lin ask you to discuss with me? I don't usually meet foreign businessmen."

Wang still spoke with a bright New York patter. He walked like an American, leaning backward slightly, splay-foot, rather than forward on the balls of his feet, as people do in cultures where they must always be wary.

"Professor Cao wanted us to talk business. Just as you and I did many years ago in China. He thought that maybe you would be more interested now. Easier for you to think about traveling, after, you know, your son. You have some room to maneuver. Professor Cao has some room, too. He's trying new things."

"What is your business, if I may ask? Remind me. It's been a long time."

"Short version, okay? We supply the commercial and government satellite market. We got lucky. We were in at the takeoff of commercial space with good, cheap products. We kept expanding our product line. On the hardware side, we sell dishes, antennas, routers, signal processors, cabling, and specialty chips. We're even a reseller of atomic clocks, for satellites. In software, we sell satellite solutions: Telemetry, tracking, safety assurance, end to end. We manufacture now in China, Taiwan, Singapore, South Korea, India, and America, of course."

"Sorry to be stupid. But are you a Chinese company or an American company?"

"American, of course. Our chief executive is Roger Birken, one of the cofounders with me. I got out of senior management. I'm a sales guy, really. Our board is entirely American. We register with the SEC and the Commerce Department. We don't break anyone's rules."

"But you manufacture in China?" Volkov was still feeling his way.

"Sure. Who doesn't? Apple makes phones in China. Microsoft writes software. Oracle designs databases. Things may get a little noisy in global business these days. But we get by. We sell to America, Russia, China. We are the United Nations of satellites."

"And what role does Professor Cao Lin play? Is he your investor? Your partner? Your friend?"

Wang got a wry look and tilted his head. His unspoken answer was: Give me a break. Don't ask so many questions. Then he shrugged.

"Well, Professor Cao is mostly a friend now. He was an investor before. And he was a partner in some early joint ventures. But that was a long time ago. We separated. There are all these rules in America. Completely separate now. Firewall."

"Ah," said Volkov. He didn't believe a word of it. But his curiosity was mounting. "What did Professor Cao, as a friend of the business, want us to talk about?"

"Hey! Good question. Don't waste time. Get to the point. American-style. So, like I said, one of our product lines is atomic clocks. I'm sure you have them on your GLONASS satellites, right?"

"Certainly we have atomic clocks," answered the Russian. "Every positioning satellite system does. We use rubidium, which is stable because it has a single electron in its outer orbit. So does GPS, BeiDou, Galileo. All the same."

"You're beyond me here, technology-wise, my friend. I'm just a salesman. So, the thing that Professor Cao wanted your help on is error correction. He thinks you know how to make it go on and off. That's what he told me, at least."

"Why did he think that?" Volkov's skepticism was as intense as his curiosity.

"I don't know, honestly. But he said that because of your work on GLONASS, you could help us think about some problems with this 'error correction.' What does that mean, anyway?"

"It means correcting the errors on satellite clocks that make them unreliable."

"Yeah, well, he wants some help. He wants to talk to you."

Volkov found this new turn in the conversation uncomfortable. Error correction of atomic clocks was one of the most sensitive issues involved in satellite navigation. He didn't talk about it with anyone, outside of a few trusted colleagues at the institute. He was intrigued that Cao Lin wanted his assistance, but he couldn't give it through this intermediary.

"I'm sorry, Mr. Wang. I can't help you with that one. Too complicated.

Sorry. Tell Professor Cao I appreciate his interest. But I am not, what, his 'guy' on this."

Wang was disappointed. You could see the downcast look on his face under the embankment lights just below Red Square.

"Well, maybe something else, then?" Wang asked. "Professor Cao sounded pretty eager to make friends again. He said he's been trying to hire you for twenty years."

"Longer than that, actually. But as I told you, I'm not his man. Not anybody's. I'm not for sale."

"But you don't like Russia, correct? How could you? I mean, your son and everything. So maybe it's a good time to move."

"I like Russia fine. I'm stubborn. I told Professor Cao long ago that it was my home. It still is."

"Look, Mr. Volkov, Cao really wants to see you. He thinks there's trouble coming. He could meet you somewhere. Not here, in Russia, but somewhere else. He could explain better than me. He says he needs you. If he were here, I think he would say that he's different now, from what you remember. He wants a smart guy like you on his side."

Volkov shook his head. "Sorry. Give my respects to Professor Cao Lin. Tell him I appreciate his interest, but I can't help him."

Wang knew he was failing his assignment. Volkov was slipping away. "Well, maybe you and I could meet again. I'll take you to lunch tomorrow. Or dinner. Best place in town. What about that?"

"I don't mean to be rude. But no, I don't want to see you again, for lunch, dinner, or anything else. I met you this afternoon because I wanted to understand why Professor Cao was reaching out to me. Now I know. I can't help him or you. As we say in Russia, this is how the story ends."

They had reached the Bolshoy Moskvoretsky Bridge. Across its span was the Kempinski Hotel.

"See, I've brought you home. Safe and sound." Volkov gestured toward the brightly illuminated entrance of the hotel. Then he turned and walked back toward the domes of St. Basil's Cathedral and was soon lost in the crowd.

47

Moscow, February 2022

As fall ground toward winter in Moscow, Ivan Volkov kept to himself even more than usual. The authorities left him alone. If his meeting with the American businessman had caught anyone's attention, it had been forgotten. Russia had more important things to worry about. There were rumors of war in Ukraine, and then the mechanics of actual preparation for conflict. The director of the Central Intelligence Agency visited Moscow in November to warn the Russian president against invasion. Across Europe there was a flurry of meetings, as the Americans tried to convince skeptical leaders that the Russian president was actually contemplating an attack.

Volkov tried to ignore the daily news and focus on what had become a matter of intense personal interest. Cao Lin had sent him a message via his American salesman. He was gathering expertise on the error-correction process for the specialized clocks used aboard positioning satellites. What could explain that? This was an arcane scientific topic, usually of interest only to engineers. He had sought Volkov's help. What was he planning?

So Volkov went to work, using the resources of the Lebedev Physical Institute and the GLONASS system on which he'd been a consultant for nearly two decades. The work was technical, but Volkov had liked solving problems since he was a boy. As always, he started with the basics—the straight edges of the puzzle, so to speak, so that he could eventually fill in the rest.

Volkov kept a notebook for each of his projects to help order his thinking, and now he started a new one. He wrote a first question in the neat Cyrillic penmanship he had learned as a boy: "Why are satellite clocks so important that any error must be corrected?"

The basics were familiar enough. Since the earliest days of navigation, location had been a matter of time and distance. Seafaring navigators carried the most accurate clocks of their day, chronometers they were called, and they would locate their position by comparing the local time, measured by sighting the sun or stars and planets, with the Greenwich Mean Time recorded on the chronometer.

Satellite navigation was about time and distance, too. Satellites could determine the position of a receiver on the ground, like a cell phone, by measuring their distance to the receiver. GLONASS required four satellites in sight of the receiver. GPS was the same. When Volkov explained it to non-scientists, he told them to imagine four lengths of string, each cut to the length of the distance from one of the satellites to the receiver. The point where they all fit tight on earth was the receiver's location.

"Why is time so important?" Volkov underlined the sentence. It mattered because the way that satellites measured distance was by recording the precise length of time it took a signal to travel from the satellite to the receiver. So the two clocks, on earth and in space, must be perfectly synchronized.

Volkov wrote in his notebook a formula he had remembered from his early days working on GLONASS: "1/300." That was shorthand for saying that a clock difference of just one microsecond, a millionth of a second, could produce a position error of three hundred meters. That was the distance that light traveled in that microsecond. In a far quicker nanosecond, an unimaginably brief billionth of a second, light traveled thirty centimeters. That meant that if the clock was ten nanoseconds off, the position error would be three meters. *Vazhnyy.* Important.

Volkov wrote another question in his notebook. "How do we synchronize clocks?" That sounded simple, but it wasn't. Usually, the quartz clocks on ground receivers aren't as accurate as the atomic clocks onboard the satellites.

So the receiver has to measure signals from the four satellites in its constellation to get a precise range and set its clock. But even then, the clocks are fallible.
There are elaborate ways to check and cross-check: Against the master clock at
a control station; against dispersed receivers and mobile rovers; and against a
half dozen other exotic systems. The simple question—what time is it? —was
not simple at all.

Volkov inscribed one more question in his catalogue: "What can produce
clock errors?" He made a list: First, even the atomic clocks in space could vary
slightly from the even more precise time calculation of the master control station. The likely error range from this clock imprecision was two meters, plus
or minus. Then there were orbit errors. Even the fixed, medium-earth orbits of
the GPS satellites wobbled a bit, and that could add an error range of another
2.5 meters. As the satellite's radio signals passed through the atmosphere, they
were distorted once again. The upper ionosphere could add an additional error
range of five meters. The lower troposphere, closest to the earth, could distort the signal and the resulting distance measurement by another half meter.
And there were other possible errors, harder to predict: Noisy receivers could
distort the signal; signals that bounced off buildings might skew it more. The
sources of error lay, quite literally, in every direction.

Volkov turned a page in his book and wrote: "Error correction." He listed
the basic methods, each with its particular benefits and drawbacks. A simple
but imprecise way was to average different error measurements and then send
the best estimate back to the satellite; another imprecise approach was to
model the factors causing distortion and predict the correct time. The most
accurate techniques involved using a range of base stations to resolve ambigui-
ties and could generate accurate, reliable error messages for transmission to the
satellites. Technicians depended on machine-generated warnings to tell them
when errors arose, when the correction wasn't precise enough, or when the
clocks remained in variance despite correction.

Volkov closed his notebook and let himself think. Scientists had long
understood the vulnerability of their clocks. They had devised an array of elegant solutions for detecting and correcting errors. Each GPS satellite had three
atomic clocks, to ensure redundancy if one failed. And for each GPS satellite,
there was a backup one in orbit ready to fill any gap. The technicians had fore-

seen that jammers might try to overpower GPS signals with electronic noise, and they had devised subtle anti-jamming antennas and other techniques. They had anticipated that "spoofers" would try to trick a receiver by broadcasting incorrect time or location data on the same frequency as a GPS signal.

Volkov wondered: Where was the weak spot? How might the wooden horse enter the walls? So many precautions had been taken by the United States government, which had created the system and was still its master controller. What had they missed, that Cao Lin might seek to exploit?

* * *

And then Volkov had an odd, fleeting insight. He thought of his automobile, and the red warning light that flashed on the dashboard, indicating that the battery was weak, or the gasoline supply was low, or the water in the radiator was overheating. The light signaled a potentially dangerous malfunction. The driver was supposed to fix the problem immediately or, failing that, stop the car.

And the thought formed itself in Volkov's mind: If someone wanted to disrupt a person's car travel, they didn't have to interfere with the battery, or the gas tank, or the radiator. It was the same for airplanes. They could be grounded for hours or days because of a pesky light warning of danger, even if the cause couldn't be identified.

And that was the answer—the magic bullet! An attacker just had to illuminate that red warning light. People would begin searching frantically for an error that might not actually exist. The attacker didn't have to sabotage the system itself, which would be difficult and easily detected. He simply had to have access to peripheral components that would create the appearance of a malfunction—or better yet, a random string of them. Human nature would take care of the rest. People would be wary of using a system until they were sure the apparent faults had been cured. It was, in its devilish capacity to introduce crippling uncertainty, a "kill switch."

* * *

Volkov had authority to review GLONASS's chain of suppliers. That was one of the many technical areas that he sometimes examined, as part of Lebedev Institute's technical advisory contract with Roscosmos. It wasn't a secret. These items were purchased, for the most part, in the global marketplace. GLONASS was a global resource, positioning signals were shared with the world, even the United States.

He made an appointment to visit Roscosmos, which still oversaw Russian space programs, even after all the thievery and mismanagement of the past. Its headquarters were in a tall, ugly skyscraper in the Meshchansky District between the two ring roads. His visit was routine. He entered his name on the visitors' logs and showed his credentials, but nobody paid much attention. The flurry of action that week involved satellite signals over Ukraine. It was increasingly obvious that war was coming.

Volkov looked for three words, Satellite Supply Systems, as he checked the computer records for GLONASS's contractors and vendors. The company, headquartered in Northern California, had been cofounded by Arthur Wang, now a sales executive who was all but invisible in subsequent corporate records. It was tedious work. But he began to find items that had been purchased from "SSS," as the company abbreviated its name.

He compiled a list, as always, to record what he found. Satellite Supply sold dishes and cables for GLONASS ground stations across Russia, Brazil, and Nicaragua. It resold atomic clocks under a licensing agreement with a California company that produced ninety percent of them.

Volkov searched the website for Satellite Supply Systems. The section "About the Company" boasted that it was a long-term supplier to America's GPS array, as well as to China's BeiDou, Europe's Galileo system, Japan's Quasi-Zenith Satellite System, and the Indian Regional Navigation Satellite System—as well as GLONASS.

Volkov wanted to double-check the GPS link, just to make sure. This was the central trunk of the tree. It took him forty minutes of searching GPS online records to find the American suppliers of components for the key corrections technologies. And there, on a list of subcontractors, was the name of the trusted American vendor, Satellite Supply Systems. He did the same for BeiDou; its global contracts were a matter of public record, too.

Cao Lin was the ghost in the machine. If Volkov was right, the Chinese professor had developed the power to stop time, or at least make people believe it had stopped. He had the ability to make mischief across the global system, in every backup as well as the main array. His target must surely be the United States—the country whose flag graced his Trojan horse, Satellite Supply Systems. Volkov felt a chill run down his spine. This was an unimaginable power of disruption, in the hands of people who were radically untrustworthy. He needed to tell someone. But who in his past or present could help him make a connection?

48

Moscow, February–April, 2022

In the last weeks of February, the mood in Moscow became a kind of giddy panic. It was obvious now that the country was going to war. The Russian social media channels, VK and Telegram, were streaming with cell phone videos of Russian tanks moving by train toward Ukraine, grainy images taken at night of flatcars topped with metal hulks painted with the letter z, one after the other, for miles, it seemed. The commentators on Russian state television, normally mimicking cosmopolitan Europeans, were sputtering about a supposed Nazi threat in Kyiv. Moscow's airports were jammed with Russians who sensed what was coming and wanted to get out before the hammer dropped.

The military bloggers on Telegram feasted on one detail that especially interested Volkov. The Russian military was poorly prepared for its invasion. Bases near the Ukrainian border, in Russian cities such as Voronezh, weren't ready. Transport networks that were supposed to have been completed were still unfinished. Procurement of supplies had been inefficient; weapons and other gear were found to be missing from their stores—looted by thieves or perhaps never purchased in the first place.

The mil-bloggers dared to say it out loud: The Defense Ministry was corrupt. The *siloviki*, the "people of force," were thieves. Growing public recognition of that fact, and anger at the thugs who were euphemistically known as the "polite people," was oddly comforting to Volkov. It showed anyone who cared to remember that his son Dmitry had been right. He had died trying to stop the thievery that now left the nation's soldiers so vulnerable.

Volkov continued traveling through the February chill to his office at the institute. People spoke to their colleagues quietly now as if they were afraid of being overheard. A darkness was descending. There was no surge of patriotism, only dread, as people watched the television news in their offices or checked the latest updates on their phones. A frozen conflict on the border that had seemed an obsessive personal hobby of the country's leader had now become red-hot.

Volkov watched the crisis envelop his own world. Lebedev scientists were receiving notices that their fellowships or speaking engagements abroad had been canceled. Roscosmos was in an uproar: Volkov's colleagues told him that the company had been tasked with preventing Ukraine and its friends from jamming GLONASS signals, even as Russia tried to jam GPS. Volkov had never worked on military jamming systems. He was glad of it now.

Late that month, as the invasion was imminent, Volkov and his colleagues at the institute received a secret directive, in a briefing from a member of the "special services." The issue of satellite communications had become a matter of survival for the motherland. Ukraine was using Western commercial satellite networks to coordinate its forces. Commercial satellite imagery was providing locations of Russian targets, and commercial broadband satellites were beaming internet connectivity to Ukrainian soldiers in the field.

Russia dispatched a special scientific delegation to Beijing, to discuss satellite communication issues with the PLA unit that now oversaw all space activities. The Chinese had the expertise, and the Russians needed it. Volkov feared that he would be tapped for this assignment because of his time in Beijing, but it was deemed too sensitive for any who lacked the very highest clearances.

The Lebedev Institute's space tracking and telemetry team was secretly tasked with two requirements: First, study the orbits of American commercial satellites and calculate with precision when their imagery and signal footprint covered Ukraine. And second, make contingency plans for coordination between GLONASS and the BeiDou global-positioning system in case America's GPS system was disrupted.

As Volkov digested this news, he felt that he had been very stupid. He hadn't seen what was in front of his eyes. Russia was going to war, on the ground and in space. It was struggling to block the commercial satellite networks that gave little Ukraine the power of a giant. Russia was looking for ways to freeze the Western system, and it had the secret assistance of China. If Russia were pushed to the breaking point, the Chinese might flash the false red light of the "kill switch" Volkov had postulated.

Volkov had been so careful to protect himself, and then so stricken by his personal loss, that he hadn't seen the catastrophe that was taking shape—and that he was standing on the wrong side. He knew what Dmitry would have told him: You must take action.

*   *   *

The president of Russia announced the invasion of Ukraine in an early evening broadcast to the nation. His face was a prison tattoo on Russia's skin: cold blue eyes, a face purged of emotion. He spoke with anger, as if he felt cheated and demeaned by the West and this invasion was forced on him by NATO powers determined to humiliate Russia. "Why is this happening?" asked the wounded voice on the television. "What is the explanation for this contemptuous and disdainful attitude to our interests and absolutely legitimate demands?"

There is a kind of parallel rationality that is indistinguishable from madness. Volkov heard the voice, coming from a place where words lost their normal meaning: "The purpose of this operation is to protect people who, for eight years now, have been facing humiliation and genocide perpetrated by the Kiev regime. To this end, we will seek to demilitarize and de-Nazify Ukraine." Volkov couldn't watch anymore.

*   *   *

In the refuge of the institute, amid the phantoms of Russia's past, Volkov struggled to think about what to do in the present. He knew that he must act upon the frightening insight he had gained. What would happen to this chaotic world, now riven by war, if its central nervous system suddenly became paralyzed because of uncertainty about its integrity? Systems functioned only if people trusted the reliability of the underlying technology; if that vanished, the systems would begin to wobble and break. The ordered clockwork of life would freeze, and with it, the operation of stock exchanges, banks, power grids, transportation networks, communication systems.

When we know a secret that could have devastating consequences, what should we do? Often people choose to do nothing, especially in countries like Russia, where passivity and stoicism are embedded in the culture. Sometimes people tell "the authorities," the people with power. But Volkov knew that Russia's leaders were part of the conspiracy he had glimpsed or were unwitting but obedient coconspirators.

Sometimes people with secrets choose to share them with "the enemy." A criminal will break ranks and talk to the police. A military officer will report a superior who commits war crimes. Or a scientist will share a secret with the intelligence agency he had been taught from his youngest days is his country's enemy. Betrayal is not so much a cognitive decision but an action of the limbic system. You decide to share information because, really, you have no other choice.

* * *

Volkov was left with a practical question. How should he send his message of warning to the Central Intelligence Agency? He knew from browsing the internet over several decades that the CIA had a website. But how could he access it securely, in a way that wouldn't identify him? He was ready to take risks but not commit suicide. So he began looking for secure laptops that wouldn't disclose his IP address. The institute kept a stack of loaners in the basement. Volkov borrowed several. He identified internet cafés around Moscow that had Wi-Fi signals.

He found the CIA website easily enough, browsing on a Wi-Fi network at a café near the Moscow Zoo. *"We are the Nation's first line of defense. We accomplish what others cannot accomplish and go where others cannot go,"* read the opening screen. Okay. That was the right address. He signed off and left. He wore a hat and scarf that obscured his face, when people tried to identify who had signed on to that address from the coffee shop's network. The next day, he signed on to the same address from another coffee bar on the Arbat.

This time he went a little deeper, to the page marked "Contact Us." "*People from nearly every country share information with the Central Intelligence Agency daily, and new individuals contact us daily. If you have information that might help our foreign intelligence collection mission, there are many ways to reach us.*"

Volkov clicked a link deeper, to the page designated "Report Information." He was just beginning to read the message when someone came down and sat at the next table. The page continued: "*The best method to contact us depends on your personal situation. We will work to protect all information you give to us, including your identity. Our interactions with you will be respectful and professional. Depending on what you provide, we may offer you compensation.*" Volkov quickly closed the CIA site, powered down his computer, and left the coffee bar, wrapped tightly in his scarf.

It was unsafe. He was spending too long on the CIA site, accessing it from public places that kept records of their Wi-Fi traffic and surely had hidden security cameras. He needed something more secure. Volkov had a spare laptop at home. It had belonged to one of Dmitry's friends who had left it with him and then moved overseas without ever collecting it. Volkov had salvaged it from his son's possessions thinking that someday he might need a clean computer. Now he did.

Volkov composed the message on this anonymous laptop that he would send to the CIA. He tried many versions. But the one he settled on began: "I am Anonymous. I live on a street with no entrance or exit."

Volkov needed the most secure location from which to send this message. He decided that, paradoxically, the safest place was his own institute, which was such a protected environment that its internal security was fairly lax. The institute had a cavernous library where the fellows did their research. Since they often needed to consult American and European research journals, the library had a special VPN plug-in channel to allow unimpeded access to the global internet.

It was through this access point, using a laptop that could not be traced to him and an Ethernet cable to plug into the VPN router, that Volkov sent the CIA site his final draft. He read the admonition: "*We go to great lengths to keep these channels secure, but any communication sent using the internet involves some* risk. You can reduce some risk by using the Tor browser, a virtual private network, and/or a device not registered to you."

"Do it," he whispered to himself. He typed the fifty-five-character string provided by the agency, and then the site ".onion." He closed his eyes, took a deep breath, and then sent the message:

> I am Anonymous. I live on a street with no entrance or exit. Here is my information: You are blind to the danger from above. Satellites are your enemies, especially your own. You have 16 ground monitors and 11 antennas to run your global navigation system. Do you trust it? That is only the beginning. Hidden codes can seem to make time stop and turn north into south. They will freeze your world and everything in it. Warning messages may be tricks. Beware. A war has already begun in space. You think you understand, but you do not. The worst has already happened. Only a few people know what I know. If you are smart, you will find me.

Volkov had been careful. He had hinted, but not stated directly. He had placed signposts pointing the Americans in the right direction and encouraged them to find him if they wanted more. He had been brave, but not foolish.

* * *

Weeks passed with no answer. Why didn't they respond? Volkov admitted the answer to himself after the first days. They couldn't find him. He had been too cautious. His extreme care in hiding his identity would prevent the CIA from locating him and learning what he knew. By the end of the opening month of the Ukraine war, he began to feel a gnawing in his gut.

Russia was trying to break Ukraine in space, as well as on the ground. The rumors flew at Lebedev Physical Institute. Specialists in electromagnetic energy had been transferred on urgent temporary assignment to the Ministry of Defense. The team that had visited the PLA satellite specialists in Beijing had made a second emergency trip. The ordered world was crumbling around Volkov. He thought he knew what was coming if matters reached an ultimate crisis point. There was a disabler, a panic button. The reckless leaders in Beijing would use it, to save their Russian friends.

* * *

Resistance required courage. The president of Ukraine was a humble man, nobody's hero. But he had stood his ground, refusing to buckle, when even the Americans encouraged him to evacuate. That act of defiance empowered his countrymen and helped them to be braver than they thought possible.

Volkov considered ways he could reach the agency more directly, so that he could share precisely what he knew. He could think of only one CIA contact he'd ever made. "Likely" contact would be more accurate.

It was painful to recall those events more than two decades before in Beijing. He had believed that he loved the woman, and that maybe she loved him, too, until he concluded that she was playing a game to bring him into her net. Maybe there had been some of both. That was what he had decided.

Volkov had kept the small strip of paper on which she had inscribed her name and her parents' address and phone number in Massachusetts, in block letters, and at the bottom, below the address, the words: "I'm sorry." He stored it in a secret hiding place he never visited, but never forgot. Now, he retrieved it.

A letter mailed through the post to an address in America. It sounded too easy and direct to work. But in the internet age, this was perhaps the most secure means of communication. The Russians didn't check most letters posted to the United States, and even if they opened a message, it could be composed in a way that wouldn't arouse suspicion. That was the simplest way to ring the CIA's bell. Through the mailbox.

Volkov made his decision at the beginning of April, when the media, even in Russia, showed the horror of what had happened in the town of Bucha, as Russian troops began retreating after their inability to seize Kyiv. It was sickening to see the civilian bodies, old men and women, young children, murdered by the Russian soldiers. And it was worse still to hear the official Russian response. The Western claim of such atrocities was a fabrication.

"None of it happened." What you can see with your eyes you are not seeing. That was how stupid and frightened the "people of force" thought their fellow

Russians were, that they would accept these cowardly lies to cover crimes conducted in the name of the motherland.

Volkov thought again of what his son Dmitry would do. But he didn't have to think very long. His son would run toward danger to do what was right.

Volkov took up his pen and began to write:

Dear Miss Ryan:

Perhaps you remember me. I am Ivan Volkov, who studied aerospace engineering at Tsinghua University when we were young and very poor. I am sorry I haven't written for so long. I am 51 years old now, and my son, my only family, is gone. I am quite alone. I work now at the Lebedev Physical Institute. I am always happy to meet old friends. Perhaps you could contact me.

Yours sincerely,
Ivan Volkov

BOOK TWO: LANDING

SUNDAY

APRIL 17, 2022

Nearly two months into Vladimir Putin's brutal assault on Ukraine, the Biden administration and its European allies have begun planning for a far different world, in which they no longer try to coexist and cooperate with Russia but actively seek to isolate and weaken it as a matter of long-term strategy.

At NATO and the European Union, and at the State Department, the Pentagon and allied ministries, blueprints are being drawn up to enshrine new policies across virtually every aspect of the West's posture toward Moscow, from defense and finance to trade and international diplomacy.

—THE WASHINGTON POST, Sunday, April 17, 2022

49

Vnukovo Airport was a stampede of frightened faces on the morning in April when Ivan Volkov left Russia. Most international flights had been halted by sanctions after the Ukraine war began, but Turkish Airlines was still flying four flights a day to Istanbul. Volkov booked a seat on one of the morning flights, so that he could transfer in Istanbul and reach Paris that Sunday night.

He arrived at Vnukovo very early, taking a train in the middle of the night to the sprawling airport in the southwest suburbs of Moscow. He had his Istanbul reservation, his signed travel approval from his bosses at the institute, and the exit papers stamped by the Lebedev security chief, who was skeptical at his invitation but hungry for any information he might bring back. Still, the long queues at baggage check-in and passport control made him worry that he would miss his flight.

Volkov had one week. The institute had granted him a five-day leave from work and given him a special security briefing. He was expected back in the office the following Monday. If he wasn't on the return flight to Moscow, Volkov knew that they would find him and bring him home, dead or alive. It was a small miracle that he had any time at all. All around him was the chaotic scatter of people trying to escape a war on earth. Volkov was trying to stop a disaster in space.

Volkov made his way through the crowd. He was still tall and command-ing, his hair slate-gray now but his body taut like an animal's that has sur-vived amid predators. He tried to be polite, even as others pushed their way forward in the queues. The clamoring horde of people rushing to get out were the ones who had dreamed of a modern Russia. Many were young men in their twenties and thirties. Russia hadn't announced a mobilization yet for the "special military operation," but people sensed it was coming. From the looks on the faces of those departing, Volkov could see interwoven emotions of fear and defiance. They didn't want to fight for this Russia. But would they fight against it? Volkov doubted it. These were the soft ones who thought of Europe as an entitlement.

Vnukovo was a gleaming gateway to the West. Its Terminal A had been rebuilt in the modern airport style. It was a palace of space and light, with vaulted steel beams and struts supporting a canopy of glass. Like so much of Russia, it was almost there. The moving walkways were often broken, and the bright displays had computer glitches and sometimes failed to show accurate departure and arrival information. Computer systems periodically crashed, forcing the men and women at the check-in counters to frantically scan paper records. Given this jumble, departure times were a fiction, but it was remark-able that planes were taking off at all.

Volkov emptied himself of emotion as he approached passport control. The FSB border guards were suspicious of everyone, always, but now they were especially truculent. They despised the young Russians who were fleeing the war and the motherland. As Volkov approached the booth, he pulled up the sleeve of his sweater to reveal the tattoo on his forearm with the name of his hometown hockey team, Metallurg. The guard looked at the tattoo and then at his passport.

"Magnitogorsk?" The place didn't fit the cosmopolitan man in the queue.

"I was born there. My father was a steelworker."

"Shithole," the guard muttered. He said that he was from Chelyabinsk, another industrial city from the Russian rust belt, farther north. He looked Volkov in the eye, curiously at first and then with a stony glare.

"Why are you leaving Russia?" he asked. He looked at Volkov's papers and shook his head. He called his superior in the guard station and asked for assistance.

* * *

An odd letter had arrived in early April at the home of Katharine Ryan in Holyoke. It fell through the mail slot of her old family house on Harvard Street. Mrs. Ryan had been meaning to sell the house, but during the Covid pandemic she hadn't wanted people trooping through. Now it was simply inertia. She had lived there so long that she didn't know where else to go. She was teaching school now part-time. The only thing she really wanted in life was a grandchild, but it was too late for that.

She took the peculiar letter in her hands. The stamps had a foreign writing that she realized must be Cyrillic after staring at the envelope. The letter was addressed to her daughter Edith. The return address didn't give a name, just a street number in Moscow. Mrs. Ryan debated whether to open the letter but decided against it. She knew that her daughter had worked for the CIA; the early fiction that she was a "foreign service officer" had melted away long ago. For Edith to receive a letter from Moscow was eerie, especially when every night's news brought reports of Russia's war in Ukraine.

Mrs. Ryan put the letter on the hall table and went to the phone. She was curious who might be trying to contact her daughter, but this was a private message, perhaps a secret one. She reached Edith at her office in California. It was morning there. Edith had come in early. With the war, Apollo Space Laboratories was working on Washington time; sometimes, it seemed, on Kyiv time, trying to keep satellites operating.

Edith's mother described the letter with the Russian stamps, the careful handwriting on the front, the vague return address. There was a slight tremor in her voice.

"What should I do with it?" she asked. "Is it dangerous? Should I send it to you?"

Edith's mind raced as she listened to her mother. Who in Russia could know her parents' address in Holyoke, Massachusetts? Who would send a letter out the blue from Moscow, at a time of crisis, addressed to a former CIA officer?

And in the same instant, the memories cascaded back, and she was certain who the letter must be from.

"Open the letter and read it to me," Edith said. "But first, go in the kitchen and get some plastic gloves. Don't touch the letter with your hands. Open the envelope carefully with a knife. Bring a baggie to put the letter in when you've read it to me. I'll wait while you go get the gloves, okay, Mom?"

Mrs. Ryan laid down the phone, scurried to the kitchen, and returned thirty seconds later.

"I have the gloves on. I'm cutting the letter open now."

"Read it," said Edith.

Mrs. Ryan slowly recited the brief message. Edith murmured assent when her mother read the name Ivan Volkov and the part where he recalled that they both had been graduate students in China. Mrs. Ryan stumbled over the name of his workplace, Lebedev Physical Institute. Edith asked her to read the last line twice: "Perhaps you could contact me."

"Do you know him?" asked Katharine Ryan.

"I did. When I said goodbye in China, I gave him our address and phone number."

"Ah!"

"Mom, here's what I want you to do. Put the letter and the envelope in the baggie. I'm going to call someone in Washington where I used to work. Okay? I am going to ask them to send a courier from the Federal Building in Boston to collect the letter. The courier will show you a badge. He will tell you that he is with National Resources. That's a part of the CIA that deals with Americans."

"What do I do then?"

"Give him the letter. And get a signed receipt, with his name and badge number. If he won't do that, don't give him the letter. Understood? And don't tell anyone about this. Anyone."

"Yes. Of course. Is this something bad?"

Edith thought a moment before answering. "No. I think it's something good."

50

The CIA moved quickly to respond to Volkov's letter. The Support team at the CIA base in Boston checked the letter for fingerprints and other DNA as soon as it arrived, and the base chief immediately sent the hard copy to Washington. By early evening of the day the missive arrived at the Ryan home, a small compartmented team had been created to craft a plan for contacting the Russian. The Europe and Eurasia Mission Center had responsibility for the case, but it was handled by a tight group in what the agency still called Russia House.

Edith Ryan was on a plane from California back to Washington within hours after she had alerted the watch officer at National Resources. An operations officer in the mission center gave her the address of an office building in Arlington and asked her to meet two former colleagues there at nine the next morning. When Edith said she didn't recognize the address, the watch officer told her that it was a clandestine location. "Don't discuss this with anybody, especially within the agency," said the officer from the mission center.

Edith arrived at the Arlington rendezvous wearing a blue suit, a white blouse, and low heels, the kind of bland office uniform that she had adopted in her years at the agency but had dropped when she moved to California. She was dyeing her hair the auburn color it had been when she was young, and she had started wearing glasses, thin black frames, that made her look more youthful.

Looking in the mirror as she dressed that morning, she performed the kind of self-evaluation people do before a college reunion, or a meeting with an old boyfriend. How do I look? Am I one of the cool kids or the losers? She hadn't slept well the previous night. It was partly jet lag, but more, she felt a return of the sense of failure and embarrassment that had surrounded her earlier encounter nearly three decades before with Ivan Volkov.

Tossing in bed, she had thought that perhaps the only thing that she had done right with Volkov was to give him her parents' address. But what could have prompted him to reach out so many years later to a woman he had seemed to regard with such anger in their final days? She badly wanted to know, but she feared she didn't have a "need to know."

* * *

The meeting in Arlington was more like a murder board than a welcome-home party. Two officers from Russia House, a man and a woman, led the conversation. The man identified himself as Jerry Hunt and said he was an operations officer; Edith assumed the name was an alias; the woman, who said her name was Amy Gray, described herself as an analyst. An officer from Support was also in the room; she said she was a polygrapher.

The meeting lasted six hours. They talked from nine to noon, when sandwiches were brought in from a restaurant across the street. The agency team let Edith eat alone, while they retreated to another room to talk over the case. They resumed at one and the questioning continued until four.

The inquisitors asked Edith to review every detail of every interaction she could remember with Ivan Volkov, including every intimate moment of their sexual relationship. Edith told them it was all in the files that had been gathered during two investigations in the 1990s, but they wanted it all over again. They asked her to describe Volkov's meeting with Larry Hoffman, the deep-cover officer who had briefly tried to develop Volkov as an asset. That was surely in the files, too, but they wanted Edith's version.

The Russia House team also queried Edith about a Chinese intelligence officer named Cao Lin. Had Volkov ever spoken about meeting with him? Had he discussed his work on projects with Cao Lin's contacts in the Chinese aero-space industry? Edith said Volkov might have known someone named Cao Lin, and that she had recognized his face in a photograph in an intelligence report she had chanced to see when she worked in S&T. She had asked the East Asia Division for more information about him back then, but they wouldn't explain further.

Jerry Hunt nodded; he wouldn't explain, either.

The two officers pressed Edith, prodding her with events and dates, and she remembered things that had been dormant in her memory. She recalled Volkov's questions after the failure of a Chinese rocket that was carrying an American-made satellite. She remembered how the Russian asked her questions about a crisis that was happening in Taiwan while they were students; he cared little about politics and hadn't known any of the background, but when he realized how seriously the Chinese took Taiwan, he began to read about it in the newspapers.

"Why did Volkov reach out to you now?" The CIA team asked that question at the start of their interrogation, and they came back to it repeatedly later. Had Volkov been in love with her? Yes, Edith told them, he probably had been in love. And she had felt a deep affection for him, too. Had Volkov realized that Edith worked with the CIA? Yes, she told them. He must have realized it. That was part of why he had been so angry. He felt that she had been manipulating him.

Edith said what surely was obvious to all of them. The reason Volkov had written to Edith was that she was the only CIA person for whom he had an address. He didn't want to walk into the U.S. Embassy because he knew he would be spotted. She was his only safe contact point with the agency.

"He's tried to message us before," confided Hunt, the operations officer. "A few weeks ago, when the war started. An anonymous message came in via the website from a VW who was spun up about space. We didn't know how to answer. Last night, doing a scrub in the back room, we realized that it must have been him. He talked about a threat to satellite communications. Do you know anything about that?"

"Satellites were his thing," answered Edith. "He loved to doodle with equations about locating objects in space. He wanted to be a new Kepler."

"Who's Kepler?" asked Hunt.

Edith shook her head. Her former colleagues could be as thick as concrete blocks. They didn't know Volkov, and they didn't understand science. They needed her.

"I want to be part of this operation," she declared. "Ivan contacted me personally for a reason. I'm the person he knows. I can help."

"Hey, I'm sorry," said Hunt. "That won't be possible. We've talked about this. The reason you're the right person is also the reason you're the wrong person. We don't want the wires to get crossed again."

They polygraphed Edith that afternoon, in the final hour of the meeting. They didn't tell her if she had registered deception, but she knew she had passed. She had been honest in every answer; there was nothing more to hide about her relationship with Volkov. And she could tell from the body language of the two officers as they said goodbye that they had relaxed a bit. Edith wasn't going to be part of the operation, but she wasn't going to blow it up, either.

Edith asked if she should stay in Washington and they told her, No, go back to Apollo Labs. There's a war going on. They need you.

*   *   *

Ivan Volkov had been assigned a cryptonym long ago. The Operations Directorate had opened a 201 file on him, back when they imagined that he was a "developmental" in China. Now Russia House logged a new crypt for the operation to contact him. Officers debated whether it was safer to try to arrange a first meeting in Moscow or outside. They knew where he worked now, and it had been easy to find his home address.

But meeting a new recruit in Moscow right now would be like trying to tie a knot in a matchbox. There was no operational space, no freedom of movement. Most of the operations officers in the embassy had been expelled. For the few that remained, the surveillance had become a choke hold. Sending in a deep-cover officer on whom the FSB had no traces, posing as a foreign businessman, say, might have been possible before the war. But nobody got into Russia now. Inviting Volkov to a meeting in Moscow would be like giving him a suicide pill.

"Don't forget, this may be a dangle," Hunt admonished his colleagues. "A guy contacts us out of nowhere, wants to push us information about space war. This could be a phony, start to finish. Plus, the Russians would love right now to catch us in the act, arrest one of our officers and hold him hostage. Better than a woman basketball player, any day."

Colleagues debated the bona fides of Volkov's offer. Nobody disagreed that this was a moment when the Russians would want to feed false information about space operations. America's network of government and commercial satellites was its secret weapon to support Ukraine. The Russians were trying to jam or disrupt that network any way they could, and Volkov's message seemed weirdly timed. He says nothing for more than twenty years, and then, poof, he materializes at a moment of high tension.

Maybe it was a scam, but the consensus among the handful of people told about the case was to find a way to download this Russian space expert and consider what he had to say. The question was how best to do it.

Russia House rejected a meeting inside the country. So the debate turned to ploys that could draw Volkov out of Moscow to a safe place where they could talk with him. The team whiteboarded a half dozen different schemes before settling on one they thought might work: A prestigious, non-American organization should invite Ivan Volkov to a conference in his field of satellite telemetry. The invitation should offer an irresistible chance for Russia to gather useful intelligence.

Jerry Hunt, the officer who would run the operation, flew to France to plan the scenario with a trusted officer in the Paris station. They met in the CIA corner at the U.S. Embassy on Avenue Gabriel. Fortuitously, NASA maintained an office in the embassy to conduct liaison with European space programs. The NASA rep had a security clearance; she was vetted and invited to the meeting, too.

The NASA liaison officer suggested the right convenor. The University of Paris Cité had recently established a space research center at their campus at Grands Moulins, at the southeast edge of Paris. The Paris station had a long-time contact at the university, who affirmed that Cité wanted to make a name in "new space" and connect with the companies that were launching thousands of commercial satellites into orbit.

An urgent meeting was organized between a Cité University dean and an

American "venture investor" who supposedly funded space start-ups. The CIA team devised a proposal for a quick conference on "Tracking and Telemetry of Commercial Satellites in Low-Earth Orbit." Hunt tapped an operational fund to make a covert grant of $200,000 to support the meeting, nominally provided by the American venture capital firm.

The Cité space center loved the idea. Who doesn't want quick money to support a hot research topic? The conference was scheduled for the third week of April at the Cité campus. Hunt's operations team had obtained Volkov's email address at the Lebedev Physical Institute soon after receipt of his letter. Now they used it.

The team crafted an invitation for Volkov and several dozen other global scientists who had published papers on the minutiae of tracking satellites in orbit. They proposed a two-day conference to discuss the particular tracking problems that had emerged as the number of satellites in the low-earth orbit band had proliferated. With the Ukraine war, that was a hot topic for space geeks.

The agency team needed to signal to Volkov that they were answering his message. So, in describing the conference agenda, they included the phrase: "Making Time Stop and Turning North into South." Volkov had used that phrase in his initial anonymous message. Surely he would recognize it now. And he did, evidently. Several days after the University of Paris invitations were emailed, a response arrived from "I. V. Volkov" at the Lebedev Physical Institute, accepting the space center's invitation.

Hunt was delighted and skeptical. He was the sort of intelligence officer who mistrusted anyone who said yes too quickly. He sent a "Restricted Handling" cable to the back room at Russia House saying that he suspected the operation was a Russian dangle. The man who claimed he wanted to provide information had teased the agency once before, several decades ago, and he was doing it again. It was too easy.

But the meeting was set, whether it was a forum for a real sharing of intelligence or a provocation. Hunt and his colleagues began preparing for the covert debriefing of Volkov when he arrived in Paris.

Each step along Volkov's pathway was monitored: Signals collectors at NSA picked up his inquiry to Turkish Airways about connecting flights to Paris. They confirmed two days later that he had made a round-trip reservation for a five-day visit to France. They intercepted his email exchanges with Lebedev Institute colleagues asking if they wanted him to bring anything special back from Paris.

The SIGINT specialists even tracked Volkov's cell phone as he made his way to Kievsky Station just after midnight to catch the Aeroexpress train to Vnukovo Airport. They got worried when the phone's geolocation froze at the passport control line, but after a few minutes' wait, they tracked the phone's movement toward the gate. The watchers registered when Volkov switched his phone to airplane mode as he began his journey to the West—nearly an hour late, but with enough time to make his connection in Istanbul.

* * *

Volkov arrived at Paris Charles de Gaulle just before eight p.m. Sunday night. His delay at passport control at Vnukovo had been ordinary harassment, no more. When his plane rumbled down the concrete runway in Istanbul and lifted into the air, Volkov had let his body relax, at last, and drifted off into several hours of sleep.

The flight landed on a rainy April evening and taxied to the concrete donut of Terminal 1 at Charles de Gaulle. Volkov and the other passengers waited in a long line at passport control. Volkov had to show the passport officer his invitation to the conference and the address of his hotel. When he cleared customs, he bought himself a new French SIM card, to use later if needed. As he stood in the taxi queue, he assumed that people were watching him, perhaps from several different intelligence services.

Volkov checked into an inexpensive hotel near the university campus, which was located on the banks of the Seine in an old working-class district east of the city center. This was not the grand luxe Paris of the guidebooks, but Volkov was excited nonetheless. It was late, but he took the Metro to Notre Dame and then walked to Place de la Concorde. He caught the last elevator ride to the top of the Eiffel Tower and gazed out through the mist at the dazzling quilt of light far below. This was his best cover, that his actions were so completely predictable in a city where he was a stranger.

MONDAY

APRIL 18, 2022

WASHINGTON—*Russia's halting efforts to conduct electromagnetic warfare in Ukraine show how important it is to quickly respond, and immediately shut down, such attacks, Pentagon experts said Wednesday....*

Brig. Gen. Tad Clark, director of the Air Force's electromagnetic spectrum superiority directorate, said modern wars will increasingly involve electromagnetic warfare, particularly to shape the battlefield when conflicts begin.

Dave Tremper, director of electronic warfare for the Office of the Secretary of Defense, pointed to SpaceX's ability last month to swiftly stymie a Russian effort to jam its Starlink satellite broadband service, which was keeping Ukraine connected to the Internet. SpaceX founder Elon Musk steered thousands of Starlink terminals to Ukraine after an official sent him a tweet asking for help keeping the besieged country online.

"The next day [after reports about the Russian jamming effort hit the media], Starlink had slung a line of code and fixed it," Tremper said. "And suddenly that [Russian jamming attack] was not effective anymore. From [the] EW technologist's perspective, that is fantastic ... and how they did that was eye-watering to me."

—DEFENSE NEWS, April 2022

51

When Ivan Volkov's alarm rang at six the next morning, he wondered in the first moment where he was. He showered and shaved. The tap water tasted odd when he brushed his teeth. Russia had its own tastes and smells. Nowhere else was the same. He ate some cereal in the hotel restaurant and then set off for a walk along the Seine before the conference opened at nine. The rain showers of the previous day had stopped, and the morning air had the clean stillness that comes after rainfall.

The conference took place in the university's main academic building, on the site of an old flour mill. A sign posted outside a salon on the first floor announced the gathering: "Tracking and Telemetry of Commercial Satellites in Low-Earth Orbit," and below it, an additional tease: " 'New Space': Tracking a Crowded Commercial Zone." A student assistant checked Volkov's name on her log and registered him as an attendee. She gave him a conference badge to wear around his neck on a tricolor band. As he was about to enter the salon, a dark-haired man in his forties walked toward him.

"Dr. Volkov, I'm Professor Green," he said in English. "We're so glad you're here. We've been waiting for you. Edith Ryan sends you her best wishes."

Volkov smiled broadly at the name and shook the man's hand. This Professor Green was wearing a conference ID, too. With his athletic build and close-cropped hair, he looked more like a military officer than a professor, and, as Volkov scanned the room, he saw several other men, incongruously wearing sunglasses, standing nearby.

"Very good," said Volkov. He hadn't been sure what would happen when he arrived at the conference site, but he was reassured. This man knew about his letter to Edith, and he and the people around him seemed to be professionals.

The man who called himself Professor Green gently steered Volkov by the elbow away from the reception desk toward a nearby door that was marked TEST DIAGNOSTIC—COVID. Volkov resisted at first, he never liked to be pushed anywhere, but then he followed.

"We'll have a talk, you and me," said the American. "But first you need to get your Covid test. Right through this door."

He led Volkov to a masked nurse. "This is Dr. Volkov from Russia. V-O-L-K-O-V. He needs an antigen test."

The nurse gestured for Volkov to take a seat. She swabbed his nose and prepared the test kit. "Just fifteen minutes and we'll have the results," she said, pointing Volkov toward a seat by the wall. Professor Green waited by the door.

Fifteen minutes later, the nurse approached Volkov with a baby-blue surgical mask in her hand and a sorrowful look in her eyes. She stopped three feet from him and extended the mask.

"I regret to inform you, Dr. Volkov, that you have tested positive for the coronavirus. You'll have to quarantine in Paris until you test negative. Until then, you can't attend the conference. We will notify the organizer and the other delegates right away. Do you have anyone who can take you back to where you're staying?"

The American who had brought Volkov to the test center moved toward him and the nurse. He had donned a mask, too. He gave a quick nod to the nurse, who reciprocated.

"I'll take Dr. Volkov back to his hotel. You go notify the folks at the conference that he had to leave," said the American. He turned to Volkov. "Follow me."

They exited the university building by a back door and into a waiting car. As the car pulled away, Volkov looked gravely at the American. "I'm sorry to be sick. I don't have any symptoms. I tested myself yesterday morning before I left Moscow."

The American smiled. "You're fine, Doctor. You tested negative. We just had to get you out of there to someplace where we can talk. Keep your mask on, though. Officially you're sick."

The car took them to Volkov's hotel through a maze of streets in the 13th Arrondissement. As they pulled up to the entrance, the American leaned toward Volkov.

"Here's what I want you to do," the American said. "Walk through the lobby. Take the elevator to your room. Get whatever you need for a night away. Toothbrush, pills, underwear. Put a DO NOT DISTURB sign on the door and then leave. Walk down the stairs to the back door of the hotel, just past the men's and women's toilets. The door opens onto an alley. Another car will be waiting there. A blue Peugeot. He'll take you to a place that's safe. I'll be there when you arrive. Are we cool?"

"Yes, I am, okay, cool. Thank you."

52

The Peugeot transported Volkov along a circuitous route to a building in Montparnasse. The driver didn't speak a word through the twenty-minute journey. He parked the car in the garage and led Volkov to an elevator that lifted him to the seventh floor. The driver escorted the Russian down the hall to a brightly lit but windowless room. A coffee urn and an electric teakettle sat atop a sideboard along with sodas, sandwiches, pastries, beer, and a bottle of vodka on ice.

In the middle of the room stood a wooden table with two hard-back chairs. Sitting in the chair at the far end was the American who had organized Volkov's artful escape from the conference. In the center of the table was a microphone.

"Hello again, Professor Green," said Volkov, taking his chair.

"My name isn't Green," the American answered. "You can call me Jerry Hunt, but that's not my name, either. I work for the Central Intelligence Agency. We organized this meeting because we want to hear what you have to tell us. Sorry for the hocus-pocus at the university."

"It was good. Very smooth. I'm happy to be here."

"So are we. We are pleased that you reached out to us through Miss Ryan. She can't be here, but she sends greetings. Are we okay? Am I talking too fast? We can get a Russian translator for you."

"My English is good enough. I am giving thanks that you found a way to talk safely with me. I trust you." Volkov was not an emotional man, but he spoke each word gravely.

"Okay, so, thank you, Dr. Volkov. Before we begin, let's agree on the next meeting place. If something happens here and we are interrupted, we will meet tomorrow at nine a.m. at Apartment 408, 237 Rue de Montreuil, near Place de la Nation." He handed Volkov a card with the address and told him to memorize it.

Volkov repeated the address twice and handed back the card.

"We should get started."

"Yes, please," said the Russian.

"We know that you sent us an earlier message that we couldn't answer. We apologize for that. To refresh your memory, in the earlier message you said: 'Satellites are your enemies, especially your own. You have sixteen ground monitors and eleven antennas to run your global navigation system. Do you trust it? That is only the beginning. Hidden codes can seem to make time stop—'"

Volkov raised his hand. "Those are my words. I wrote them. You are in danger. This is what I have come to explain."

"Well, then, let's hear it," said Hunt. "We want the information you can give us. You understand, I'm sure, that we have to be careful. Sometimes Russians who want to speak to the CIA are liars. They are sent to deceive us. We try to establish good faith. Bona fides."

"I am not a liar."

"I'm going to assume that, for now. I want to hear your story. All of it. I want you to start with the specific warnings. The urgent stuff. What did you mean when you said, 'Hidden codes can seem to make time stop and turn north into south. They will freeze your world and everything in it'? Be specific."

Volkov took a deep breath and extended his legs. His body was too big for the chair. He tried to speak slowly and carefully, but the words tumbled out.

"I am talking about your Global Positioning System, GPS, and everything that depends on it. I believe it is poisoned by malware. Companies run by China are inside your supply chain. I don't know all the points of entry. But I believe their bad code will warn you about errors in time, location, everything. People will panic. Everything that depends on GPS will be unreliable. Finance.

Airplanes. Communications. Everything will stop, while you try to figure it out. But you won't be able to find what's broken. Because there are no errors. The warnings will be wrong. Unless you listen to me and take action, you will be crippled."

"Whoa! You're going to have to break that down. Start with the Chinese malware. Who makes it?"

"There is a company called Satellite Supply Systems. They are pretty big. I know them because they tried to hire me when I lived in Beijing. And then they tried again when I was in Moscow. And one time after that. You know them, right? They must be in your files."

"I'll ask the questions. You give the answers. Who runs Satellite Supply Systems?"

"One of the founders is named Arthur Wang. I first met him in Beijing when I was a student at Tsinghua University. The man who introduced me to him was a member of the Chinese Academy of Sciences named Professor Cao Lin."

"Does this Mr. Wang work for the Chinese government?"

"I don't know. He talks with Cao. He accepts his money and advice."

"Okay. We'll check those names out. Have you personally met with these two, Arthur Wang or Cao Lin, since then?"

"Yes. I met Arthur Wang last September in Moscow. Cao Lin had contacted me after my son was murdered. Cao asked me to meet Wang. He wanted me to work with him, as he had asked me to do before."

"We'll come back to your son later. Stick with Cao Lin. Had he been in contact with you in the years since you returned to Russia?"

"Yes, several times. As I told you, he wanted me to work with him, or with Satellite Supply Systems."

"But you didn't cooperate."

"Yes, I did. One time. At the request of the special services."

"The FSB, that would be, correct? You were working for them?"

"Yes. Briefly. I had no choice. But Cao Lin broke it off. He said he would wait for a better time. I didn't know what that meant. I think they are working together now. China and Russia. On satellites. Everybody was talking about that in Moscow before I left."

Hunt closed one eye and tilted his head as he asked the next question.

"Why should we believe anything from someone who used to work for the FSB? Are you working for them now?"

"No. But it's Russia. The FSB touches everything."

"Did they send you here?"

Volkov sat up sharply in his chair. "No. Of course not. I risked my life to come here." He shook his head. "You don't believe me."

"Dr. Volkov, we'll decide later what we believe and don't believe. Right now I'm just listening. We're happy you're here. We want to hear your story. Do you want a break? Do you want to use the toilet?"

"Yes, toilet, please." Volkov stood. He was a head taller than Hunt. He relieved himself in the toilet adjacent to the room, returned, and took a cup of coffee and an almond pastry from the array on the sideboard.

"Continue," Hunt said when Volkov was seated again. "Tell me how this malware works."

"I don't know exactly. But the Chinese can get inside the most precious piece of equipment on a GPS satellite. It's called an atomic clock. They keep very precise time. Satellite Supply Systems resells those clocks as a contractor, vendor, I don't know. They sell so many things. You can see their business online. They sell satellite dishes and cables for ground stations. They sell error-correction systems, to back up the clocks. They sell all the little pieces that make the big pieces work."

"This is too technical for me, Doctor. Honestly. I don't know the difference between a Timex and an atomic clock. But we'll get some experts who can talk with you, maybe tomorrow. Right now I need all the actionable intelligence you can share. The stuff that could get people killed."

Volkov was warier now that the CIA man had said he wasn't sure he believed him. The CIA didn't own him, any more than the FSB.

"What do I get if I tell you all these things? Talking to you is treason for me in Russia. I would be killed. What do I get?"

"We'll protect you if we decide your information is accurate and useful. We'll pay you. Maybe we'll find a way for you to leave Russia and find a new home. If we don't believe you or can't use what you're saying, then you can go back home and sort things out for yourself."

"I'm taking all the risk."

"Yeah. But like I said, if we come to an understanding, we'll take care of you. We've done a pretty good job so far, right?"

"Yes, you have." Volkov nodded.

"So, tell me some secrets. Actionable. Real-time. There's a war going on."

"Okay. Real-time. The Russians are working very hard to stop American commercial satellites over Ukraine. They want Chinese help. I don't know if they're getting it. Our institute has been crashing to help with locating the broadband and optical satellites and jamming their signals over Ukraine so the Ukrainians can't see what's on the ground, can't communicate with their troops, all that."

"Did your institute get specific tasking? Coordinates?"

"Yes, all that. It's very technical. I can discuss it with your specialists."

"What's the big thing? The big secret that you know, that can help us?"

Volkov thought a moment. He wanted to give a true answer.

"The big secret is that the Russians need Chinese help in space. China has the tools to stop the commercial satellites. The Russians don't. And if it comes to a big crisis, where Russia may lose in Ukraine, the Chinese have their big trick, that I told you about. Where they make you believe that GPS and all the systems that depend on it, and all the backups, are failing. I call that the 'kill switch,' because the panic would freeze everything in the West."

"The 'kill switch.' Are you kidding me?"

"I am telling you the truth. I tried to say it in code in my message. 'Turn north to south.' 'Freeze your world.' That's what I meant. They have a kill switch."

Hunt nodded. He said he needed to leave the room for a moment to make a call. He exited by a side door to an adjoining office. He was gone for a long while. Volkov drank his coffee and ate his Danish pastry. When he was finished, he poured another cup and took another pastry, this time cinnamon apple.

* * *

Eventually Hunt returned. "Okay, my friend. Business done. I'm your concierge, not just your case officer. I've lined up some people for you to talk with tomorrow, who can make better assessments of all this than I can. How does that sound?"

"Good. Very good. Thank you, Mr. Hunt."

"Right now I want you to continue. Tell me the details of your story. Your time in Beijing. Your jobs. Your son. Your work. All that stuff. It will take us a few more hours. When I'm done, I'll ask you to take a polygraph test that will measure whether you are being deceptive on any of the key things you've told me. Is that acceptable?"

"Yes." Of course it was acceptable. Volkov had no choice.

They began a detailed reconstruction of Volkov's life. Names, places, dates. Information that could be put in the database and checked and cross-checked. It was a journey over the arc of Volkov's lifetime, from his birth in Magnitogorsk to the moment he left his apartment in Moscow and took the train to Vnukovo Airport.

Volkov started cautiously, but he rolled into the narrative. For a quiet, reserved man, there is something about sharing your story that opens a door. The contents spill out. There is a relief in talking about events and people that have gone unspoken.

When they were done with the narrative, Hunt summoned the polygrapher. She was an American woman, round as a bowling ball, with muscular arms and a body that looked like it could withstand a hurricane. She strapped Volkov to her machine and asked some simple questions to establish a baseline. Then she and Hunt walked Volkov back through the elements of his story, asking if he was lying about them, item by item.

It was after seven p.m. when they finished. Volkov was exhausted. Hunt opened the bottle of vodka. Although Volkov wasn't usually a big drinker, he helped Hunt drain the bottle in forty minutes, laughing and talking about sports. Hunt wasn't a hockey player, but he had lived in Washington when it won the Stanley Cup, and he adored Alexander Ovechkin.

A Support officer brought them both a hot meal. Steak and french fries, with a Caesar salad on the side. Volkov devoured it, along with the ice cream they brought him for dessert. When he was finished with his meal, Hunt took him to a bedroom in the suite and told him to get a good night's sleep. Tomorrow would be a busy day.

53

Edith Ryan drove down Route 1 from Santa Monica to her office that Monday morning. She started her trip before the sun came up, just as she did most workdays now. They say war stops time, but really it speeds it up. Every day was a new stack of problems, requirements, queries. She turned on the FM radio, her connection to ordinariness in this stressful time. The country station was playing yet another Luke Bryan song. She switched to an alternative pop station and listened to Lizzo rasping her new song, "About Damn Time." Edith turned up the volume. Yes, ma'am. Exactly right.

Edith was wearing a hoodie, over a black T-shirt and a pair of tight jeans. Her version of fatigues. During her CIA years, she had volunteered for the big stations in Baghdad and Kabul and for the dangerous little bases, too. But she was a bit too old, with a few too many asterisks in her file, and her friends in management told her to stay put in the Directorate of Science and Technology. Supporting the Ukraine war from the ops room at Apollo Space Labs was probably as close as Edith would get to a real deployment.

She turned away from the coastal highway toward the warehouse district where the Apollo campus was nestled. This was the Los Angeles that people didn't imagine. Secretive and unglamorous, closer to a military installation than a film-studio lot. Edith checked her badge with the security man at the entrance to the parking lot, and then again at the space operations center. It was just six-thirty a.m. when she entered her building, but most of the lights were on.

Space was the hidden battlefront. America might not be fighting on the ground in Ukraine, but it was most certainly active in space operations. And Apollo was part of the support team for the U.S. government agencies and the dozens of commercial satellite companies that had become Kyiv's lifeline. That was one of the deep secrets about this war: Beyond the weapons that America was providing, its assistance to Ukraine centered on a public-private technology platform that most people didn't see. Apollo Space Labs, as a "federally funded research and development corporation," could work with both the military intelligence agencies and the commercial companies.

Edith entered the surveillance-protected room known as a Secure Compartmented Information Facility and downloaded the classified overnight message traffic. The broadband satellites of a big American space communications company called MegaZone were being jammed again. The Russians had tried that in the first days of the war with old-fashioned ground jammers, but the company had quickly rewritten its code to bounce its signals among so many frequencies that the Russian jammers couldn't keep up. But this jamming was something new.

Space Command in Colorado Springs proposed a three-way meeting with Apollo and MegaZone the following morning. Edith's task was to prepare brief recommendations about the security of "mesh networks" in space.

Edith closed her office door to concentrate. On the wall was a tacky poster for *The Wild Blue Yonder*, a 1951 movie whose title had appealed to her. Space was supposed to be clean and empty. But it was wild: Cluttered with satellites and debris; laced with electronic signals; menaced by orbiting pirates. People imagined the heavens as the ultimate peace, but it was a war zone.

* * *

Edith went down the hall to make herself a cup of coffee. This was going to be a long day. She took her cell phone into the ladies' room outside the secure area and called the CIA landline of her friend Simone, with whom she had worked in S&T and who had since been promoted to the executive director's office, which had always been a clearinghouse of agency gossip.

Simone was the big sister Edith never had. She knew every detail of Edith's career and personal life. She was the first person Edith had called after she received the letter from Ivan Volkov, even before she called the watch officer in National Resources to get the agency to retrieve Volkov's letter.

"Just checking in," Edith said. "Any seventh-floor chatter about my letter-writing friend? Did he get out of Russia?"

"I don't have anything for you, sweetie," answered Simone. "This is super-tight hold. Restricted handling on all the cable traffic. Even the Ex Dir hasn't been read into it."

"I want to help. I know the Russian guy. I worry about him."

"I understand, Edith. But on this one, keep it zipped. Don't ask me again. This case gives people the willies. I don't know why. Stay clear."

"Got it."

"Love you, 'bye," said Simone. Usually she liked to stay on the phone with Edith awhile, talking with her about men, shopping, cooking. All the important things. But not today.

* * *

Edith took her time walking back to her office, thinking about Ivan Volkov. He had been a continuous baseline in her mind since his letter arrived, playing below the notes of whatever else she was doing. She found herself remembering gestures, silly jokes, the press of him against her when they kissed.

When she had first mentioned him long ago to her handler in Hong Kong, she had described him extravagantly: Handsome, manly, tall, cerebral. "Very Russian," she said several times, even though she had never met a Russian before him, only seen them in movies.

She had been so enthusiastic about the brilliant student she had "spotted" at Tsinghua that her Hong Kong handler had asked at one point, "Are you sure you know what you're doing?" He had explained that in operations, control was essential. Emotional involvement was poison. Edith hadn't understood his warning. She thought she was in control. Near as she could tell, Ivan Volkov adored her. But she had feelings for him, too, and that wasn't control; it was more like love.

Over the years she had thought about him more often than she liked to admit. Part of what had made him special was that beneath the disciplined manner of an ex-athlete and aerospace student, he was sentimental. Once the Tsinghua film society had held a special showing of *Dr. Zhivago*. Volkov had never seen it. As he watched Julie Christie and Omar Sharif and their doomed love, he kept reaching for a Kleenex to wipe the tears away.

In moments like that, Edith had felt an overwhelming attraction to him. She had once blurted out, after an intense conversation, "I could fuck you right now!" He was prudish like most Russians, and unsure what to do. She hastily retreated and told him that it was an American joke, not to worry about it. She had continued drifting toward the edge of the waterfall until that last night, when she realized that she was about to betray both herself and him and finally pushed him away.

She had wondered whether he had forgiven her. Whether he had married someone else, raised a family, lived like an academic prince. It had never occurred to her that he had lived a mostly solitary life, was betrayed by a Russian woman he grew to despise, and fended off other women who thought about money but too little about life. All she really knew was that through it all, he had kept the piece of paper with Edith's contacts and the words, "I'm sorry."

* * *

When Edith returned to the SCIF after calling Simone, a new crisis had erupted in the space domain above Ukraine. Edith and her boss, Anna Friedman, the head of space operations, received an urgent request from one of their commercial clients, a company called VIZZO Systems. The company's chief technical officer wanted an urgent videoconference that morning. Members of Friedman's team bristled; they had projects for other clients.

"There's a fucking war going on!" Friedman told the grumblers. She called Edith into the secure VCR area and had an assistant dial up the numbers. Friedman had just returned from a rock-climbing trip to Yosemite and was limping slightly.

"Hurt?" asked Edith.

"Hell, no," answered Friedman.

The face of the VIZZO chief technical officer came on the screen. He was an Indian American, parents born in Chennai, now on his way to his first hundred million. He had buzz-cut hair, a two-day growth of beard, two piercings in his ear.

"Thanks for doing this on short notice," he said when the screens came into focus. "We have a problem."

"We're listening," said Friedman. She was rubbing her calf as she talked.

"You know the basics on VIZZO, right? We run an earth-observation network. We're one of the biggest private imagery providers to the National Geospatial-Intelligence Agency. As of today, we have eighty-two satellites in GEO and a hundred twenty in LEO. We've got the best commercial coverage right now of Kherson in the south, Kharkiv and Bakhmut in the east, and Zaporizhzhia along the Black Sea coast."

"Understood. You're helping Ukrainians kill Russians. How can we help?" asked Friedman.

"We got hit by a malware attack last night that infected our network and has stopped transmissions from all the satellites in both constellations. This is mission-critical. Our constellations feed the targeters in Germany and the SOF guys at the front."

"What's the malware bug?" interjected Edith. "How was it transmitted?"

"That's the problem. We don't know. We're hardened against malware that could be uploaded through ground systems. We use relay systems that bounce signals among different satellites in the network. Let me be blunt: There was no obvious source of this attack. We've looked and we can't find anything. That's why we called you."

"Let's start with a checklist," said Friedman. "Implanted malware. Malware uploaded from ground stations. Bad code in the original system software and applications. Sleepers in the satellites that someone turned on from the ground. Have you checked all those possibilities?"

"Yup. We've run diagnostics and simulations on each pathway. We've tested the source code using a twin in our software lab, looking for holes or exploits. We've mirrored the failure in our cloud backup to see if we could find the glitch. Nothing, nothing, nothing."

Edith closed her eyes. She put her head in her hands to think for a moment. Her years at S&T had taught her to look for the anomalous explanation, the thing that hadn't been previously observed. She raised her hand.

"What about high-powered microwaves?" Edith asked the CTO.

"Say what?" he replied. He tugged at the ear with the piercings.

"High-powered microwaves. HPM, people call them. They can insert malware if they're close enough. They can put a signal through a brick wall that can disable a laptop. I've seen it tested at you-know-where."

"So, Edith, explain who has high-powered microwaves in space." Friedman nodded to her colleague.

"Well . . ." Edith paused. This was delicate terrain. "The PLA in China has been testing high-powered microwaves for nearly twenty years. They filed their first patents in 2009. They were big clumsy machines back then. But the Chinese are smart enough to figure out how to make small ones that could fit on a satellite. So they could do it. And nobody would see."

"Bad!" said the VIZZO executive. "How can we check it out?"

"Give me a few minutes," said Friedman. "Keep the line open." She stepped out of her videoconference space into another part of the SCIF. She called a number at the Space Command's operations center in Colorado Springs.

"Hey, man," she said confidentially to her contact. "I need a quick count of the number of Chinese satellites that have recently passed within five kilometers of any satellites in the VIZZO constellations, LEO and GEO. I know you track that stuff. We need it. Quick. VIZZO's system has crashed. They have no imagery for Ukraine."

Space Command provided the answer twenty minutes later. Friedman returned to the VCR cubicle and brought Edith and the VIZZO technology chief back on-screen.

"Maybe we have an answer," said Friedman. "In the past forty-eight hours, two Chinese satellites were in range of your sats. Both altered their orbital planes to make these flybys. I'd guess that's the source of your malware."

"That sucks!" said the VIZZO man.

"Definitely," said Friedman. "Can you fix it, if you assume that's how the malware was transmitted?"

"Maybe. Is there any signature for an HPM code?"

Edith thought a moment, back to work she had done at the agency.

"I think so," she said. "I haven't studied this for years, but my recollection is that HPM leaves tags."

"Can you get me details?"

"Let me call someone in Washington and see if we can get it cleared for you to use. If you know where the bad code was inserted in the software, could you rewrite it and create a quick work-around?"

"Probably," answered the CTO. After a moment's thought, he revised that. "Definitely," he said.

Edith gave him a thumbs-up sign.

"Will we ever have any proof that it was the Chinese who hacked us?" asked the VIZZO engineer.

"Microwaves don't carry flags," answered Edith.

"This would be a lifesaver," said the VIZZO engineer. "Not just for us. People on the ground. What do we owe you?"

"I'll save that for accounting," said Friedman.

Twenty-four hours later the VIZZO satellites were back in operation, sending imagery and precise coordinates that allowed Ukrainian artillery and rockets to resume their normal intelligence analysis and targeting of attacking Russian forces. Russia's problems, whatever they were on the opening day of the war, were increasing.

* * *

That day's interaction with VIZZO rang bells in the national security community. From the start of the Ukraine war, analysts had worried that China might assist Russia—perhaps not in obvious ways that would be visible, but hidden assistance in domains where actions couldn't be attributed to China and blame couldn't be fixed.

And with the VIZZO attack, that cascade of events might have begun. The invisible attackers had been blocked this time. After trying to advance on the measureless Go board of space, they retreated.

When Edith called her former CIA colleague in S&T, who had been helpful when she had queried him earlier about the high-powered microwave signatures, he warned Edith not to call again. "The China door is shut. Especially
to you." She tried Simone, but her friend wouldn't answer.

Edith received a secure message late that Monday afternoon. It was nearly
six when the text came through to her in the SCIF. It was from an official in the
National Reconnaissance Office, which worked with top managers at Apollo
Labs. Edith rarely heard from NRO directly, and never from a senior official.
But the text was encrypted uniquely for her.

The message was brief and to the point. "Miss Ryan: Please be more careful
in matters involving China's activities in space. As I told you several years ago
when you were on temporary assignment to the NRO, this is one of the most
sensitive areas for the intelligence community. Let me be frank: It is a matter
of life and death. Don't go poking around. There are things that you do not and
cannot know."

It was signed by Robert Gallant, the NRO deputy director for strategy.

TUESDAY

APRIL 19, 2022

The war in Ukraine has underlined the growing importance of space to armies on the ground.

In an interview with the BBC, the head of the US Space Force, General Jay Raymond, describes it as the "first war where commercial space capabilities have really played a significant role." It's also the first major conflict in which both sides have become so reliant on space.

Gen. Raymond—whose service is the newest branch of the US armed forces—avoids giving precise details of how the US and its allies have been helping Ukraine.

But he gives a clear indication of what it's been doing. "We use space to help strike with precision, we use space to provide warnings of missiles, of any threat that could come to the United States or to our allies or partners," he says.

—BBC News, October 6, 2022

54

Ivan Volkov was awakened Tuesday at seven a.m. in Paris by Jerry Hunt. The Paris weather, always fickle in April, had brightened. Outside the closed cube of the safe house, the buildings were bathed in orange from the rising sun. Hunt didn't look as genial as the night before when he and Volkov had consumed a bottle of vodka together. He was wearing a suit and carrying a small suitcase. Hunt turned on the bright ceiling light. Volkov was at first startled by the glare, then he relaxed and smiled at his handler. He had slept soundly after the vodka and the reassurance that he had done what he intended and delivered his message.

"Wake up, Doctor," said Hunt. "You're going on a little trip."

"*Da*," said Volkov. Yes, of course. He rose, showered, and dressed. Coffee and cold cereal were waiting in the living room. Hunt looked at his watch. "Eat up," he said. "You have a plane to catch."

Hunt handed Volkov a bulky gray coat and a black cap and told him to wear them. He escorted him down the hall to the elevator, which took them to the basement. A blue van was waiting by the elevator. Its windows were shaded gray. The back doors were open, revealing an empty space where the seat would normally be. Hunt took from his coat pocket what looked like a black cloth bag.

"I'm sorry," Hunt said. "Put this over your head."

Volkov did as he was told. Hunt tightened a strap around Volkov's neck so that he couldn't remove the hood. He led him to the vehicle and lowered his body to the floor of the van. Even with the seat removed, it was uncomfortable for the Russian's long legs.

They drove for nearly an hour, along the Périphérique that circles Paris and then north toward Charles de Gaulle. The van exited the motorway at Le Bourget, a smaller airport that handles private jets. At the perimeter, the driver showed an embassy credential and diplomatic passport, and the van was cleared to drive onto the taxiway to where a Gulfstream jet was parked. The plane was unmarked except for its tail number.

The van parked alongside the boarding ramp. Hunt opened the vehicle doors to shield the hooded passenger from view. He helped Volkov up the ramp and into the plane. Still hooded, Volkov was placed in a seat.

"Can you please take the hood off now?" the Russian asked through the muffle of the fabric.

"No," answered Hunt. "Not possible."

*　*　*

The Gulfstream jet landed sixty minutes later at a small airport in Gloucestershire, northwest of London. In the parking area off the runway was another Gulfstream, also unmarked. Near it were two large helicopters.

Volkov was bundled into another van. This time he was allowed to sit on the bench seat.

"Where am I?" Volkov asked from under the hood.

"Another country," said Hunt. "You aren't here, officially. You aren't anywhere, really."

The van rumbled out of the perimeter of Gloucestershire Airport toward the old spa town of Cheltenham. In the far distance stood the Promenade and the Pump Room, where fine ladies and gentlemen came for the mineral baths in Regency times. But that wasn't the town's premier attraction now.

Volkov was silent, struggling to make sense of what was happening. He was a captive. How had that happened? The day before, he had been treated with respect, as a source of useful information who had bravely traveled from

Russia. Now he was wearing a black hood in a place whose location nobody would disclose.

"What have I done?" shouted Volkov. "I came here to help you, Mr. Hunt. You welcomed me. Now you act like I am a member of Al Qaeda. Why am I a prisoner?"

Hunt didn't answer. Volkov sat in blinded, manacled silence for the rest of the short trip.

On the outskirts of Cheltenham loomed an immense building; it was so bizarre amid the verdant English countryside that it at first seemed a mirage. An immense circular ring of offices enclosed an inner courtyard so that the structure resembled a giant automobile tire, or perhaps, as locals described it, a donut. It was clad in sleek silver-gray metal.

This strange, forbidding building housed the headquarters of GCHQ, the British communications intelligence agency and heir to the celebrated codebreakers of Bletchley Park. Its very existence had been a secret until the 1960s. Now it almost screamed its presence as Britain's palace of electronic espionage.

The van stopped briefly at the gate, where Hunt displayed his credentials. The vehicle dipped down a rampway that passed beneath the giant oval. In the bowels of the building, two British security guards removed Volkov from the vehicle and escorted him to an elevator that took him to an upper floor. He was seated in small room that faced large opaque glass. Volkov's hood was finally removed, but all that he could see was the reflective pane of the one-way mirror.

55

Ivan Volkov steadied himself. This was what special services did, everywhere. They operated behind opaque panels. They were an engine of disrespect. That didn't matter now. The only thing he cared about, even after the ordeal of his travel that morning, was that the members of this group, whoever they were, should believe him and take action.

He waved awkwardly to the invisible inquisitors.

"Hello," he said. "I am Ivan Vladimirovich Volkov."

Volkov's interrogators sat silent on the other side of the one-way mirror. Hunt had taken the chair on the far left. He was the junior member of the team. Next to him was Joan Nevil, a senior CIA counterintelligence officer. Beside her was Robert Gallant from the National Reconnaissance Office. The last figure in the front row was a military officer wearing the cross-buttoned uniform of the U.S. Space Force. Behind them were representatives of Britain's Secret Intelligence Service, better known as MI6, and GCHQ, the agency that was hosting this hastily assembled meeting.

Hunt spoke first. His voice, like those of the others, was amplified through speakers into Volkov's room.

"Dr. Volkov," Hunt began, "we have brought you here because some senior officials of the United States government would like to ask you some questions. They have all been briefed on what you told me yesterday. Obviously we have some concerns that we need to resolve."

Joan Nevil, the counterintelligence officer, opened the questions. Volkov couldn't see her through the opaque glass, but she was tall and slender, with the poise of a woman who had been a dancer long before she joined the secret world. She retained a ballerina's insistence on precision and an intolerance for the detail that didn't match: a foot in the wrong place, a gesture out of synch with the musical score.

"Let me explain something, Dr. Volkov," Nevil said. "In the intelligence world, we await people like you who come to us with secrets. They sustain us. But we also treat them with caution, because very often they turn out to be controlled agents, false friends, who intend to mislead us or disrupt our operations. Sometimes such false agents are unwitting and are being used by others. We must be careful. Do you understand what I am saying, Dr. Volkov?"

"Yes, madam. I do."

"That's reassuring. Now, then, let me ask you: Have you ever worked with the Russian or Chinese intelligence services?"

Volkov looked at the frosty glass, covered with reflective tape. What was the answer?

"Yes, I probably worked with both, sometimes witting, sometimes not."

"Tell us the details, please."

"Well, first the Russians. In Beijing, in 1995, a Russian Embassy officer named Krastev wanted me to work against the Chinese. I said no. When I returned home to Russia in 1996 after my mother died, someone in my hometown, Magnitogorsk, wanted me to stay in Russia and the special services arranged for me to rejoin Moscow State University, which I had left before because I had no money. Later the same Krastev from Beijing, who had returned to Moscow, pressured me for information, and I gave him some, yes. I was broke. Finally, I told him no, I refused a specific request, and he told me I would regret it." He paused, gathering his thoughts.

"And you served a sentence in prison, is that correct?"

"Yes." They knew everything, it seemed. "I was a fool. I needed money for this crazy wife I had married, and I offered to smuggle something from Helsinki. I was caught, of course, and again, it was Krastev who offered to rescue me, for a price. I was to do secret work in an institute. A scientist, but not quite, if you know what I mean."

"Not really. You are a scientist, or you are not."

"Please, this was Russia."

"Let's move on. What did Krastev and the others ask you to do?"

"They wanted information about China. A Chinese professor had tried to find me a job in Beijing when I was a graduate student there. He saw something in me, I suppose. He tried to hire me again when I went back to Moscow, several times. Krastev told me to accept one of his offers, as a way to gather information about China. I agreed, and I asked this professor questions to see what they knew about the American GPS system. But I think the professor realized that I was under control of the Russians, and he ended contact."

"Tell me about this Chinese professor," demanded Joan. Her voice had tightened a notch.

"His name was Cao Lin. He said he was a member of the Chinese Academy of Sciences. He knew everyone in the Chinese scientific establishment. He seemed, how to say, his own man. People did what he wanted. He gave me a very generous gift. A first edition of a book by Johannes Kepler. My hero. The Russians took it from me, of course."

"So did you work for Cao Lin?"

"Not really. He asked many times. He wanted me to join an American company that was founded by a man named Arthur Wang. A very American Chinese man. He came to see me last fall in Moscow. I told all this to Hunt."

"I want to hear it again," said Joan. "Did you ever talk to people about your relationship with Professor Cao Lin or Arthur Wang?"

"Not really. I mean, the Russian services knew Cao wanted to hire me when he sent me the book. They tried to play me. But I don't think they knew when Wang came to Moscow in September."

"Did you think Cao and Wang were Chinese agents?"

"Yes, of course. Cao was connected to everyone. Wang, because he was so American, I thought at first maybe he was CIA. Then I realized he must be working with the Chinese, because he was so close to Professor Cao. But really, madam, this isn't my business. I am better at solving equations than following these spy games."

"And you never reported to anyone that Arthur Wang had come to you last year with a message from Professor Cao."

"No. I was very angry with Russia by then. They had killed my son."

"And what was Wang's message, exactly?"

"He wanted my help. Let me restate that. Professor Cao wanted my help. They were selling atomic clocks for satellites, along with their other equipment. Atomic clocks don't work without, we call it, 'error correction.' They have to be the same as the receiver clocks on earth. Professor Cao wanted my assistance. That's when I began to understand the danger."

A new voice intervened in the conversation. It was the man Gallant from the NRO.

"What threat are you talking about, Dr. Volkov?" His voice had the smooth finish of polished leather.

"Maybe danger is the wrong word. Risk. I know about atomic clocks because I worked on the Russian positioning system, GLONASS. And I know that without the error-correction process, the clocks would be unreliable. That's why all the satellite architectures have so much, what, extra things."

"Redundancy," offered Gallant.

"Yes, just as you say. So I began to think, Why would Professor Cao and his Chinese friends want my help with error correction? What are they doing with their company that can touch every part of the space networks?"

"Satellite Supply Systems is the name of the company, I believe."

"Yes, whatever. It's theirs, Cao and the Chinese. Why did he care so much about correcting these atomic clocks that he would reach out to me in Moscow? And the more I thought about it, it was obvious that Cao wanted the capability, yes, to disrupt that system and bring down global positioning. So I asked myself: How would they do it, if everything in these systems is so protected? And then I realized: They don't have to break it. They just have to make it look like it's broken."

"You are a clever man, Mr. Volkov. I will say that. Did you tell anyone about your theory?"

"Just you. The CIA. In my message."

"My goodness. That's hard to imagine. You're a Russian. By your own admission, you have worked on numerous instances with your country's security services. Why would you decide to share this big secret with the United States? And why would you implicate this man in particular, Cao?"

"I wanted to tell America because, I will be frank, I hate Russia's leaders. They killed my son, but really, they killed my country. And now they are allied with China. They say it out loud. 'No limits.' They are trying to destroy little Ukraine, and next it will be somewhere else. Taiwan, Estonia. India. I don't know."

"Well, that is admirable," said Gallant. "But it is not credible."

Volkov bowed his head. For the first time that day, he felt he had truly hit a wall.

"What can I say?" he answered quietly. "If you don't believe me, I am ruined."

Gallant waited a few moments before responding.

"We have to protect ourselves, Mr. Volkov. That is the law of life. Let me return to something that you said earlier. You were talking about Professor Cao and Satellite Supply Systems. Did you identify anyone else in this company, other than Arthur Wang?"

"No, sir."

"Do you know any of the people in the Chinese space program, other than Professor Cao?

"Not really. I met some people when I was studying in Beijing. I had a part-time job at the Academy of Space Technology, so I met people there. But the only person I knew well was Professor Cao."

"And why did you two get along, do you suppose?" asked Gallant.

"Because I respected him. I thought he wasn't a party hack, like some of the others. He introduced me to one of China's great scientists, Chen Fangyun. He told me once that he thought we were 'kindred spirits.' He was flattering me, I guess. I thought he wanted a better China, like I wanted a better Russia. I was stupid. What can I say? He wanted to use me."

"Yes, evidently he did," said Gallant. He went silent for a moment.

"Who did you tell in Russia about Professor Cao?"

"I talked with Krastev, after Professor Cao sent me the Kepler book. Krastev wanted me to work with him to get information about the Chinese."

"But did he want information about Cao in particular?"

"Not so much. Russians are, I am sorry to say, quite racist when it comes to Chinese people, sir. They don't distinguish very much."

"And you don't think that Krastev was trying to recruit Cao, or blackmail him in some way, when he suggested that you work with him."

"He wanted intelligence. That's what he said. China makes Russia nervous. Krastev and the others wanted to understand what China was doing in space."

"Very well." Gallant cleared his throat. "I think that's all from me."

"Let's talk about Ukraine," proposed a new voice. It was the U.S. Space Force representative. He asked Volkov detailed technical questions about the work the Lebedev Physical Institute had done since the Russian invasion in February. He was particularly interested in jamming operations against commercial satellite providers, like VIZZO and MegaZone, that were operating over Ukraine,

Volkov told the Space Force officer everything he knew, but the American seemed disappointed that his knowledge was limited.

"Shouldn't you be able to give us more information, Mr. Volkov? Your institute had some of the best brains in Moscow."

"This is Russia. I'm sorry. Nothing works the way it's supposed to. Maybe that's on purpose. I don't know."

Volkov shook his head. It was as if he had brought a gift, but it wasn't enough. Or, worse, that the people to whom he had given the gift thought for some reason that there was a bomb inside.

The questions continued for another ninety minutes. Volkov was tired. He hated speaking in this closed box of a room to people he couldn't see, who were able to watch his every fidget and gesture. He tried to cooperate, but his voice was weakening, and he worried that he was repeating himself, or in his fatigue unintentionally contradicting something he had said earlier.

The Space Force representative wanted more details on technical issues, involving the satellite projects of the Lebedev Physical Institute and Roscosmos. He asked about GLONASS capabilities.

Joan Nevil, the CIA counterintelligence officer, posed a long string of questions about his interaction with Edith Ryan that concluded with a blunt query: "Were you in love with her?"

"Yes, maybe," answered Volkov. "That was why it hurt me when I realized that she was working with the CIA."

"The CIA is the enemy for you, isn't it, Mr. Volkov?"

"I didn't think so. That's why I contacted you. Now I don't know who are my friends and who are my enemies."

"Yes, it's perplexing, isn't it?" said Nevil. The tone in her voice was almost mocking. "That's our problem, too."

56

The interrogation of Ivan Volkov finished in late afternoon. Jerry Hunt looked at his colleagues, who nodded that they had the information they needed. Hunt came back on the speaker. "Thank you, Mr. Volkov. Please remain in your seat." The Americans retired to a private conference room to confirm their decision. Then the senior officials departed GCHQ headquarters for the airfield a dozen miles away and their flight back to Washington on their unmarked government jet.

Hunt opened the door of the interrogation room and walked toward Volkov, who had been resting with his head in his hands. He asked the Russian to sit up, and then he placed the hood back over his head. Volkov rose unsteadily. He was weak in mind and body. He asked to use the toilet, and Hunt walked him down the hall to a men's room. "Piss or shit?" he asked.

"Shit," said Volkov. Hunt opened a stall, unbuckled the Russian's trousers, pulled them down, and sat him on the seat, still hooded. It was a level of personal humiliation that Volkov, in all his days, had never experienced.

"What have I done?" he asked plaintively, waiting to clear his bowels.

Hunt didn't answer.

"Close the fucking door," Volkov said. Hunt retreated, and Volkov could hear the sound of the latch closing.

Hunt marched Volkov back to the van, which took him to the Gulfstream jet. The Russian slept for most of the flight back to Le Bourget in Paris and awakened only when the airplane wheels skidded against the runway. The van with the missing seat was waiting at the bottom of the ramp, and Hunt guided Volkov down the steps and toward his place on the floor of the vehicle.

When they reached the security gate to exit Le Bourget, Volkov thought to cry out for help. But he knew that could begin a cascade of events that would end with him in prison, or worse.

As the van accelerated on the motorway, Volkov moved to a seated position. He turned toward the front and spoke as loudly as he could at the end of this dreadful day.

"I am helpless," he said. "What are you going to do with me?"

"We're going to throw you back into the stream," answered Hunt. "Let you swim home."

"They will kill me in Russia."

"Maybe. Or maybe they'll give you a medal. We just don't know, do we?"

"I know. My flight back to Moscow leaves Friday. If I'm not on it, they will find me and bring me back."

"That's not our problem. It's your problem."

Volkov felt a sadness beyond words. He had been courageous. He had risked his life. And he was being spurned. Worse than that, humiliated and then discarded.

"Why don't you believe me? I don't understand. Your people talked as if I were threatening them. I'm doing the opposite."

"Hey, Mr. Volkov, I didn't make the decision. Whatever it is you're selling, my colleagues didn't want to buy it. Maybe they just don't like you."

Volkov was silent. He listened to the whir of traffic as they reached the Périphérique and drove southeast. When the van exited the highway into the city, slowly and stopping at lights, Volkov spoke up.

"Where are you taking me?"

"Back to your hotel. Home again. I have a Covid test, so you can show everyone that you're negative."

The van came to a stop a few minutes later. Hunt stepped into the back and removed Volkov's hood. They were parked in a dark alleyway. He handed Volkov the Covid test and pointed toward a building two hundred yards away.

"That's your hotel," he said. "You still have your key card for the room?"

"Yes," said Volkov.

"All right, then." He patted Volkov on the back. "Happy landings, brother."

Hunt walked back to his van, which sped off down the alley.

Volkov steadied himself. The clock was ticking. He had worried before that he had five days to share his secret before the Chinese could use their kill switch to disorient the West as the Ukraine war deepened. But now he was focused simply on staying alive.

What was the next move? Volkov had played chess games like this, where the slide toward checkmate seemed inevitable but could sometimes be averted through bold strategy. He needed to recalibrate. He walked back into the hotel, dressed in the baggy coat and black cap that Hunt had given him so early that morning. He entered the front door and walked to the elevator. Nobody stopped him.

The DO NOT DISTURB sign was still hanging from his doorknob. But when Volkov entered the room, he could see that someone had searched it. A curtain was askew. The alignment of his suitcase on the luggage rack was different. He sat on the bed, thinking about his options.

After many minutes had passed, Volkov rose and took his wallet from his pocket. He opened it and removed an old piece of paper, so worn by time that the words were fading.

Atop the sheet Edith Ryan had written her home address in Holyoke, Massachusetts. At the bottom was an apology. In the middle, so long ago, Edith had written a telephone number.

57

Edith Ryan was summoned to an urgent early morning meeting at Apollo
Space Labs. MegaZone, the broadband satellite network that was the Ukrainian military's lifeline and also an Apollo client, was in trouble. Its new ground
terminals in Ukraine weren't working. The invisible satellite war in the heavens
above Ukraine was escalating, and Russian jammers had found a way to choke
the signals on which the Ukrainians depended for their survival.

Edith arrived at six a.m. on Tuesday to prepare for the video conference
with MegaZone. She wore her version of dressy, a blouse and sweater. She
would be presenting a brief primer on the security of the "mesh networks" used
by MegaZone. She wanted to get it right, especially after the sharp message
she had received the night before from Robert Gallant, the deputy director at
NRO. She didn't understand the forces at play in the shadow war in space, but
she wanted to be careful.

Edith knew the order of battle: MegaZone was as important to Ukraine as
artillery and ammunition. The company had quietly joined the industry giant
Starlink soon after the war began in providing broadband internet service. At
first MegaZone had just a few receivers deployed forward near the front. But
in April, as Ukraine prepared a counteroffensive, it had pushed thousands of

terminals into Ukraine to receive more signals. The system was beautifully designed. It had such low power requirements that it could run on a car battery; sometimes it could even operate through an automobile's cigarette lighter.

The MegaZone constellation dazzled Edith as a piece of engineering. The company had more than a thousand satellites operating in space, on twenty different orbital planes. The satellites in this incredible ever-spinning gyroscope communicated with each other through laser signals that created a "mesh network" linking each individual satellite with all the others. The laser signals moved back and forth, creating an interdependent router system in space.

This magnificent space network had been crippled by something agonizingly simple: The new MegaZone terminals in Ukraine couldn't be turned on. Once the signals were actually flowing from space to ground, they could connect targeters with armed drones and artillery and rocket launchers. For a desperately outgunned Ukrainian army, this software connectivity was a matter of survival. But the new terminals weren't connecting with the satellites, and the company wasn't sure why.

Edith joined Anna Friedman in the secure videoconference space just before ten a.m. MegaZone was based in Oregon, in the same time zone, but the call was joined by a MegaZone engineer in Germany, too.

The MegaZone team leader was named Max. He had a frizz of curly hair and a chin-puff goatee. He was wearing a Hawaiian shirt with an American flag pin on one lapel and a button that read NEED TO KNOW on the other. He looked as if he hadn't slept in a week. He got right to the point.

"We have a new Russian jamming problem," said Max. "We can't turn on our new receivers. Our sats are beaming the signals, but the new terminals we sent in aren't picking up the signals. They're just dead boxes."

"Oh crap," said Anna. "Are you sure?"

"Very sure. And it's not normal jamming where you overwhelm the signal with noise. We beat that when the war started by jumping frequencies. Now they're trying something different."

"Like what?" asked Anna.

"The Russians are jamming GPS signals over Ukraine. Big-time, not like at the beginning of the war. Most Ukrainian applications can switch to other navigation systems, like Galileo or BeiDou. But not ours."

"Why do you care about GPS? You're MegaZone. You have your own time and position signals, right?"

"Yes, but there's a stupid, mundane problem. Our terminals need to register with our system to get turned on, so they can receive the broadband signals from the sats. For registration, we geolocate them with GPS signals, so we have an address and can confirm who's getting what. We need the location information for boring things like billing customers."

"Why not recode the software in the receivers, so they can register via Galileo?"

"We thought of that. But it's too much code. We can't transit that much data to the receivers because they're not connected to our broadband system, right? It's like trying to stream video when you have three bars on your phone. No can do. We can only send very simple messages."

"Meaning that you can't turn the terminals on because they're not already 'on.'"

"Correct," said Max. "We can't do it the 'right' way. So we're looking for crazy ideas. Off-the-wall stuff."

Anna looked at Edith. As a graduate of the CIA's Directorate of Science and Technology, she was the resident expert in off-the-wall solutions.

Edith moved her chair closer to the camera.

"Hi, folks, I'm Edith Ryan. I worked for a three-letter agency in another life. I'm not as wild in the creative department as I should be, but I had one thought while I was listening. It's probably dumb. You guys are the A-team."

"Nothing's dumb. Right now we're fucked. What's the idea?"

"Well, why don't you just turn off the code that requires the receivers to register themselves before they receive signals? Can you do that?"

"That would be, like, free signals. No registration. No nothing."

"I guess so. But someone in the government would probably pay you. And if they don't, so what? It's a war, right? The Ukrainians need those signals."

"The Russians will crap in their pants. They've warned us not to provide signals that could be used for drones or targeters. The Chinese will be pissed, too. They don't want the Russians to lose."

"Tough shit," said Anna. "You don't work for the Russians or Chinese."

"Not yet."

"Could you do the override, technically?" asked Edith.

Max tugged on his chin puff. "Yes. I mean, hell, yes! It will take a quick audible, but it's simple once we figure out how to push out the override."

"Well, let us know," said Anna.

"We'll get back to you. Or maybe we won't. Thanks, Eleanor."

"It's Edith. Don't mention it. Just win the war."

By noon, Max and his team had begun sending the simple signals that switched off the MegaZone terminals' usual activation requirements. They weren't "registered" in the system, but they worked just fine. The signals were flowing once more to the Ukrainian military, supplementing Starlink, and the Russians and their Chinese friends had been frustrated again in space.

*   *   *

Late that crazy afternoon, the small galaxy of people who carefully followed space systems had a new worry. Space Command in Colorado Springs reported that a half dozen Chinese satellites had begun repositioning their orbits. Movements take time in space, and the operational significance of the new orbits wasn't clear yet. But this was what an adversary would do if it was planning an offensive maneuver. It was the equivalent of raising the alert status.

Edith and her boss Anna Friedman weren't cleared for all the intelligence, but they could see much of it. Their own space-tracking systems, displayed on the giant screen in the Ops Lab, showed the movement of the Chinese satellites.

Maybe it was a bluff, or an exercise. But at midday, the National Security Agency sent an urgent alert summarizing new signals intelligence from China that the PLA Strategic Support Force command had held an urgent meeting. The intel summary provided to Apollo Space Labs didn't give any details, just the ominous evidence that as Russia stumbled in Ukraine, China might be preparing deniable support activities in space.

The Pentagon's first move was to secure the systems on which the United States depended, especially GPS. The network had experienced some minor wobbles over the past twelve hours, but no more than would be caused by sunspots.

Still, the Pentagon decided to sound a quiet warning. The committee that oversees GPS sent a request for a security update to a United Nations organization that coordinates satellite systems so that one network can back up another when a glitch happens. The committee notified GPS, Galileo, BeiDou, and GLONASS to check security. Engineers were instructed to report any problems in their systems immediately.

It was the satellite version of a police BOLO notice. Be on the lookout.

* * *

Through the late afternoon, in the most secret enclaves of the U.S. government, the concerns continued to mount. The Chinese satellites kept moving position. Some of them were transiting toward orbits that, within twenty-four hours, would bring them close to commercial satellites in the VIZZO and MegaZone constellations—and also close to several critical U.S. intelligence-collection satellites.

NSA reported that afternoon, in an intelligence brief that was restricted to a few dozen of the most senior U.S. officials, that top Russian and Chinese security officers had been conferring about the deteriorating situation in Ukraine. The Russians had pleaded for help in halting Ukraine's advance, and Chinese officials were considering the request.

* * *

Wars begin with ambiguous actions. They can be feints, or they can signal actual "preparation of the battlefield." The agony of being a national security planner is that you often don't know which. If you act too quickly, you can trigger the very crisis you hope to avoid. If you delay, it may be too late for action.

Washington had no "hotline" for crisis communication with Beijing. But in this instance, the White House tried to invent one. The chairman of the Joint Chiefs of Staff called his Chinese counterpart to inquire about "unusual Chinese satellite movements." The Chinese general declined to take the call. The White House inexorably moved up the ladder to the next rung.

The National Security Council ordered Space Command to begin preparations for possible offensive and defensive actions by U.S. satellites and ground systems. The initial campaign measures were part of a careful playbook: Deploy space jamming systems; deploy low- and high-energy laser systems; begin moving satellites to "perch" positions, from which they could attack.

The options in the "Notional Space Attack Scenario" prepared for the président included one that was captioned: "Conduct intentional near miss as warning." The president ordered Space Command to prepare this anti-satellite warning shot, but he didn't pull the trigger. Yet.

The Pentagon also raised the broader alert status for U.S. conventional and nuclear forces—not all the way to DEFCON 1, called "Cocked Pistol," but to DEFCON 2, known as "Fast Pace," where U.S. forces could deploy within six hours if necessary.

None of this was visible to the public. But the Chinese and Russians would see the changes.

* * *

One more unusual notification was made late that Tuesday. The Pentagon sent details of the Chinese satellite movements and the worrying NSA signals intelligence to a very senior delegation of officials aboard a Gulfstream jet that was returning from a brief trip to England. Because the information was top secret and compartmented, it was transmitted on the government's most secret channel, known by the anodyne designation the Joint Worldwide Intelligence Communications System.

Robert Gallant from the NRO, who led the team aboard the Gulfstream, received the JWICS message first. He immediately contacted Space Command in Colorado Springs and the National Security Council at the White House. Gallant urged them to delay any response until the Gulfstream landed and he could join senior officials in the Situation Room. The United States had an operational capability, unknown even to the most senior officials, that would be useful in this crisis.

Gallant made other secure calls in the remaining hours before the flight landed, to make sure that key assets of the United States were protected.

* * *

Edith stayed late at her office in Manhattan Beach, trying to do some additional work on anti-jamming measures that might be useful for MegaZone. She had left the SCIF and was sitting at her desk in the main building of the space operations center when her phone rang. It was a distant voice, but with a sudden shiver, she recognized it.

"Hello, Miss Edith? This is Ivan Vladimirovich Volkov. Your mother gave me this number."

She tried to respond, but the words caught in her throat, blocked by joy, shame, and fear. All that came out was, "Hello."

And then: "Where are you? Are you all right?"

"I need help," said the Russian voice. "I am in France. But I am not all right."

"What's wrong? They have your letter. I gave it to them."

"Your friends won't listen to me. They treat me like a Russian spy. They must think I have been sent to deceive them. It's not true."

Edith's voice choked for a moment.

"Of course it's not true. I read the letter. I know you. What can I do?"

"Help me," he said. "Talk to your friends."

"I don't think they'll listen to me. They've shut me out of anything that involves you. Maybe I can find someone who can help you. Where can you go now?"

"Maybe only Moscow. The French won't help me, I am sure. The Americans will tell them I am a Russian spy. My ticket back home is Friday. I feel that I am a dead man. I don't know what to do. I don't know."

Edith deliberated, but only for an instant. This was her chance to undo the past.

"I'll come to Paris," she said. "I'll get you out."

"Is it possible? It's too much. Can you?"

As Edith talked, she had been checking her phone for flights to Paris from LAX. There was an Air France flight that left at 9:00 that night. She was close enough to the airport that she could just make it. The flight arrived at 4:50 the next afternoon. She had her passport in her purse, where she always kept it.

"Listen to me, Ivan: I can be in Paris tomorrow afternoon. I'll meet you at seven p.m., after I clear passport control and take a taxi into the city. We need a secure location. Someplace where two people can talk."

She paused, as she tried to remember quiet locations in Paris. After a moment, she was back.

"There's a restaurant near the Eiffel Tower. It's called the Fontaine de Mars, on a street called Rue Saint-Dominique. You can sit outdoors, and it will be dark then. Face away from the street. I'll meet you there at seven tomorrow night. Try to make sure that nobody follows you. Okay? We'll figure out what to do then."

"I want to say, from my heart . . ." He couldn't finish the sentence.

"Turn off the location services button on your phone. In fact, turn off the phone. Now. I have to go, or I'll never make my flight. Goodbye until tomorrow."

Edith ended the connection. As she rushed out of the office, Anna Friedman called out to her, asking where she was going.

"A quick trip. I'll be in touch," said Edith. She started running toward her car in the parking lot. It had taken more than twenty-five years, but she was finally going to do right by someone she had wronged.

WEDNESDAY

APRIL 20, 2022

We would like to underline an extremely dangerous trend that goes beyond the harmless use of outer space technologies and has become apparent during the events in Ukraine. Namely, the use by the United States and its allies of the elements of civilian, including commercial, infrastructure in outer space for military purposes. It seems like our colleagues do not realize that such actions in fact constitute indirect involvement in military conflicts. Quasi-civilian infrastructure may become a legitimate target for retaliation.

—KONSTANTIN VORONTSOV, Russian Foreign Ministry, statement at
United Nations, September 12, 2022

58

Ivan Volkov was afraid to stay in his hotel. He was afraid to check in anywhere else. So he slept under a big shrub in the rambling Bois de Vincennes, in the eastern part of Paris near where he had been staying. He didn't check out of the hotel. He just left by the back door. He turned up his coat collar and pulled down his cap and walked, staring at the ground, across the bridge that spanned the Seine near the university and along a road toward the park entrance. The park closed at eight. Volkov had to jump a fence at a far corner where the surveillance cameras might not see him.

He skirted the shadows until he found a place deep in the woods, shielded by a thick overhang of foliage, and made a space for himself in the brush. The earth smelled of mulch and decay. Volkov laid out his big coat on the ground and wrapped himself in a sweater. It was almost comfortable. He had camped in places like this with his father, running away to the wilderness beyond the Ural River to escape the smoky air and the party bosses and all the other things his father despised about Soviet life but didn't dare to challenge.

Volkov awoke with the sun. He dusted the leaves and dirt from his clothes and walked a few dozen yards to another part of the enclosure to relieve himself. He found a water fountain a hundred yards away, along a gravel path, where he brushed his teeth and gave himself a sponge bath with one of his undershirts. Then he returned to his hideaway to think.

His phone had exploded in the days before he had turned it off, with text messages and missed calls and voice mails. First they came from his boss at the Lebedev Physical Institute, then from the Lebedev security officer, and finally from the FSB officer who had taken over his file when Krastev died.

They must know he was on the loose. They had surely noted his absence from the conference on "Tracking and Telemetry of Commercial Satellites in Low-Earth Orbit," which they had allowed him to attend. They had searched his room. They must have realized the day before that he was missing, but it would take them a while to start looking in earnest. They would need permissions and cross-departmental clearances. It was Russia.

Volkov knew he was a hunted man. He suspected that his enemies were coming from at least three directions: The Russians, certainly; the Americans, probably; the French, alerted by both the Russians and Americans, very likely. Perhaps the Chinese were hunting him, too; maybe Cao Lin thought this was his chance to kidnap Volkov back to Beijing.

Invisibility was Volkov's best protection until he was able to meet Edith Ryan that night. He would hide in the Vincennes woods as late as he could. But it's hard to disappear in public spaces. The French were annoyingly fastidious about their parks, and just after nine a.m., a gardener in a green suit saw Volkov in his lair and told him to move on.

Volkov traversed the park, a mile east, a half mile north, then back. He was famished but didn't dare approach the food vendors; he drank water from fountains along the main pathways. His ambling carried him past noon. With the warm sun overhead, he found a sheltered spot in the woods and slept for an hour until he was roused by another park attendant who assumed he was a vagrant and told him to leave.

Volkov walked as slowly as he dared toward the exit. When he got there it was three p.m., and he still had four hours before his meeting with Edith. He saw the beaux arts decoration of a Metro station at the southwestern corner of the park. He started down the stairs, but as he neared the bottom, he could see two members of the French national police, in their baby-blue shirts and round caps, checking the papers of people entering the subway.

The Russian edged out of view and quickly climbed back up the stairs. He was truly hunted now.

Volkov chose a zigzag route west across the city. His real enemies were the surveillance cameras on every block. He turned his cap inside out and pulled the brim down to his nose. He walked in the shadows and hoped he would be lucky.

*   *   *

Edith boarded her flight at LAX dressed in the same blouse and sweater she had worn to work that morning. In her tailored blue and white she looked like one of the Air France flight attendants.

Edith had bought a seat in business class so she could relax and think in private. Now, in the perfect anonymity of her cubicle, she pondered what must happen in the hours ahead. She would need somewhere for Volkov to stay after they met. Sneaking him into a hotel would be risky, and also emotionally jarring for them both.

What hideaway existed in Paris? She didn't dare contact the American Embassy. What else? The last time she had been to the city was on a business trip to visit the European Space Agency. Its headquarters were on the Left Bank, past the Napoleon monument at Les Invalides. Since her visit, Apollo Space Laboratories had rented an office nearby for its local staff who were doing consulting for the Europeans. Maybe Volkov could stay overnight in that space.

When the Air France plane reached cruising altitude and Wi-Fi service was available, Edith composed a message to Anna Friedman, her boss at the space operations center. She had done a good job for Anna and the Apollo team that day. Now she wanted something in return. She composed the message.

Hi Anna: Sorry for the quick departure tonight. I had to fly to Paris to help a friend who's in trouble. Yes, Paris. I need to ask you for a favor. My friend needs somewhere to crash Wednesday night. His papers are messed up. Don't ask. My recollection is that we rented an office in Paris last year near the European Space Agency. Can my friend stay there Wednesday night and then, on Thursday, can we make some secure calls from Apollo's Paris ops center?

I know this is a super-big favor, I wouldn't ask if it wasn't really important. Could you send me the address and door code of the Paris office? You'll need to clear it with our security people in California and Paris, which is a pain at this hour. But it matters. Message me back ASAP. Edith

PS: Don't forget, I helped Ukraine win the war today.

Anna responded an hour later, after Edith had eaten her meal and nearly dozed off.

Edith: The short answer is yes. The address of our office is 123 Rue Duroc. It's a few blocks from the European Space Agency. The front door code is 537711. The office number is 416. Someone will be upstairs to let you in. The long answer is you're out of your mind. Don't ever ask me for anything as screwy as this again. Anna

* * *

Volkov made his way up the back streets of the 7th Arrondissement toward the restaurant on Rue Saint-Dominque. Several times he had to duck into alleys or enter stores when police cars or foot patrols passed. It was nearly seven p.m. He walked slowly down the commercial street, looking in the store windows at the wildly expensive products on display, as the last minutes ticked away.

He arrived at Fontaine de Mars just at seven. It was a long spring twilight; the sun wouldn't set completely for another ninety minutes. The outdoor seating area around the fountain was nearly empty; it was too chilly outdoors for most diners. Volkov scanned the tables and didn't see Edith. Maybe she had missed her flight. Maybe she had decided, once again, to pull back from him.

Volkov chose a table in the rear of the terrace and sat so that he faced the back wall. A waiter arrived and tried to get Volkov to move to a nicer table closer to the street, but Volkov waved him off. A woman would be joining him, he said.

"Ah, oui, monsieur," said the waiter, as if that explained everything. He dropped two menus and brought some bread, which Volkov devoured.

Edith arrived twenty minutes later. She approached him from behind, and he didn't realize she was there until she put her hands on his big shoulders. He stood and turned and embraced her.

"It's you," he said, shaking his head in wonder. "Impossible."

Edith stood on her tiptoes and kissed him gently on both cheeks. "Turn around," she whispered in his ear, "so that people can't see you from the street."

Edith urged him to eat quickly, so she could get him out of the restaurant to safety. As they ate, Volkov began to narrate the path that had brought him to this place. He kept returning to the same paradox.

"I can save them from disaster. But they don't care. Why?"

"It's my fault," Edith answered. "They don't trust you because I didn't, what, 'recruit' you. They must think that you work for someone else."

Volkov paused to think. Edith was probably right. He drank some of the Beaujolais the waiter had brought with his steak.

"Why did you stop that night in Beijing? Why did you pull back from me?"

Now it was Edith's turn to reflect. There was only one answer. She had known it that night in 1996.

"Because I was in love with you. And I thought you would never forgive me if you believed that I had slept with you to seduce you into becoming a spy."

Volkov shook his head ruefully. "I wish you had made me join the CIA. Then I would have had a home. Now I have nothing."

"Not true," she said. "I'm here." She wanted to say more, but she was done with easy promises.

He smiled. She had come all this way. They were sitting together in a restaurant in Paris. He took her hand.

"We need to go soon," she said. "I've found somewhere for us to stay."

Volkov nodded. As he sat in the darkening night, relaxing his mind and body for the first time in many days, he was lost in thought for a moment, as if he were trying to solve a particularly complicated set of equations.

"There is a mystery here that I don't understand," he said eventually.

"Come on," said Edith, pulling at his arm. "We need to go."

59

Edith nestled close to Volkov as they walked to the street. It was past eight-thirty, and the sun had nearly set. In the shadows on Rue Saint-Dominique, she handed Volkov her sweater. "Put this over your shoulders," she said. "And as we walk, hold me tight. It's good cover. The police are hunting for one man. They'll look right past a couple."

Volkov followed her instructions. He whispered to her, "How do you know about these things?"

"You forget. I used to be a spy."

Volkov smiled. He had hated her for that once. They walked, bodies entwined, along the narrow streets of the 7th Arrondisement, avoiding traffic and pedestrians. They skirted the busy avenues around the Hotel des Invalides and remained on side streets as they made their way toward Rue Duroc. Several times, when Edith saw police in the distance, she turned toward Volkov and kissed him.

Traveling in a cross-hatch, street to street, they neared the commercial building where Apollo Space Laboratories had its Paris office. As they passed the European Space Agency, all the lights were blazing. That was odd. It was past nine now.

Edith and Volkov walked to the door of the building at 123 Rue Duroc. The lobby was empty. Edith punched the code that Anna had sent into the pad: 537711. With a click, the door opened. Edith pushed Volkov toward the elevator and pressed the button for the fourth floor.

Edith knocked on the door marked 416. A security guard opened the door but left the chain in place. He wanted to see identification. Edith showed him her passport. The guard scanned it, handed it back, and then asked for Volkov's.

"Not now," said Edith. "Let us in."

Standing behind the guard was another man, thinning hair, dressed in a cardigan sweater and wire-rimmed glasses.

"*Ça va,*" he told the guard. "*Laissez-les entrer.*" The guard unchained the door and Edith and Volkov entered the brightly lit office. Through a glass window was a room with many small computer monitors and a big video display. It looked like a smaller version of the space operations center at Apollo Space Labs.

"Hi, Edith," said the man in the wire-rimmed glasses. "I'm Felix. I run the Paris office. Anna said you would be coming. With a friend."

"Thank you so much," said Edith. "This is Ivan. I'm sorry to keep you up late. You can go home now. We'll be fine."

"Anna said I should stay here overnight. The security people are a little worried, I guess. We have three small rooms. I'll take one, and each of you can take one of the others. There are men's and ladies' bathrooms down the halls. With showers. How's that?"

"That's great, Felix. But are you sure you need to stay? I hate to inconvenience you."

"Boss's orders. Plus, all hell is breaking loose in space. I should stay and monitor it in the ops room."

Edith was concerned by this last bit of information. When she had left Los Angeles, the space trackers had been monitoring movement by Chinese satellites. She didn't know about the alert to global GPS providers, much less the Pentagon's heightened state of readiness.

"Where is hell breaking loose?" asked Edith. "Is Galileo down? I saw the lights on at the European Space Agency. And what about GPS? What's going on?"

Felix took a breath. "GPS is fine. So is Galileo. BeiDou is down in China. From what we've heard, their systems are haywire. They grounded flights out of Beijing and Shanghai today, because they don't trust the navigation readings. The Chinese are keeping it quiet. But the satellite world knows."

"Holy shit! What happened? Has the system bricked?"

"I have no idea. You're welcome to watch our feed. But all we've got right now is mostly rumors."

Edith looked at Volkov. He looked exhausted, suddenly, after so many days of stress. She felt tired, too. It was a blessing, in a way, that they would sleep in separate rooms. This wasn't the night to leap back across time.

"Listen, Felix, we're not going to fix whatever's wrong with BeiDou. I didn't sleep much on the flight. I'm going to turn in. Ivan is tired, too. Show us to the rooms that we can use, and we'll get out of your hair. We've got some crazy stuff to sort out, but we can do that tomorrow."

Felix seemed relieved that his babysitting duties would be painless. He led the two down the hall, pointing out the bathrooms along the way. At the rear of the suite were two small offices. Each had a couch, overlaid with a sheet, blanket, and pillow.

Volkov stood awkwardly next to Edith.

"You saved me," he said.

She shook her head. "This isn't over yet. Let's get some sleep."

Edith retired to her room and closed the door.

Volkov walked back to the men's bathroom. He was filthy after his days of running and hiding. He smelled the animal fear on his body. He stripped off his clothes and stood under the hot shower for many minutes, his mind still processing the puzzle of events and the pieces that didn't fit.

THURSDAY

APRIL 21, 2022

What Happens If GPS Fails? Despite massive reliance on the system's clocks, there's still no long-term backup

It only took thirteen millionths of a second to cause a whole lot of problems. . . . As the U.S. Air Force was taking one satellite in the country's constellation of GPS satellites offline, an incorrect time was accidentally uploaded to several others, making them out of sync by less time than it takes for the sound of a gunshot to leave the chamber.

The minute error disrupted GPS-dependent timing equipment around the world for more than 12 hours. While the problem went unnoticed by many people thanks to short-term backup systems, panicked engineers in Europe called equipment makers to help resolve things before global telecommunications networks began to fail. In parts of the U.S and Canada, police, fire, and EMS radio equipment stopped functioning. BBC digital radio was out for two days in many areas, and the anomaly was even detected in electrical power grids.

—DAN GLASS, *The Atlantic*, June 13, 2016

60

Edith Ryan rose before Volkov the next morning. There was a dazzling ray of sun that lased her windowpane and spread to illuminate the City of Light. Edith showered and put on the same plain ensemble from the day before. She borrowed toothpaste and toiletries from Felix and vowed that she would buy new clothes and niceties when the shops opened. She let Volkov sleep until nearly nine and then knocked on his door. The Apollo Labs staff would be arriving soon. "Wake up," she said. "Big day."

Felix had sent out for breakfast, and they shared fresh croissants, raspberry jam, orange juice, and grainy French espresso. Volkov's eyes were clear with the new morning. It was as if a storm had passed overnight.

They gathered in the Paris office's small operations room to monitor what had become an increasingly uncertain situation in China. News from inside the country was fragmentary, but systems that depended on satellite positioning, timing, and navigation appeared to be affected. More flights were now grounded. Some Huawei communications networks were down. The Alipay automatic payments system had become unreliable. Weibo social media was crashing for some mobile applications.

Apollo's Paris office was linked on a secure videoconference line with the company's offices in Los Angeles and Chantilly, Virginia. Those feeds gave a rolling update of events as China passed through its Thursday. Some of the best information came from European television correspondents on the ground in Beijing, Shanghai, and Hong Kong who were able to file reports through their own satellite uplinks. They described a scene of growing concern. The authorities weren't making any public comments, but Chinese people sensed that something was wrong.

China had requested an urgent meeting of the United Nations International Committee on Global Navigation Satellite Systems. That was scheduled to start at nine a.m. in New York, five hours hence. The European Space Agency had offered backup coverage through Galileo, and Japan had offered the same through its Quasi-Zenith Satellite System. So far, China hadn't responded to those offers.

As the hours passed, China struggled to maintain digital order. Police were deployed in several cities to assure "calm," the reports said, and one French channel reported that army units had been mobilized outside Beijing in case they were needed. A correspondent in Hong Kong said that sources inside China believed that the country's network of surveillance systems, operating though omnipresent cameras, might cease functioning. Small crowds had formed in some cities, but they quickly dispersed; people were tentative, still uncertain whether facial recognition would capture their identities.

*　*　*

Volkov watched the reports, sitting beside Edith in Felix's now-teeming operations room. Felix hadn't wanted to admit Volkov to the ops center, but Edith had vouched for him and cited her years at CIA as her trump card. Felix kept Volkov out of the SCIF, where the most sensitive conversations were happening, but the Russian was able to monitor the flow of events. There was a growing look of consternation on his face. He took notes, paced the room, began to speak several times, and then stopped to consider further. Finally, in the early afternoon, he walked to Edith and took the chair next to her.

"I know what's happening," Volkov said.

"You do?" she said in astonishment. That seemed impossible.

"These are like the disruptive systems that my Chinese patron, Professor Cao Lin, was developing. Now someone has turned them against China. That is what we are watching. I'm happy to see this. China is nobody's friend. But Cao Lin will take revenge for these attacks. There is great danger ahead for America."

"What's the danger?" asked Edith.

"The kill switch. Everything I warned the CIA about. The power to freeze our world. They will make America think every satellite system it has is failing. China's problems today will seem like nothing if Cao Lin turns the switch for America and makes the lights flash red. They haven't listened to me so far. But I would be ashamed of myself if I did not try one more time."

Edith studied his face. She knew his brilliance and passion. But there was so much that she didn't know.

"Are you sure that you're right?" she asked. "Morally certain? I don't want to scare you, but your future is at stake. They could arrest you and charge you as a Russian spy if you mislead them."

"The time when people could scare me ended a long while ago," said Volkov, taking her hand. "And I am not a Russian spy. I am trying to be an American spy."

* * *

Edith knew who she should contact. There was one person in the intelligence community who had truly seemed to focus on China. For a decade, he had been warning Edith to stay away from matters involving Beijing. He was protective of his secrets. He had told her, several times, that she didn't understand the sensitivity of the operations she was discussing. Probably he would ignore what Volkov had to say now. But Edith should at least make the attempt.

Edith buzzed into the SCIF and signed on to her secure account. She scrolled her recent email messages until she found the one she wanted. She reread the text:

Please be careful in matters involving China's activities in space. . . . Let me be frank: It is a matter of life and death. Don't go poking around in this area. There are things that you do not and cannot know.

Edith addressed a reply.

Dear Mr. Gallant:

I am in Paris with a Russian defector named Ivan Volkov. He has tried this week to share with the CIA information of urgent importance about China's capabilities in satellite warfare. He has personal knowledge of a Chinese scientist named Cao Lin who he believes can do great harm to America. He wants to prevent that harm. I have brought him to the Paris office of Apollo Space Laboratories for his safety. I hope you can talk with Mr. Volkov as soon as possible. He only wants to help the United States. Would you be willing to speak with Mr. Volkov by secure VCR here in Paris?

Edith Ryan

Edith remained in the SCIF, hoping and praying that Gallant would get her message. Thirty minutes later, a response arrived.

Miss Ryan:

I have ordered that you and Ivan Volkov be brought to the United States immediately. A security team from the U.S. Embassy will enter your offices shortly after this message arrives. Please do not resist. The team will take you to a U.S. government plane that will bring you both to Washington Dulles and from there to a secure location where an interagency team, including representatives of the Department of Justice, will discuss what further action should be taken in this matter.

Let me repeat: Do not resist the security officers. They have the authority to arrest you and bring you home in handcuffs.

Robert Gallant

Edith read the message in shocked silence, and then reviewed it a second time to make sure what it said. As she was finishing the second reading, shaking with anger, there was a loud pounding at the main door and a sudden entry into the Apollo Labs office by a team of four men. They showed their badges to Felix at the door. He nodded assent.

* * *

Edith quickly emerged from the SCIF and stood by Ivan Volkov as the team approached. The team leader showed Edith his badge and revealed a holstered weapon. He and his team members had the anonymous, menacing look of the CIA's Global Response Staff, the "Scorpions," they called themselves, whom Edith had seen occasionally in her days as a case officer.

"Miss Ryan and Mr. Volkov, I have a lawful order to bring you both to the United States. If you do not obey this order voluntarily, I have the authority to compel you to return by force."

Tears were streaming from Edith's eyes. She didn't want to be crying at this moment when she needed to be strong, but she couldn't help it. She felt that she had betrayed Volkov twice over, first in Beijing and now in Paris. Volkov was tense, his fists clenched. He looked like the enforcer in a hockey game who's about to take a wild swing.

"Do what they say, Ivan," Edith admonished him. "If you fight them, you will end in prison for sure. We have no choice."

"Just to warn you both," said the lead security officer, "if you resist at any point, I am going to apply handcuffs and leg restraints."

"We won't resist," said Edith. "Tell them that you won't do anything, Ivan."

"I won't resist," said Volkov.

He looked at Edith with an odd smile. "I am going to America."

61

Robert Gallant's black SUV left NRO headquarters in Chantilly late Thursday afternoon and sped toward the White House. Next to him on the bench seat was a freshly laundered shirt that an aide had brought from his home, along with a change of underwear. Gallant tried to be dainty, covering himself with his suit jacket while he changed; he quickly pulled on the new pair of boxer shorts, his bare bottom resting only briefly on the black leather of the seat.

The crispness of the starched white shirt was reassuring. He inserted his collar stays and gold cuff links. He knotted his tie, but the thin end was too long, and he had to try again twice before he got it right. He still hadn't had a chance to shave since returning from England, but perhaps the stubble would distract his colleagues in the Situation Room from the gray circles under his eyes.

Gallant was exhausted but oddly elated. He had been to the White House twice since returning from his brief trip to England. For once, the NSC's crisis management procedures seemed to be operating as designed. The plans he had worked so hard to prepare were holding. There had been no leaks.

The Defense Department alert status was still at DEFCON 2, "Fast Pace." The Pentagon spokesman had fended off the first press query about the elevated alert. He read a statement that the United States was "concerned about recent reports of instability in China" and taking "appropriate precautions." He refused to take questions. That elliptical explanation wouldn't hold up for long, but if things went as Gallant hoped, they wouldn't need much more time.

Gallant arrived at the White House from the south. He had to pass through two security barriers to enter West Executive Road. His driver navigated the diagonal row of parking spots between the White House and Eisenhower Executive Building. It was unusually empty for a weekday afternoon. This was a crisis in which so few people had access to information that the group in the Situation Room would be small.

Gallant climbed down from his vehicle and walked under the awning into the White House basement. A guard opened the door to the Situation Room. A dozen men and women were seated around the table. Most of them looked as tired as Gallant, but the men had at least managed to get a shave.

Jason Wolf, the national security adviser, opened the meeting. He was a slender man, thin-faced and balding, who looked at once very young and very old. Gallant didn't trust many people in the White House, but since the Ukraine crisis began, he had grown to respect Wolf. He was the right mixture of smart and cunning.

"Let's review the China situation, and what has changed since our meeting this morning," Wolf began. "The NSC warning officer says the Chinese have moved their satellites back into their previous orbits. No more 'perch,' ready to pounce. Is that right, Bob?"

"Yes, sir," said Gallant. "The Chinese sats began moving position last night, after your first warning message to Beijing. That repositioning continued through our night and morning. It was nearly completed when I left Chantilly. We don't see them playing any games."

"Roger that," said a uniformed military officer who represented Space Command in Colorado Springs.

"What about the domestic situation in China?" asked Wolf. "Still crazy, or is it calming down?"

Laura Oden, the CIA director, handled that one. She handed classified computer screens that displayed the latest intelligence reporting to the people gathered around the table.

"Still pretty crazy," Oden said. "Everything linked to satellites is flashing red. Technicians think the systems are broken so they're doing patchwork fixes that make the problems worse. The PLA doesn't know what's happening, and when they get nervous, the Politburo standing committee freaks out."

"How dangerous is this?" asked Wolf.

"Very," said Oden. "The Chinese don't do very well with uncertainty. And they're flooded with it now. The Russians can't help. They're overwhelmed in Ukraine. So the Chinese leadership is feeling isolated and spooked. They backed down on the satellites, but they're pissed."

"What's happening with their leadership?" asked Wolf. "What's the decision timetable?"

"They've had a bad night. Rumors everywhere. They debated last night whether to mobilize troops to maintain order but decided that would make things worse. It's very early there now. The Central Military Commission has a meeting scheduled for eight a.m. our time, in about two hours."

"So this would be a good time for some hand-holding?"

"Yes, sir," said Oden.

Wolf looked to Gallant. "What say?"

"I agree," said Gallant. "Time to help them find their way out of the woods. Is the president on board?"

"Yup," said Wolf. "Who's the right person for me to talk to in Beijing?"

"Teng Guomeng," answered Oden. "He's the secretary of the Central Military Commission. Ex–intel officer. Slippery character, but he's the closest thing in China to your counterpart as national security adviser. We think he's the person who processed the president's warning message last night."

"Let's try to get him on the phone," said Wolf. "See if we can get him soon, before the Central Military Commission meeting."

"What are you going to tell him?" asked Oden.

"To calm down. Everything's fine. Daddy's here to help."

Gallant nodded. Just right. But he added a caution.

"Remember, Jason, that you are a snake handler. Not a snake charmer."

* * *

The NSC communications staff spent a frantic twenty minutes trying to get a secure line to the Zhongnanhai leadership compound in Beijing. The line kept dropping, which was a sign of how chaotic communications were. The United States didn't have a formal "hotline" with China, but Wolf had been using the same channel to send messages for the past year. Sometimes the Chinese answered and sometimes they didn't.

A good line was finally established to Qiansheng Hall, where the Chinese president and the Politburo had their offices. The NSC's senior director for China, who spoke good Chinese, got on the phone. He said that National Security Adviser Jason Wolf wanted to talk to CMC Secretary Teng, on behalf of the president of the United States.

That elicited an audible gasp in Beijing, followed by a pause of perhaps thirty seconds, and then a request for more time to see if such a call was convenient.

The line went dead, amid frantic consultations on the Chinese end. The audio, now muted, was piped into the Situation Room. Everyone realized that it would take time to find Teng, and then more time to rouse the general secretary and get his approval.

Wolf left the room to get a Diet Coke. Gallant asked the Navy mess steward if he could find a disposable razor. When it was delivered, he went into the men's room for a quick shave. He emerged looking magisterial. A steward brought sandwiches and coffee from the Navy mess.

* * *

Teng Guomeng came on the line at seven-fifteen Washington time. He offered formal, empty greetings to the national security adviser. There was a break for translation, then Wolf reciprocated, but more warmly, expressing greetings from the president. Teng made a sound, which the translator conveyed as, "The secretary grunted."

"The president has asked me to say that the United States would like to be helpful to China," Wolf continued. "We noted that Chinese space vehicles have moved their orbits, following the president's expression of concern. We are encouraged by this demonstration of mutual respect."

Teng responded carefully when the translator finished. "The PLA Strategic Support Force has conducted normal maneuvers in the past twenty-four hours. America's concerns about Chinese satellite movements were groundless.

China rejects any American claims that our satellite forces were positioned in an aggressive manner. It is the United States that is the aggressor in space."

Wolf rolled his eyes, drawing nods of agreement from his colleagues. Propaganda was part of any exchange with China, but it was annoying now, when the clock was ticking. Wolf spoke again, ignoring the barb.

"Because of China's responsible and statesmanlike actions in space, the president's concerns about security are reduced," Wolf said. "For that reason, he has asked me to tell you that the United States is lowering its military alert status, which, as you know, was at DEFCON Two, to DEFCON Three."

A long pause followed, as Teng presumably sought confirmation of the reduction in alert status and guidance from members of the Central Military Commission. When he came back on the line, his voice was livelier, conveying interest rather than suspicion.

"Please tell the president that the members of the Central Military Commission are pleased to know of this reduction in military posture, which had been raised in an unnecessary, warlike provocation," he said. When the translator had conveyed the formal response, he added a phrase that could only have come from the general secretary himself. "We are glad that you have backed down."

Wolf didn't take the bait. He continued in the same solicitous tone with which he had begun the call.

"The president understands that China is experiencing some difficulties with BeiDou and some other satellite-based systems," he said. "The United States would like to assist China in making sure that these satellite systems are restored to normal operations."

"Please repeat," said Teng Guomeng when he'd heard the Chinese translation. This was one message the Chinese weren't expecting.

Wolf made it simple this time.

"We would like to help. That's the president's message."

Again, a very long pause, followed by a non-answer. "The chairman of the Central Military Commission would like to consider the president's offer before giving you a response."

Wolf took that as a yes. He leaned back in his swivel chair and took a long swig of his Diet Coke.

FRIDAY
APRIL 22, 2022

From its first satellite launch in 1970 . . . China has quickly become one of the most capable space nations. To enable its growing space and counterspace capabilities, China operates four spaceports and a family of Long March launch vehicles with a range of sizes and capabilities. . . . Civil, intelligence, and military space capabilities are a priority for China as it continues to invest in and plan for greater access to space in the coming decade, successfully executing on the vision statement of the 2016 white paper on space activities: "To build China into a space power in all respects."

—CENTER FOR STRATEGIC AND INTERNATIONAL
STUDIES, "Space Threat Assessment 2022"

61

The small jet was like a flying prison. Edith and Volkov were put in separate compartments, each enclosed with metal bars, so they resembled cages for traveling animals. They were instructed not to talk with each other. Burly guards sat in front of each of them. None of the people on the flight had recognizable uniforms from any military service or law enforcement organization.

They sat on the runway for hours before taking off. The guards brought bottles of water and granola bars, and eventually some tasteless premade sandwiches. Edith tried occasionally to talk with her guards. She asked them their names. She told them she had worked at the CIA. She asked if they had any children. These questions elicited nothing but an occasional, "No talking, lady."

Volkov didn't speak to anyone through the long flight. He was attentive but lost in thought, as if reviewing in his mind a long chess game, and the different strategies forking from each move, past and future.

The plane landed at Dulles early Friday morning. The window shades were drawn but the passengers could hear the screech of the tires on the concrete and the roaring backwash of the jet engines. The plane taxied into a big hanger. A transport van with blacked-out windows was waiting. When Edith and Volkov emerged from the plane and were standing on American soil, they were handcuffed and led from the plane. Edith asked if she was being arrested and on what charge. The guard just laughed. "Protective custody, ma'am," he answered.

The transport van left the Dulles compound and headed toward Chantilly and the NRO site but then veered down a side road that was protected by a chain-link fence and barbed wire. A sign at the gate warned U.S. GOVERNMENT FACILITY; ENTRY STRICTLY PROHIBITED, but no more. The car drove several miles down this road, past what appeared to be warehouses and training sites, and then came to a stop at a brick complex marked GUEST QUARTERS.

*　*　*

Edith and Volkov were marched into the building. Guards led them through a charmless lobby, decorated with furniture so blandly immaculate that it seemed never to have been used. To the left of the main lobby was a dining room, with a long table whose chairs still had their plastic seat covers; to the right was a television room with a large-screen TV and, at the back, a folded ping-pong table. The quarters were so weirdly antiseptic and free of adornment that they might have been prepared for a visitor from outer space.

At the back, beyond the kitchen, was a large windowless room, painted a dull gray. Fluorescent lights above diffused an eerie glow. At the four corners were surveillance cameras. There were two cots, one on either side of the room. Edith was led to one side, Volkov to the other. Their escorts instructed them not to speak, and then removed their handcuffs. A guard pointed to a buzzer at the front of the room by the door.

"If you need to use the toilet, press the buzzer," the guard said.

The guard retreated toward the door. Edith had been cooperative all the way across the Atlantic and into this strange place of detention, but her patience was exhausted.

"What the fuck is going on?" she shouted at the guard.

Volkov watched her, relishing her anger.

"Sorry," the guard said. "I can't answer any questions."

"Don't give me that shit. I see your face. And you know what? I have a photographic memory. That's right. And you will be personally liable. Not the government. You, and your family, your kids."

"Stop threatening me, Miss Ryan. We have our orders and we're following them."

"I want to talk to a lawyer. Right now, goddammit."

"Not possible. And there's no need for a lawyer."

"What am I being charged with?" Edith screamed. "What the hell is going on? Charge us or release us. This is America, if you'd forgotten."

"Take it easy, ma'am. You're not being charged with anything. We just have some business to do."

"What are you talking about? Why are we here? What's the delay?"

"We're waiting for a plane to land, ma'am. That's all I can tell you. Sit tight."

* * *

Edith and Volkov had been in their holding cell for two hours when there was a knock and the door swung open. Into the room walked a man dressed in a trim suit and a striped tie. He looked very tired. Aides brought four chairs into the room, which were assembled in a square, as if for a card game with no table. The visitor gestured for Edith and Volkov to take two of the chairs. He took the third and left the last one empty.

Edith spoke first.

"Hello, Mr. Gallant," she said. She turned to Volkov. "This is Robert Gallant. He's from the National Reconnaissance Office."

Volkov studied the man's face.

"We've met before, actually, Mr. Volkov," said Gallant. "Three days ago. But I was behind a glass partition."

Volkov nodded. He looked almost serene. "I recognize your voice, Mr. Gallant."

Gallant took a deep breath and then exhaled, almost a sigh. "You two. Jesus! We're on the brink of World War Three, and the two of you are bouncing around like ping-pong balls. Really! The problem with smart people is that they figure out the things that stupider people are trying to keep secret."

Gallant pointed at Volkov. "And I mean you, sir!"

"The kill switch," said Volkov. He still had that odd smile on his face. "That was yours."

"Correct. Ours."

Edith put up her hand. "Back up a minute. I think I heard you mention World War Three."

"Not happening," said Gallant. "Averted. Thanks to one of the most delicate intelligence operations in American history, which the two of you kept tripping over. Some people will say we were lucky. Nonsense. Luck is the residue of good planning."

"I have no idea what you're talking about," said Edith. "You have to speak a version of English that's going to make sense to a girl from western Massachusetts. Please."

Edith was flustered. But Volkov was still smiling and nodding to himself.

Gallant snorted. "Oh well. The easiest way is simply to introduce our guest. He arrived an hour ago, and he's had a chance to rest. But he's eager to meet Mr. Volkov."

Edith said nothing. She was beyond stupefaction.

Gallant called to one of the guards outside the room that it was time.

* * *

Into the room walked Cao Lin, formerly a member of the Chinese Academy of Sciences, now a defector who had just been granted asylum in the United States. He was wearing a pair of black slacks and a black cashmere sweater.

Professor Cao immediately walked to Volkov and gave the Russian a long hug.

"I was afraid you knew," said Cao.

Volkov shook his head. "I am not so smart as you think. I only figured it out a few hours ago when there was no other explanation."

"I need the version with subtitles," said Edith. "I'm still not sure I understand what's going on."

Robert Gallant spoke up. Despite his acidulous manner, he had something of the magician, too. But like an ancient conjurer, his charms were now all overthrown. The play he had helped create had run its course.

"Professor Cao Lin is the most valuable intelligence asset the United State has had in this century," he said. "For many years, I won't say how many exactly, he has been working with us, under the impenetrable cover of working *against* us. He is the master of Chinese space systems, and the innermost secrets of those systems, I am happy to say, he has shared with us."

Edith nodded. Some of the scales had fallen from her eyes. "And you were afraid that I would expose him, by asking too many questions about China operations?"

"Just so," said Gallant.

"But here I am," said Cao Lin. "Very ready to begin a new life. My real life."

"Amen," said Gallant. He pointed to the Russian.

"But you, Mr. Volkov, bless you, sir, you were our nightmare! You figured out Professor Cao's plans. You understood his 'kill switch.' You didn't know he would turn it against China, but you figured out how it would work. When I realized that, I admired you, but I was frightened what you might do—or might have already done—that could jeopardize our agent."

"You had nothing to fear. I hate Russia. And the part of China that my friend Cao Lin despises, I hate that, too."

"We didn't know," said Gallant. "We were terrified to the very last second that you might have betrayed Professor Cao. Perhaps unintentionally. That's why we decided we had to send you back home. It was to protect your friend Cao. It was too big a secret for us to risk."

"I am Russian. I play chess. We know pawn sacrifice. I would have done the same thing."

Gallant turned to Professor Cao. He had a question of his own.

"We'll be talking though this for weeks in debriefings, you and me," Gallant said to the Chinese man. "But one question, while we're having our celebration party. Why on earth did you turn to this Russian? That was reckless."

Cao Lin shook his head. "You don't understand."

"Evidently," said Gallant, "so explain it to me."

"We were scientists. We wanted the same things. Free minds. Free people. I knew that Mr. Volkov had a very good brain, but it wasn't just that. I could see that he rejected the same parts of his system that I rejected in mine. I needed someone who could operate for me outside China. Someone who had nothing to do with China—or with America. My insurance, you could say. I thought that this person could be my friend Volkov. I tried one final time, last year, but Ivan was too suspicious."

"I thought you were one of the destroyers," said Volkov. "I wanted to stop you. I reached out to the CIA. I never imagined, really, until today, that you were already working for them. And that they would kill me to save you. As I said, I am dumber than you think."

"Let's go back to World War Three," said Edith. "BeiDou crashed. Why didn't the Chinese retaliate?"

"Ah!" said Gallant. "The brink. But it wasn't, really. The Russians were begging China for help, and Beijing made some provocative moves to intimidate us. They moved satellites. So did we. We raised alerts. They took note. Their bluff didn't work. The result: Standoff. Deterrence established. End of story."

"And their attack satellites?" pressed Edith. "I saw them moving into place in the ops center at Apollo Labs."

"They moved those satellites back," answered Gallant. "We knew they would. They had some glitches, I'm afraid. Bad software. Unreliable ground stations. You have to be very careful about supply chains. Am I right?" Gallant looked at Cao Lin and tipped an imaginary cap.

"And as for BeiDou," he continued, "they could hardly blame us. It crashed because their own software was indicating difficulties. Red lights. System down. Alert! Alert! We're helping them fix things, actually."

"You're kidding," said Edith.

"The president, through the national security adviser, offered assistance to China yesterday in repairing the BeiDou system. Secret assistance, to save face. They agreed today to accept our help, and they will use GPS as a backup until BeiDou is stable again."

"And Professor Cao? Do they know that he has defected."

"We worked very hard to make it appear that Professor Cao died in a car accident in Shenzhen. But the Chinese authorities aren't stupid. They'll figure it out. They will be terrified when they realize that he is gone."

Ivan Volkov stood. He was taller than the others. A commanding presence, even in this humble place. In truth, of all of them, he had come the longest distance.

"I want to speak to my friend Professor Cao. You know that I loved the work of the German scientist Kepler."

"Certainly," said Cao. "That was where we began."

"Kepler said once that 'nature uses as little as possible of anything.' And that's true with inanimate objects. But it's not true, so much, with human beings."

He stopped and drew his breath.

"I am sorry. I don't make speeches. But I think, maybe, human beings should use each other more. All of us, here. We should have used the parts that make us human. More. As much as possible."

Edith moved toward him, the emotion showing on her face. She reached out to embrace him, but Volkov first took her hand and spoke quietly to her.

"You have to help me with this. I have grave doubts about happy endings."

Acknowledgments

A caution for the reader: This is a novel, and the characters, companies, government agencies, and plot events exist in a fictional landscape only. To make this fiction believable, across an arc from China and Russia to the "high ground" of space, I turned to many experts for advice. Any mistakes are all mine.

At U.S. Space Force, my thanks to General Jay Raymond and his successor, General Chance Saltzman; Colonel Jeremy Renker; Colonel Catie Hague; and her husband, Colonel Nick Hague.

At the Aerospace Corporation, a national treasure, special thanks to the amazing Rebecca Reesman and James R. Wilson, whose essay "The Physics of Space War" inspired my character's version; to Steve Isakowitz, the company's president and CEO, for an enlightening discussion; and to Sabrina Steele and Dianna Ramirez for arranging a day at Aerospace's headquarters in El Segundo and a series of other fascinating interviews there. I also drew on their excellent in-house publication: *The Aerospace Corporation: A History, 1960–2010.*

From current and former members of the intelligence community, my thanks to Glenn Gaffney, Sean Roche, and Stephanie O'Sullivan, formerly with the Central Intelligence Agency; Robert Cardillo, former director of the National Geospatial-Intelligence Agency; and Dr. Troy Meink, principal deputy director of the National Reconnaissance Office, who offered a rare visit to its headquarters.

Other space experts who generously shared their thoughts included: Jim Baker of the Pentagon's Office of Net Assessment; General Paul Selva, former vice chairman of the Joint Chiefs of Staff; Representative Jim Cooper, one of the earliest critics of America's space policy; Jim Bonomo of Rand Corp.; and John Hamre, head of the Center for Strategic and International Studies, who understands space issues better than most. My descriptions of Chinese and Russian attack satellite maneuvers draw heavily from the CSIS's excellent annual "Space Threat Assessment" series.

I am also grateful to "commercial" space experts Jared Isaacman, Alden Munson, Anthony Vinci, Alex Karp, Dmitri Alperovitch, Brian Schimpf, and Palmer Lucky. To go to school on space (kindergarten, for me) I consulted the textbook *Understanding Space: An Introduction to Astronautics*, by Jerry Jon Sellers. My understanding of Johannes Kepler is primitive, but it was aided by Sellers's text.

For help in explaining GPS and other global positioning systems, I would have been lost without Paul E. Ceruzzi's monograph, "GPS," and NovAtel's *An Introduction to GNSS*, from which I borrowed the metaphor of imagining four lengths of string to position a ground receiver and four satellites. Curious readers will also find a wealth of data on the GPS.gov website. The arcana of atomic clocks are carefully explained in *Rubidium Atomic Clock: The Workhouse of Satellite Navigation*, by G. M. Saxena and Bikash Ghosal.

My account of China and its space scientists is drawn principally from Chinese government documents available on the internet, including detailed biographical information about the great scientist Chen Fangyun, a fictional character in this book inspired by a real giant in modern Chinese scientific history. My character's interest in Go was animated by introductory books by Cho Chikun, and by Janice Kim and Jeong Soo-hyun.

My Russian research was complicated when I was sanctioned by Russia and banned from traveling there after the Ukraine war began. I had planned to visit Magnitogorsk, but had to rely on Stephen Kotkin's book *Magnetic Mountain: Stalinism as a Civilization* and other works. Thanks to Google Earth, you can walk the streets there and in Moscow. I drew on Mark Galeotti's excellent study *The Vory: Russia's Super Mafia* and many Russian government resources online. For Russian space history, a useful book is Brian Harvey's *Russian Planetary Exploration: History, Development, Legacy and Prospects*, which describes the Mars 96 fiasco.

The scathing Russian intelligence portrait of Chinese national characteristics is drawn verbatim from a document in *Comrade Kryuchkov's Instructions: Top Secret Files on KGB Foreign Operations, 1975–1985*, edited by Christopher Andrew and Oleg Gordievsky.

Several other Russia notes: My fictional Lebedev Physical Institute is a shadow of the real place with its roster of Nobel Prize winners. My larcenous character Danil Kuzmin doesn't exist, and the defense contracts agency where he works was abolished long before this book's fictional description of it begins. In writing about Russian corruption, I was inspired by the heroic Aleksei Navalny and his revelatory and bitingly caustic videos. May he live again in freedom.

This book was written in the dark shadow of the Ukraine war and the tragic collapse of free and humane society in Russia. Between the lines, there is a love letter to the Russia that once was and might be again.

Finally, I thank the friends who read and commented on this book, starting with my wife and first reader Eve. My friend Lincoln Caplan read each section in draft and helped me focus and clarify plot and characters. This book, like my last few novels, wouldn't exist without Linc's generous help. My friend Garrett Epps read a later draft carefully and made some valuable suggestions. It's intimidating to deliver any manuscript to a great editor like Starling Lawrence at Norton, but, as always, his pencil notations were sharp and often wickedly funny. I am grateful to the Norton team for many years of support, especially to their wonderful publicist, Rachel Salzman. Thanks finally to my agents, Raphael Sagalyn, Bruce Vinokour, and Matthew Snyder, who thanks to merger magic are all now at Creative Artists Agency. Bruce's notes were especially helpful, and Rafe's counsel has been unfailing for four decades.

I have been lucky through my career to have support from the *Washington Post* to pursue the twin paths of fiction and fact. My new boss, Opinions Editor David Shipley, has been an especially wise and supportive colleague. This book is dedicated to my three siblings, Sarah, Amy, and Adi Ignatius, and the deep bond we've formed in caring for our parents.